THERE WAS
A LITTLE GIRL

Also by Ed McBain

McBAIN

THERE WAS A LITTLE GIRL

A Matthew Hope Novel

Hodder & Stoughton

Copyright © Hui Corporation 1994

First published in Great Britain in 1994 by
Hodder and Stoughton
A division of Hodder Headline PLC
Published in the United States of America by Warner Books, Inc.

The right of Ed McBain to be identified as the author
of this work has been asserted by him in accordance with the
Copyright, Designs and Patents Act 1988.

10 9 8 7 6 5 4 3 2 1

British Library Cataloguing in Publication Data

A CIP catalogue record for this title is available
from the British Library

ISBN 0 340 59886 7

Typeset by Hewer Text Composition Services, Edinburgh
Printed and bound in Great Britain by Mackays of Chatham plc

Hodder and Stoughton
A division of Hodder Headline PLC
338 Euston Road
London NW1 3BH

THIS IS FOR
my son and daughter-in-law,
Richard and Patty Hunter

1

There was a little girl . . .

THE FIRST bullet hit Matthew Hope in the left shoulder.

The second one hit him in the chest.

He was a lawyer, and therefore subject to a deep-seated American animosity for the legal profession. But he was not normally a target for shooters. Well, he'd been shot once before, but this time hurt more than the last time. People who made movies should tell a person how much it hurts to get shot.

The last time he'd got shot, he had just shoved himself off the fender of a car and was trying to intercept a person being chased by a detective. This time, he was just coming out of a bar, in the same section of town, come to think of it, just stepping outside to see if he'd got the telephone message wrong – were they supposed to meet *inside* the bar or *outside* on the sidewalk? – when all at once the shots erupted.

The last time he'd got shot, he was still conscious when the ambulance arrived. This time there was first the searing pain and then a feeling of complete helplessness, his shoulder leaking, his shirt wet with blood, legs going weak, arms flapping, mouth gasping for air as he flailed backward through the swinging doors that led into the bar, everything swimming out of focus like in a cheap detective novel, everything getting darker and darker, and somebody screamed. People who made movies should tell a person that getting shot was so painful it caused you to scream aloud.

Everything went black.

Matthew was in the emergency room when his partner Frank Summerville arrived at ten thirty-seven that Friday night. He was told by the attending intern that Mr. Hope had been admitted unconscious at ten twenty-two and was at the moment awaiting emergency surgery. X rays had revealed a relatively insignificant bullet wound in the left shoulder, just above the clavicle, fortunately missing the apex of the lung, passing through the soft tissue of the shoulder instead. The other wound was more serious. The massive loss of blood indicated that the bullet had ruptured at least one major blood vessel – one of the main pulmonary arteries or veins perhaps – or numerous smaller arteries, causing Mr. Hope's present state of shock. They were currently pouring in saline to bring his blood pressure back up, which at the moment was reading only thirty over palp. Blood for transfusion had been ordered from the blood bank. A sample of his own blood had been sent to the lab for a CBC, a medical screen, and tests of his arterial blood gases. Regardless of what the tests showed, he would be removed to the O.R. as soon as it was ready for him. A thoracic surgeon and two resident surgeons were standing by.

The intern's smock was bloodstained. Victims of accidents or attacks were being carried in on stretchers. Stainless-steel tables kept wheeling past, bottles dripping into long plastic tubes. Police officers kept moving in and out of the entrance door. Outside, ambulances blinked furiously. Bewildered, Frank stood with the intern in the midst of this noisy, swirling maelstrom. Everywhere around them was the detritus of the start of a weekend's mayhem in any American city or town.

"How did this happen?" Frank asked.

"I have no idea, sir," the intern said.

Matthew was distantly aware of people fluttering everywhere around him. He was vaguely aware of motion and light. There were voices speaking in tongues. He did not know where he was or what was happening to him.

They talked in solemn whispers in the hospital waiting room. Warren Chambers wanted to know where Matthew had been that night. Frank said he didn't know. Whispers.

Warren checked with Admissions and got the name of the Calusa P.D. officer who'd accompanied the ambulance to the hospital. The cop was long gone. This was now ten past eleven; Matthew had been in the operating room for almost a half hour. Warren called the Calusa Public Safety Building from a wall phone. A nurse wheeling a cart shouted, "Coming through!" and hurried on by. Warren put a finger in his free ear. The sergeant he spoke to told him that Officer Parks would be relieved there at the facility at 2345 hours. Warren asked if he could raise him on the radio, this was important. The sergeant asked who this was.

"Warren Chambers," he said. "I'm a licensed private investigator. I do a lot of work for . . ."

"What's this in reference to, Mr. Chambers?"

Suddenly alert, ready to protect his behind. Or anyone *else's* in the police department.

"It's about a shooting victim admitted to Good Samaritan at ten twenty-two tonight. White male named Matthew Hope. Officer Parks signed him in."

"So?"

"I'd like to talk to him."

"Why?"

"I've done work for the victim."

"Come on over, maybe you can catch Parks when he rolls in."

"Well, I'd appreciate it if you radioed him first, tell him I'll be waiting."

"Who'd you say this was?" the sergeant asked.

"Warren Chambers. Check with Detective Alston. He knows me."

"Nick Alston?"

"Yeah."

"I'll check with him."

"And then radio Parks, okay?"

"I'll talk to Nick," the sergeant said, and hung up.

Warren went back to where Frank was still pacing the hallway. They spoke again in whispers.

"Will you be all right here alone?" Warren asked.

"Fine, fine," Frank said.

He didn't look fine.

"I want to get on this right away," Warren said.

"Yes, sure, go ahead."

"You might want to call Patricia."

"Patricia?"

"Demming."

"Yes. I will."

"I'll see you," Warren said.

In the city of Calusa, Florida, in spite of the rash of tourist shootings elsewhere in the state, police officers still drove their motor-patrol sectors alone. Officer William Parks pulled his car into the parking lot behind Calusa Public Safety at twenty-five minutes to twelve that night of March twenty-fifth, took his peaked uniform hat from the seat beside him, got out of the car, and only then put the hat on his head. He was wearing the regulation blue nylon jacket with the blue imitation-fur collar. March in the state of Florida was sometimes chancy; if you wanted guaranteed sunshine and tropical temperatures, you didn't choose a so-called semitropical climate where frost on the pumpkin was a distinct possibility during the winter months.

Apparently, the sergeant *hadn't* radioed Parks.

The man reacted just the way any white cop would when confronted with a tall, healthy-looking black man in the semi-darkness of an isolated parking lot, even if it was behind a police station.

"Who's that?" he said, and placed his hand on the butt of the weapon holstered at his waist.

"Warren Chambers," Warren said at once. "I called . . ."

"What do you want?"

Hand still resting on the butt of the .357 Magnum. Not yanking the weapon yet, still respecting the guidelines, but ready to use it if Warren so much as looked at him cockeyed. Warren wasn't the least bit surprised. What Parks was seeing here was a black man, plain and simple, in a state where black men and white cops often viewed a mutual problem from opposite ends of the spectrum. Never mind that Warren was well-dressed and well-groomed, his hair trimmed in a neat Bryant Gumbel cut these days, wearing gold-rimmed specs that gave him the appearance of a scholarly accountant, never mind that Warren stood with his hands open, palms outward at his sides, his body language clearly signaling anything *but* aggressive behavior, never mind any of that. Warren Chambers was black. And therefore a threat.

"I'm a private investigator," he said.

"Let me see your ticket," Parks said. "Slow and easy. I hate surprises."

Warren gingerly fished his wallet from the left-hand side pocket of his trousers, took a laminated card from that, and handed the card to Parks. Parks leaned into the dim light coming from a stanchion some twelve feet away. The card, issued in accordance with Chapter 493 of the Florida Statutes, gave its recipient the right to investigate and gather information on a great many criminal and noncriminal mattters listed in detail in the statute. Warren's actual Class A license to operate a private investigative agency in the state of Florida was framed and hanging on his office wall. The card simply affirmed that he had paid a hundred bucks for the license, had renewed it on the thirtieth day of June, and had posted a five-thousand-dollar bond as required by subsections 493.08 and 493.09.

Parks seemed satisfied he was talking to a bona fide individual and not somebody about to hit him on the head with a lead pipe because his sister had been arrested for dealing dope two weeks ago. Handing the card back, he said, "What can I do for you?" but his tone said Make it fast, pal, I'm just coming off a long, hard day.

"You signed in a shooting victim at Samaritan earlier tonight," Warren said. "His name was Matthew Hope, he . . ."

"Yeah?"

"Where'd you pick him up?"

"Why?"

"I'd like to know who shot him. I've done work for him in the . . ."

"Leave it to the police, okay?" Parks said, and was starting away when Warren gently placed a hand on his arm.

"He's a friend," Warren said.

Parks looked at him.

"Detectives are already on it," he said.

"I won't get in their way."

Parks studied him for a moment.

Then he said, "The Centaur on Roosevelt and G."

"What do you mean?" Patricia said.

"He's been shot," Frank said. "I'm here at . . ."

"*Shot?*"

"Yes. He's in surgery right this minute, they're . . ."

"Where?"

"Good Samaritan."

"I'll be there."

Oh, Jesus, she thought.

Warren did not recognize either of the two detectives who were still canvassing the neighborhood outside the Centaur Bar & Grill on Roosevelt Avenue and G Street. He said hello to them, introduced himself, told them the victim was a good friend of his for whom he'd done a lot of work . . .

"Yeah?" one of them said, totally uninterested.

. . . and would they mind if he asked a few questions? "Like what?" the other one said.

This was a little past one in the morning and they had a shooting on their hands that might turn into a homicide at any moment, and they didn't feel much like bullshitting with a friend of the victim, who, by the way, they now surmised was a black man like his good buddy here.

"Well, for openers," Warren said, "what was he doing in this shitty neighborhood?"

"What *kind* of work?" the first one asked, suddenly interested.

"Investigation. He's a lawyer."

Both cops nodded knowingly, as if they felt it served lawyers right, white *or* black, to catch one in the shoulder and another in the chest. One of them started writing in his pad; apparently they hadn't known before now that the victim was a lawyer. Warren wondered what they *did* know. He was beginning to wish Nick Alston had caught the squeal. Or even Bloom and Rawles, with whom he'd also worked in the past. These two . . .

"Name of the firm?" the second cop asked.

He was the bigger of the two. Wearing a plaid topcoat that had gone out of style in the sixties. Lots of people came down to Florida to stay, they stored their winter clothes, dragged them out whenever the thermometer dipped. In any cold winter, half of them looked like they were dressed for a costume party.

"Mine or his?" Warren asked.

"The lawyer's."

"Summerville and Hope."

"And yours?" the first cop asked.

He was wearing an L.L. Bean jacket that looked fairly new. Green and blue, with a zipper front. He looked warmer than his pal in the plaid topcoat.

"Warren Chambers Investigations."

"Here in town?"

No, in Singapore, Warren thought, but did not say.

"On Whittaker," he said, and nodded.

"Who do you want to talk to?"

"Anybody who might have seen anything."

"In *this* neighborhood," the one in the jacket said, "that means nobody."

This neighborhood was black.

He was still in the operating room when Patricia got to the hospital.

"How is he?" she asked at once.

"One of the nurses came out a few minutes ago," Frank said. "There's a lot of bleeding from the bullet that went through his chest. It's going to take time. There are major arteries involved."

"Who did this?" she asked.

Frank shook his head.

It all kept passing in the dark like a parade, all the circuses blaring, the elephants and clowns, the wild-animal acts and high-wire artists, the flyers and the girls in their sequined tights and tops. All the girls Matthew had ever kissed or never kissed, passing in the dark while voices whispered we've got a bleeder and the band played brass and gold. He'd never met a circus he'd liked, even when he was a kid, he'd always hated circuses, always.

"So what was he doing here?" Warren asked.

"I guess he was waiting for somebody," the bartender said, and shrugged.

He was black, like Warren. But in this neighborhood, you didn't get involved in police business. Warren had identified himself only as a friend of the victim. The bartender was wary nonetheless, brother or not. This section of the city was called Newtown, exclusively black until recent years when an Asian population had begun moving in, causing a somewhat volatile mix in a neighborhood already seething with racial unrest. Warren wondered when the hell it would ever end.

He was not a black man who chose to call himself African-American. He had been born in this country, as had his mother and his father and his grandparents, and if that didn't make him one-hundred-percent American, then he didn't know what did. One of his liberated slave ancestors who'd been carried here in chains from the Ivory Coast might have reasonably called himself *African*-American – which was what he'd been, after all – but the label simply did not apply to Warren, and he wasn't having any of it, thanks. Nor did he believe, the way some black people did, that *every* black act was justified, any more than every *human* act was. In fact, he would have *hanged* those bums who'd beat up that truck driver in Los Angeles.

The way Warren looked at it, black men like the ones out there only made it harder for black people like himself to get a taxi when it was raining. It was as simple as that. Get *any* black man breaking the sacred covenant – or so he considered it – and *all* black men suffered. Warren Chambers was a hard-working man dedicated to the "faithful and honest conduct and performance" of his business. Those were the words that had come along with the $5,000 bond he'd posted: *Conditioned upon the faithful and honest conduct and performance by the licensee of the business so licensed*. Warren Chambers Investigations. That's me, he thought. And he was damn good-looking besides.

"Did he *say* he was waiting for someone?" he asked the bartender.

"No, but he kept checking his watch."

"What time did he come in?"

"Around ten."

"Came to the bar?"

"Yes."

"Ordered a drink?"

"This is a bar, ain't it?"

Warren looked at him.

"I don't think I got your name," he said.

"Mister, the cops already asked me all this."

"I'm not a cop. And I *still* don't have your name."

"My name's Harry, and I *still* told the cops all this."

"Harry, my friend was shot bad, *twice*, outside your place of bus — "

"It ain't my place, I just work here. And I didn't see who shot your honkie friend. First I knew there was any trouble, was I heard shots and he come falling back through the doors."

"What kind of drink did he order?"

"Beefeater martini on the rocks, pair of olives."

Warren knew what Matthew drank; he was simply confirming that he and the bartender were talking about the same man. The only white men who came to the black section of Calusa were here looking for pussy or crack.

"We don't carry the Beefeater, I made it with Gordon's," the bartender said.

"So the man sat down," Warren said, "and he ordered a drink. Did he say anything *after* he ordered the drink?"

"Said the Gordon's would be fine."

Like pulling teeth, Warren thought. He felt like smacking him one upside the head.

"Anything else besides that?"

"Asked me if the clock was right," the bartender said, and gestured vaguely toward the clock hanging on the wall behind him, over the mirror and the lined-up bottles of booze. Warren checked it against his own watch. The bar clock was two minutes fast.

"What'd you tell him?"

"I told him I hadn't had no complaints about it."

"Did he say who he was waiting for?"

"Didn't *say* he was waiting for nobody. That's what I sur*mised*. Him looking at his watch, looking at the bar clock, turning to look at the doors. That's only what I sur*mised*, he was waiting for somebody."

"But he didn't say who."

"No, he didn't say who. For the *fifth* time," the bartender said.

"But who's counting?" Warren said, and flashed a big, fake, watermelon-eating grin.

The bartender did not grin back.

"Did he say anything before he went outside?" Warren asked.

"Nope. In fact, I thought he was leaving."

"Why? Had he settled his bill?"

"No, but . . ."

"Then why'd you think he was leaving?"

"I don't trust nobody, this place."

"Gee, no kidding?" Warren said. "So he just got up, and without a word, he started for the doors, is that right?"

"That's right. And I don't appreciate sarcasm."

Warren swung around on his stool. The doors were the kind you'd find on a bar in a western town, or at least in a *movie* about a western town, these slatted, wooden, swinging doors hanging waist-to-shoulder high, perfectly suited to the milder weather the state of Florida advertised in its come-on catalogs and brochures, but distinctly inappropriate for a March like this one. Warren noticed that the tables just inside the doors were empty, small wonder. He turned back to the bartender.

"Did you *ask* him to settle his bill?"

"No, I did not."

"Even though you thought he was leaving?"

"I figured he was a cop."

"How'd you figure that?"

"There was a cop smell on him," the bartender said, and shrugged.

Warren wondered if he himself ever would have mistaken Matthew for a cop. It was a tough call. Matthew was around six feet tall, he guessed, weighing maybe a hundred eighty, a hundred eighty-five, in there, dark hair, brown eyes, a fox face. Most cops Warren knew had pig faces.

"What time was this? When he walked out?"

"Around a quarter past. I didn't look at the clock."

"How soon after that did you hear the shots?"

"Minute he walked through the doors."

"He pushed open the doors . . ."

"Yeah, that's the way it usually works."

Smack him *both* sides the head, Warren thought.

". . . and there were shots the minute he . . ."

"Yeah."

Which meant someone had been waiting for him to come out.

"How many shots?"

"Three."

It still felt like Friday night, but it was already Saturday morning. One-thirty in the morning by the impersonal clock on the immaculate hospital wall. Passover would start today at sundown. Patricia had called a florist earlier today – well, technically *yesterday*, Friday – to order a dozen roses for delivery to Matthew's home at nine in the morning, even though he wasn't Jewish. Seven and a half hours from now. The inscription on the card would read:

Happy Passover!
I love you, Counselor

No signature.

Matthew would not be there to accept them, of course, Matthew was still in the operating room, Matthew had been in surgery since ten-thirty tonight, *last* night, when*ever* the hell it was, she didn't know or *care* which day it was, all she knew was that her man might . . .

No, she thought.

None of that.

Stop it.

She clenched her hands in her lap.

Saturday was one of Matthew's tennis mornings. He would have driven directly from his house on Whisper Key to the club on the mainland, and there he would have played against one or another ruthless attorneys like himself, who would invariably beat him because in truth he was not a very good tennis player. Nor a very good *any* kind of athlete, for that matter. He'd once wondered aloud why pool shooters were referred to as "athletes" on television. Pool shooters? How about dart throwers? She'd shot pool with Matthew only once, in one of those new decorator pool parlors where athletic girls in fuck-me dresses leaned over the table to zero in on the eight ball while simultaneously showing a crowded bra and a tight-skirted ass. Not Patricia's style. Except in bed.

Had Matthew got home at eleven or so this morning, which was when he usually got back after his tennis game, he'd have found the roses at his front door and would have known instantly who'd sent them, despite the lack of signature on the card. Not three weeks ago, they'd had a conversation during which he'd asked why women never sent flowers to men. Didn't they know men like flowers, too? This was only *one* of the things she loved about this man, the fact that he was so unconcerned with all the macho bullshit that so burdened most other men she'd known.

She looked up at the wall clock.

She looked at her wristwatch.

Frank had gone down the hall again for coffee. The coffee came in cardboard containers. Since she'd got here, they'd each drunk three cups of the vile stuff. She did not know Frank very well. Only once had she and Matthew gone out for dinner with him and his wife. A hospital waiting room was not the best place in the world to strike up an acquaintance.

She looked at her watch again.

He had been in surgery for a bit more than three hours now. Was that normal for something like this? Should it be taking this *long*. Was something *wrong* in there?

. . . told him ten o'clock sharp, but maybe they were supposed to meet *outside* the bar. Chilly night, Matthew could feel the cold coming under the bar doors, over the bar doors, too cold a night to be out chasing lions and tigers and daring young men on the flying trapeze, too cold for little girls who dance on glittering balls, and clowns who roll in sawdust, he hated the circus. Why was it so cold in here? What were they *doing* to him? Why were they all *over* him? Let me . . . Please. Let me out of here . . . *please!* Push open the doors, feel the night air sharp and cold, see the car sitting at the curb, steaming at the curb, start for the car, no, see the window sliding gently down, swiftly down, silently down, oh God, *no* . . .

The hooker Warren spoke to thought he was looking for a good time. It was very cold for this time of year, it wasn't supposed to be this way. Many of your snowbirds had left by now, heading north again for Easter, which was only eight days away. But despite the promised unseasonal over-night lows and accompanying frost, the girl was wearing only a skintight red satin dress, a little red-dyed monkey-fur jacket, a red plastic shoulder bag, red high-heeled, ankle-strapped slippers, and a red lipstick slash to match the overall color scheme. Her own color was harder to classify. Somewhere in the beige-to-brown spectrum, more or less, but her eyes and her narrow bone structure suggested an Asian influence; Warren figured her for the daughter of a black soldier and a Vietnamese woman. She told him her name was Garnet, which meant nothing; every hooker in town had a working name. When she realized that all he wanted was information, she started walking away.

"*Were* you on the street when the shooting occurred?" he asked again.

"What's it worth?" she asked, turning back to him.

"Depends on what you saw," Warren said. "Let's start with ten, okay?" he said, and opened his wallet and pulled out two fives.

"No, let's start with twenty-five," she said, which was the going price for a blow job in Newtown.

"Sure," he said, and peeled off a ten and another five.

The girl – Warren figured she was eighteen, nineteen years old – opened her handbag, tucked the money into a change purse, and snapped the bag shut again. Cars were cruising the early morning street, trolling. Her eyes kept following them; she'd been paid for about ten minutes' work here, and she wanted to make this fast, get on with her business. A white Ford van was still parked on the street outside the bar. This was the police department's mobile crime lab, and Warren knew one or two of the technicians on the Criminalistics Unit, but he didn't see any familiar faces at the moment. Which was too bad, since he'd wanted to ask about that third bullet. It was now around two in the morning, but a crowd was still gathered on the street, huddling against the cold winds that blew in off Calusa Bay.

"I'm listening," he said.

"This was around ten-fifteen," she said. "I usually start around ten, ten-thirty, try to get a jump on some of the other girls who don't come out till midnight. I was on the corner here . . . this is my usual corner, right near the bar here, I get them going in the bar and coming out, and I also get the car traffic going both ways on Roosevelt and G. This guy came out of the bar. Good-looking white man, tall, dark-haired, wearing a topcoat, no hat. A car was sitting there at the curb. Engine running."

"Who was in the car?" Warren asked.

"I don't know. It had tinted windows."

"What kind of car?"

"A two-door Mazda. Low, sleek, black."

"Know what year it was?"

"No."

"See the license plate? Florida, out of . . .?"

"I didn't notice it."

"Okay, what happened when he came out of the bar?"

"He saw the car and started for it as if he recognized it. Then he . . . sort of hesitated. And seemed about to move back toward the bar, seemed about to turn. But the . . . the window near the curb rolled down. And a gun came out. An arm with a gun. A gun in somebody's hand."

"White or black? The hand?"

"I didn't see the hand itself. The person was wearing a *glove*. A black glove."

"Was this person male or female?"

"I couldn't see inside the car."

"Then you don't *know* whether the person was white or black."

"That's right, I don't know."

"What kind of gun was it?"

"I don't know guns. It must've been a powerful one, though. Blew him back across the sidewalk and through the doors again."

"How many shots?"

"Three. I think the first one missed."

"How do you know?"

"I saw him flinch, but he didn't act as if he'd been hit. He just sort of ducked away, looked again as if he was about to turn, or run, or, I don't know. Then there was another shot and it must've caught him in the shoulder, it knocked him sort of backward a little, and a little to the side, and the next one hit him in the chest someplace. He was like struggling to keep his balance, like thrashing all over the place, his arms, his legs, it was like he was being *carried* by the shots, do you know what I mean? Do you remember the scene at the beginning of *Jaws*, when the shark grabs her and *carries* her? It was like that. As if the shots were *carrying* him backward across the sidewalk and through the bar doors. It was very frightening. I *still* won't go in the water."

"What happened then?"

"The car drove off."

"Immediately?"

"Yes. Well . . . the hand went back in the car, the arm, the hand with the gun, and then the window went up, and then the car shot away from the curb."

"In which direction?"

"West. G's a one-way street."

"Then what?"

"Somebody came running out of the bar, yelling for the police. I took off. Cops and me don't get along."

"When did you come back?"

"Half an hour ago. I figured it'd be quieted down by then."

"You didn't see that car again, did you?"

"No."

"It didn't come back for a second look, did it?"

"No. Would you?"

She looked at the car traffic on the street again, turned back to him, and said, "Listen, that's all I saw, and I have to go now, really. I think what I told you is worth at least another dime, don't you?"

Warren gave her another ten-dollar bill.

The price of a hand job in Newtown.

"A client in *Newtown*?" Frank said, and raised his eyebrows a notch.

Matthew had once told her that many people thought he and Frank looked alike – though Matthew, personally, could see no resemblance. Neither could Patricia. Matthew was thirty-eight years old, and Patricia guessed his partner was forty, or perhaps even older. True, they both had the same brown eyes and dark hair, and were about the same weight and height – well, now that she really thought about it, Frank was two or three inches shorter and some twenty pounds lighter. More importantly, though, and using a classification system Frank himself had invented, Matthew had a "fox" face and Frank's face was definitely "pig." Moreover, Matthew was originally from Chicago whereas Frank had been born and raised in New York, and their styles were totally opposite. So, really, there was no resemblance at all. Except now, perhaps, as Frank sat solemnly sipping his coffee in the dimly lighted waiting room, hunched over the cardboard container, his face looking weary and apprehensive, all the sharp New York edges worn smooth by concern for his partner and friend.

"We had dinner together earlier," Patricia said. "I thought he'd be coming home with me, but he said something had come up, he had to meet someone. I assumed it was a client. I told him to come over later. He said he didn't know how long the meeting would take."

"But did he say he was going to *Newtown*?"

Still amazed. What the hell had Matthew been doing in *Newtown*?

"No, he didn't say Newtown," Patricia said.

"Where *did* he say?"

"Well, he didn't actually."

"Did he make any phone calls while you were in the restaurant?"

"No."

"Or receive any?"

"No."

"Then whatever had come up . . ."

". . . had to've been before dinner," Patricia said.

"He didn't tell you what this might've been, did he?"

"No. Thinking back, though, he seemed . . . well, not quite himself. Quiet. Preoccupied."

"He's been that way a lot lately," Frank said, and sighed heavily. "Ever since the Barton trial."

Mary Barton. Mary, Mary, quite contrary, for whom a jury had deliberated a verdict on three counts of Murder One. Mary had been Matthew's client. The trial had taken place in the weeks preceding Christmas. This was now close to the end of March. A long time to be brooding over what had happened, especially when one considered the circumstances surrounding it.

"He told me he didn't think he'd ever step foot inside a courtroom again," Frank said.

Patricia looked at him. This was news to her. She herself was an assistant state attorney for Florida's Twelfth Judicial District here in Calusa, and she knew Matthew was a damned *good* litigator. Then again, she loved the man.

"Not after what happened with Mary Barton. He won't take on anyone he believes is guilty, you know . . ."

"I know."

". . . and he was *so* convinced of her innocence. Then to have happen what happened . . . which, really, you know, was something beyond his control . . ."

"I know."

"But he doesn't. And that's the problem. Frankly, Patricia, I think he *meant* what he said. About trying another case. He's turned down half a dozen criminal cases since the trial, and I think it's because he's lost faith in his own judgment. If he won't defend anyone he thinks is guilty, how can he trust he's making the right decision about someone's *innocence*? After *Mary*? How can he trust *anything* after Mary?"

"That was an unusual situation, Frank. Surely he knows . . ."

"No, he doesn't. He blames himself. For taking her on in the first place, although she *was* innocent as it turned out, wasn't she? And for having it turn out the way it did in the second place, which was the goddamn *irony* of it. You know what he's been doing since you guys got back?"

"Yes, but I thought . . ."

"Real estate," Frank said.

"I know, but I thought that was only temporary."

"Trying to buy the state *fair*grounds," Frank said, and shook his head.

"Yes, he mentioned that."

"Something nice and safe. No crazy ladies under the bed or in the bushes."

"Well, there *was* a suicide involved, wasn't there?"

"A what?"

"A suicide. The woman who owned the circus. Didn't she commit suicide?"

"He never mentioned that to me," Frank said, and looked up at the wall clock. "What the hell is *taking* so long?"

Why was he remembering his sister holding a doll in her

arms, smiling in approval while he ran his electric trains under a Christmas tree? Why was he remembering Chicago thirty years ago, what was happening to him? He thought he might be dying, he thought his life was flashing by while he died. The voices were terribly concerned, someone was saying I can't see, suck up that blood, *what* blood, what were they talking about? Someone said sixty over forty, someone else said one-twenty, someone else said sponge, a gorilla was throwing gorilla shit at Gloria. They were walking up the midway where you could see the animals in their cages, Matthew was eight and his sister was only six, and a gorilla threw his own shit at her. It stained her bright yellow dress and splattered on the ground, eighty-seven over fifty, he reached down and picked up a handful of straw and shit and threw it back at the gorilla who began pounding his chest and baring his teeth, he'd hated circuses ever since that day. There was ringing now, something was ringing, someone said Oh shit, he's flat-lined, he's in cardiac arrest, someone else said, Let's pace him, someone said, Epinephrine, someone else said Keep an eye on that clock, someone said One cc, one to a thousand, someone else said Still unobtainable, Matthew picked up the phone.

Cynthia Huellen was telling him that a man named George Steadman was on five. There was a combination digital clock-calendar on Matthew's desk. The date on the calendar read FRI 3/18. The clock read 9:27 AM.

"Who is he?" Matthew asked. "What does he want?"

"Says he wants to talk to you about a real estate deal."

"I'll take it."

Truth be known, he would have taken anything but the inside of another courtroom.

"Hello, Mr Steadman, this is Matthew Hope," he said. "How can I help you?"

"Ahhhh, Mr Hope, how are you?"

"Fine, thank you," he said. "And you?"

"Fine, just fine."

"I understand there's some real estate you want to talk about."

"Yes. I was wondering if you could come out here . . ."

"Well, Mr Steadman, I just got back from vacation on Monday, and my desk is still piled high to the . . ."

"I would come there, but we're just settling in here, too. There's a lot of work to be done before the top goes up tomorrow."

"Sorry?"

"The top, the big tent. I'm George Steadman, the Steadman & Roeger Circus, you've heard of me?"

"Yes, I have."

"So this is a busy time for me, hm? Putting it all together before we go on the road in April."

"I see."

"Otherwise, of course, I'd come there."

"I appreciate that, Mr Steadman. But . . . is there some urgency to this? Real estate isn't usually a matter of life or . . ."

"No, no, there's no *urgency*, certainly. But I'm a man of action, Mr Hope. And when I get it in my mind to do something, I want to do it right away, do you see? Where were you?"

"Sorry?"

"On vacation."

"Oh. Little Dix Bay."

"I don't believe I know it."

"On Virgin Gorda. The British Virgin Islands."

"Ahh, yes. So what do you say? Can you come out here today?"

"I don't know where 'out here' is, sir. And, as I told you, today would be out of the . . ."

"Then how about tomorrow? We're only a half hour from where you are," Steadman said. "Timucuan Point Road, do you know what used to be the old Jackson cattle ranch?"

"Yes?"

"That's where we are. We lost our lease on the land we were using for twenty years now, so I have to make do with this for the time being, hm? That's what I want to talk to you about. Please come out, Mr Hope. It's only a half-hour drive, truly. And I won't keep you long, I promise. Besides, you might enjoy seeing a circus go up."

Without mentioning to Mr Steadman that he would not enjoy seeing a circus go up or down or even sideways, Matthew agreed to go out there tomorrow at nine in the morning. The conversation with Steadman had taken exactly ten minutes. He made a note of Steadman's name and the duration of the call, though he would not bill him for the time unless Steadman actually hired him. Sinus rhythm, someone said. Gloria began shrieking at the top of her lungs. Thirty over ten, someone said. Someone was yelling that the little boy had thrown shit at the gorilla. One-forty, someone said. The gorilla was pounding his chest and bouncing all over the cage, rushing the bars, backing off again, beating on his chest, bouncing, shrilling his challenge to Matthew where he stood on the straw-covered ground almost wetting his pants in fear. Sixty over forty, someone said. Clamp it, someone said. One-twenty. What was the time? someone said. Five-forty, someone said. Silence. There's another one, someone else said. Five minutes, Jesus, someone said. And forty, someone said. Careful now, someone else said. Watch it. I've got it, someone said. Voices. Careful now. Clamp it. Steady now. Tie it. A hundred over . . .

The road leading into the temporary circus grounds was the old dirt road that used to serve as the entrance to the Jackson ranch. While Patricia and Matthew were lolling on a white sand beach in the Caribbean, it had been raining day and night here in Calusa, and so the road now was muddy and rutted and wet with standing pools and puddles of water, even though the sun was shining faintly on this moderately warm Saturday in March. As Matthew fought the wheel of the car, an Acura Legend that usually handled beautifully under almost any conditions, trying not to get stuck in the muck and mire, he could see on his right a vast field similarly awash in slime, where trucks and trailers were parked in a seemingly haphazard fashion. In the center of this evidently erratic circle of vehicles, a mass of muscled, blue-jeaned men, naked to the waist and covered with mud, were furiously struggling to erect the center pole of a huge tent Steadman had called "the top." Matthew had no idea how far along the process was. A bulky gray shape loomed on his left, and he turned, startled to see an elephant lumbering past his car. He rolled down the window, said, "Excuse me" – not to the elephant but to the man leading it – and when he'd caught the man's attention, asked where he might find Mr. Steadman.

"In the red wagon," the man said, and then grunted something to the elephant, who began moving again toward where the men were hoisting the pole.

Matthew looked in the direction the man had vaguely indicated. He could see no wagons, red or otherwise. Instead, there was only a long, tractor-trailer rig painted white, and seeming to serve not only as a means of transportation but also as a multiple poster for the show. On the cab of the vehicle, the words STEADMAN & ROEGER CIRCUS were lettered in black on the rim of a flaming hoop through which a fearsome tiger was leaping. This same ad was echoed – in much larger red, yellow, and black lettering – on the side of the rig, where more prominence was given to the word *circus* than to the owners' names:

STEADMAN & ROEGER
CIRCUS

At the far end of the rig, just beyond a door with a barred upper half, the word TICKETS was lettered in the same red, yellow, and black colors, spanning three openings now shuttered with pull-down wooden flaps painted white to match the rig. Matthew parked the car, got out, and walked through the mud toward a small platform of three wooden steps leading up to the barred door. There was no bell. He knocked on the door.

"Come in!" a voice shouted.

George Steadman was a tall, burly white man, with wide shoulders, a paunchy middle, and ham-hock hands, one of which he extended as he came around his desk. His face was broad, leathery, and suntanned, framed north, south, east, and west, by a head of thick black hair, a thick black mustache, and sideburns going white. He lumbered toward Matthew like a big ferocious bear, but his smile was friendly, and his handshake was surprisingly nonassertive.

"Come in, come in, Mr. Hope, forgive the mess," he said, "have a seat, please," and instantly offered Matthew a canvas-backed director's chair that had the word BOSS lettered in black across its back. The inside of the trailer was furnished as a traveling office, with a proper metal desk and metal filing cabinets, all painted institutional green, framed circus posters on the walls, and a metal door – open now – that could be closed to ensure privacy from the ticket-selling operation next door.

"Some coffee?" Steadman asked. "Something to eat? If you're hungry, I can send one of the boys over to the cook-house, the flag is up. Have you had breakfast?"

"I've had breakfast, thank you."

"Then some coffee, yes?"

"Not right now, thank you."

Steadman's voice was loud and resonant, perfectly suited to his huge frame and blustery manner. He was telling Matthew now that most circus owners put up their big tent a week before they set out on the road, which was usually on the first day of April. Rehearsed for a week inside the tent, most of them, then took the show out.

"Not the *Big* One, of course, Ringling rehearses for weeks and weeks. And some of your *very* small mud shows, the performers'll arrive the day before they move out, there'll be just a single run-through, and that's it."

He went on to explain that he personally liked his tent up and his performers arriving at winter quarters *two* weeks before they went out. That way he could be sure that what Steadman & Roeger was putting on the road was a hundred times better than any of the other truck shows.

"This isn't a very big circus," he said. "Ringling moves how many – eighty *railroad* cars? Altogether, S&R moves twenty-five trucks and trailers, ninety, a hundred people altogether, depending on who blows the show. But what I'm saying is this is definitely not a gigantic operation here, even though a hundred people isn't a *small* number of people to move about – *plus* the animals, of course."

"In fact, it sounds like a very *big* operation," Matthew said.

"Well, no, not really. Even so, when you've been doing it for so many years, you get the knack, hm? The reason I want the fairgrounds is so we can become a paying proposition all year round. Set up a permanent tent – Calusa is a tourist town, am I right? There are people here all winter long, looking for entertainment. How many movies can they go see?"

Plenty, Matthew thought. Some thirty first-run screens by the latest count.

"I figure if I can keep the show running here from November through March, I won't have to look all over for winter dates. Besides, I can probably get a tax benefit if I donate the tent to the local schools for the summer, to train kids who want to make the circus their life, whatever. What do you think of that idea, by the way? *Would* there be a tax benefit in doing something like that?"

"One of our tax attorneys would have to discuss that with you, Mr. Steadman. What I'*m* here for is to . . ."

"The fairgrounds, yes. They're commonly called the *state* fairgrounds, you know, but the land is privately owned, which is good for us. The state only leases the land for its fair every summer, same as anyone else who wants to use it. Carnivals, horse shows, Virginia Slims tournaments, whatever."

"How much land are we talking about?" Matthew asked.

"Thirty acres, convenient to both the Tamiami Trail *and* I-95. If I use eighteen acres for parking, and put the remaining twelve under canvas – you know what kind of a circus *that* would be? A midway, sideshows, a permanent menagerie, carnival rides, animal rides, a *three*-ring tent, what a circus! I have dreams, Mr. Hope. Very big dreams. But, of course, I have to acquire the land first. Whoever owns it is represented by a company called Florida Sun and Shore, the names they come up with down here, hm?"

"Then you don't actually *know* who owns the land, is that it?"

"I'm sorry, I don't. I would leave all that to you. Find out who they are, tell them what I want to pay, come back to me with their counteroffer, you'll negotiate back and forth for me, we'll get the land."

Maybe, Matthew thought.

Aloud, he said, "Who's Roeger?"

"Max Roeger, my former partner. He sold his fifty percent of the business ten years ago. In reality, there *is* no more Steadman & Roeger, there's just Steadman. Max died of cancer shortly after he sold out. That's why he got out, in fact. He knew he was dying. We kept the name because it had recognition value, hah?"

"Who's *we*?"

"Pardon?"

"You said Mr. Roeger sold . . .?"

"Oh. Yes. Willa. Willa Winkie. But she's also deceased now."

"I see. And what happened to *her* share of the . . .?"

"Her only child inherited. A daughter. Maria Torrance."

"Inherited her mother's share of the circus?"

"Yes. Fifty percent."

"Does she *still* own that fifty-percent share?"

"Oh, yes. But she hasn't interfered with my running of the business. She's left that entirely to me. Anyone employed by me reports directly to me. I do all the hiring, and everyone's responsible to me. The performers, the workmen, the people in charge of bookings, promotion, publicity, routing, everybody, all of them come to me. I have the final say. Maria's never said anything about the way I've been running things."

"Is this a general partnership, by the way?"

"Yes, it is."

"Does a partnership agreement exist?"

"Yes."

"Between you and the late Mr. Roeger?"

"Yes."

"Does it define what would happen if one or the other of the partners decided to sell his share?"

"We each had the right of approval over any prospective buyer. If we didn't approve, then we had the right to meet the offer on the table."

"Did you approve of the sale to Mrs. Winkie?"

"Torrance. Mrs. Torrance. Winkie was her circus name."

"Oh? Was she a performer?"

"An entertainer, actually. But a *major* attraction, very big. Here with S&R, the circus. Max and I both knew her for a long time before he decided to sell to her. We were all very good friends."

"So you approved of the deal?"

"Oh, yes, of course."

"And I'm assuming all of Mr. Roeger's right, title, and interest in the circus was then conveyed to her."

"Yes."

"She became a full partner, just as Mr. Roeger had been before her."

"Yes. A very good businesswoman, in fact."

"Mr. Steadman, can you tell me whether the original partnership agreement specified what would happen in the event of the *death* of either of the partners?"

"Are you talking about a person inheriting?"

"Yes. I'm assuming Miss Torrance inherited the same right, title, and interest her mother had purchased . . ."

"Yes."

"What I'm trying to find out is whether or not Miss Torrance would now have anything to say about how the partnership's assets are spent."

"Well, my original agreement with Max specified that if either one of us died, whoever survived was obliged to consult with the deceased's heirs on any business decisions. But, as I said, Maria's never given me the slightest trouble about how I run the business."

"But on an investment of this magnitude . . . thirty acres of choice business property . . . how much were you planning on offering for that land, Mr. Steadman?"

"Land in that part of town is going for anywhere between a hundred and two hundred thousand an acre. We'll offer very low and settle at the bottom. I'm figuring three million for the thirty acres. No mortgages, three million on the barrelhead."

"Exactly my point. How do you think she'll feel about your spending that much of the circus's assets? For your *dream*, as it were."

"The final decision is mine to make," Steadman said.

"You just said . . ."

"Yes, but Max and I thought of *that* too, Mr. Hope. Good friends make good contracts, and vice versa. Consultation is one thing, but suppose Max's daughter . . . or my daughter, for that matter . . . married some jackass, and he was the only one left when we died, and he turned out to be a plumber or a shoemaker who didn't know a damn thing about running a circus, were we supposed to worry about how *he* thought we should conduct our business? No, sir. We put in a clause that said in the event of a deadlock, the surviving partner had the right to make the final decision. We put that in for our own protection."

"Maybe I'd better have a look at that original agreement," Matthew said.

The tent was up.

Workmen stood about with their hands on their hips, admiring their handiwork, smoking, talking softly, occasionally chuckling, the way men will when they feel they've accomplished something together by their own hard labor. The canvas, blue and white in the afternoon sun, flapped in a mild breeze, the tent all aflutter with brightly colored pennants and pennoncels, an American flag flapping high atop the center pole. The man who'd earlier led the elephant past Matthew's car was now feeding the animal, who'd probably done most of the work in getting all those poles up.

Matthew could see inside the open entrance flap to where cages and chutes were being set up for the wild-animal act, trapezes and platforms hoisted high for the flyers, a wooden platform set up for the band. This – the main entrance to the big tent – was where the midway would lead when all of the sideshows and concessions were in place. It was on such a midway that the gorilla in his cage had thrown shit at Matthew's sister all those years ago. Back then, in addition to the caged menagerie, the midway had featured sideshows with what were then called "monsters" or "freaks," no longer exploited in today's traveling circuses.

While Steadman had searched in the trailer's old Mosler safe for the ancient partnership agreement between him and Max Roeger, and then for the agreement between Roeger and Willa Torrance, and then for a copy of the will granting Willa's rights to her daughter, he had told Matthew that his working nut was somewhere between $8,000 and $9,000 a day. His tent could hold 2,500 seats, and he sold those for $10 apiece. If he sold all 2,500 seats, he could take in $25,000, but kids were let in free, so he had to figure only *half* the seats were paying seats. That came to $12,500 a show. Of that, Steadman had to give anywhere from ten to forty percent of the gate to whichever town organization sponsored the show – the Lions Club or the Chamber of Commerce, or the Elks or the Shriners or whoever – and so he had to figure that doing two *capacity* shows daily, he could net after expenses something like $6,000–$12,000 a day on admissions alone. The midway, however, brought in a lot of money over that.

Gone were the days of the Siamese twins or the dog-faced boy or the fat lady or the turtle man or the mule-faced woman or the half man/half woman or the dwarf who lifted weights with a hook in his pierced tongue or the monkey girl or the tattooed lady or the rubber man or the human pincushion or the armless wonder or the midgets who could fit in thimbles or the giants taller than trees or the elephant-skin girl or alligator-skin boy or the bearded lady or the three-eyed man, gone was the entire Tarot-deck array of oddities that had bedecked the midways of the past.

But Steadman had explained that if a circus could find an empty lot large enough to put up a big top *and* a proper midway, and then open the midway an hour or two before the big show began, he could sell rides on the ponies and the camels and the elephants – all of which he owned – at two to three dollars a ride, depending on which town you were showing, and five dollars for an adult. Sell a thousand rides at each show, that came to a piece of change. Open your midway at three o'clock, say, let your two thousand or more lot lice in at that time, have your front-talkers lure them in to pay a paltry two-dollar admission fee for the privilege of watching a sword swallower or fire-eater or knife thrower or strong man or snake charmer or magician or ventriloquist or master of a thousand disguises, none of whom were monsters or freaks, all of whom were perfectly normal human beings performing amazing feats of wonder and surprise, and then have them wander all goggle-eyed outside again to buy some soda pop at a buck-fifty a can, or some hot dogs at two bucks apiece (with mustard but no sauerkraut) or some peanuts at a dollar a bag (the peanut pitch alone was a gold mine) and then maybe try the moon walk for a couple of bucks and eat some cotton candy or some snowballs and buy some souvenirs, all of this *before* these people bought their admission tickets to the big top, all of them enjoying themselves and spending their money before the big show even started! And, baby, before you could say "Step right up!" the concessionaires and attraction-operators were taking in some ten, twelve, fourteen thousand dollars a day, forty percent of which went to Steadman for leasing them the midway space.

"Who *says* the midway is dead?" Steadman had asked rhetorically. "The S&R midway is very much alive, thank you, and hopes to stay that way."

Matthew had suddenly understood why the man wanted to spend three million dollars for a piece of vacant land upon which he could erect a permanent circus.

"Hello?"

He turned to where a recreational trailer had just pulled in alongside his Acura. The vehicle was lettered in red across its side with the words THE FLYING McCULLOUGHS. A man was at the wheel, leaning on the lower part of the window frame, the window down. His hair was blond; his blue eyes squinted against the sun limning Matthew.

"Are you the lot boss?" he asked.

Matthew figured the question had been directed to him solely because he was the only man in sight wearing a jacket and tie, trappings that gave him a look of authority.

"No, I'm not," he said. "Sorry."

"Just want to know where I should park the rig," the man said.

"Mr. Steadman's in the red wagon," Matthew said, showing off.

The blond man turned to the woman sitting beside him.

"Want to go say hello to George?" he asked.

"Later," she said irritably. "Let's park."

"Let me see if anybody's laid out the lot yet," he said, and opened the car door, looked down at the mud underfoot, scowled, and stepped gingerly to the ground.

"Sam McCullough," he told Matthew, and extended his hand. He was wearing a blue short-sleeved shirt with a crocodile logo over the left breast, tan chinos, a braided leather belt with a large silver buckle, and leather sandals. The first thing Matthew noticed was the strong grip. McCullough had massive hands and thick wrists, and he took Matthew's hand as if he were catching him after a triple somersault without a net. His chest, neck, and shoulder muscles were also well-defined, giving his trim body a look of tremendous power. Matthew decided that if ever he'd want anyone to catch him after he'd left the safety of a trapeze, Sam McCullough would be a good choice.

"Matthew Hope," he said. "I'm an attorney."

McCullough nodded noncommittally, and then turned away in dismissal. "You getting hungry, Marnie?" he asked the woman in the van.

"I could eat," she said.

There was a sultry, pouting look on her face. Either they'd just had a terrific argument, or she was habitually cross. She was wearing red. A red blouse, red coral earrings, lipstick to match. Her long blonde hair was pulled back in a ponytail, fastened with a red barrette the color of the earrings. She stared ahead through the windshield, ignoring Matthew, ignoring McCullough.

"I'll see if they've set up the cookhouse," McCullough said.

"They have," Matthew said, remembering Steadman's offer to send one of the boys for food.

"Know where it is?"

"Sorry."

McCullough's look said What good are you? He glanced down at the mud again, seemed to deliberate whether he should take off the sandals or not, and then set out across the field like one of Henry the Fifth's archers at Agincourt. The blonde turned to look at Matthew. Their eyes met. Hers blue, his brown. Her glance was like the flick of a whip. She turned away almost at once.

Matthew got into the car without looking back at her, and drove through the mud and out of the lot.

They both listened intently, as if trying to memorize the doctor's words. He was still wearing a green surgical gown, a green mask still tied behind his neck and hanging around his throat. There were speckles of blood on the gown, Patricia noticed, none on the mask. This was a quarter past three in the morning, and he was telling her, telling Frank, his eyes moving from one to the other of them – no sexist pig, this one, an equal opportunity employer, this one, the eyes all inclusive regardless of sex – telling them both that they'd repaired all the ruptured blood vessels caused by the bullet's passage through Mr. Hope's chest, and that his blood pressure was back to one-ten over eighty, and his pulse down to a hundred. He was in the recovery room, and should be coming out of the anesthesia in, oh, a few hours, at which time they could see him, talk to him, the surgery had been entirely successful, and they weren't expecting any postoperative problems. He should tell them, however . . .

They both leaned in closer to him.

". . . that for a period of time during the operation, Mr. Hope suffered cardiac arrest, which meant that for some five minutes . . . five minutes and forty seconds, to be exact . . . there was a loss of blood to the brain. That is, no blood was being pumped to the brain, no blood was being circulated anywhere in the body. His EKG had flat-lined, there was no reading, his heart had stopped pumping blood, his blood pressure was unobtainable, a zero b.p. We paced him . . . we put a temporary pacemaker on the chest wall at once, and injected adrenaline directly into the heart. This got the heart pumping again, but, as I say, during those five minutes and more of the cardiac arrest, there was no electrical activity, and no blood circulating."

"What does that mean?" Patricia asked. "No blood circulating?"

She was beginning to get alarmed. She did not like the idea of Matthew's brain being deprived of blood for more than five minutes. Five minutes and forty *seconds*. That sounded very alarming to her.

"Well," the doctor said, "in some cases, loss of circulation to the brain can result in varying degrees of damage."

"Damage?" she asked at once. "What do you mean? Damage to the *brain*?"

"Yes. When the loss of circulation is an extended one."

"What do you mean by 'extended'?" she asked. "How long is *extended*?" She had fallen unconsciously into the stance she took when cross-examining a hostile witness, leaning into the doctor now, every bit the prosecuting attorney, zeroing in, wanting facts and only facts.

"Anything upward of five minutes could be considered extended."

"And Matthew's heart stopped for five minutes and forty seconds, isn't that what you said?"

"Yes, Mr. Hope's brain was deprived of blood for that period of time. His heart was not pumping blood for that period of time."

"You said *varying* degrees of damage," Patricia said. "Varying in what way?"

"The brain will tolerate a loss of circulation for only a short period of time. As a rule of thumb, if deprivation continues for more than five minutes, damage will usually result."

Five minutes and forty seconds, Patricia was thinking.

"But any interruption in the reticular activating system will be only temporary if . . ."

"What's that? Reticular acti —?"

"The interaction of neurons with the cortex of the brain. The cortex maintains wakefulness and consciousness."

Consciousness, Patricia thought.

"We're talking about coma here, aren't we?" she said.

"No, no. Well, yes, *if* the brain is deprived of blood for anywhere between five and nine minutes, coma will undoubtedly occur. But it will usually be only temporary."

"How about *more* than nine minutes?" Frank asked.

"If circulation is interrupted for from ten to twelve minutes, then recovery of consciousness would be unlikely."

"He'd be in coma permanently," Patricia said.

"Most likely."

"Permanently," Patricia said again.

"Most likely," the doctor said again.

"How about five minutes and forty *seconds*?" she asked. "Where does *that* leave him?"

"You have to remember," the doctor said, "that there was massive bleeding from numerous ruptured arteries. Mr. Hope was bleeding *continuously* until his heart stopped pumping, and the moment we got it going again, he began bleeding all over again. Quite often, such a severe loss of blood is enough in *itself* to cause a drop in blood pressure sufficient to compromise circulation to the brain. In Mr. Hope's case . . ."

"How about five minutes and forty seconds?" Patricia repeated.

"Obviously, that's at the very lowest end of the scale."

"What scale?"

"Of probability."

"Probability of what?"

"Permanent brain damage."

"Permanent coma?"

"Yes."

She could tell he was getting annoyed, he'd just spent four and a half hours awash in blood, locating and clamping and tying God knew how many ruptured vessels, and he was tired and hungry and all he wanted to do was wash up and go to a pancake house for breakfast, and then head home for some sleep, but here was a pushy broad who wanted a crash course in Thoracic Surgery 101. Well, the hell with him, this was *her* man lying unconscious there in the recovery room, and she wanted to know whether or not he'd been turned into a goddamn *vegetable*.

"I hasten to add that we're anticipating his return to full wakefulness and awareness as soon as the anesthesia wears off," the doctor said.

Then why the hell did you bring up *coma*? Patricia wondered.

"I merely felt you should be made aware of what occurred during surgery," he said, as if reading her mind, "so that there wouldn't be any surprises in the event of a worst-case scenario.

Incidentally, when you see him, don't be dismayed by all the paraphernalia. There's a tube in his nose to draw out stomach contents and another in his mouth to help him breathe, and we've got a catheter going to his bladder, and all sorts of tubes and lines feeding him intravenously and monitoring his vital signs. His condition is stable, but this was an enormously severe trauma. Getting shot twice is no picnic. So don't expect him to get up and waltz you around the room just now."

When *will* he waltz me around the room? Patricia wondered.

Aloud, she said, "How long will he be in the recovery room?"

"Two or three hours, I'd say. He should be coming out of the anesthesia by . . . what time is it, anyway?" He looked at his watch, raised his eyebrows as if surprised to learn how late it was, and then said, "Six A.M.? Around then? Maybe a little later. We'll keep him in the recovery room a while after he comes around, and then move him to TIC – the Trauma Intensive-Care unit. I must emphasize, once again, that the man was *shot*. Twice. Once of the wounds was in the chest, the path of the bullet severing a main pulmonary artery and countless other arteries before passing through. The trauma, therefore, was quite severe. We won't know for a while what damage has been done to the brain, if any . . ."

There it was again. Brain damage. What damage has been done to the brain. If any.

". . . but his condition is stable, and we've every reason to believe he'll be waking up as soon as the anesthesia wears off."

"What's the long-range prognosis?" Frank asked.

Flat-out New Yorker style; Patricia wanted to kiss him. What are we talking about here, Doc? Will he be okay, or won't he?

"As I said, his condition is stable for the moment. What happens within the next few hours, the next few days . . ."

"What *can* happen?" Frank persisted.

"I can't add anything to what I've already told you," the doctor said, and then – so softly they almost couldn't hear him – he murmured, "The man was shot."

*   *   *

There was only darkness, there was intense light. There was unfathomable blackness, there was searing glare. There was no present, all was then. There was no past, all was now. Voices gone now, concerned voices gone, lingering voices in the dark, voices swallowed in the then and the light. Whispering voices, pattering footfalls, flurries of movement, a circling of moths. Cold everywhere, hurting in the dark, shaking in the dark, sweating and hot as he came around the corner of the house. *I may be out back*, she had told him on the phone, *by the pool, just come around the house*. Sudden glare of sunlight, black slate walk set in white pebble field, darkness and light, motion and death. Was he dying, was he dead? What was today, when was yesterday? He knew that Sunday was the twentieth day of March, but that was then, and then was now, so Sunday was *today*, and he was walking into sunlight on black slate set in white, walking from deep shadow into shattering glare, walking through the valley of the shadow of death, Matthew knew he was dying or dead, *I may be out back by the pool*.

Maria Torrance wasn't out back by the pool, or at least not anywhere that he could see her. Instead, a shining bald head sliced through the surface of the glistening blue water, its partially submerged owner crawl-stroking toward the far end of the pool, head turning at regular intervals to suck in air, face dipping back into the water as Matthew came around the eastern end of the house and walked into the blinding sunlight slanting in over the Gulf.

The house was on Fatback Key, not far from where Patricia lived. He had told her, in fact, that he'd stop by after his four o'clock meeting with Miss Torrance. The property ran from east to west, a driveway snaking through it and circling to the house's front entrance, which faced the morning sun and Calusa Bay. The rear of the house opened onto the Gulf of Mexico and the magnificent sunsets that graced the barrier islands whenever it wasn't raining – which, in all fairness, was quite often, despite what Frank Summerville maintained.

Matthew had parked the Acura on a white pebble driveway, had rung the doorbell set in the entrance jamb, and had then walked around the house as instructed, circling back into sunlight to come upon the bald-headed man methodically swimming away from him. To Matthew, there was something almost hypnotic about the man's even, graceful crawl, the sunlight dappling the pool's surface, the sound of rushing surf on the Gulf beyond, the cry of seagulls somewhere in the distance. He watched as the man reached the far end of the pool, turned, and began swimming leisurely back toward where Matthew stood sweltering in the burning sunlight, wearing a proper seersucker suit, a proper shirt and tie, proper blue socks and polished black shoes, and feeling like a proper shmuck.

"Hi!" he shouted. "I'm looking for Maria Torrance."

The man did not break stroke. Steadily, deliberately, the bald head leading him like a silver bullet, head turning rhythmically to breathe, face turning rhythmically into the water again, arms pulling him, legs kicking behind him, he swam to the shallow end, found the steps with his outstretched arms, and began climbing out of the water.

The bald-headed man was wearing a woolen, flesh-colored tank suit that adorned a body voluptuous by any standards. Scooped low in the front, the suit scarcely contained the abundant bosom it timidly sought to conceal. Cut high on the thigh, the suit merely emphasized a rich curve of hip and a long expanse of leg. Matthew guessed the woman – for there was no question about it now – was some five feet eight, five feet nine inches tall in her bare feet. She pressed the palm of her right hand to her right ear, hopped up and down on her right leg, and then repeated the maneuver with left ear and left leg, bouncing on the tiled deck, shaking water loose from whatever interior canals had trapped it during her swim. Her bald head gleaming in the sun, her crinkling blue eyes catching sunlight and flashing it back like a shared joke, she grinned and said, "Hi, I'm Maria Torrance, you found me," and extended her hand toward Matthew where he stood dumfounded.

He took the hand.

It was cold from the water.

He found he could not take his eyes from her hairless head.

However much he tried to shift his attention to her truly electric blue eyes or her perfectly shaped nose or bee-stung lips, his gaze kept wandering back to that sleek, smooth dome. A thought suddenly occurred to him: she was undergoing chemotherapy. The thought shamed him, and the ensuing guilt forced him finally to confront her eyes. They were still amused. He had the sudden feeling that she was used to a visitor's shock at seeing her for the first time, and, like a mischievous child, actually enjoyed it. He supposed she was no more than nineteen years old. A girl really. A girl with a woman's body and a man's bald head.

"I'm Matthew Hope," he said.

"Yes," she said.

They shook hands briefly.

"May I offer you something?" she asked. "Some iced tea? Some lemonade? Something stronger? What time is it, anyway?"

"Almost four," he said. "I'm a little early."

"Well, then," she said, "too early, I suppose," which Matthew took to mean too early for anything alcoholic. But she went nonetheless to the sliding glass doors at the rear of the house, slid open one of them, and called, "Helen? Could you bring us . . . which will it be?" she asked Matthew. "The tea or the lemonade?"

"The tea, please."

"A pitcher of iced tea, please, Helen!" she shouted, and slid the door shut with a bang, and said, "Please sit down. And stop worrying about my head, will you? I shave it."

"Why?" Matthew asked.

"For my business," she said.

"What business?"

Was she an actress? Were they shooting a segment of *Star Trek* here in Calusa?

"I sell hairpieces."

He looked at her.

"I do," she said, "I'm serious. I go all over the country demonstrating them on television."

He thought this was action above and beyond the call of duty, but he said nothing.

"That troubles you," she said.

"No, no," he said.

"Yes, yes," she said. "Why would a young and beautiful woman shave her head for the sake of Mammon?"

"Well," he said, and shrugged.

She had called herself a woman, he noticed. Perhaps she was older than the nineteen years he'd guessed she was. Or perhaps teenagers these days had taken to calling themselves women. He had trouble with that, political correctness be damned.

"Well," she said, "because I love the smell of money, Mr. Hope, and my business brings in tons of it. Do you know how many people in the United States suffer from alopecia areata?"

"I'm sorry," Matthew said. "I don't know what that is."

"It's a common cause of hair loss."

"I see."

"Occurs in both sexes," she said, and glanced down – perhaps unconsciously – at her own swelling, water-speckled breasts in the scoop-necked top of the woolen tank suit – "male or female, usually before the age of fifty. Generally starts with one or more small, round, bald patches on the scalp, but it can progress to total body hair loss. Guess how many sufferers there are?"

"I can't imagine."

"Some two million Americans."

"I see."

"In seven and a half million American families, there's at least one person with alopecia areata. It's thought to be an autoimmune disorder."

Matthew wondered if alopecia areata was in any way related to common garden-variety baldness. He was truly interested. His father had begun losing his hair when he was forty, and Matthew was fearful he would follow in his footsteps. Forty wasn't too very far away these days. He'd been assured, though, that baldness was hereditary only through a *mother's* genes, and Matthew's grandfather on his mother's side had died with a full head of white hair. But was this information true? Or would Matthew look like Maria Torrance a few years from now?

One of the sliding doors opened and an exceedingly plain, exceptionally stout woman wearing a Hawaiian print caftan came out of the house, carrying a tray upon which were a pitcher of tea, two tall glasses with ice cubes in them, a little bowl of lemon wedges, a sugar bowl, and two long spoons. She set the tray down between the two lounge chairs, and went back into the house without saying a word. Maria poured.

"Sugar?" she asked.

"No, thank you."

"Help yourself to the lemon," she said.

Matthew took a wedge and squeezed it into his tea.

"Not many people know about alopecia areata," Maria said, "until they get it. It sounds like an opera singer's name, doesn't it? Alopecia Areata, now appearing as Mimi in *La Bohème*," she said, and threw her hands up as if the name were appearing in lights, and then grinned as if she found the allusion amusing. She lowered her hands, picked up her glass of iced tea, and sipped at it demurely, all deliberately shaven and shorn while apparently oblivious to the fact that her tits were trying very hard to escape the confines of her swimsuit. He still could not imagine her purposely shaving her own head just to further her business aspirations. But apparently this was the God's honest truth, as she now went on to attest.

"Cortisone treatments are available for milder cases of the disorder," she said, "but when it's progressed to total hair loss, a wig is the best alternative. That's where Hair and Now comes in."

"Here and now?" Matthew asked, puzzled.

"*Hair* and Now," she said. "The name of my company."

Matthew wondered why Maria felt compelled to make fun of her line of work. There were, after all, people who even sold cemetery plots. But first the opera singer and now the outrageous pun. Matthew wondered if she'd *first* shaved her head and *then* gone into business. Or had she shaved it later in guilt, as penance for taking advantage of the misfortunes of others? There was something undeniably attractive about the perverse combination of voluptuous body and shorn head. It conjured visions of collaborators and witches, vampires and dominatrices. Maria seemed well aware of her bizarre allure, twisting this way and that on the lounge to afford fleeting glimpses of breast or cheek, a bald teenager seemingly itchy in the woolen tank suit. He found himself increasingly more uncomfortable in her presence.

"And, of course," she said, "there are also women who lose their hair through radiation therapy or chemotherapy. Hair and Now provides a service for all of them. My wigs won't come off in the water . . ."

Then how'd you lose yours? he wondered.

". . . or on a sailboat or at the gym or in bed," she said, and waggled her eyebrows. "Come, let me show you," she said, and rose in a single fluid motion that afforded a view of both nippled breasts and simultaneously brought her to her feet, hand extended. He did not take the hand, but he followed her to a pool house decorated in pastel lemons and limes, where a red long-haired wig sat on a wig stand, beckoning like a traffic light.

"Human hair," she said. "European. Color approved from a sample. To match my *natural* color," she said, and arched one eyebrow, confirming his surmise that she was well aware of her own sexuality and used it shamelessly, habitually, and perhaps even unconsciously. He wondered if she was as young as he'd earlier guessed, and was tempted to ask her. But he knew that might appear as if he were picking up on her sexual allusion, the arched eyebrow, the mention of her *natural* hair color. He let it pass. She lifted the wig from its stand.

"The base is created from a plaster mold taken from your own head by one of our representatives in the field. We have representatives in every major American city. The manufacturer fashions the wig's base from your unique mold, and you try it on before our patented vacuum system . . ."

She lifted the wig above Matthew's head now, so that he could see its underside . . .

". . . is applied. The system ensures a perfect fit and perfect suction. We guarantee that under any circumstances this wig will not come off until you *take* it off. That's an iron-clad, money-back guarantee, and we make it without restrictions or . . ."

"Who's we?" Matthew asked.

"What?"

"You keep saying 'we.' Who's we?"

"Oh. Hair and Now. The company. There is no *we*. I'm the chief executive officer and sole stockholder."

"How old are you?" he asked.

"Twenty-two," she said. "How old are you?"

"Thirty-eight," he said.

"Nice age span," she said, and winked and put on the wig. Didn't look in a mirror, just slipped it over her head and onto it as if she'd done this a hundred times before, a thousand times before. She smoothed it down swiftly and firmly, probably to create the vacuum she'd talked about earlier, and where not a moment earlier there'd been a bald teenager standing there in a revealing swimsuit, there was now a twenty-two-year-old redhead standing there in the same suit.

"Now watch," she said, and stepped outside onto the tiled deck and sprinted for the pool, long legs flashing, red hair swinging, buttocks virtually naked on either side of the suit's thong, and took a running dive into the water. She stayed submerged long enough to cause Matthew concern, and then suddenly her red hair – or some European woman's red hair – broke the rippling surface of the water, and she began swimming in a faster crawl than the bald-headed man had used, coming swiftly to the pool's side, placing her hands flat on the tiled surface beyond the lip, and hoisting herself straight-armed out of the water. She executed a midair turn as she lifted herself, swinging her buttocks around and plunking them down firmly on the tile. Pulling her knees up to her breasts, and then using the same single fluid motion she'd used earlier, she rose like a dancer and shook out her long red hair. Or somebody's. Soaking wet, the suit clinging, she went back to where she'd left her tea on the table between the lounges, leaned over to pick it up, turned to him, arched her eyebrows, smiled and said, "See?"

"Remarkable," he said.

He couldn't wait to get out of here. He had the feeling he could get in very serious trouble here.

*   *   *

"I hate that son of a bitch," she said.

She was talking about George Steadman, her inherited partner. It was now almost five-thirty. The sun sinking behind the house was already casting long shadows over the pool area. She had put on a short robe the color of the tank suit. She had switched from iced tea to gin and tonic. Matthew had politely refused a drink. He was thinking that the first thing he'd do when he got to Patricia's house was mix himself a Beefeater martini. Here with Maria Torrance, he wanted to keep his wits about him.

"I wouldn't agree to *any* deal he came up with, and you can tell him that."

"He says you have no quarrel with how he's running Steadman & Roeger."

"That's right. But only if he keeps sending me statements and a check every month," Maria said, and took another swallow of the gin.

"Besides, he has the right to make the final decision regarding any business matter."

"No, he doesn't."

"Yes, he does. I've read the agreement between him and Mr. Roeger. The terms of that agreement have carried down to . . ."

"I don't care what his original agreement says. You come here telling me he's planning to spend three million dollars for a piece of land . . ."

"That's right."

"And I'm telling you there's no way I'll let him do that," she said, and nodded emphatically. She was still wearing the red wig. *This wig will not come off until you take it off.* Apparently, she did not wish to take it off just yet. Matthew wondered what determined when she swam wigless and when she swam otherwise. Did she ever go out in public without the wig? When she did those television presentations she'd mentioned, did she show how she looked Before and After? When she made love, did she take off . . .?

It was very dangerous here.

"I have the right of consultation," she said. "If he thinks . . ."

"But not approval," Matthew said. "Mr. Steadman has the

final word. In any case, I'm here only to tell you what he's proposing. I'm here to *consult* with you, Miss Torrance, as per the terms of the agreement."

"The hell with him *and* the agreement," Maria said, and drained her glass. "Let's go inside," she said. "It's getting chilly out here."

She set her glass down on the table between the lounges, and rose again with that same swift dancer's motion. Matthew followed her to the sliding glass doors that led into the house. They opened onto a living room decorated in cool whites and blues, a particularly gorgeous Syd Solomon painting on the white brick fireplace wall, colorful throw pillows softening the white tile floor, a huge John Chamberlain sculpture sitting against a window wall that opened onto a deck facing the Gulf. The sun was quite low on the horizon now. The Chamberlain was almost in silhouette.

"I'm still wet," she said. "I'll be right back. Make yourself a drink, the bar's right there."

He did not make himself a drink. He sat in the serenely cool, serenely beautiful living room and watched the sun sinking lower in the western sky, dipping toward the water, the sky turning to the colors and shapes of many of Solomon's paintings, though the one on the fireplace wall was aglow with cobalt blues and emerald greens. The sky was changing swiftly now, from the fiery reds and oranges and swirling shapes of a moment earlier, to a roiling reddish violet, and then a flatter purple. A thin line of color lingered on the horizon. The living room was dark.

A light snapped on behind him.

He turned.

Maria was adorned in the colors of the sunset, her red hair echoed in a thousand subtle ways by the threads woven into the silk caftan she had put on, red and gold high-heeled sandals adding two inches to her already impressive height. Glancing toward the sea, she said, "Beautiful, hmmm?" and then walked swiftly to the wall bar, obviously naked under the flowing garment, and mixed herself another gin and tonic. She squeezed a lime wedge into the glass, dropped it into the drink, raised the glass and then one eyebrow, and asked, "Sure?"

"Sure," he said.

"Cheers, anyway," she said with a shrug, and sipped at the drink. "Very good," she said. "You're missing something." She came to where he was sitting, sat beside him. "What do *you* think of the deal?" she asked.

"I think it has merit. *If* I can get the land at his price."

"Do you think you'll be able to?"

"I don't know yet. I haven't approached anyone. But I don't feel you'd be going wrong, if that's your question."

"I hate the son of a bitch, you see."

"I gather. Why's that?"

"I loved the circus, it was my whole life when I was growing up, and I loved Max, too, but I couldn't stand George. My mother was an entertainer with S&R, you know, very well known, quite famous, she had offers from Ringling, Beatty, Vargas, all of them. But she chose to stay with George and Max, finally bought half the show from him, Max, when he found out he had cancer. I must've been twelve, thirteen years old at the time. My mother kept entertaining after she bought Max out, but she became a hardheaded business-woman as well. Well, after all, half owner of Steadman & Roeger? This wasn't some cheap little mud show. It was small, but highly respected. My earliest memories are of moving out, moving on, setting up, tearing down, moving on again . . ."

The booking agents did all the advance work long before we moved out on the first of April. There were four agents, they'd be on the phones day and night calling potential sponsors, your Kiwanis Clubs, your Jaycees, who got ten, twenty, sometimes forty percent of the gate for furnishing locations and getting the necessary permits, the basic lots and licenses. George set up all the routes, sometimes keeping them secret even from Max. There are a lot of mud shows out there, you know, ready to take advantage of the paper you put up, the clowns or elephants you send out ahead, steal all your promotion and advertising, move in as if *they're* S&R, set up on a supermarket parking lot and take all your customers. The routes varied year to year, but in Florida we started here in Calusa and then hit Sarasota, Naples, Bradenton, St. Pete and Tampa on our way north. Then we'd move through the Carolinas and Virginia, swing west through Kentucky and Missouri, and then head back south again through Tennessee, Alabama, Georgia, and then home in October, November, depending on the schedule. We tried to keep the jumps no longer than a hundred miles, moving at night or else very early in the morning, four, four-thirty A.M., when there wasn't much traffic on the roads. Twenty-five percent of our tickets were usually sold before we got there. We counted on paper to bring in the rest.

Paper is what circus people call the posters we put up, the streamers, or the banners, or the guttersnipes – that's the paper they paste on rain gutters – these are all different kinds of circus posters, circus paper. The billing agent is the person who makes sure a town is well-papered long before the circus gets there, goes out with a billing crew a week, sometimes ten days before the show opens in any given town. Your twenty-four-hour man is the one who puts up the arrows the trucks follow. While you're still showing a town, he's gone twenty-four hours before anyone else, leading the way. He knows where the next lot is, some of them are really in the boonies, and he staples arrows to telephone poles or pastes them to lampposts, so the trucks'll know which turns to take to get there. I can remember, sometimes, there'd be *two* circuses playing the same town at the same time, although this was something you tried to avoid in your routing. Whenever that happened, there'd be different colored arrows up for each of the circuses, telling the trucks which way to go, you'd sometimes end up on the *other* circus's lot by mistake, you'd have to retrace your steps. Your twenty-four-hour man laid out the lot, deciding where the midway and the big top'd be – S&R still has a great midway, you know, not many small circuses do. He orders hay for the elephants and ice for the snowballs, and he's there ready to tell you where to park when your truck or your trailer pulls in. My mother was a star, so we always got to park at the front of the lot, near Max and George's trailers.

"I always loved the circus," Maria was saying. "All the confusion, all the ballyhoo, all the noise and excitement, I really loved it. Even after what it did to my mother, I still loved it. I could have sold my share, you know, the fifty percent she left me. But I held on to it because of my love for her. And my love for the circus."

Matthew hesitated a moment. Out on the Gulf, there was only the thinnest line of color now the sky above it a virtually black blue. A single star was shining.

"What *did* the circus do to your mother?" he asked.

"It killed her," Maria said without hesitation.

Warren Chambers had joined Patricia in the hospital waiting room at four-fifty A.M., and the clock on the wall now read six o'clock sharp. Frank was asleep in the chair beside her, snoring. Matthew still hadn't come out of the anesthesia, but Patricia figured that was okay because the doctor had said two or three hours, six o'clock, maybe a little bit later, so they were still within the outside limit. She filled Warren in on what the doctor had told them, about all the bleeding the bullet had caused, all the ruptured arteries. Warren told her he wasn't surprised. He'd finally got one of the Criminalistics techs at the scene to tell him they'd recovered three .22-caliber bullets, one of them in pristine condition, the other two badly deformed . . .

". . . most likely the two that hit Matthew and went on through," he said. "People have the misconception a low-caliber gun doesn't do much damage, but that isn't true. The bullet hasn't got as much force as a slug from a forty-four, or a forty-five, or a nine, but that means it doesn't just go through clean. Instead, it bounces around inside the body in there, like a rubber ball bouncing off all the furniture in a house before it flies out a window. By that time, it's broken a lamp and a vase and knocked a picture off the wall, it's the same as that. The bullet goes caroming around inside the body doing all kinds of damage before it exits."

Patricia hadn't yet mentioned possible brain damage.

"The thing I've been trying to figure out is what he was doing in Newtown," Warren said. "Even *I* don't go to Newtown."

"Frank asked me the same thing," she whispered.

They were both whispering. A hospital waiting room encouraged whispering. Six o'clock in the morning encouraged whispering. She looked at the clock again. Six-ten. Six A.M., the doctor had said. *Around then? Maybe a little later*. Still okay, she supposed. She hoped. She prayed. Six-ten was still *around* six o'clock, it was still only a *little later* than six o'clock. When will it get too late? she wondered. She said nothing to Warren.

"He never mentioned Newtown to *you*, did he?" he asked.

"No," she said.

She did not want to look up at the clock again.

"Did he tell you what he was working on? It wasn't a *criminal* case, was it?"

"No, he was trying to acquire some land for the circus."

"What circus?"

"Steadman & Roeger."

"Oh? Really? That's a good circus."

"Yes."

"Where? What land?"

"The state fairgrounds."

"Mmm."

She looked up at the clock. Twelve minutes past six.

"What is it?" Warren asked.

"There's a possibility of brain damage," she said, and sighed heavily.

"Oh shit," he said.

He looked up at the clock, too.

"When's he supposed to be coming around?"

"Now," she said.

They both looked at the clock. The minute hand lurched visibly as if conscious of their scrutiny.

"Wasn't there something about that circus?" Warren asked.

"What do you mean?"

"Some kind of scandal, I forget. In St. Louis? Wherever? Didn't something happen?"

"Yes," Patricia said. "But I don't think it was a scandal, it . . ."

"What was it?"

"One of their stars committed suicide."

"Was that it?"

"If that's what you're thinking of."

"I only remember a big fuss in all the papers down here. I'd just moved here. It was a big story."

"I was still living in New York at the time."

"Wasn't it in the New York papers?"

"I guess it was. But that's not why I remember it."

"Then why do you?"

"Matthew told me about it."

"About this woman who committed suicide?"

"Or *whatever* it was."

"What do you mean?"

"He was only telling me what her daughter said."

"Well, what'd *she* say? When was this, anyway?"

"A week ago. Right after we got back from the Caribbean, the Sunday after we got back."

"How'd he happen to start talking about it?"

"He'd just come from a meeting with the daughter."

"What about?"

"The circus deal he's handling. She's part owner."

"I see," Warren said.

Patricia looked up at the clock, and then looked immediately down at her hands. They were folded in her lap, as if in prayer. Frank suddenly snored sharply, awakening himself.

"What time is it?" he asked.

Time, Patricia thought.

"Six-twenty," she said.

"Should be coming around soon," Frank said, and checked his own watch against the wall clock.

"What did Matthew tell you?" Warren asked. "About the suicide. About what the daughter said about it."

"I'm going to find someone," Frank said, and stood up abruptly. "See what the hell's going on here." He hiked up his pants, looked at the clock once again, and went off toward the nurse's station.

Patricia did not want to report all this to Warren, Patricia wanted to scream instead. It was already six-twenty, going on six twenty-one, the clock ticking noisily on the wall across from where she sat with Warren playing detective while her man lay unconscious somewhere down the hall, he'll be out of the anesthesia by six o'clock, the doctor had said, around then, maybe a little later, but it was *already* a little later, it was already starting to get a *lot* later. She sat with her hands clenched in her lap, Warren not prompting her, not urging her, just sitting there quietly in stately expectation, waiting for her to tell him how Matthew had happened to begin talking about a circus lady who'd committed suicide quite some time ago in a city other than this one, five years ago, was it? Six years ago? Boston, was it? Atlanta, was it? Place and time were here and now on this hard sofa in a barren room with a clock relentlessly throwing minutes onto the floor. Time and place were the twentieth day of March at seven P.M. in Patricia's house on the beach, Matthew sipping the Beefeater martini she'd mixed for him, telling her that a bald, nearly naked woman had swum for him this afternoon in order to demonstrate the staying power of a wig fashioned from the hair of countless redheaded European women . . .

No, she didn't, Patricia says.

She did. Only twenty-two years old, too.

You're thirty-eight, Matthew.

Mm, yes. She thought that was a nice age span.

I'll kill her, Patricia says.

It was strictly business, he says.

For Matthew, in fact, it *was* strictly business, until young Maria Torrance mentioned that the circus had killed her mother, at which juncture something odd clicked in his mind, something he realized at once was even more dangerous than the bewigged temptress sitting beside him jiggling a shapely foot encased in a red and gold high-heeled sandal that had slipped off her heel and was dangling by its toe. The something more dangerous was his own curiosity, lulled to near death by what he visualized in the near future as interminably boring negotiations for a three-million-dollar piece of dirt, not to mention the necessity of convincing a twenty-two-year-old twit that the deal was truly an excellent one, lest (despite documents to the contrary) she decided to sue for the right of approval, raising all sorts of legal problems that could cast a cloud over clear title and create a chilling effect in the seller's mind – on a deal for which Matthew had no heart, anyway.

But here was this same twenty-two-year-old twit stating with all the certainty of a bona fide adult that the circus had *killed* her mother, which prompted the natural question, "Why do you say that, Miss Torrance?" to which Maria replied, "That was no fucking *suicide*, Mr. Hope."

Her answer startled Matthew in any number of ways.

First, he hadn't even known there'd *been* a suicide, or possibly a mere *apparent* suicide, as Maria's response now seemed to suggest.

Moreover, if Willa Torrance's death hadn't been either a suicide or an apparent suicide, then it had to have been death either through natural causes, accident, or murder. There were no in-betweens, no other possibilities. The tone of Maria's voice and the use of the strong epithet indicated that she was hinting homicide. Despite his own better judgment, Matthew was immediately intrigued.

"Tell me about it," he said.

Famous last words.

It seemed that the "suicide"—

Each time Maria used the word, her lip curled in disdain, giving her the appearance of a bald Teutonic fencing master rather than a gorgeous twenty-two-year-old woman in a red wig and matching caftan—

The "suicide," then, had taken place in Rutherford, Missouri, before Rand McNally had chosen that town as one of the more desirable places to live here in the United States of America. "It's quite lovely now," Maria said, and asked Matthew if he would like to see the newspaper reports of her mother's "suicide"; she had copies of all of them, including the *Enquirer* and the *Star*, both of which had carried front-page stories on it. She went to a modern sideboard on the same wall as the bar, knelt to open a drawer, and brought out a good-sized gray cardboard box which she carried back to the sofa. She was about to remove the lid when Matthew said he would look at them later, if she didn't mind. Right now he was more interested in knowing why she was suggesting that her mother's apparent suicide had, in fact, been a homicide.

"I'll tell you why," she said, and put the box beside her on the sofa, and pulled her legs up under her, and turned to face him. "Three years ago come May," she said . . .

The Steadman & Roeger Circus had been showing Rutherford for three days and was scheduled to tear down and move
out on the eleventh of May, a Saturday . . .

"There's something eerie about a tent coming down in the
middle of the night," Maria said, "everyone moving in silence
as though afraid they'll wake up the sleeping town they've
just entertained . . ."

. . . seats and rigging disassembling in the empty hours of
the night, pacing animals in cages loading onto trucks, the
smell of early morning coffee from the cookhouse, morngloam
not yet here, trailers and trucks and recreational vans starting
before the sun comes up, puffing carbon monoxide exhaust
onto the early morning air, something still, serene, and sur-
realistic. The Torrances, mother and daughter, were living
in a . . .

Matthew noticed that not once had Maria yet mentioned her
father . . .

. . . large trailer in a choice location on the lot, a ten-acre
parcel of land with plenty of space for parking, close to a major
thoroughfare, and convenient to a huge shopping mall, from
which they'd drawn a great many walk-in customers during
their three-day stand.

Maria had set her alarm for four-thirty in the morning, her
mother having told her she wanted them both to be ready
and on the road by six, before the morning rush-hour traffic
started. Willa enjoyed her sleep, and generally allowed herself
the absolute *minimum* amount of time necessary to shower,
dress, and grab a cup of coffee at the cookhouse. She was still
asleep when Maria left the trailer at five. Her own alarm was
set for five-fifteen. It never went off because the bullet Willa
presumably put in her forehead passed through her skull,
ricocheted off the metal side of the trailer, and then went
through the clock where it sat on a metal dresser bolted to
the floor near the rear entrance door, stopping it dead at ten
minutes past the hour.

At the very moment of her mother's death, Maria was
in the cookhouse tent, sitting on the short side, as it was
called . . .

"This didn't refer to the short side of the *tent*," she explained to Matthew now. "It's where the shorter *tables* were, the better ones, reserved for George and his various managers and toadies, all of whom sat closest to the front door. There's a pecking order in the circus, you know, same as everywhere else in the world. Your performers and entertainers are next in rank, and even *there* the seating's according to importance. Your equestrian performers are the top of the order, God knows why, you'd have thought it'd be your flyers or high-wire people, or your wild-animal trainers. The tent that morning . . ."

It is a miserable morning, thunder and lightning punctuating the steady rain that blows in over the lot in slanting sheets. The ground underfoot has not yet turned to mud, but the rotten weather has tempted many of the people who will not physically be tearing down the circus to stay in bed a while longer. The cookhouse tent, at this early hour, is packed with men on the other side of a curtain that divides performers and top management from workers, crew bosses, and gazoonies. Maria sits at one of the shorter tables with Davey Sheed, who's awake and around because it takes a bit of time and care to load cats without spooking them, especially with all this lightning, and he wants his animals calmly packed away before the hubbub of moving out really starts.

"I was having an affair with Davey that season," Maria said. "He was the first man I'd ever known intimately."

Nineteen years old back then, Matthew thought.

"We picked each other on Choosing Day," Maria said.

"The first dress rehearsal is usually Choosing Day. That's when everyone decides who they'll pair off with for the season."

Matthew took mental note of the grammatical lapse, but said nothing.

"We were the only two people on the short side of the tent . . ."

Otherwise that side of the tent is empty. All the noise, all the buzz of conversation and laughter, the clatter and clink of cutlery on cheap china, is coming from the other side of the curtain. Over the noise in the cookhouse tent, no one hears the gunshot from the other end of the lot. Or so they will all later claim. Over the crackle of lightning and the booming of thunder, no one hears the gunshot from the Torrance trailer. Or so they will all later claim.

The chief medical examiner testified at the inquest that the autopsy report had been premised on certain indisputable facts consistent with a finding of suicide. To begin with, the bunk in which Willa had been sleeping was located on the right-hand side of the vehicle. Willa's head was facing the front of the trailer, her feet the rear. She was lying on her right side when the body was discovered at 5:35 A.M. by her daughter. The shoulder straps of her white baby doll nightgown were flecked with spatters of blood. The sheet that had covered her to the neck when Maria left the trailer at 5:00 A.M. was rumpled below her waist when Maria returned.

The entrance wound of the bullet was in the center of the forehead, which was consistent with findings of suicidal shootings to the head whether the victim was right-handed or left-handed. In most such cases, the gun muzzle was held in close proximity to the skin, leaving brownish burn marks around the bullet hole and sometimes singed hairs above it. In Willa's case, these indications were consistent with a finding of suicide. Moreover, a black coat of powder residue smeared the area of the entrance wound, and the coroner recovered unburnt powder grains from the skin around the site. Most convincing, the murder weapon – a .32-caliber Colt Detective Special – was found in Willa Torrance's right hand, her right forefinger inside the trigger guard and resting against the trigger. All of these indications were consistent with a finding of suicide – apparently the chief M.E.'s favorite expression.

The Medical Examiner's Office concluded that while lying on her side, Willa Torrance had placed the muzzle of the suicide weapon against her forehead, and fired a fatal bullet into her head. The bullet had moved upward and in a slightly lateral direction to burst through the skull, ricochet off the wall behind the bunk, and then tumble across the interior space toward the rear of the vehicle to smash the face of the dresser clock and become embedded in its mechanism, which was where it was finally recovered in a highly deformed state.

"Trouble is," Maria said, "my mother never owned a gun in her life."

"Was this brought out at the inquest?"

"It was."

"And?"

"These days guns are easy to come by in America. Even then, three years ago, they concluded that my mother – leading the life of a circus entertainer – could easily have obtained a gun in any of the towns we showed."

"Were there any blood splashes on her hand?"

"No," Maria said. "Just on the straps of her gown. And the wall."

"Mmm."

"We carried her home in a coffin and buried her here in Calusa. The newspapers were full of it. There were headlines all over America. I'll show you," she said, and reached for the gray box beside her.

Matthew tried to remember where he'd been in the month of May, three years ago, not to have seen headlines about the suicide of a well-known circus performer, especially here in a circus town like Calusa. But, no, they'd never said *performer*, both Steadman and Maria kept referring to Willa Torrance as an *entertainer*, however that may have differed from someone who trained elephants to stand on their heads. Were those elephants, in fact, performers or entertainers? Matthew hadn't the faintest idea. He knew only that he could not remember any headlines announcing the suicide of Willa Torrance. Had he been away at the time? Was that the year he'd gone to Spain for his vacation? Or perhaps it was the name Torrance that was throwing him. Steadman had mentioned her circus name, but he couldn't quite recall it now. Wendell? Was it Willa Wendell? Or Wagner? Willa Wagner? No, that wasn't it, either. Winkler?

"Mr. Steadman mentioned your mother's circus name," he said, "but I've . . ."

"Winkie," she said.

"Yes, that was it, thank you."

Maria nodded, and smiled, and then lifted the gray box onto her lap. She removed the lid, and took from the box a framed photograph of a little girl of three or four, wearing a short pleated skirt, a white blouse, and black patent-leather tap shoes. The little girl was beaming at the camera in a smile very much like Maria's own. The little girl was standing alongside a caned wooden chair that gave scale to the picture; she could not have been taller than two and a half feet. In the photo, the little girl's hair appeared lighter than Maria's; she could have been a strawberry blonde. Matthew wondered if Maria was showing him a picture of herself as a child.

"Wee Willa Winkie," Maria said. "That's how they billed her, Mr. Hope."

Matthew looked again. The little girl in the photo had the mature face and eyes, the lipsticked mouth, the knowing smile of a woman. The little girl in the photograph had the firm breasts, full hips, and shapely legs of a woman. Matthew was looking at Willa Torrance, he was looking at Wee Willa Winkie.

"My mother was one of the little people," Maria said. "My mother was a midget."

Frank Summerville came stamping into the waiting room.

"Nobody knows a goddamn thing," he said angrily.

2

And she had a little curl . . .

WARREN ARRANGED to meet Toots Kiley at a little past one that Sunday afternoon. They met in one of those beer and burger joints designed to look like an old-fashioned New York saloon, but succeeding only in looking like some Florida decorator's notion of an old-fashioned New York saloon. Everything was just a wee bit off. The cut-glass panels were too glittery, the brass too strident, the wood too mellow. The only authentic touch was in the shopworn St. Patrick's Day decorations still hanging from the seventeenth.

In Calusa, Florida, there'd been no St. Patrick's Day parade; in fact, down here the holiday passed each year with hardly any notice at all. Except in the bars. The bars always decked themselves out in green. Some of them even served green beer. Presumably, this was in tribute to the widely circulated notion that Irish people drank a lot. Warren didn't know if the concept was sheer myth or absolute fact. Frankly, he didn't give a damn either way. Neither he nor Toots were here to drink. Matthew Hope was in serious trouble at the hospital, and Warren needed her help in finding whoever had shot him.

"When he didn't come around by seven," he told her, "they started running all these tests on him. The doctors. They didn't let us know till later, it must've been eight o'clock, by then we were . . ."

"Who's this?" Toots asked.

"Me, Patricia, and Frank."

"Patricia?"

"Demming. An assistant S.A. Matthew's been seeing."

Toots nodded and picked up her cheeseburger. She'd have loved a beer with it, but she'd been clean for three years now, and she wasn't going to let a lousy beer tumble her right back into the cocaine habit. Toots was twenty-six years old, a tall, slender, suntanned, brown-eyed blonde who'd let her frizzed perm grow out and who now wore her hair long and falling straight to her shoulders. On this chilly Sunday, the twenty-seventh day of March, celebrated simultaneously as Palm Sunday and Passover by Christian and Jew respectively, Toots was wearing a pink sweater with a white bib collar showing above the crew neck, faded blue jeans, and cowboy boots. Warren had to admit she looked healthy. She was chewing on the hamburger like a starving wolf.

"What they did," he said, "first they checked his arm and leg reflexes, there's a word they have for that, but I forget what term he used, testing the extremities. They got very faint neurological reflexes, so they . . . they . . . I find this hard to talk about,' he said, and brought his hand up to cover his eyes, and sat very still for several moments, his hand covering his eyes, his head bent. Toots said nothing.

Warren swallowed and then took his hand away from his eyes, and wiped them with the back of it, and then he said, "They told us they'd pulled back his eyelids then, and shined a bright light into his eyes, first one eye, and then the other, to see if the pupils would react. They did, thank God, which meant his reflexes weren't entirely lost, the back of the brain was . . . was still functioning. The cortex or the brain stem, I forget which is . . . which is . . ."

He's about to lose it again, Toots thought.

But he didn't.

"Then they . . . they ran a piece of cotton over the cornea, touching it to see if there'd be a protective reflex, and there was, but he was just . . . just barely responding. He's not in coma, you understand, there's still brain activity, but he's still not entirely awake and aware. Those are the two terms they use, awake and aware. Being awake relates to the *level* of consciousness. Being aware relates to the *content* of consciousness. These are altered states of consciousness, you see. Coma's the worst, a person in coma is completely out of it. But there's also stupor and obtun . . . I don't remember what they called it, obtunation? Oduntation? Lethargy is another one. That's the mildest one. These are all terms they use to . . . to describe the . . . the various levels of wakefulness and awareness. Matthew isn't completely awake, and he isn't completely aware, either."

"When *will* he be?" Toots asked.

"They want to watch him for another day or so, see if the brain wave pattern improves. They're not getting a *flat* EEG, but there's not much electrical activity, either. They have to wait and see. What happens. Tomorrow or the next day. Peripheral, is what it's called. Examining the arms and legs. Peripheral neurological exam."

Warren sighed, and then nodded, and then looked down at his plate, where his eggs were already cold. He picked up a fork, and poked it into one of the yolks. Yellow ran onto the plate.

"I want to get the son of a bitch who did this," he said.

"Amen," Toots said.

"We're running a week behind Matthew," he said. "Everything he did, everything he learned, we're running a week behind him. Last Sunday, the twentieth, he went to see the daughter of a woman used to be part owner of the circus, name's Maria Torrance. I want you to go see her today, find out what she told him, find out what could've led him from there to wherever he went next, whatever it was he was following. Cause, Toots, I feel positive *whatever* he was onto, that's what got him shot last night. He wouldn't have gone to Newtown without it was something *took* him to Newtown. And whatever took him there got him shot."

"I'll call her," Toots said, and stabbed a forkful of fries. "Have you got a number?"

"Patricia told me she lives on Fatback Key, I looked it up in the directory. Her name's Maria Torrance . . ."

"You already told me that."

"Here, I'll write the number down for you," he said, and took a slip of paper from his wallet and began copying the phone number onto a page in his notebook. "Incidentally, on Friday night he had dinner with Patricia, told her something had come up, and then left her to go somewhere. He didn't say where, but it was obviously Newtown, the way things've turned out. Also, the shooter was driving a black two-door Mazda."

"Got it," Toots said, and took the page he tore from his notebook, glanced at the number, and then asked, "Where will you be later?"

"I'm heading over to the newspaper right now," he said, "check the morgue for that suicide three years ago. I'll be home after that, whenever that'll be, long as it takes me to find anything."

"I'll call you later, fill you in," Toots said. "I know you want to get started, go ahead. I'll pick up the check."

"No, you got it last time."

"No, you did. Anyway, go on."

"Toots . . ."

"I know. You want to nail this son of a bitch."

He hadn't known that Willa Torrance was a midget until he began perusing the *Calusa Herald-Tribune* articles on her suicide. Wee Willa Winkie was what they'd called her. He tried to remember the way the nursery rhyme went. But the name wasn't *Willa*, was it? What . . .? Willie. Yes. Wee *Willie* Winkie.

> *. . . runs though the town*
> *Upstairs and downstairs*
> *In his nightgown.*

Willa Torrance had been wearing a baby doll nightgown when she'd shot herself. Blood spatters on each of the shoulder straps.

> *Rapping at the window*
> *Crying through the lock*
> *"Are the children in their beds*
> *For it's now eight o'clock!"*

Her bedside clock had been stopped by a .32-caliber bullet at exactly 5:10 A.M., the bullet entering through the back of the clock, and then lodging itself in the works without exiting. She'd been lying on her side at the time, but had opted for shooting herself in the forehead. The alarm had been set for 5:15 A.M.. Her daughter had discovered the body at 5:35. The various newspaper accounts quoted Maria as saying that her mother had planned to be on the road by 6:00 A.M., "before the morning rush-hour traffic started." Maria had further stated that her mother was still asleep when she'd left the trailer at five.

Warren wondered if he'd have to go to Missouri on this, talk to the coroner's people there.

He hoped not.

There were wonders galore to explore in Missouri, joys unimaginable to be found there, but not while he was running a week behind whatever discoveries Matthew had made, discoveries Warren was sure had led to the attempt on his life.

All of the newspapers referred to the suicide as a "tragedy" and talked about the great loss to the circus world. Apparently, Wee Willa Winkie had been something more than a sideshow midget sitting on a sideshow giant's lap, the better to exaggerate the differences in their respective heights. She'd been an uncommonly beautiful woman in miniature, a perfectly proportioned, captivating enchantress who sang as well as danced. Many of the articles referred to her as "The Lilliputian Queen of the Midway," and described her act as superior to anything then showing on Broadway – but Calusa, and the *Calusa Herald-Tribune* in particular, tended to wax overly enthusiastic when touting the cultural aspects of the town, often claiming as a "native" any artistic visitor who spent as short a time here as a month in the winter.

All of the obituaries and feature stories reported Willa's age as thirty-seven at the time of her death, her height as thirty-three inches, and her weight as twenty-nine pounds. Only one of the articles went into detail about the condition that had caused her diminutive size. The fact that she had stopped growing at the age of six was attributed to a malfunction of the pituitary gland, which produces the growth hormone. The clinical term for this condition was "hypopituitary dwarfism," a definition that distinguished Willa's type of dwarfism from the other ninety-nine types in the United States. Many of these entailed some sort of bone disorder that resulted in disproportionately short people with large heads and small limbs. Others involved painful spinal irregularities. In common speech, as opposed to medical terminology, Willa was a "midget," a mature adult who looked like a tiny woman, her proportions similar to those of any normal, fully grown female.

The article went on to say that not very many midgets were currently in evidence because semiweekly injections of a growth hormone could result in a normal growth pattern, if the treatment was maintained over a period of ten years. The article had been written three years ago, at the time of Willa's death. It explained that such treatment was now readily available throughout the United States. But as late as 1979, when Willa would have been twenty-five, only a handful of research programs were offering the treatment, and by then she would have been well past the age when treatment should have been started.

All of the obits mentioned that she'd been born Willa DeMott, and raised in the town of Lancaster, Ohio. All of the obits mentioned that it was there in Lancaster that she'd been discovered by Max Roeger, while she was performing on a float in a high school pageant, twirling a baton bigger than she was. All of the obits mentioned her brief marriage to someone named Peter Torrance, "a circus man." All of the obits said, "Ms. Torrance is survived by her only daughter Maria Lovelock Torrance," or words to that effect. Warren wondered how the daughter had got her middle name. And whereas the obits remained otherwise silent on Maria's physical condition, *all* of the feature stories mentioned that she was perfectly "normal" in size.

It was not until sometime after three that afternoon that Warren came across the first substantial reference to Willa's former husband. For several days in March last year, the *Trib* had run a series of features on the circus scene in Calusa and environs. The first issue outlined the history of circuses from the time of the Roman era to the present, and gave a glossary of circus talk for the uninitiated. Warren had not known before he read the article in that issue that a "grab joint" was a hamburger stand, a "perch act" was a pole balancer's act, and three acrobats lying on their backs and tossing around a fourth one was called a "Risley act," live and learn.

The second issue highlighted some of the old Big Bertha performers who still made their homes in Venice, Calusa, Sarasota, or Bradenton. Warren learned here that Big Bertha was circus talk for the *Big* One, which of course was Ringling.

Finally, in the last issue devoted to the series, the paper zeroed in on the smaller Steadman & Roeger show, which – at the time of the article's appearance – had made its winter quarters here for the past nineteen years.

No retrospective of the S&R Circus would have been complete without mention of the "tragic" death of Willa Torrance, who'd entertained under the name of Wee Willa Winkie. In fact, much of the article was devoted to her untimely death in the town of Rutherford, Missouri, which – again, at the time the article appeared – had been two years back. But whereas all of the obituaries had noted that Willa Torrance was discovered in Lancaster, Ohio, when she was a mere seventeen years old, none of them before now had mentioned that shortly after she joined the circus, she met the man who would become her husband.

Peter Torrance, the "circus man," had actually been the marketing director for S&R when Willa Torrance came aboard at the age of seventeen, some twenty-three years ago. He was described in the article as "a tall, rangy man with an air of old world charm and sophistication," an account that left no ambiguity as to whether or not he, too, had been a midget, but left dangling the origin of his old world manners. *Torrance* did not sound particularly European. Perhaps he was British. Or perhaps, as had been the case with countless immigrants seeking America's streets of gold, his name had been changed upon arrival by immigration authorities too burdened or harried to deal with a Polish *Trzebitowski*, a Japanese *Tsuboi*, a Norwegian *Tønnesen*, or an Icelandic *Tryggvason*.

The piece went into great detail on what Torrance's duties had been when he first met Max Roeger's most recent discovery and immediate star. Apparently, a circus's marketing director was an expert at public relations, a man expected to arrive in any given show town several months after the booking agents had made telephone contact, usually two to three weeks before the show itself arrived. He was the essential link between townie and clownie, so to speak, the man who paved the way for a mutually enjoyable and profitable encounter. As the last one to leave any show town, sometimes lingering a day or two after everyone else was long gone, it was his task to make certain the circus had cleaned up after itself and left a favorable impression, its calling card for the next season's return.

That Torrance could find the time to court, no less to win the heart of the midway's new queen, was an equal tribute to his management skills and his ardor. Court her he did, and win her heart he did – all in the space of a single season, which by all accounts had been S&R's most successful one in all its years. The pair was married six months after Willa joined the circus, when she was just eighteen and Torrance was twenty-five. Their first and only child, Maria, was born ten months later.

They were divorced a year after her birth.

When you're on dope, you do everything there is to do, you know people you'd never wanted to know before, you learn to despise yourself for what you are doing to yourself. You learn very quickly to lie, and almost as quickly to steal. Male or female, you learn that you can always barter sex for the drugs you need to sustain yourself. Well, not yourself, really. Not really yourself. This stranger you're supporting is merely someone else inhabiting your body, clamoring inside your body for what this stranger needs to survive. If lying and stealing are not enough to satisfy this stranger inside you, then you must sometimes physically hurt people to get what you need. Hurt them badly, take from them what you need to buy the cocaine to satisfy the stranger residing somewhere inside this body of yours that somehow looks the same on the outside – oh, a little thinner perhaps, a trifle gaunt, in fact; a somewhat driven, almost haunted look in the eyes; the mouth a little tight, perhaps even a bit drawn – a body you know has been confiscated by this stranger inside, a body being abused by this stranger you would not spit upon if you were sober.

The stranger you would not spit upon is yourself.

You revile yourself for what you have become, what you have allowed yourself to become, and you tell yourself if *only* I had the willpower to stop, if *only* I could get a decent job someplace, I would quit this shit in a minute, I would not go down on strange men in alleys stinking of urine, I would not beg anyone for a free hit just this one last time I promise you, I would clean up my act, I would become sober again, if *only*.

For Toots Kiley, the 'if *only*' was when Otto Samalson, the private investigator for whom she was working, discovered she was tooting coke and fired her on the spot. She'd respected Otto, thought of him as almost a second father. Her own father had become a living ghost the moment her mother died. Otto taught her everything there was to know about investigation, turned her into one of the best private eyes in this town. A cop named Rob Higgins taught her everything there was to know about cocaine, turned her into the biggest nose in this town. Sniffed cocaine day and night. Preferred cocaine to eating or to sex or to anything else on this planet, preferred cocaine to being herself again, the innocent young girl her father had named Toots after the harmonica player Toots Thielemans. She wanted to marry cocaine, live with cocaine for the rest of her life, love, honor, and obey cocaine till death us do part. Cocaine was her be-all and end-all. Cocaine or snow or C or blow or toot or Peruvian lady or white girl or leaf or flake or happy dust or nose candy or freeze or even $C_{17}H_{21}NO_4$, a derivative of *Erythroxylon coca*. Or any of the other darling little euphemistic pet names Higgins taught her for a drug that could fry your brain whether you sniffed it up your nose or smoked it in a crack pipe.

Took her two years to kick the habit.

She was planning to go see Otto again, ask him if the old job was still available, when he got killed tailing a wayward spouse. It was Warren Chambers, instead, who'd given her the first job she'd had since her nosedive two years earlier.

Tell me about the job, okay? she'd said.

First tell me you're clean, Warren had said.

Why? Do I look like I'm not?

You look suntanned and healthy. But that doesn't preclude coke.

I like that word. Preclude. Did you make it up?

How do you like the other word? Coke?

I used to like it just fine. I still think of it every now and then. But the thought passes. I'm clean, Mr. Chambers.

How long has it been?

Almost two years. Since right after Otto fired me.

And now you're clean.

Now I'm clean.

Are you sure? Because if you're still on cocaine, I wish you'd tell me.

I am not on cocaine. Or to put it yet another way, I do not do coke no more. I am clean. K-L-double-E, clean. What do you need, Mr. Chambers? A sworn affidavit? You've got my word. I like to think it's still worth something.

There was a time when it wasn't.

That was then, this is now. Mr. Chambers, are you here to offer me a job, or are we going to piss around all morning?

Call me Warren, he'd said, and smiled.

After all her years of experience with cocaine, Toots Kiley thought she could recognize a cokehead whenever she saw one.

But she didn't realize Maria Torrance was one until the lady offered her a toot.

It was close to four o'clock. They were sitting on the deck facing Calusa Bay and the intercoastal waterway, Toots wearing a denim skirt, blue sneakers, and a yellow blouse, Maria wearing tight white shorts, white sandals, and a white T-shirt without a bra, her red hair pulled back into a ponytail. A matching red Mercedes-Benz convertible with an MT-1 vanity plate had been parked in the driveway when Toots arrived.

The water was choppy this Sunday afternoon, but that didn't stop any of Calusa's weekend boaters. The intercoastal was thronged with powerboats, the bay beyond teeming with bloated triangular white sails. Toots would never understand the lure of boating. Far as she was concerned, the best way to enjoy boats was the way she was enjoying them right this minute: just sitting onshore *watching* them. Maria had spent the past half hour educating Toots about her mother, and then she'd shifted the conversation to her father, Peter Torrance.

"I hardly knew him," she was saying. "He left when I was only a year old, still an infant really. In a sense, I've never really known him at *all*."

"Know where he is now?" Toots asked.

"For all I know he's dead," Maria said. "There was a letter from him when Mother died, wanting to know if he'd been mentioned in her will, can you imagine? Wanting to know if she'd *left* him anything. Gone for all those years, wants to know if she *left* him anything! I turned it over to her lawyer."

"*Had* she left him anything?"

"Not a cent."

"I gather the parting wasn't a pleasant one."

"Pleasant? He ran off with one of the McCulloughs, behaved like some damn *gazoonie* you hire for the season. This was supposed to be a respected person on the staff. The *marketing* director. A married man with a baby daughter! Didn't even leave a note. Just disappeared in the night with Aggie McCullough, one of the flyers, would you like a drink?"

"Thank you, I don't drink," Toots said.

Maria looked at her.

"How about a toot instead?" she asked.

Toots wondered how she'd known. Was there something on her face, something in her eyes that said *I'm a sober cokehead, test me*? Or was Maria misreading her name? Surely Toots had pronounced her own name correctly when introducing herself, the Toots rhyming with "puts" and not with "boots." But if Maria had mistakenly heard her, then mightn't she have assumed the name was merely a nickname earned because the lady *did*, in fact, toot? If the lady toots, why not *call* her Toots?

"Thanks, no," she said.

"Sure?"

Still watching her steadily, blue eyes fastened to her face.

"Positive," Toots said.

"I think I'll have one," Maria said, and turned away, and walked back into the house. Toots sat watching the boats out on the water, wondering whether Maria was mixing herself a drink or snorting a line. When she came back out of the house, it was obvious she'd done both. There was a gin-tonic in her right hand, but her eyes were brighter than they'd been five minutes earlier, her smile more dazzling, her stride more confident, her mood one of keen exhilaration. Her nipples under the white T-shirt were puckered.

"Sure now?" she asked again, and jiggled the ice in her glass, and waggled her eyebrows.

"Positive," Toots said again, and hoped this time the emphatic plosive made her meaning clear. "How'd they meet?" she asked. "Your parents."

"Through the circus. He was from Ireland originally, worked circuses on the Continent before he came to America. Do you know the Marateo Circus in Italy? Very famous. He was a booking agent with them for four years. Torrance is an Irish form of Terrence. It's from the Latin, means 'tender, good, and gracious.' Isn't *that* a hoot, man who leaves his wife with a year-old child? I was cute as a button, they say. My father was a very tall man, from what they tell me, but everyone was scared to death I'd stop growing, the way Mother did when she was six. But I turned out pretty normal, didn't I?" she said, and jiggled her sandaled foot and grinned mischievously at Toots over the top of her glass.

Images of a very tall man making love to a midget immediately filled Toots's mind. She was reminded of a ribald joke she'd once heard and almost started telling it, until she remembered that the woman sitting opposite her happened to be the *daughter* of a pair as unseemly as the couple in the joke. Her mind lingered on the premise. Visions of maypoles danced in her head.

"Did you tell all this to Mr. Hope?" she asked.

"About my father, you mean? Yes."

Toots wondered if she'd also offered him a few lines of cocaine.

"When your father wrote to you," she said, "where was he living?"

"L.A."

"With the woman he'd run off with?"

"Aggie? No, that didn't last more than a minute. She was back with the circus the very next season."

"How'd your mother feel about that?"

"They became very good friends, in fact."

"I take it the McCulloughs are an act."

"High flyers, yes. Aerialists. Aggie's brothers and some of their children are still with S&R. So's her son and daughter-in-law. They're really very good. Aggie's retired now, she lives in Bradenton with her third husband, man who used to be a bear trainer. Worst animals in the world to train. Very dangerous. Bite you in half soon as look at you," Maria said, and snapped at the air, clicking her teeth together sharply, and smiling at Toots immediately afterward. Toots suddenly wondered if she was lesbian. No pierced ears with a multitude of earrings in them, no such blatant signal, no subtle ones, either, a tentative touch, a brief exploratory resting of a hand upon an arm, nothing like that. But still . . .

"Was that the last time you heard from him? After your mother died?"

"Yes."

"Had he tried to contact her at any time before then?"

"Not that I know of."

"After she bought her share of the circus, for example?"

"No. Why?"

"Well, a man reappears out of the blue to ask if his divorced wife left him anything in her will, you've got to wonder if he tried to hit her up for cash while she was still alive. Is all I'm saying. Hears she's part owner of a circus now, figures she might be an easy mark. But you don't know that he had any contact with her after he left, huh?"

"No. My mother never mentioned having heard from him."

"Were you very close with her?"

"Very."

"She'd have told you, huh?"

"Yes, she told me everything."

"Ever tell you she was planning suicide?"

"No. It wasn't suicide. Someone killed her."

"Did you tell *that* to Mr. Hope?"

"Yes."

"How did he react?"

"He wanted to know if I had any idea who might have done it."

"And did you?"

"Yes."

"Did you tell him?"

"I did."

"What'd you tell him?"

"I told him Davey Sheed had shot and killed my mother."

"Davey . . .?"

"Sheed. S&R's cat trainer."

The nurse monitoring Matthew Hope's blood pressure and pulse was getting essentially normal readings on both. A hundred over seventy for the b.p., ninety-five for the pulse. But she knew that his EEG had shown disorganized electrical activity, and that the doctors were already talking among themselves about coma. If he flat-lined on his next EEG, this would indicate that the cortex of the brain had stopped functioning. The longer he stayed in a comatose state, the fewer were his chances of waking up. If he flat-lined for two days in succession, they could assume he was brain-dead, and that his chances for recovery were essentially zero. That was when they would call in the family and ask what they chose to do about life-support systems.

The nurse wondered what was going on inside his head.

Inside his head, there was a blackness as vast and as empty as a Siberian plain. Inside his head, there was a cold, keening wind sweeping in over the pebbled plain. In the darkness, there were crackling sounds and sudden bursts of light. An electrical storm was crashing in over the cold, dark plain. Each time lightning crackled and spit, he saw a black whip snaking out of the blackness. Each time the wind howled, he heard the roar of a tiger. Images flashed and were gone.

Now a blue and white tent. Now a black and monstrous generator truck rumbling in the darker black. Voices echoed in a vast echo chamber. There was more lightning. And the electric crackle of the whip. And a tiger's head hanging in the midnight sky, flashes of lightning striping her magnificent head . . .

. . . jaws opening wide as Davey Sheed approached her. Matthew was standing just outside the cage, George Steadman at his side. The showman was leaning in close to him, yelling over the crack of the whip and the roaring of the cats, and the scolding, cajoling, encouraging patter of his cat trainer. Steadman smelled of Old Spice aftershave. The cage smelled of tiger piss and human sweat and something less identifiable, perhaps fear.

"It takes a long time to put up the cage and chute," Steadman was saying. "That's why the wild-animal act is always the first one in the show. Davey Sheed, King of All the Beasts. That's how he bills himself. Soon as he's done, the clowns come out while we're taking down the cage, and then we go off the ground and up in the air for the high-wire act, sometimes while we're still taking down the . . . oops!" he said, and snapped his full attention to where the female tiger Sheed was working had jumped off her pedestal and was moving dangerously close to him.

"There's a line they know they can't cross," Steadman whispered. "It's the length of the whip or the stick the trainer is using. They're taught not to come any closer than that. She's moving in on him, see that? And he's letting her know he'll have none of it. Listen to him."

"*Sakti!*"

Snapping her name like a whip.

"*No Sakti!*" Sheed yelled, as if scolding a tabby who'd peed on the carpet instead of a three-hundred-pound beast who tossed her head disdainfully, and clawed for the whip again with her right paw. Sheed, a handsome, dark-haired, muscular man of medium height, was working bare-chested in blue jeans and boots. There were four other tigers in the cage; the trio of young male lions hadn't yet been brought in. Steadman had explained to Matthew that male cats were less aggressive, which was why cat trainers used females for their so-called fighting acts. Of the five tigers in the cage with Sheed, Steadman had pointed out a young male, two mature females, and two elderly males. The two to watch were the females, he'd said, one of them on the ground with Sheed now, quarreling over turf. The other one seemed keenly interested in what was going on, shoulders hunched, neck craning, eyes intent on the action. Matthew had the feeling she might join the argument at any moment.

"Up where you belong, Sakti," Sheed said, and relaxed his tight grip on the whip's handle, refusing to get into a tug-of-war with a clawed opponent. He had lowered his voice now, having caught her undivided attention with his earlier shouting, reducing the argument to a one-on-one personal bickering that had nothing to do with any of the other animals in the cage, particularly the other female who was crouching the way Matthew had seen household cats do before they lunged at a backyard lizard.

"Get up there now," Sheed said, and Sakti watched him, tail flicking, but she did not paw at the whip again. He lowered the whip entirely. Took a step toward her. He's crazy, Matthew thought. Another step. Closer now. The other female's ears were back flat against her head. Matthew felt she would go for him in the next instant. Apparently Sheed's two outside men felt the same way. They were moving restlessly on either side of the cage, ready to join him if push came to shove. One of them had a pistol in his hand.

"Come on now," Sheed said, moving in very close to the tiger now, his voice soft, "enough of this, we have work to do. *Up!*" and he snapped his fingers an inch from Sakti's nose, and the big cat turned and leaped up onto the pedestal again. The other female watched a moment longer, and then seemed to lose interest entirely. Yawning, she turned away. The yawn seemed contagious. Both elderly males joined her, and then one of the younger tigers.

"We never feed them before the act, you know," Steadman said. "We keep them hungry while Davey's putting them through their paces. They don't get fed till he's finished with them."

Matthew did not think he would like to be a wild-animal trainer.

As Sheed put the cats through the routines they'd rehearsed and rereheared a thousand times already, as he called for his outside men to let the three young lions in through the chute, and then worked them into the act so that now there was a volatile mix of tiger and lion and one sole brave human, Matthew told Steadman that he'd gone to see Maria Torrance the day before, to talk to her about the proposed land offer. He was now confident she would not oppose it, which cleared the way for him to approach Florida Sun and Shore with Steadman's opening bid. In fact, he had an appointment with a man named Lonnie McGovern there, later this afternoon.

"I want to ask Mr. Sheed a few questions first," Matthew said, "and then I'll be . . ."

"Oh?" Steadman said. "What about?"

"I understand he knew Willa Torrance pretty well."

"*Everyone* knew Willa pretty well," Steadman said. "What's that go to do with acquiring the fairgrounds?"

"Maria suggested I talk to him," Matthew said vaguely, "see what he thought about it."

"About what?" Steadman asked.

"In fact, it might not be a bad idea if you called her yourself within the next few days," Matthew said, sidestepping the question, not for nothing was he a twinkly-toed shyster. "Fill her in on what you plan to do, treat her like a real partner with a good head for business."

"Maria?" Steadman said, and raised his brows. "A good head for *business*?'

"I think so," Matthew said, and suddenly recognized his own unconscious pun. A good head for business. Maria had, in fact, shaved her scalp entirely bald, giving herself the undeniably good head she needed for demonstrating the effectiveness of the wigs she sold. He felt a smile starting, but the smile froze on his face when the other female tiger leaped off her perch and came rushing at her trainer.

Sheed did not hesitate a moment.

He turned the leaded handle of the whip so that he was holding it like a club, and just as the animal seemed ready to leap, he whacked her on the nose with it, *whap*, and yelled her name like a cannon shot, "*Rahna!*" and whacked her again, and shouted "*Rahna!*" and gave her yet another whack, backing away from her all the while, easing himself toward the cage door, where one of his outside men was already standing, ready to pull it open the moment he reached it. Rahna was crouched low now, ears flat, tail flicking, watching him from eyes that seemed to have gone as yellow as her coat.

One of his outside men, a burly guy with muscular tattooed arms and a weight lifter's chest bulging inside a grimy T-shirt, yanked open the cage door. Sheed slipped through the narrow opening, and the outside man slammed the door shut just as Rahna sprang, hitting the door with all the uncoiled force of four hundred plus pounds. Sheed turned to look into the cage. He was breathing heavily. Rahna was pacing back and forth some six feet back from the door now, tail flicking angrily, eyes grazing him like twin yellow lasers. Sheed extended his hand, palm up, toward the second outside man. Initially, the man seemed not to understand him. Then he looked at the pistol in his own hand, grasped what Sheed was wordlessly saying, and placed the pistol onto the trainer's outstretched palm.

He's going to shoot her, Matthew thought.

Sheed nodded to the first outside man, who shook his head. No, he was saying. Sheed nodded again, insistently this time. Yes. Again, the outside man shook his head.

"*Open* it!" Sheed snapped.

He's going back in, Matthew thought. He's crazy.

The outside man reluctantly threw back the bolts on the cage. Rahna whipped around when she heard the metallic clicking. Cautiously, the outside man opened the cage door. Rahna snapped her head toward Sheed the instant he slid through the narrow opening and into the cage. Her ears went back again. She was going into a crouch again.

"No, Rahna!" he shouted, and raised the gun over his head. "*No!*"

The word seemed to mean nothing to her. She opened her jaws and roared in defiance, still crouched low, shoulders hunched, ears back.

Sheed fired into the air.

Rahna sprang out of the crouch, seemed to whirl in midair, landed on her feet again some four feet from where she'd been crouched, and then turned immediately to face Sheed again.

"Now stop this," he said.

Rahna cocked her head is if listening.

"Get back up there," he said.

She blinked.

"Up," he said.

She opened her jaws but the roar was more like a growl.

"Let's go," he said, "Now," he said, "*Up!*" he said, and cracked the whip at her, and she turned instantly and ran toward her perch and leaped up onto it. Sitting like a docile house cat on her favorite cushion, Rahna blinked again, and twitched her ears, and then yawned as she had earlier.

"Good girl," Sheed said, and then spun away from her, disdainfully showing the tigress his back. Lifting both arms over his head, he faced each sector of the tent in turn, as though acknowledging applause from an invisible, adoring crowd.

"Bravo," Steadman said in soft appreciation, and Matthew suddenly realized that the entire dispute between Sheed and the two huge females had been staged and rehearsed God knew how many times, a carefully choreographed brawl that involved the trainer, his two boisterous female cats, the other observant but essentially uninterested animals in the cage, and the two fearful outside men – an artful performance designed to demonstrate how recklessly courageous was the King of All the Beasts, Davey Sheed.

Matthew couldn't wait to talk to him.

Warren found him in a white trailer lettered in red on its side with the words:

DAVEY SHEED

★ *KING OF ALL THE BEASTS* ★

He mounted the several steps leading to the door near the rear of the vehicle, knocked, waited, knocked again, and then called "Mr. Sheed?"

Silence.

"Mr. Sheed?"

A rumble from inside the trailer, somewhat like the low growl of one of Sheed's own cats.

"It's me," Warren said, his face close to the door. "Warren Chambers. We talked on the phone just a little while ago."

"Mrff," from inside the trailer.

"Mr. Sheed?"

"Yes, wait a goddamn minute, will you?"

Warren waited.

He thought he heard someone peeing inside the trailer. He thought he heard a toilet flushing. He kept waiting. He heard water running. Sheed washing his hands. Warren *hoped*. A moment later, the door opened.

Davey Sheed looked somewhat older than one would have expected the king of all the beasts to be. For no good reason, Warren had anticipated a man in his late twenties or early thirties; who else would have been foolhardy enough to step into a cageful of wild animals? But the man standing in the doorway to the trailer, a scowl on his sleep-sodden features, looked to be in his mid-fifties. Dark-haired and beetle-browed, hazel eyes prying through the portage of the head like brass cannons, so to speak, he stood barefoot and muscularly bare-chested in skimpy jockey shorts, glowering at Warren as though they hadn't arranged a meeting for one-thirty that Monday afternoon, which time it now happened to be. His chest and arms were interlaced with old scars, perhaps the result of altercations with cats he had known, and perhaps a contributing factor to his somewhat surly demeanor.

"Mr. Sheed?" Warren asked.

"You woke me up," Sheed said.

"I'm sorry, I thought we'd said . . ."

"Come in, come in," Sheed said, and stepped aside to permit Warren entrance, scratching his balls as he moved deeper into the trailer toward the dining and cooking area up front. Lie down with cats, Warren thought, and you start behaving like cats.

"We *did* say one-thirty, didn't we?" he asked.

"I dozed off," Sheed said, dismissing the question. "Sit down. Would you like a beer?"

"No, thank you," Warren said, and looked for a place to sit. Almost every flat surface in the trailer was strewn with dirty laundry. The stench of cats rose from much of it. Lie down with cats, he thought again. He was damned if he was going to touch any of Sheed's dirty underwear or socks.

"Where?" he asked.

"Anywhere," Sheed said, and swung his hand across the dinette table, sweeping the clothing on it to the floor. Walking to the refrigerator opposite the table and its banquettes, he opened the door, took out a can of beer, popped the cap, closed the door, and brought the can to his mouth. Warren noticed that the drainboard on the sink counter alongside the range was stacked with soiled paper plates and plastic utensils. He wished he was Sheed's mother; he'd send him to his room without dessert.

"Mr. Sheed," he said, sitting carefully on the banquette to the left of the table Sheed had cleared, "as I told you on the phone . . ."

"Yeah, yeah."

"I'm trying to track Matthew Hope's . . ."

"Yeah, yeah."

". . . movements last week in an attempt . . ."

"Yeah," Sheed said.

". . . to find out why someone shot him. Policemen usually concentrate on the twenty-four hours before a homicide . . ."

"Why?" Sheed asked. "Is he dead?"

"No," Warren said, "but he's in very serious condition at Good Samaritan."

"I'm sorry to hear that," Sheed said, and belched.

"Yes," Warren said. "And the twenty-four hours *following* it, because those are the most important times. The *pre*-twenty-four because they tell us where he went and who he saw . . ."

"But you're not a cop," Sheed said. "I understood . . ."

"That's right, I'm a private investigator. Who worked with him. He's a close friend of mine."

"Okay," Sheed said, and nodded.

"But I *used* to be a cop. In Boston."

"Uh-huh."

"Which is how I happen to know this stuff," Warren said, feeling like a jackass for having to explain. "Anyway, the *post*-twenty-four's important because that's when the perp is widening his edge, that's when a trail can start getting cold."

"Um-hmh," Sheed said, scratching his balls again, bored to tears. He'd probably read all this shit in some cheap paperback cop novel, and didn't care to hear it all over again in the sanctity of his cat-piss trailer. He put down the beer can, picked up a pair of jeans from where they were tossed onto the other banquette, and began putting them on.

"I figure I'm following him by a week," Warren said. "Today's the twenty-eighth, I'm a week behind him. Which gives whoever shot him a very *big* edge."

"Yeah, that's a shame, all right," Sheed said.

No sarcasm in his voice, no boredom, just saying the words flat out, no inflection, no emotion, no anything. Maybe working in a cage with wild animals did that to a man. Left him incapable of reacting emotionally to *anything*. Show any emotion *outside* the cage, then you were liable to lose your cool when you were in there with the cats and it counted. Show them anything they could see or smell or sense, and they'd claw you to pieces. Witness Sheed's scars.

"You told me on the phone that he'd come to see you last Monday," Warren said.

"Yeah, that's right," Sheed said, and zipped up his fly, and then slipped on a pair of loafers without socks, and picked up the beer can again, and took another swig.

"Can you tell me what you talked about?"

"Willa mostly."

"Torrance?"

"Yes. What's this about, anyway?"

It was about Maria having told Toots that Matthew planned to talk to Sheed as soon as he possibly could. It was about Matthew having been here last Monday. It was about Maria having told first Matthew and then Toots that the guy swilling beer over there by the sink had killed her mother. That's what it was really about. But that was the one thing Warren could not reveal.

"Didn't Mr. Hope tell you?" he asked.

"He told me someone was challenging her will . . ."

"That's right," Warren lied.

"And he wanted to know about her state of mind before the suicide."

"You knew her back then, did you?"

Taking him back to the then and there, three years ago, when Willa Torrance allegedly put a bullet in the middle of her forehead, a conclusion her daughter rejected in favor of a theory that had Sheed shooting her and then placing the gun in her lifeless hand.

"Listen," Sheed said, "you mind if we get out of here? I hate being cooped up in this dump." He tossed the empty beer can onto the stack of already accumulated debris, adding measurably to the dumpiness of the trailer, and then moved immediately to the rear door, not waiting for an answer. Wearing only jeans and loafers, still bare-chested, he went outside. Warren followed him.

What ten minutes earlier had been a big blue and white tent surrounded by what appeared to be a trailer park on a mud lot caked and hardened by a week of baking sunshine; what at one-thirty had, in fact, seemed like a graveyard for vehicles – not a human being in sight, not a leaf stirring on this breezeless, steamy, Florida day; what had then been somnolent and still, had now transmogrified to a bustling open-air carnival. It had been siesta time, Warren supposed, but now everyone was awake and alive.

As Sheed led him toward where he said his cats were caged at the far end of the lot, the field swarmed with performers in leotards and tights, blue jeans and bikinis, halters and shorts, sweat suits and – in at least one instance – an actual tutu tattered beyond belief. Like a wide-eyed child moving through a circus wonderland magically stripped of its shimmering trappings, its performers nonetheless immediately recognizable in rehearsal clothes, Warren followed Sheed toward the tent, moving through and past bouncing acrobats and scurrying clowns, ballet girls painstakingly practicing steps, jugglers tossing balls and clubs and fiery torches, men and women leaping on teeter boards and rolling on glittery globes, a trainer putting half a dozen scrappy little dogs through their frantic scurrying paces, another trainer trying with little success to coax a pony to jump over a hurdle . . .

"The horse won't do it," Sheed explained. "That's all part of the act, it gets a million laughs. Let's cut through the tent."

. . . a midway ventriloquist working with a dummy who looked like Groucho Marx, talking to the air as he drank a glass of water – the ventriloquist and not the dummy – talking all the while, leapers and vaulters and tumblers and balancers, all bounding and jumping and prancing and hopping and sprouting from the field like energetic weeds.

"Shortcut through the tent," Sheed further explained, and walked through the wide entrance where the flaps were fastened back, into yet another area of frantic activity, this one multileveled like a three-dimensional chessboard. Rehearsing on the ground in one of the two rings, was a woman putting a half-dozen riderless horses through their paces . . .

"Your liberty horses," Sheed commented. "No riders."

. . . first in single file, and next two by two, and finally three by three, the magnificent animals thundering around the ring, hooves flying in unison as the brunette trainer in jeans and cowboy boots coaxed them along with cooing words of encouragement. In the second ring, a trainer – assisted by a tall brunette wearing shorts and a pink T-shirt – was urging three huge elephants to sit on their haunches and raise their front legs and trunks.

"The bull hand is his wife," Sheed said.

Close by both rings, but outside of them, web girls were relentlessly climbing ropes, and ladder-walkers were dangling upside down and hanging in space, one of them from a bit clenched between his teeth. On the second level, midway between the ground and the trapezes way up high, a pyramid of wire-walkers moved steadily, precariously, cautiously but certainly across a steel-strand cable that stretched some thirty feet from platform to platform. Two men on bicycles, each holding a long balancing pole, formed the base of the triangle. Above them was a third man perched on a narrow plank supported by a pole strapped at either end to the chests of the cyclists. He, too, held a long balancing pole. Standing on his shoulders, wearing leotard-and-tights rehearsal clothes, was a long-haired redhead, her hands spread toward the top of the tent like the wings of a large bird in flight.

"The Zvonkova family," Sheed said. "From the Moscow State Circus. They knew Willa much better than I did."

High above the ground, higher still than the wire-walkers, the flyers rehearsed. Craning his neck, eyes sweeping the top of the tent, Warren watched as a blonde woman in black tights and a pink top concentrated on an empty trapeze swinging back toward her platform, gauging her timing against that of an equally blond man dangling head-downward on another swinging trapeze, and off she went, catching the bar and flying out into space, back, forward again, back, forward, timing herself, and finally releasing her grip on the bar, somersaulting once, twice, and yet another time, reaching for her catcher's outstretched hands – and missing.

As she fell like a stone for the net far below, Sheed shrugged and said, "Going for the Big Trick, the triple. Marnie knows it like her own name, her timing was just a hair off."

The blonde bounced up out of the net, arms outstretched, hit the net with her feet, bounced up again, walked swiftly to the side, flipped out of the net and onto the ground, and walked immediately toward the runged stanchion leading up to her platform. Glancing up to where the blond man was now sitting upright on his trapeze and looking somewhat bored, she called, "Sorry, Sam!" and began climbing.

On the far side of the tent, an eight-piece band – all of its musicians in jeans and T-shirts – was tuning up. The keyboard player, a woman, hit a B flat over and over again for the trumpet, tuba, trombone, and tenor-sax players. The reed man doubled on alto and clarinet; he tuned the clarinet from the same B flat, and then the woman plinked him an E flat for the alto. The bass and guitar players, in a world of their own, kept a running string dialogue going between them, while the drummer banged out paradiddles and ruffs, trying to drown out the universe. Sheed and Warren came through an open tent flap into bright sunshine just as the band struck up a lively marching tune. It felt like the first day of May, but it was still only the twenty-eighth of March.

The big cats had just been fed, they lay dozing in their

cages. Sheed went from cage to cage, slipping his hands casually through the bars, gently scratching the massive heads of the tigers and lions, murmuring each one's name in turn, mentioning to Warren that there was no such thing as a *tame* animal, these cats were simply *trained*.

"I think of them as my friends, though, isn't that right, Simba?" he asked, scratching one of the male lions behind his left ear, the lion nuzzling his hand. "Lions are easier to work with than tigers," he said, "yes, Simba, yes, they're social animals, they travel in prides. Your tigers are solitary hunters, they don't like being part of a pack. They make their own decisions, won't give any kind of signal before jumping you, very dangerous animals, yes, Simba, that's a good boy. I got most of my scars from leopards, though, they're worse than your bears, I won't work with them anymore."

"Your bears?" Warren asked, picking up the possessive.

"No, your leopards," Sheed said. "Your panthers, too, for that matter. Quick, untrustworthy, more unpredictable than all your other cats. But your bears are from another planet entirely. 'A bear bears a grudge,' that's an old circus saying. You insult a bear, you treat him badly in any way, give him any kind of excuse to build up steam inside, he'll *remember* it, he'll bide his time till he can get even. You've got to be crazy to get in a ring with a bear. You ever see a circus bear without a muzzle? You know how pit bulls clamp onto a leg? Or moray eels grab a hand when you stick it into wherever they're hiding? That's your bear. Won't let go till he's chewed it off. Nothing in his eyes, nothing on his face, no sign whatever he's about to attack, and *whammo*, he's on you in a minute and he won't let go."

Warren wanted to talk about Willa Torrance.

"So what can you tell me about her state of mind?" he asked, jumping in again with both feet.

"Willa, you mean?"

No, your bears and your tigers and your lions, Warren thought, but did not say.

"She seemed okay to me," Sheed said, and shrugged, "but who knows what goes on in a woman's head, huh? Shoot herself that way? Never would've thought it."

"Nothing depressing her at the time? Nothing bothering her?"

"Not that I knew of. There was that thing with Aggie, you know, but that was ancient history by then."

"Aggie?"

"McCullough. Sam's mother, you just saw him catching for Marnie up there. Best hands in the business. Willa's husband ran off with her. Or so I understand. I wasn't with S&R at the time, I only heard about this later."

"What was his name, do you know?"

"Peter Torrance, a twenty-four-hour man or something, I really don't know."

"But you say this was long before . . ."

"Oh, yeah, *ages* ago. Aggie came back to the circus, though, and she and Willa became close friends. So there wasn't any kind of hard feelings there, this wasn't like a bear nursing a grudge."

"What happened to Torrance?"

"I have no idea."

They were walking back toward the trailer now. Everyone they passed seemed eager to greet Sheed, flattered when a celebrity of his stature responded with a wave or a smile. Here on his home turf, the trainer seemed as supremely confident as he was in a cageful of wild animals – Davey Sheed, indeed King of All the Beasts.

"How well did you know her?" Warren asked.

"Willa?" he said. "Or Aggie?"

"Willa."

"Pretty well."

"How well is that?"

"Figure it out," Sheed said, and smiled.

They were at his trailer now. Sheed was starting up the steps to the door; as far as he was concerned, the interview had ended.

"When did you last see her?" Warren asked.

"Why?"

"I'm curious."

"I've been through this before, you know," Sheed said, and reached for the doorknob. "You're giving me a lot of bullshit about somebody challenging her will, but you're really here to ask me did I kill her, aren't you?'

"Did you?" Warren asked.

"Sure. Which is just what I told the police in Rutherford. I killed Willa Torrance, fellas, so take me away and lock me up. Come on, willya? She shot herself three years ago, who the hell would be challenging her will now? You and your pal should think up a new story.'

"My *pal* is in the hospital," Warren said.

"Yeah, that's too bad," Sheed said. "But I'm not the one who put him there."

"What kind of car do you drive, Mr. Sheed?"

"A yellow Cougar," Sheed said, and opened the door. A faint whiff of cat piss wafted out on the still sunlit air. "In keeping with my line of work," he added, and smiled again, and stepped inside.

Detective Morris Bloom had not returned from his vacation until that Monday morning, and what with one thing and another, it was not until two-thirty that afternoon that he learned Matthew Hope had been shot on Friday night and was in serious condition at Good Samaritan Hospital.

He got there at three o'clock. Patricia Demming was still in the waiting room. He knew her well, had worked dozens of cases for her since she'd joined the S.A.'s Office. She filled him in on Matthew's condition, told him he should be coming around any minute now. She did not look too terribly convinced. She looked up at the clock, sighed, and then asked, "Which of your people are on the case?'

"Kenyon and Di Luca *were* on it," Bloom said. "I've taken over personally."

"Good," she said, and nodded.

"Any idea what he was doing in Newtown?"

The same question, over and over again. What the hell was he doing in Newtown?

"No," she said. "Warren Chambers went there Friday night, canvassed the neighborhood . . ."

"Anything?"

"Hooker saw the shooter's car. All she could tell him was it was a black two-door Mazda."

"No year?"

"She didn't know."

"License plate?"

"Didn't notice it."

"Did she see the shooter?"

"Just a hand. Wearing a black glove."

"I'll call Warren, see what else he's got."

"Toots is on it, too."

"Couldn't ask for better. I just don't want us duplicating whatever . . ."

"Yeah, you should talk to him."

She fell silent again.

She was thinking of the first time she'd laid eyes on Matthew Hope . . .

. . . a cat appearing suddenly out of the driving rain, a swift, gray, emaciated creature that looked like the scrawny raccoons they had down here, darting off the curb and into the gutter. She slammed on her brakes at once, and the little red Volkswagen she'd been driving back then went into a sidelong skid and smashed into the left rear fender of a sleek blue car parked at the curb. "Oh dear," she said, and got out of the Volks and was looking at the banged-up fender when a barefooted man wearing a white terry cloth robe came thundering down the front walk from the house, coming through the pouring rain like a fury intent on strangling her. She stood in her little red silk dress and red high-heeled shoes, soaking wet, rain spattering the roadway, rain pelting everywhere around her, long blonde hair getting wetter and wetter and wetter, and all she could think of saying in the face of his monumental anger was "I'm awfully sorry."

"Sorry, my ass," he said.

He was six feet tall or thereabouts, she noticed, with dark hair plastered to his head now, dark brown eyes smoldering in rage.

"I didn't want to hit the cat," she said.

"What cat?" he said.

And naturally, the damn cat was gone by then, so much for motivation.

"He ran out into the road," she said lamely. "I hit the brake and . . . I'm sorry. Really. I am."

He didn't look as if he gave a good goddamn whether she was sorry or not. He merely kept staring at his expensive car, which she figured was brand-new or close to it, while she looked from the fender of the car – which she now saw was an Acura – to the grille of her lowly VW, and then to the skid marks on the wet asphalt. The marks clearly defined the course her little car had taken before wreaking its havoc. Guilty as charged, Your Honor. She shook her head as if amazed by the wonder of it all, but he wasn't buying innocence or guilelessness, he was fuming mad, even if he was sort of cute.

"I'm an attorney," she said at once, figuring she'd better pull some rank here pretty damn fast before he . . .

"So am I," he said.

That had been the beginning.

"Matthew was heading over to Sun and Shore soon as he finished talking with Sheed last Monday," Warren told her on the telephone.

"You get that from Sheed?" Toots asked.

"Steadman. Sheed wouldn't give me the right time."

"What's the guy's name there? Sun and Shore?"

"Lonnie McGovern."

"I'm on my way," Toots said. "Where will you be?"

"The hospital. See what they took from Matthew when they checked him in."

"Then where?"

"Depends what I get. By the way, Sheed drives a yellow Cougar."

"Maria drives a red Benz."

"So much for that."

"I'll call you at home later."

"Right," Warren said, and hung up.

*　　*　　*

The man at Florida Sun and Shore appreciated blondes.

He told Toots Kiley almost at once that his wife was blonde and his three daughters were blonde, and he had favored blondes his entire life long – though he himself was unlucky enough to have brown hair, as she could plainly see.

Thinning brown hair, Toots noticed, but did not say.

"It's always a pleasure to talk to a blonde," he said, and smiled broadly.

In addition to the thinning brown hair, he was also unfortunate enough to possess water blue eyes, a thin-lipped mouth, and a nose out of a catalog that sold funny noses with black-rimmed eyeglasses and a shaggy black mustache attached. It happened that he was wearing black-rimmed eyeglasses and sporting a shaggy black mustache. His name was Lonnie McGovern, and he told Toots that in addition to appreciating blondes he also appreciated Cincinnati, Ohio, which is where he was from originally.

"The wife and I moved down with the kids six years ago," he told her, and glanced admiringly at her legs and then her breasts and then the blonde hair he appreciated so much. Toots wondered why he figured he had the right, but she said nothing about it. She was here to find out what McGovern and Matthew had talked about during their meeting last Monday.

"You told me on the phone," McGovern said, "that you were investigating . . ."

"Yes . . ."

"The shooting . . ."

"Yes, this past Friday night," Toots said.

"Yes, but I don't see what that has to do with Sun and Shore. Or with me, for that matter."

"We're walking in his footprints," Toots said.

"I beg your pardon?"

"Trying to determine if anything he did or said could have provoked the shooting."

"Well, I can assure you," McGovern said, his bushy eyebrows rising closer to his receding hairline, "that nothing said in this office could have even the *remotest* bearing . . ."

"Perhaps if you tell me just *what* was said," Toots suggested, "I can judge for myself."

McGovern seemed suddenly not to appreciate blondes as much as he had earlier. It was okay for her to sit there with her cute little fanny planted in the leather chair opposite his desk, her splendid legs crossed, the blonde hair he had recently appreciated falling straight to her shoulders, an object to be admired and perhaps ogled – until one encountered the eyes. The eyes were brown and unflinching. The eyes accompanied the unsmiling mouth, letting McGovern know that this was a serious meeting here, however blonde Toots may have been, however much blondness was a flavor McGovern particularly liked. Until now, at any rate. Now he was studying her across the desk and wondering how that soft blonde hair of hers could have turned so suddenly into a burnished gold helmet.

Women, he thought, and sighed heavily, and said, "Mr. Hope came here with an offer. On behalf of George Steadman and the Steadman & Roeger Circus."

"Could you tell me . . .?"

"I don't feel at liberty to discuss the terms of the offer."

"I already know that Mr. Steadman was hoping to buy the state fairgrounds."

"How do you know that?"

"Maria Torrance told me. She's half owner of the circus, she's well aware . . ."

"Then ask *her* what the offer was."

"I'm not truly interested in dollar amounts, Mr. McGovern."

"Mr. Hope came here with an offer," McGovern said again. "I really feel that's all I can divulge at this time."

"At which time do you feel you may be able to divulge more?" Toots asked.

"I'm sorry, Miss Kiley, but I'm sure you must realize that whatever financial matters were discussed in this office . . ."

"I'm not asking you to tell me how much *money* was offered for the land," Toots said. "I'm trying to find out if Mr. Hope mentioned anything *besides* the land."

"Like what?"

"Like anyone or anything that might have hindered the purchase."

"He didn't mention any obstacles. I don't see why he should

have. Man comes here wanting to buy a choice piece of property, he's certainly not going to forewarn the seller of any . . ."

"How about the seller forewarning *him*?"

McGovern looked at her.

"*Are* there any obstacles to the purchase of that land?"

McGovern kept looking at her.

"Mr. McGovern," she said, "did you and Mr. Hope discuss any obstacles to the purchase of that land?"

"Yes," McGovern said. "As a matter of . . ."

. . . fact, the problem came up shortly after Matthew arrived. On the phone, he had told McGovern only that he represented a party interested in the purchase of the thirty acres of land commonly known as the state fairgrounds. He understood that Florida Sun and Shore . . .

"Yes," McGovern had said.

". . . represents the owner or owners of that land, and I was wondering if I could stop by sometime Monday afternoon . . ."

"Only time I've got free on Monday is four o'clock," McGovern told him.

"I'll be there," Matthew said.

Ten minutes after Matthew got there, McGovern told him there was a cloud on the title. The owner of the property, a Florida investor given to land speculation . . .

"What's his name?" Matthew asked.

McGovern hesitated a moment, debating whether it was okay to reveal the name of the party his firm was representing. Apparently, he'd had no directives to the contrary. He took off his black-rimmed glasses . . .

Matthew expected the nose and the mustache to come off with them.

. . . wiped the lenses on his tie, put the glasses on again, said, "John Rafferty," and raised the bushy eyebrows in anticipation, as if he expected Matthew to recognize the name. Matthew did not.

"Fifteen months ago," McGovern said, "Rafferty got in way over his head on a tennis club he was buying in Lauderdale. He went to a friend here in Calusa, and asked to borrow two million dollars . . ."

Matthew did not have any friends who could lend him two million dollars. He said nothing.

"Very successful businessman down here," McGovern explained, "you'd recognize the name in a minute if I told you."

"Well, why don't you just tell me, then?" Matthew said, and smiled encouragingly.

Again, McGovern seemed to be debating whether or not this was information he could safely reveal. Apparently, he decided once again that there was no danger involved. "Andrew Byrd," he said, "owns half the real estate on Lucy's Circle, plus acres and acres of property near the airport."

Matthew nodded. He had not recognized Byrd's name in the promised minute, but Lucy's Circle was a man-made island that served as a luxurious stepping-stone between the mainland and two upscale barrier-island communities. If Calusa could claim a Gold Coast shopping area, Lucy's Circle was it. The rest was all malls. Matthew kept listening.

It seemed that Rafferty had asked Byrd for the loan of two million dollars, promising to pay simple interest for the use of the money, at the maximum legal rate of twenty-five percent per annum. Byrd had considered this a good deal. He'd done business with Rafferty in the past, and the man had always paid him back on the button. But as security for the loan, he asked Rafferty for a first mortgage on the thirty-acre parcel . . .

". . . of land on Barrington and Welles, the so-called state fairgrounds," McGovern said.

Matthew was already ahead of him. Rafferty had undoubtedly defaulted on the loan, and Byrd had sought a foreclosure judgment against him. Since there was now a "cloud on the title," as McGovern had just told him, Matthew assumed a judgment had not yet been entered and filed, but that litigation was in progress. Otherwise, McGovern would have told him there was a *lien*, and not a *cloud*, on the property. In short, McGovern was warning him that . . .

". . . there *is* a first mortgage on the property, and this would have to be satisfied before a transfer of the land could be affected."

"An existing mortgage isn't the buyer's responsibility," Matthew said.

"That's correct. Mr. Rafferty would have to satisfy the mortgage."

"For two million dollars, you said."

"Yes. Plus twenty-five percent interest for the fifteen months the mortgage has run. Plus a reasonable profit on his investment."

"I'm prepared to offer two million dollars for the parcel," Matthew said.

"That wouldn't even satisfy the mortgage," McGovern said.

"Will you discuss it with Mr. Rafferty?"

"I know he would refuse such an offer."

"I don't see why. Land in that part of town is worth only a hundred thousand an acre."

"More like *two* hundred thousand," McGovern said.

"Six million dollars would be an outrageous price for that property."

"Mr. Rafferty has already turned down offers of four."

"How did Mr. *Byrd* feel about that?"

"Mr. Byrd hasn't yet been granted a judgment. You're not even in the ballpark, Mr. Hope."

"Define the ballpark," Matthew said.

"Byrd is looking for his two million plus interest and legal fees to date. And, as I said, a reasonable return on his money. If you made an acceptable offer right this minute – and truly, Mr. Hope, two million dollars is ridiculous – we still wouldn't be able to close till *when* . . . a month from now? Perhaps longer? For the sake of convenience, let's say we could close by the first of May. By then, the interest would have run for sixteen months at a bit more than forty thousand a month, give or take a few pennies, for a total of six hundred and sixty-six thousand and change *plus* legal fees – and we all know what lawyers charge these days, don't we? Add, let's say, a safe return on the two million at six-percent prime, and I'd say we were already somewhere close to the four-million mark."

"I'd say closer to the *three* million mark," Matthew said. "How would Mr. Rafferty feel about that? Payment in full, no mortgage."

McGovern looked at him.

"Figure your client takes home half a million, and Byrd gets the rest," Matthew said. "Both of them would save a lot of time and money on endless litigation, and . . ."

"I don't represent Mr. Byrd," McGovern said.

"Well, how do you think Mr. *Rafferty* would feel about taking home half a million? If Byrd prevails, and there's a foreclosure sale, your client may end up with nothing."

"Mmmm," McGovern said.

"What do you think?"

"I would have to ask him."

"Could you please? And if you tell me where I can reach Mr. Byrd, I'll contact him directly."

"His office is in Newtown," McGovern said.

Late afternoon sunlight was streaming through the windows behind McGovern. Toots blinked.

"Newtown?" she said.

"Andrew Byrd is a black man," McGovern said.

The battle-ax nurse in charge of the hospital's Storage Section was wearing a white uniform like any of the other nurses at the hospital, and her little black plastic name tag read DOROTHY PIERCE, R.N., so Warren guessed she was a bona fide nurse, though why they would waste a qualified person in a section that stored the personal belongings of patients was something beyond his ken.

He had stopped at the main desk to check on Matthew's condition, and then had taken the elevator down to the very bowels of the hospital, where Dorothy Pierce, R.N., held sway. Dorothy Pierce, R.N., was now telling Warren Chambers, P.I., that he could *not* have a look at Matthew Hope's appointment book.

"Why not?" he asked. "You just told me he had one on his person when they checked him in."

"Exactly," she said. "On his *person*."

"Huh?" Warren said.

"Which makes it *personal* property," she said.

"All I want to do is *look* at it," Warren said.

"For what purpose?"

"To copy the . . ."

"That would be a violation of the patient's rights."

"You didn't let me finish my sentence."

"I heard enough of it to know what . . ."

"But you don't know what I want to copy."

"What is it you want to copy, Mr. Chambers?"

"His calendar appointments for last week."

"That would be a breach of regulations," she said. "I don't even want to *hear* about it."

"Miss Pierce . . ."

"*Mrs.* Pierce."

"Mrs. Pierce, a very good friend of mine is very sick upstairs, and I'm trying to find out what he did last week that might have got him shot. If you won't let me have his appointment book . . ."

"I won't."

"Then I'll have his law partner apply for a court order . . ."

"Don't snow me, kiddo," she said.

"Either his law partner or any one of a dozen police detectives I happen to know."

"Like who?" Mrs. Pierce said.

"Like me," Morris Bloom said from the doorway behind her.

Matthew's appointment book was a fine, brown leather Ghurka he'd bought in one of the shops on Lucy's Circle. Measuring some four inches wide by six and a half inches long, the book when opened to its calendar section displayed each week split approximately in half, the four days from Monday through Thursday on the left side of the dividing binder, the remaining three days on the right side. Warren copied those pages on a Xerox machine in the hospital's Clerical Office, where the objections of a second battle-ax nurse were finally overcome when Bloom showed her his detective's shield.

In the first lined space for Monday, March 21, Matthew had written the words *Call Felicity Codlow, FSU.* Several spaces below that, he had written *Circus 2:00 P.M.* and just below that,

Lonnie McGovern, Sun & Shore, 4:00 P.M. Studying the entries now, Warren figured that Matthew had written his telephone reminder *after* he'd seen Maria Torrance on Sunday, but before he'd gone out to the circus grounds on Monday. Warren had no idea who Felicity Codlow was, but he knew that FSU stood for Florida State University, and he further knew there was a branch of the school in Sarasota, near the new Calbrasa airport that serviced the tri-city area.

At twenty minutes to six that evening, after Bloom had gone back to his office with Matthew's actual appointment book in hand, Warren scanned the Sarasota/Bradenton/Calusa telephone directory for an FSU listing, dialed the number, and asked the woman who answered the phone for Miss Codlow, please.

"*Mrs.* Codlow, yes," she said, "just a minute, please."

Warren waited.

"History," a woman's voice said.

"Yes, hello," Warren said. "Mrs. Codlow, please."

"Who's calling, please?"

"Warren Chambers."

"May I tell her what this is about, sir?"

The *sir* didn't mollify Warren; he hated when they did that. Nurses in doctors' offices were the worst offenders. You called a doctor because you wanted to speak to the *doctor*, and not some nurse-twit wanting to know what this was about. Warren was always tempted to say, "I have a leaky penis."

"I'd like to talk to her personally," he said.

"Moment."

He waited again.

"Stuart England," a no-nonsense voice said.

"I wanted Mrs. Codlow," Warren said.

"This is Mrs. Codlow."

He was certain she'd announced herself as Stuart England, but he plunged ahead regardless. "This is Warren Chambers," he said, "I'm an investigator who's done work for Matthew Hope . . ."

"Yes, my God, how *is* he? I saw the news on television the other night, what on earth *happened*?"

"Well, as you know . . ."

"I spoke to him only last Monday. What . . .?"

"That's why I'm . . ."

". . . could have possibly taken him to *Newtown* at that hour of the night?"

"I know he was planning to call you . . ."

"Yes, he did."

"About what, Mrs. Codlow?"

"Well, he knows I teach English history . . . my husband and I know him socially, you see, him and Susan both, knew them even before they were divorced, actually. I suppose he assumed I'd know something about lovelocks."

"I'm sorry, something about . . .?"

"Lovelocks."

"What . . . I'm sorry, Mrs. Codlow, but I don't know what that means, lovelocks."

"Lovelocks were a men's fashion of the seventeenth century. A way of wearing the hair."

"The hair?"

"Yes. The style became popular in England when James the First . . . I teach Stuart England, you see . . ."

"I see."

"Sixteen-oh-three to seventeen hundred."

"I see."

"James the First allowed a lock of hair on the left side of his head to grow much longer than the rest of his hair. A lovelock, it was called. It was combed forward from the neck, and it usually hung casually over the front of the shoulder. Some men decorated it with a ribbon tied in a bow. It was all the rage."

"I see. And . . . Matthew called to ask about this . . . uh . . ."

"Lovelock, yes. The Puritan writer, William Prynne, wrote a long discourse on the style. He called it "The Unloveliness of Lovelockes," spelled with an 'e' back then in 1628. Would you like to hear what he wrote?"

"Well . . . uh . . . yes," Warren said.

"He wrote, and I quote exactly, 'Infinite and many are the sinfully strange and monstrous vanities which this inconstant, vain, fantastic, idle, proud, effeminate and wanton age of ours hath hatched and produced in all parts and corners of the world . . ."

"Yes, but how did he *really* feel?" Warren said.

"Indeed," Mrs. Codlow said, and trilled a delightfully girlish laugh. "He went on to say, 'I have resolved for the present to single out one sinful, shameful and uncomely vanity with which to grapple, which hath lately feigned on many effeminate, loose, licentious, singular, fantastic and vainglorious persons of our masculine and more noble sex; to wit, the nourishing and wearing of unnaturally shameful and unlovely locks, or *love* locks, as they style them. These lovelocks had their birth from the very Devil himself!' He went on and on in like manner for a good sixty-three pages that defy all sense or logic, the more *noble* sex indeed!"

"Did Matthew say why he wanted to know about a *hair* fashion?"

"Well, apparently he'd done a bit of homework beforehand."

"What sort of homework?"

"I expect he'd been to the library. He told me that he knew Lovelock was a town in Nevada, and that Lovelock was also the name of a thirty-nine-year-old Olympic track star who was killed under . . ."

"Killed?" Warren said at once.

"Yes, under a subway train in Brooklyn. Back in 1949. Dr. John E. Lovelock was his full . . ."

"Ah," Warren said.

"Pardon?"

"He was going for her middle name."

"I'm sorry, what . . .?"

"He was chasing down her middle name. Lovelock. That's someone's middle name."

"It is?" Mrs. Codlow said.

"Yes. A woman he'd seen the day before."

"I see," she said, but the tone of her voice indicated she wasn't quite following Warren. "In any case, he called *me* because he'd also found a reference to lovelock as a *fashion*, and he wanted to know more about it. Remembering that I taught Stuart England . . ."

"Yes."

"He thought I might know something about the style."

"And you did."

"I did. History does have its amusing sidelights, you know. Besides, James's quarrel with the Puritans was of enormous historic importance."

"So what you told Matthew . . ."

"I had no idea he was tracing a name, you understand."

"Yes."

"I simply told him what a lovelock was."

"You said . . ."

"I said it was a sort of curl. A tress of long, curled hair."

"A curl," Warren repeated.

"Yes. Quite simply, a curl."

3

Right in the middle of her forehead . . .

BLOOM HAD met Matthew Hope for the first time right here in this office on the third floor of what the city of Calusa discreetly and euphemistically called the Public Safety Building. This was your basic cop shop, though, a police station constructed of varying shades of tan brick, its architecturally severe face broken only by narrow windows resembling rifle slits in an armory wall – not a bad innovation in a climate like Florida's.

You entered the building through bronzed entrance doors, and you went up to the third-floor reception area, where an orange-colored letter-elevator rose like an oversized periscope from the floor. You told the uniformed police officer sitting at a desk in front of the paneled wall facing you that you wanted to talk to Detective Morris Bloom, and she buzzed him from the newly installed "communications center" equipment on her desk, and then told you to follow the hallway to the office at the far end, and there was Bloom, a heavyset man in his mid-forties, an inch over six feet tall, and weighing close to two hundred pounds after his recent trip up north.

The day he'd first met Matthew, if he recalled correctly, Bloom was wearing much what he was wearing today, a rumpled blue suit, a wrinkled white shirt, a blue tie. A total picture of sartorial elegance, but that's the way he looked, take it or leave it, whenever he slept in his clothes as he'd done last night. He was probably a few pounds heavier than he'd been back then, but the fox face was the same, and so was the nose that had been kicked around the block a few times, and the shaggy black brows and dark brown eyes that made him look as if he were about to weep even when he wasn't feeling particularly sad – a bad failing for a cop.

He was, in fact, feeling particularly sad this Tuesday morning because he'd just called the hospital and they'd told him that Matthew Hope's condition was still "stable but critical," whatever the hell that meant. Now he sat here waiting for a man named Andrew Byrd to arrive, looking up at the clock – he'd be here in five minutes – and remembering the very first words Matthew had ever said to him: "I'm an attorney. I'm familiar with my rights."

Bloom had known a great many streetwise bums who were *also* familiar with their rights, so it didn't cut much ice with him that his particular rights-aware person happened to be an attorney. Attorney or not, the night before Bloom had ever laid eyes on him, Matthew Hope had slept with a woman who'd subsequently been beaten to death.

"Well, Mr. Hope," Bloom had said, "the way I look at it, you're technically in custody here, and I'm *obliged* to advise you of your rights. I've been a police officer for close to twenty-five years now, and nothing gives me a bigger pain in the ass than interpreting Miranda-Escobedo. But if I've learned one thing about interrogations, it's that it's better to be safe than sorry. So, if you don't mind, I'll just reel off your rights to you, and then we'll be over and done with it."

"If it makes you feel better," Matthew said.

"Nothing about murder makes me feel very good, Mr. Hope, but at least this way we'll be starting off even, everything according to how the Supreme Court wants it, okay?"

"Fine," Matthew said.

Snotty bastard, Bloom thought.

But sometime during the course of the interrogation, he'd

changed his mind. Winding down, he'd asked, "And you say she was alive when you left, huh?"

"She was very much alive," Matthew said.

"I think maybe she was," Bloom said, and nodded.

Matthew studied him.

"Mr. Hope," he said, "this line of work, you develop what Ernest Hemingway used to call a built-in shit detector. You familiar with Ernest Hemingway? The writer?"

"I'm familiar with him."

"You learn to sense whether somebody's telling the truth or somebody's lying, I'm sure it's the same in your line of work. I think you're telling me the truth."

Matthew kept studying him.

"If I'm wrong, sue me," Bloom said.

He had not been wrong.

The buzzer on his desk sounded.

He picked up.

"Ballistics on six," a woman's voice said.

"Thanks, Lois," he said, and hit the six button, and said, "Bloom."

"Maury, it's Ed Raines, how are you?"

"Fine, Ed, what've you got?"

"Depends what you already know," Raines said. "Way I have it, your people at the scene already nailed the slugs as twenty-twos, which is exactly right. All three bullets are twenty-two-caliber long rifles, two of them badly deformed, one of them clean as a whistle. No recovered casings, is that right?"

"Yes."

"Which ties in with our findings here."

Meaning Raines knew the gun hadn't been an auto. Whenever an auto is fired, it tosses out a spent cartridge case. These cases are usually recovered at the scene, since the shooter rarely has the time or the inclination to pick up after himself. When a revolver is fired, however, the empty shell stays in the cylinder. Bloom knew that the people in Ballistics could identify an unknown firearm either from a bullet *or* a cartridge. *How* they did it was quite another matter.

In much the same way that lawyers and doctors had invented secret languages only they could understand, thereby making it possible to charge exorbitant fees for what was essentially basic translation, so had ballistics experts come up with an arcane tongue that utilized code words like twists and grooves and lands and pitch and angle and breech and muzzle and rifling and direction and axis and extractor and rim and ejector and snot.

Nonetheless, Bloom knew that four factors were constant in every pistol of the same caliber and make. The ballistics people measured the width and number of the grooves on the bullet, and the direction and degree of the twist. Width, number, direction, and degree. WNDD. Like a sixty-watt FM radio station somewhere in the wilds of New Jersey. One, two, three, and four, which they then checked against their various charts and tables, and *voilà* . . .

"The gun was an Iver Johnson Trailsman Snub," Raines said, "model sixty-six. It's available as a thirty-eight caliber, a thirty-two, or a twenty-two long rifle – which is what this one was. Eight-shot cylinder capacity . . ."

Three of which were fired at Matthew, Bloom thought.

". . . tempered, blue-black, finished steel throughout, chrome lining in the barrel, top break frame. The snub weighs twenty-five ounces, and she's got a two-and-three-quarter-inch barrel. That's it for now. Let us know when you've got something we can test-fire."

Aluvai, Bloom thought.

"Thanks, Ed," he said.

"My pleasure," Raines said, and hung up.

The instrument buzzed again almost the moment Bloom put the receiver back on its cradle. He picked up at once.

"Mr. Byrd here to see you," Lois said.

"Send him right in," Bloom said.

She had known about Matthew since Saturday morning, when she heard the news on the radio while driving to her aerobics class, but although she'd called the hospital to inquire about his condition, she hadn't decided to come here till today.

She still wasn't sure she should be here.

Their roller-coaster marriage had been followed by an acrimonious divorce. Even two years later, when they'd met again at a party, they could barely manage civil conversation.

"Are you still angry?" she'd asked.

"About what?"

"Joanna's school."

Their separation agreement had given her the right to send their daughter to any school she chose. She'd chosen one in Massachusetts. Now she was asking him if he was still angry.

"Actually it might be good for her," he said. "Getting away from *both* of us."

"That's what I was hoping," she said.

She was wearing a fire-red gown held up by her breasts and nothing else. Dark eyes in an oval face, brown hair newly styled in a wedge, black pearl earrings dangling at her ears. He had given her those earrings on their tenth wedding anniversary. Three years later, they were divorced. Now, two years after that, they stood on a deck overlooking a beach that spread to the shoreline. A full moon above laid a silvery path across the water. From somewhere below the deck, the scent of jasmine came wafting up onto the night. Some kids up the beach were playing guitars. Just like that summer on Lake Shore Drive in Chicago. Except that on the night they'd met long ago, it had been mandolins and mimosa.

"I knew you'd be here tonight," she said. "Muriel phoned and asked if it was okay to invite you. Did she tell you I'd be here?"

"No."

"Would you have come? If you'd known?"

"Probably not," he said. "But now I'm glad I did."

She almost told the woman behind the reception desk that she was his wife. All these years later, and somehow she still thought of herself as his wife. "We were married," she said instead. "I was hoping . . ."

"Mr. Hope isn't allowed visitors yet," the woman said.

"Can you tell me what his condition is?"

"Stable."

"Is his doctor here at the hospital?"

"I'll check," the woman said, and picked up a telephone. She hit several buttons, waited, and then said, "Mary, is Dr. Spinaldo on the floor?" She listened, nodded, and then said, "I have Mr. Hope's ex here, she'd like to talk to him. Spinaldo, yes."

Susan said nothing.

"Right here at the desk," the woman said into the phone. "What's your name, ma'am?" she asked.

"Susan Hope."

Still Susan Hope, she thought. After all these years, still . . .

"Susan Hope," the woman said into the phone. "Shall I send her up?" She listened again, and then said, "No, his *ex*. Can Spinaldo talk to her? Good. I'll send her right up." She replaced the phone receiver, said, "TIC waiting room, fourth floor," and handed Susan a card that read VISITORS PASS.

"Thank you," Susan said, and went past a uniformed security guard, and walked swiftly toward the elevator. The doors opened, disgorging a gaggle of nurses in crisp white uniforms.

The party was black-tie, all the men in white dinner jackets, all the women in long slinky gowns. The band's drummer had gone up the beach to disperse the kids playing guitar and then had come back to join the piano player and the bass player on the patio below the deck. They were now playing "It Happened in Monterey." The moon was full. The Gulf of Mexico glittered beneath it like shattered glass.

"What are you thinking?" Susan asked.

"I'd get arrested," Matthew said, smiling.

"That bad?"

"That good."

". . . a long time ago," the lyrics said.

"You look beautiful tonight," he said.

"You look handsome."

"Thank you."

". . . lips as red as wine," the lyrics said.

"But then, Matthew, you always *did* look marvelous in a dinner jacket."

He was staring at her again.

"Something?" she said.

"Yes, let's get out of here," he said in a rush.

The elevators swished open. A nurse wheeled out an old man on a stretcher, and Susan followed her out into the fourth-floor corridor. She searched for a sign, found one telling her that the trauma intensive-care unit was to the right, and began walking down the hall. She was suddenly very frightened, suddenly fearful that the doctor would tell her Matthew was either dying or already dead.

The first person she saw in the waiting room was Patricia Demming. She debated leaving. Instead, she went to her, extended her hand, and said, "Hello, Patricia, how are you?"

"*Did* you have this meeting Mr. Hope had arranged?" Bloom asked.

"I did," Byrd said.

He was a tall, brawny man in his mid-thirties, Bloom guessed, conservatively dressed in a tan tropical-weight suit, a shirt the color of sweet corn, and a chocolate-brown tie fastened to his shirt with a simple gold tie tack in the shape of a tiny shield. The letters *AB* emblazoned the shield like an ancient scroll writ small in curlicued script. Andrew Byrd was the color of his tie.

He sat before Bloom's desk, his long legs casually crossed, his manner indicating a complete willingness to cooperate. Hanging on three walls of the room, or otherwise resting on shelves fastened to those walls, virtually surrounding Byrd with impressive exploits of derring-do, were framed photographs of the detective squad Bloom had commanded up north; and a citation plaque from the Nassau County chief of detectives; and a pair of laminated front-page stories from the New York *Daily News* and Long Island's *Newsday*, headlining the daring capture of two bank robbers in Mineola, Long Island, by a young police officer named Morris L. Bloom; and a boxing trophy Bloom had received while serving in the U.S. Navy; and a Snoopy doll his then-nineteen year-old son had given him on a Father's Day some years back, the hand-lettered sign around its neck reading: *To the best bloodhound in the world. Love, Marc.*

All of this might normally have intimidated and/or disarmed the bad guys Bloom interrogated in this office, but Andrew Byrd was not one of the bad guys. Instead, he was a reputable and highly esteemed Calusa businessman worth some six hundred million dollars according to an issue of *Forbes* that Bloom had found in the stacks of the Calusa Public Library. Trim and fit in his well-tailored suit, speaking in a voice somewhat reminiscent of the Islands – a faint Jamaican lilt, was it, a Bahamian pulse? – he told Bloom that Matthew had called him late Monday afternoon, the twenty-first, and had arranged to come to his office early the next morning, the twenty-second.

On Bloom's desk, Matthew's appointment calendar was open to the page showing those dates. In the space for March 22, he had first written, in blue ink, *Andrew Byrd, 9:00 AM* and below that, in pencil, *John Rafferty, 12 Noon*. Below that, he had written, again in pencil: *Phone MEMO* What the hell was a phone memo?

"He came to see you at nine, is that right?"

"On the button," Byrd said.

"Where *is* your office, Mr. Byrd?"

"In Newtown. 1217 Kensington Circle. In the mall there. I built that mall, Mr. Bloom. It's one of the most successful malls in all Calusa. The one downtown is still empty, built five years ago, you can't *give* away space there. Kensington's in *Newtown*, mind you, not exactly the garden spot of Florida, but my mall is *full* of upscale shops. I've even got Lord & Taylor in there, do you know of any other Lord & Taylor in Calusa? Lord & Taylor, Victoria's Secret, The Coffee Connection, The Sharper Image, Laura Ashley, Barnes & Noble, you name it, anything you'd expect to find in a Palm Beach mall, I've got in Newtown. I don't have to tell you that in some sections of Newtown, it's worth your life to go out after dark. Well, look what happened to your Mr. Hope. The Kensington Mall draws people from all over the tri-city area, though – white, black, purple, they all come to my mall. The security there is the best in all Florida, bar none. You can park a Caddy, a Lexus, a Beemer, a Mercedes, the most luxurious car you can name, a Rolls even, you name it, when you're finished with your shopping you'll find it just the way you left it. I myself drive a Jag, Mr. Bloom, I park it in the mall garage when I go to work every morning, it's safe there all day long. There're no rowdies in my mall, no teenagers looking for trouble. Kensington isn't a place for hanging out, it isn't a street corner. It's a place for people to come to and do business in a safe and pleasant environment. I'm very proud of what I've accomplished there. I've built places all over Calusa . . . hell, all over *Florida*, for that matter, I own half the property on Lucy's Circle, I guess you know that . . ."

"Yes, I do."

"Sure, it's what everyone mentions, the jewel in the crown. But I'm proudest of what I accomplished there in Newtown. I created a place where blacks and whites can shop together in peace and comfort. Before I built that mall, what white man in his right mind would go to Newtown? Sure, okay, on the way to the airport, but that was all. Now they come flocking there. And the blacks come, too, not because it's close but because it gives them something they can be proud of, right there in Newtown, something that makes them hold their heads high in self-respect."

Byrd was telling the truth in a slightly embroidered fashion. Kensington Mall *was*, in fact, one of the most profitable malls to have opened in Calusa during the past several years. It *was* safe and clean and well-lighted and every bit as upscale as Byrd had claimed. And, too, it *did* draw customers from all over the tri-city area, black and white alike. But the mall was situated a good four miles from where Matthew had been shot last Friday night, and it was doubtful that anyone who hung out in the neighborhood of Roosevelt and G would be shopping Godiva Chocolatier on any given Friday night.

"What'd he come to see you about?" Bloom asked.

Toots Kiley had already told him what Matthew had earlier learned, that Byrd was suing the owner of the land, hoping to have a foreclosure judgment entered.

"The land on Barrington and Welles," Byrd said. "What they call the state fairgrounds. He had a party interested in buying it. Sun and Shore told him – Florida Sun and Shore, big realtors over on Pineapple – told him I'd taken the owner of the land to court. They knew he'd find out, anyway, the minute he began asking around, this wasn't an act of generosity on their part. I told Mr. Hope that, in any event, the problem wasn't with me. The problem was with Rafferty."

"Rafferty?" Bloom asked.

"John Rafferty. Sole owner of the thirty-acre parcel before he mortgaged the land to me. Mr. Hope seemed to understand that *I* wasn't the one standing in the way of any prospective purchase of the land. It's *Rafferty* who's been . . ."

. . . holding this thing up in court, Byrd told Matthew, because he wasn't about to let him *give* the land away just to square a bad debt.

Matthew was sitting across from Byrd in his office on the top floor of the Kensington Mall, the digital calendar on Byrd's desk reading MAR 22, early morning sunlight streaming through the windows behind him, a veritable jungle of greenery planted on the rooftop deck beyond. The mall would not open until ten. Byrd had been here since eight, he'd told Matthew, his daily habit except for Sundays.

"I've been trying to get a foreclosure judgment for the past three months now. I've got a two-million-dollar mortgage on that land, and I want my goddamn money back. *Plus* interest to the date of foreclosure, if and when *that* ever happens, *plus* the money I've spent on legal fees trying to *collect*. The mortgage is for twenty-five percent per annum simple interest, which is the legal limit for any business loan of five hundred thousand or more . . . well, I guess you know how the law works."

"I do," Matthew said.

"Of course you do," Byrd said. "I loaned the money to Rafferty's corporation, which made the higher interest rate acceptable. Made it a *business* loan, you see. Anything over twenty-five percent simple is usury in this state. They're very tough on usury down here . . ."

"Yes, I know."

"Of course, you do. They not only send you to jail, but you lose all the money you loaned. Which is even *worse* than going to jail," Byrd said, and burst out laughing.

Matthew believed him. To Andrew Byrd, losing money *would* be a fate worse than going to jail.

"The original loan was for a year," Byrd said, "two million

bucks at twenty-five percent simple, which made it a decent investment. That's five hundred thousand dollars in interest, that's good money for a year. Okay, when Rafferty defaulted, he *already* owed me the half mil, and in the three months *since*, he's piled up almost *another* hundred and twenty-five thou. That's what it comes to at the stipulated two-point-oh-eight points a month."

"Are you a lawyer?" Matthew asked.

"No, thank God," Byrd said, and burst out laughing again when he remembered he was in the presence of one. "What makes you think so?"

"Well, you used the word 'stipulated,' which . . ."

"But that's a word in *English*, too, isn't it?" Byrd asked, and began laughing louder when he realized he'd just deprecated legalese.

"I suppose it is," Matthew said, smiling. "But you won't find a lawyer on earth who'll agree to 'agree to' rather than 'stipulate'."

"I have a feeling you're not one of those lawyers," Byrd said.

"Only in court," Matthew said.

The way Byrd looked at it, Rafferty was already into him for $2,625,000 *plus* the legal fees it had cost him in his struggle to get a judgment for foreclosure. The day he was looking forward to was the day the sheriff stood on those courthouse steps at eleven in the morning, which was when all foreclosure sales were held in Calusa County, and conducted a public sale for the thirty-acre parcel on Barrington and Welles. At that time, Byrd would bid the $2,625,000 plus he'd already spent on the goddamn fairgrounds, be awarded the land, and get his deed in the mail a week later, after which he would turn the land over to a broker for sale. If the broker got the asking price, Byrd would call it a day. If he got *less* than he'd already laid out, he would once again go against Rafferty, this time for a deficiency judgment. He may not have been a lawyer, but Byrd sure as hell knew his remedies at law.

"As I understand this," he told Matthew, "your client is offering three million for the land. I'd take it in a minute. Pay me back everything I've laid out, let Rafferty have whatever's left, sure, that'd be wonderful. But until I get that damn judgment, my hands are tied. *Rafferty's* the one who's . . ."

"I realize that. But I thought, if I could go to him and tell him you were ready to drop the suit and settle for . . ."

"You don't understand. Rafferty doesn't *want* that land sold right now. He'd like to hold on to it till doomsday, watch it go up in value, the way *everything* goes up in value sooner or later in Florida."

"Not everything," Matthew said.

"*Almost* everything," Byrd conceded. "The point is . . . well, figure it out. In reality, *I* own more of that land than *he* does. It's just a matter of getting the court to hand down a judgment. I recorded that mortgage the minute I made the loan. There's no one behind me on it, I'm Rafferty's sole creditor. But I can't go after the land, or anything *else* he owns, even though he personally guaranteed the loan. I can *forget* the five-million-dollar house he owns on Whisper, that's protected by the Homestead Act. But he's got property all *over* Florida, and I can't touch any of it till I win the court case. It's ridiculous, the way his lawyers keep stalling this thing along. Excuse me, but I *hate* lawyers, I really do. You'd think they'd want to save their client all those legal fees . . . this is costing *him* money, too, am I right? Give me a deed in lieu, let the thing rest. But no, Rafferty's going to fight this thing till we're both old and gray."

"Unless I can tell him you'll settle for the two million five. That'll leave him . . ."

"You *still* don't understand," Byrd said, and shook his head. "The son of a bitch is doing this because – well, never mind."

"What were you about to say?"

"I'm black, all right? That's what I was about to say. And I'm more successful than he is. Who put up Kensington? Was it Rafferty? Oh, sure. Rafferty put money in the *down-town* mall, that's what he did. Lost his shirt along with everybody else. He doesn't want a successful *black* man to take his land, that's all there is to it. My black money was good enough for him when he needed it, but he doesn't want my black hands on land he still thinks he owns."

Matthew said nothing.

"Which he does, in fact, till the court decides otherwise. That's the way it is, Mr. Hope. If your client wants that land, he'll have to deal with Rafferty. Right now, he's the only one who has the right to sell it. And he won't, I promise you. Accept your three-million-dollar offer, and then hand most of it over to me? No way. He'd rather fight this out till the cows come home. You go talk to him. You'll see."

Matthew was silent for several moments.

Then he said, "You're telling me this is a personal thing . . ."

"You don't know *how* personal."

"You're saying the man's prejudice would stand in the way of . . ."

"Oh, he doesn't even *know* he's a bigot," Byrd said. "You ask him, he'll tell you I'm his best friend. Hell, we went to high school together, I've known him forever."

"But you say he's *not* your friend."

"I say he hates me."

"Then why'd he come to you for money?"

"Nowhere else to go. He was at the end of his rope. Look, I *have* loaned him money in the past – which he's always paid back, by the way. This time, though, he's in too deep. He keeps pouring money into that tennis club, it's like a bottomless pit, there's no way he can salvage it. That's what rankles, that's why he's fighting me in court. He *knows* he defaulted, he *knows* I should be granted that damn foreclosure judgment, he *knows* all that. But it rankles that *I'm* sitting here in this fancy office on top of the most successful mall in town, while he hasn't got a pot to piss in. That's what twists inside him like a poison snake. And that's why he'll *never* accept your client's offer."

"I'm obliged to make the offer, anyway," Matthew said.

"Go right ahead. It won't do you any good."

"Because you feel this is a personal matter."

"Yes."

"But this wasn't a personal *loan*."

"No, no, my company made the loan. Lawson-Byrd Investments."

"Who's Lawson?"

"My wife. That's her maiden name. She's also my partner."

"In actuality, then, Rafferty owes the money to both of you."

"And don't think *that* doesn't rankle, too."

"How do you mean?"

"It rankles, that's all. With him, everything rankles."

"Enough to turn down an offer that'll settle his debt . . ."

"Doesn't care."

". . . get him off the hook . . ."

"What does he care?"

". . . and relieve him of any further legal costs?"

"The man just doesn't care."

"You really think he'd slit his own throat just to . . .?"

"My throat first," Byrd said.

Patricia wondered why the good Dr. Spinaldo was directing most of his conversation to Susan Hope rather than sharing it between them. Did the good doctor believe Matthew and Susan were still married? Did he believe that the holy bonds of matrimony were sacred and eternal, once husband and wife, always husband and wife? His manner was unmistakable. He was treating Susan as the wife, ignoring Patrica exactly as he was ignoring her now.

What?

In this day and age?

". . . no perceptible change in his condition," he was telling Susan, his body actually *turned* toward her, his back virtually to Patricia. "His vital signs are still stable, and his responses to externally applied stimuli remain unchanged. You must understand, Mrs. Hope, that . . ."

Patricia noticed she did not correct him.

". . . we are dealing here with altered states of consciousness, in which the *alert* state and the *comatose* state are at extreme ends of a behavioral continuum. Your husband . . ."

Again, Susan did not correct him.

". . . isn't alert, but neither is he comatose. The other two points on the continuum are lethargy and stupor. We use the term 'stupor' to define a state from which the patient can be awakened only by forceful and frequent stimuli. I would suggest that your husband's condition would fall somewhat higher on the continuum than stupor. Semicoma is a highly unscientific term, and I'm loath to use it. Nonetheless, it would possibly best describe his condition."

"Thank you, Doctor," Susan said, and then, as an afterthought as she started out of the room, "It was nice running into you, Patricia."

Patricia wanted to strangle her.

"Mr. Rafferty, please," Bloom said into the phone.

"This is Rafferty."

"Detective Morris Bloom, Calusa P.D.," Bloom said.

"Yes?"

"Mr. Rafferty, we're investigating a shooting that took place last Friday night . . ."

"Matthew Hope, right."

"You're familiar with the incident, sir?"

"It's all over television. In fact, I was wondering when you'd get to me."

"Why is that, Mr. Rafferty?"

"I just assumed you'd be checking on anybody he had anything to do with recently."

"That's right, sir, we are."

"And I'm further assuming you know he came to see me last Tuesday afternoon."

"That's what it says in his appointment calendar, sir."

"So there you are."

"Yes, sir. Mr. Rafferty, I wonder if *I* could stop by there sometime today, go over some of . . ."

"Sure, that's what I was expecting."

"What's a good time for you, sir?"

"How about right now?"

"Well, I'm waiting for a long-dist — "

"I'll be here all morning," Rafferty said. "When do you think you'll be free?"

"Can we make it for eleven?"

"Fine, I'll look for you. Do you know where I am?"

"I know where you are," Bloom said.

Warren and Toots were walking the loop. This was a favorite pastime in Calusa, especially on rainy days, when you couldn't go to the beach, and you had a choice between the movies and shopping. It wasn't raining this particular Tuesday morning. It was, in fact, quite a nice sunny day for a midmorning stroll around Lucy's Circle. Warren didn't like meetings in his office because the place was about the size of a shoebox and it made people feel claustrophobic. He had called the hospital from the office first thing this morning, and then he'd called Bloom, and finally he'd called Toots and asked her to meet him on the Circle for coffee. They were walking the loop now, Toots in yellow denims, sandals, and an orange-colored top, Warren in gray tropical-weight slacks, blue sneakers, and a short-sleeved, dark blue shirt. They were both wearing sunglasses. Neither of them looked into any of the shop windows. What they were trying to do was lay out what they already had and then figure where they should go from here.

The thing that was troubling Warren was what he called the Double Two-Step. What they were doing here, essentially, was duplicating everything Matthew had done last week. By walking in his footprints, they were hoping to learn what *he* had learned. Once they knew that, then maybe they could figure out why someone had shot him. But Matthew had been following two *separate* trails, the land purchase in the here and now, and a questionable suicide three years ago.

Maria Torrance had stated without compromise that someone – in fact, someone quite specific, someone named Davey Sheed, in fact, King of All the Beasts – had killed her mother. If this was true, then probing a case the Missouri police had closed as a suicide three years earlier could very well have proved dangerous to Matthew. On the other hand, the purchase of the state fairgrounds was turning out to be a complex situation in its own right.

On the phone this morning, Bloom had recounted Byrd's recitation of his meeting with Matthew last week, and it now appeared that Matthew had uncovered a festering situation he'd intended to pursue further. The penciled notation in his appointment calendar had undoubtedly been written in *after* his meeting with Byrd. He had seen Byrd at nine last Tuesday morning. His appointment with Rafferty was for noon that same day. He had also made a note to himself that read . . .

"Does 'phone memo' mean anything to *you*?" Warren asked.

"No."

"Anyway, Bloom's seeing Rafferty later today," Warren said. "I'm eager to know what the hell's going on between those two. Man hates another man so much, but he asks him for two million dollars?"

"And *gets* it, don't forget."

"And then refuses to pay it back. How does that figure?"

"Why'd Byrd lend it to him in the first place?"

"Twenty-five percent interest, that's why."

"The limit before it becomes usury."

"Damn good return on the dollar."

"But would you lend it to a man who hates you?"

"Byrd says it's cause he's black."

"If you hate black men, don't go to one for money," Toots said, and shrugged.

"But he did."

"And he *got* the money. Despite the fact that Byrd *knows* he's a bigot."

"Or *claims* he's one." "Love to know what's going on there," Warren said.

"Love to know what Bloom gets from Missouri."

"What do you *think* he'll get? He'll get 'Case Closed, don't bother us.'"

"Maybe not."

"Let's go out to the circus again," Warren said. "See if anybody remembers just what did happen in Rutherford, Missouri."

"That was three years ago, Warren."

"If somebody blew her brains out in the trailer next door to me, *I'd* remember three years ago, wouldn't you?"

"Not if I was the one shot her," Toots said.

"Right in the middle of the goddamn forehead," Warren said.

The collect return call from Rutherford, Missouri, came at seven minutes past ten that morning. The caller asked to speak to Detective Morris Bloom, and then identified himself as Dr. Abel Voorhies, one of the physicians who'd prepared the Medical Examiner's Office report on Willa Torrance three years back. Bloom accepted the call. Voorhies went on to say that at the time he'd had some doubts about the conclusion the M.E.'s Office had drawn, but the majority opinion . . .

"Majority?" Bloom asked. "How many people were involved in the autopsy?"

"Well . . . excuse me, but was it Mr. Hope who put you onto me?"

"No. What do you mean?" Bloom asked at once. "Are you talking about *Matthew* Hope?"

"Yes. Because he called here last week, you see, and asked virtually that identical question. I thought . . ."

"You spoke to Mr. Hope last week?"

"Last Tuesday, yes."

So *that* was it. Phone MEMO. Phone Medical Examiner Missouri.

"What'd he want?" Bloom asked.

"Well, he told me Mrs. Torrance's will had come up in some sort of real estate negotiation . . ."

"I see," Bloom said.

"Yes, and he wanted to know the details of her suicide three years ago. Apparently a clause in the will . . . well, it doesn't matter. We get similar requests every year, on the anniversary of her death, newspaper and television reporters digging up the past, we're quite used to it here in Rutherford. This is the county seat, you know . . ."

"I didn't know that," Bloom said.

"Yes, which means we're relatively well-staffed and therefore able to handle such requests. Mr. Hope wanted to know whether we'd been concerned about the lack of a suicide note . . ."

"Yes, what about that?" Bloom said.

"I told him what I've told anyone *else* who asks me. And there are plenty of askers, believe me. I told him, yes, I *had* been concerned about the lack of a note. Then again, not all suicides leave notes, I'm sure you know that."

"That's true, but . . ."

"And not all right-handed suicides shoot themselves in the right temple. I'm sure there're plenty of them who shoot themselves in the middle of the forehead. The way Willa Torrance did. Have you investigated many suicides, Mr. Bloom?"

"My fair share."

"Well, wouldn't you ask, if someone was intent on killing herself, and if this person actually had a gun in her right hand – which was where the gun was when her daughter discovered the body at five thirty-five A.M. – and if this person was lying on her back contemplating what she was about to do, deciding that she was finally and irrevocably going to *do* it, wouldn't you ask why she'd chosen such an *awkward* position?"

"What position was that, Dr. Voorhies?"

"Well, she was lying on her right side, you see."

"Yes?"

"So why would she have contorted her wrist into such a clumsy position in order to shoot herself in the *forehead*? Why hadn't she simply turned her head and shot herself in the right temple? Or even turned her entire body to lie on her back, either of which positions would have made the act easier to execute – and, incidentally, would have conformed more closely to statistics for gunshot suicides by right-handed people: the gun in the right hand, the wound in the right temporal region. Are you following me?"

"Yes, I am. Go right ahead, Doctor. I'm listening and taking notes."

"I simply wondered why she'd chosen to bend her arm up from the elbow, twist the wrist at an almost ninety-degree angle to the arm, and put the bullet in her forehead from that odd position. Don't you think that's odd?"

"Yes, I do."

"The alarm clock bothered me, too."

"The alarm clock?"

"Yes. She'd set her alarm, you see. Now, in my experience – and admittedly I'm a mere country doctor, Mr. Bloom – but in my experience, someone contemplating suicide does not normally decide to do it at such and such a time the *following* morning. Gosh, I think I'll kill myself at five-fifteen tomorrow, better set the clock for it, get up bright and early to shoot myself in the forehead while lying on my side. No, Mr. Bloom. In my experience, suicide is most usually the result of months and months of desperation, the final decision coming suddenly, after a bleak and lengthy period of uncertainty and delay."

"That's been my experience, too, Doctor."

"Yes. But the alarm was nonetheless set. Her daughter had set her own alarm for four-thirty, and she testified at the inquest that her mother was still asleep when she'd left the trailer at five. Yet ten minutes after that, Mrs. Torrance was awake enough to twist her hand into the awkward position necessary to shoot herself in the forehead while lying on her side. Five minutes *before* her alarm went off. This did not sound like suicide to me, Detective Bloom."

"But suicide was the M.E.'s finding."

"Three of us examined the body, Mr. Bloom. My two colleagues concluded it was suicide. I wrote a minority report, but the majority prevailed."

"What did your report say?"

"It said that I considered homicide a distinct possibility. I recommended further police investigation."

"Did the police ever . . .?"

"No, there was a coroner's inquest, and then the case was closed."

There was a long silence on the line.

"I told Mr. Hope all of this last week," Voorhies said. "You should've asked him. Saved yourself a long-distance call."

News of Matthew's shooting had been broadcast on the radio shortly after it occurred last Friday night. The television news shows had carried it on Saturday morning, and the Saturday newspapers had headlined it in both their editions that day. But then the hubbub had sort of died down over the weekend, and there'd been nothing more on it till this morning, when a front-page story in the *Trib* appeared. The story was headlined LAWYER IN COMA. The subhead read NO CLUES TO SHOOTING. The story was written by a staff writer who thought he was Jimmy Breslin or Pete Hamill, but who was in reality only George N. Marley.

Calusa wasn't a tiny little fishing village; it was a bustling community of some fifty thousand permanent residents, and not everyone in it could be expected to know Matthew Hope. But Marley's piece apparently touched some kind of chord out there because all at once the hospital switchboard was lit up with calls from strangers wanting to know how the lawyer was doing. The callers were told that Mr. Hope's condition was stable but critical. A lot of people thought "critical" meant he was about to die. Some of them said, "Oh, the poor man," or words to that effect. None of them knew Matthew, and none of them knew the person impersonally reporting on his condition. But they felt it necessary to let *someone* know they were feeling *something* for this person who, like so many other people in America, had been senselessly shot and was now lying in coma, as Marley had erroneously reported it.

"What is his condition?" the callers asked.

"Stable but critical."

"Oh, I'm so sorry," the callers said.

They didn't know Matthew from a hole in the wall.

They were saying something quite else.

John Rafferty was a man in his mid- to late thirties, Bloom supposed, some two or three years older than Andrew Byrd, which made it entirely possible that they'd gone to high school together, as Byrd had mentioned. A portly man with a fringe of graying brownish-red hair around his balding pate, his freckled face gave evidence that he might have been completely redheaded back then. He was wearing a lime-colored sweater over a white open-throat shirt and darker green slacks. White loafers. No socks.

They were in the living room of his luxurious home on Whisper Key, the one Byrd had said was protected by the

Homestead Act. Blueprints were open on the huge glass-topped coffee table in front of a sofa upholstered in a nubby white fabric. Sliding glass doors opened onto a vast patio, a huge swimming pool, and the waters of Calusa Bay beyond. Byrd had said the house was worth five million. Bloom believed it.

"Did you go see Andy, too?" Rafferty asked.

"Andy?"

"Byrd."

"Oh. Actually, he came to see me."

"Of his own accord?"

"He had business near my office, so he agreed to stop by."

"Nice of him," Rafferty said dryly. "I figured you'd have called him. Your Mr. Hope came here right after seeing him, so I figured you'd be following the same pattern. Hell of a thing, what happened, isn't it?"

"Yes," Bloom said.

"Now the lunatics'll start yelling about more gun control. What they don't realize is that gun control doesn't take guns out of the hands of criminals, it takes guns out of the hands of people like Matthew Hope."

Bloom said nothing.

He was wondering if John Rafferty owned a gun.

More specifically, he was wondering if John Rafferty owned a twenty-two-caliber Iver Johnson Trailsman Snub, model sixty-six.

"What did you and Mr. Hope talk about?" he asked. "When he was here last week?"

"A client of his wants to buy the land I own over near I-95. The state fairgrounds. He came here with an offer."

"Did you accept it?"

"No, sir, I did not."

"Was it a reasonable offer?"

"Is this just curiosity, Detective Bloom? Cause I know damn well I don't have to answer that kind of question."

"You don't have to answer *any* kind of question, Mr. Rafferty. This is just a friendly visit."

"I'm sure it is. Which doesn't mean I have to disclose any of my personal business dealings."

"Of course you don't," Bloom said, and smiled pleasantly. "But I already know that three million was offered for the property."

Rafferty blinked.

"I also know you're in litigation over a bad debt," Bloom said.

"That's for a judge to decide," Rafferty said.

"No, the bad debt is a fact. It's for a judge to decide whether Andrew Byrd gets a foreclosure judgment against you. If he does, he'll snap up Matthew Hope's offer in a minute."

"Meanwhile, he hasn't got the judgment."

"Meanwhile, he hasn't, that's true," Bloom said. "How'd Mr. Hope react to your rejection, by the way?"

"He's a lawyer, how do you *think* he reacted? A lawyer's job is to convince you his client's right. Hope tried to convince me the three mil was a good offer. As if I don't know what that land's worth."

"That's right, you'd already turned down *four* million, hadn't you?" Bloom said, nodding.

"That's right," Rafferty said, and blinked again. "How'd you know that?"

"Did you tell Mr. Hope you'd turned down four million?"

"He already knew it. Have you been talking to him?"

No one's talking to Matthew just now, Bloom thought.

"Or was it Andy?" Rafferty said. "Did *Andy* tell you I turned down the four?"

"He may have mentioned it in passing," Bloom said.

"None of his fuckin business, anyway," Rafferty said, and began pacing in front of the long glass wall. Outside, beyond the swimming pool, a stately blue heron walked delicately toward the bay. "What Andy wants me to do is sell that land for whatever'll get him his money back. I guess you know the sum he loaned me was two million . . ."

"Yes."

"He wants that back, naturally, plus interest, naturally, and now *legal* expenses cause he took the thing to court, instead of just letting it rest awhile. He knows he'll get his money back sooner or later, what the hell's he worried about?"

"I gathered he would prefer having it sooner," Bloom said.

"Yeah, well, fuck him. We'll see what the judge has to say about it. Meanwhile, I'm not selling that land to *anybody*. Not Hope's client, whoever he might be . . ."

"Didn't he say?"

"No. Big secret. *Lawyers*," Rafferty said, and rolled his eyes. "Two, three years from now, that land'll be worth ten, twelve million dollars. Why should I sell it now? Just to satisfy *them*?"

"Who do you mean by 'them,' Mr. Rafferty?"

"*Them*, who do you think? My *creditors*. Andy and Jeannie. They can just wait, they've got plenty of money as it is."

"Who's Jeannie?"

"His wife. Years ago, neither of them had a pot to piss in."

The same expression Byrd had used to describe Rafferty's current financial situation. Except for the five-million-dollar house.

"So now they've got a little money, they start putting on airs," Rafferty said. "I drive a fuckin Pontiac, they both drive *Jags*. A white one for her, a black one for him. Cute, am I right? Lawson was her maiden name. Jeannie Lawson. I knew her when she was still in high school, I gave her a part-time job in the office, she must've been sixteen, seventeen. She worked for me one whole summer. I was the one talked her out of running away with the circus."

Bloom was suddenly all ears.

"When was this?" he asked.

"I told you, when she was still in high school. I was the only one'd give Andy the right time of day. Florida's the *South*, you know, no matter *how* many beaches or palm trees we've got down here. Never mind civil rights, down here a nigger is still a nigger. I was the only one befriended Andy. So he pays me back by stealing her away from me."

Bloom was listening harder and harder.

"Nobody'd have anything to do with her anymore. This was five or six years ago, and here's a white girl starting up with a *black* man? In the *South*? Who's fifteen, twenty years *older* than she is? He used to work on a construction crew for a housing development my company was putting up, that's how they met. They call themselves African-Americans now, I wish they'd make up their fuckin minds. A blonde, you should see her. She's still blonde, but I think she's partners with Revlon now."

Five years ago, Bloom was thinking. Maria Torrance would've been seventeen, about the same age as young Jeannie Lawson.

"And you say she wanted to run off with the circus?" he asked.

"Yeah. Crazy idea. Well, she was crazy altogether, am I right? Starting up with Andy?"

"Which came first?" Bloom asked. "Starting up with Andy, or wanting to run off with the circus?"

"Andy. All the kids at Calusa High were ready to run *both* of 'em out of town on a rail, you know. Cut off Andy's balls, tar and feather 'em both, run 'em both out of town. She called me one night, told me she was going to run away with the circus. She said she could become an elephant girl, ride around the ring on an elephant's back. I asked her where she'd got such a crazy idea, she told me she'd talked to the owner, he said she had good legs, with practice he could make her a good elephant girl."

"Which circus?" Bloom asked.

"Ringling, I guess. Why?"

"Are you sure?"

"Maybe the other one down here, the small one. Who remembers? This was a long time ago."

"You said five or six years . . ."

"Yeah, at least."

"Would you remember which?"

"I'm thirty-seven now, so it must've . . . Andy's younger than me, that's another thing that pissed me off, her starting up not only with a *nigger*, but with a guy *younger* than me! He must've been twenty-eight, twenty-nine at the time. She was seventeen. So how long ago was that?"

Bloom waited.

"I was thirty-two, so, yeah, it was five years ago. What happened was Andy and Jeannie *both* left town . . . well, Andy had to. Really. They'd've killed him."

"Where'd they go?" Bloom asked.

"*He* went to South America. *She* left with the circus a few months later."

"But . . . they're married now," Bloom said, puzzled.

"Yeah, they're married, all right. Jeannie came back to town soon as the season ended. She'd had enough of shoveling elephant shit. Andy came back two years later. With a fortune. Told everybody he'd come back to claim his little bride. Only trouble was, she was already married by then."

"Who was she married to?" Bloom asked.

"Me," Rafferty said.

He knew he wasn't dead because he kept remembering things. You couldn't remember anything when you were dead, could you? He didn't think so. He kept seeing things flashing yellow and jagged across the blackness in his head, but he remembered things, too, all the conversations he'd had, all the things they'd told him. Snatches of talk floated in the darkness, whispers, secrets, things they'd said, things he'd been piecing together bit by bit, a flash of yellow, and then another, and another, and he was falling, he remembered everything.

The circus grounds.

Bustling with activity on this Tuesday afternoon, Steadman behaving like the lord of the manor as he led Matthew through, performers greeting him, interrupting their rehearsals to chat. There was still a sense of tentativeness here. They would not be moving out until the second day of April, which meant the performers still had almost two weeks in which to perfect their routines. So they approached their separate acts – and indeed each other – like old friends who would nonetheless take some getting used to. The roller ball girls fell from their moving perches far too often, the jugglers missed far too many unlighted torches, and here under the big tent – where Steadman, puffing on a cigar, sat beside Matthew – ten performers known collectively as the Toy Chen Acrobatic Troupe, practiced their entrance over and over again.

The opening stunt was visual as well as physical. The youngest of the Chens, a pint-sized little girl rehearsing in leotards and tights, came bursting through a pair of hanging red silken curtains, hit the ground running, and went into a series of somersaults that took her to the opposite side of the ring. As she popped to her feet again, arms opening wide to the top of the tent, the second of the Chens came running through the parted curtains. This one was a few inches taller than her younger sister. She hit the ground and did the same series of somersaults, and was followed by a slightly taller Chen coming through the curtains, each of the family escalating in size until at last the three oldest Chen brothers came bouncing out in succession, followed by Papa Chen, tallest of the lot, all of them somersaulting to the end of the line, the tiniest Chen up front, the tallest Chen bringing up the rear.

The trick, Steadman explained, was to keep a sense of momentum going so that it almost seemed the same performer was coming through those curtains each time, having grown a few inches each time. Timing was essential here – as it was in every circus act – the new tumbler popping through those curtains and leaving his feet the instant the preceding performer rolled out of the last somersault and jumped to his feet.

"They're from Shanghai," Steadman said. "Best acrobats in the world come from China. They're starting to develop some good aerial acts over there, too. That's not a tradition with them, you know, like acrobatic arts, but they're becoming very skilled at it. Two, three years from now, I'll have Chinese flyers every bit as good as the McCulloughs, you'll see."

Matthew suddenly realized why he didn't like circuses.

He didn't like them because they were boring.

Watching the Chen family repeat its opening sequence God knew how many times, over and over again, until it seemed that not ten but ten *thousand* Chinese of graduating sizes were tumbling out in numbing succession from between those parted red curtains, repeatedly somersaulting across the tent, incessantly popping onto their feet, arms snapping ceaselessly skyward, grins magically appearing on ten beaming Oriental faces, Papa Chen snapping his fingers and flipping his hand palm-upward to initiate the next stunt – but, no, the next stunt was to be delayed yet another time while all the Chens swarmed once again behind those secret silken curtains (some secret by now) and prepared to perform one more time (Matthew hoped) an opening he had now seen at least a dozen times.

This time, the band was here.

Hooray for the band, he thought.

And this time, there was a snare-drum flourish and then a brassy trumpet blast as the first of the Chens, that tiny three- or four- or five-year-old darling, popped through the curtains with her arms high in introduction and leaped immediately into the first of those damn somersaults, cascading across the tent as the snare drum rolled, once, twice, three times, four times, five times and *bingo*! Up onto her feet with a trumpet's red blare just as the next slightly taller Chen overlappingly popped through the curtains with a grin that said *Hi-Folks-I'm-Here*! Surprise! Matthew could almost do it himself by now.

He was reminded of the old joke about the stranger in New York stopping a man on the street and asking, "How do I get to Carnegie Hall?"

"Practice," the man replies.

It was all a matter of practice, Matthew figured. Practice and repetition. Which, in the long run, was what made it so boringly predictable. If you've seen one circus, he thought, you've seen them all. You know that there's going to be the big opening number – what Steadman had already told him they'd begin rehearsing next week and perform in full costume at the dress rehearsal next Friday, what they called the "spectacle" or simply the "spec." And then there'd be the animal act, and then the diverting clowns while the cages were dismantled and removed from the ring, and then something up in the air, and then some more animals, either dogs, horses, seals, elephants, or unicorns, and then all the jumpers, rollers, flyers, leapers, prancers and dancers and blitzen and all, all calculated to stun you with acts of derring-do and double dare, while meanwhile stunning you to sleep with sameness.

Practice, practice, practice.

Matthew wanted to know about the seventeen-year-old runaway named Jeannie Lawson. Was *Steadman* the "owner" who'd told her "with practice he could make her a good elephant girl?" And did he know that she was now married to a man named Andrew Byrd, who was seeking a foreclosure mortgage on the very land Steadman was trying to buy?

Steadman looked surprised.

He had taken his cigar from his mouth, and was holding it in his hand an inch from his lips, looking very much like an unskilled actor simulating clichéd astonishment, his mouth open in a small O, his eyebrows rising as the Chens moved into the second routine in their act, similarly rehearsed ten thousand four hundred and twenty-seven times in order to achieve the high level of perfection essential to complete boredom. Matthew suddenly remembered a dirty limerick about boredom, and almost grinned aloud as it flashed through his mind.

> *There was a young girl in Peru*
> *Who had* absolutely *nothing to do.*
> *She sat on the stairs*
> *Counting crotch hairs*
> *Four thousand three hundred and two*

Steadman must have detected the half-smile on Matthew's face. His look of surprise changed to one of faint puzzlement. Or was he trying to forge a connection between the long-ago elephant girl named Jeannie Lawson and the here-and-now prospective judgment creditor named Andrew Byrd?

"*Who?*" he said.

Which one? Matthew wondered.

"Jeannie Lawson," he said. "Jeannie Byrd. Andrew Byrd's wife."

Covering all the bases.

"As I told you earlier, I don't know *who* owns the fairgrounds. My information was that Sun and Shore . . ."

"Yes."

"Are you now saying that someone named Andrew Byrd . . .?"

"Doesn't own the land, no. He's seeking a foreclosure judgment."

"And you say he's married to a woman who was once an *elephant* girl with Steadman & Roeger?"

"Perhaps."

"How long ago?" Steadman said, and began puffing on his cigar again. It had gone out. He took a book of matches from his vest pocket – Matthew wondered how many other men in America still wore vests – and began lighting the cigar again. Great billows of smoke polluted the air. In the ring, the Chens were jumping through hoops again and again and again and again. Four thousand three hundred and two.

"She would have joined you five years ago," Matthew said. "For a . . ."

"And you expect me to remember . . .?"

". . . for a single season. She said the owner told her he could make her a good elephant girl."

"The boss *bull* man is the one who hires any performers in his elephant act," Steadman said. "*Not* the circus owner."

"Did you *have* an elephant act back then?"

"We've *always* had an elephant act. I believe I told you . . ."

"Yes."

". . . that elephants and cats bring in maybe forty percent of our audience."

"Yes. Do you remember *which* elephant act was with you back then?"

"Five years ago," Steadman said, and puffed thoughtfully on the cigar. The drummer was trying to bring down the tent with a series of bass-drum explosions as the Chens bounced up onto each other's shoulders. "So that would've been . . . let me see." He puffed on the cigar again, let out a wreath of smoke. Matthew fully expected one of the smaller Chens to jump through it. "I guess that would've been Rudi Kroner. Best elephant man in the business. His son's with the Beatty-Cole show now. Hans Kroner, almost as good as his father was."

"Where's the father now?"

"Dead."

"Would you remember him hiring a young girl named Jeannie Lawson?"

"Rudi had an eye for the young girls," Steadman said, "dressed them in next to nothing, draped them all over his bulls. Blue costumes, he . . . wait a minute, wait a minute. Was she the one in some kind of trouble with a *black* man?"

"I'm not sure you'd call it trouble, but . . ."

"Had to get out of town before they skinned her alive? Is that the one?"

"Yes," Matthew said.

"Oh, I remember *her*, all right," Steadman said. "Jeannie Lawson, absolutely. Wild little thing. Came on in March, quit at the end of the season. Willa tried to take her under her wing . . . well, you know, she mothered every young chorus girl in sight . . ."

And now, as Steadman sent clouds of bilious smoke on the air, and the Chens incessantly rehearsed routine after routine, the trumpet, drums, tuba, and trombone punctuating every complicated move they made, Steadman searched through his memory to a time five years ago and Matthew tried to visualize the woman who was Willa Torrance, all of thirty-three inches tall, *mothering* these young kids who were far from home. The circus's famous little girl, so to speak, offering solace, guidance, and comfort to girls littler than she, fifteen- and sixteen-year-olds, some of them younger than that, traveling with a *circus* – which was not quite the same thing as being a novitiate nun at the Convent of the Sacred Tears of Mary. You sometimes had . . .

. . . twelve- or thirteen-year-olds hanging upside down on a rope, wearing costumes tight enough to show every crack they owned. Jeannie Lawson was a pretty little thing, blonde as brass, cute little figure, long legs, good breasts, came to the circus with a reputation that preceded her like a cannon shot. Rudi dressed all his chorus girls in blue, a good color to complement the gray of his bull elephants. Kept his animals shaved close so the girls' costumes wouldn't rip on the tough bristles, used a blowtorch to give them their haircuts.

The prime requisite for any so-called chorus girl or show-girl or ballet girl was a figure that looked good in tights. An *elephant* girl needed the additional attribute of courage. It might have appeared a simple task to sit smilingly between an elephant's ears on his domed head, wearing next to nothing, one arm prettily raised to the crowd, but when you considered the indisputable fact that a good-sized African bull elephant could weigh anywhere between four and five tons and could trample you in an instant without batting an eyelash, then perhaps it was understandable why a hundred-and-twenty-pound slip of a thing might consider twice before climbing onto its back. Which was exactly what made elephant girls appear so delicately desirable. Not that Jeannie Lawson needed any Beauty-and-the-Beast assistance.

On Choosing Day, if Steadman recalled correctly, Jeannie chose not one but *two* young boys. Having narrowly escaped being shorn of her golden locks, branded with a scarlet S, covered with hot tar and fluffy white feathers, and then rail-ridden out of her tolerant hometown of Calusa, Florida, she now seemed to take some kind of obstinate pride in her notoriety. It was not every white girl in the South who could boast of having bedded a black man. There were two black gazoonies working for S&R back then, and Jeannie started her burgeoning career with them, literally taking them to her bosom, first one at a time and then in tandem, and then tossing them out of her trailer when Rudi Kroner claimed her for his own; not for nothing had he promised the seventeen-year-old high school dropout that "with practice he could make her a good elephant girl."

Apparently they practiced all through April, May, and June, in *and* out of the ring. But by the fifteenth of what was already a very hot and sticky July, Jeannie tired of what amounted to a virtually married existence with a much older man, and took up first with Evgeny Zvonkova – uncle to Boris, who now headlined the Zvonkova family act with his wife, Rimma – and next with the resident cat trainer, Davey Sheed, King of All the Beasts. The miracle was that Rudi did not throw young Jeannie out of the elephant act on her cute little ass, but by then the season was well under way, and he *had* trained her, after all, and it would have been difficult if not impossible to replace her at this late stage of the game. Besides, she still favored him with her presence in his trailer whenever the spirit moved her.

In circus parlance, Jeannie was known as a "specialist." This did not mean that she rode elephants well – which apparently she did, by the way, seemingly possessed of an immediate natural affinity for the huge beasts. It *did* mean that she was reputed to have engorged organs larger than the one in the Ringling band, Andrew Byrd's included, a distinction that endeared her to the hearts of every man within a circus mile, her scent seeping into their nostrils as surely as did the sticky substance secreted from the temporal glands of female elephants when they were aflame with desire. Jeannie Lawson seemed *continuously* aflame with desire. Which was perhaps what prompted Willa Torrance to take her aside for a little heart-to-heart, mother-to-daughter chat.

Willa had no idea that most of the people traveling with S&R referred to her as Little Miss Goody Two-Shoes, a sobriquet premised on (1) an unflinching devotion to God, drummed into her by her Methodist parents back in Ohio, both of whom were perfectly normal in stature, by the way; and (2) a missionary zeal for conducting social work among the alcoholic gazoonies and pubescent teenagers who formed a part of any circus, large or small.

Young Jeannie Lawson would have none of it.

In no uncertain terms, she told Willa she was a *grown* woman who didn't need advice from someone who hardly came up to her kneecaps, or words to that effect, and suggested that Willa leave her alone unless she wanted one of Davey's big cats to swallow her in a single gulp one dark and stormy night. Willa may have been co-owner of the circus, but she did not have the clout to fire the circus's biggest star and main attraction, with whom Jeannie happened to be sleeping. She backed off. Or so the story went.

Jeannie stayed with the circus until it returned to Calusa in October. She then said so long to her various bedmates – including, by season's end, some of the younger girls, or so it was further rumored – and went smiling off into the sunset. Steadman never saw her again.

"I assumed she went back to being a townie," he told Matthew now. "Though I have to tell you, once you get a taste of the mud, it isn't always easy to return to civilian life. But now you tell me . . ."

"Yes. She's married to a man named Andrew Byrd, who's . . ."

"I don't know the name."

"He's the black man you mentioned earlier."

"Well, you know what they say, don't you?"

"No, what do they say?"

"Once a woman acquires a taste for licorice . . ."

Steadman let the sentence trail. He raised his eyebrows,

smiled knowingly, and tried to puff on his cigar again, but it had gone out. Matthew watched him lighting it. The Chens were taking down their red silk curtains. The elder Chen, as befitted his patriarchal station, walked regally out of the ring, two of the women following several steps behind. The smallest of the Chens began rolling up the silk. Two web-and-ladder girls in leotards, tights, and ballet slippers stamped flat-footed across the ring to where one of the ladders was hanging several feet above their heads. One of them loosened a rope from its cleat, and began lowering the ladder while the other one watched, her hands on her hips. Neither of the girls was older than fifteen. Matthew was still thinking about Jeannie Lawson's single season with the circus.

"You may be seeing her again," he told Steadman.

"How so?"

"If Byrd gets his foreclosure judgment, and you still want that land . . ."

"I still want it," Steadman said.

"Well, she's not only his wife, she's a partner in his company."

"Small world, isn't it?" Steadman said.

Susan placed the call to her daughter at two thirty-seven that Tuesday afternoon. She had left the hospital at ten this morning, but it had taken her all this time to muster the courage. She listened now as the phone rang on the other end. The last time she'd spoken to Joanna, she'd been told that it was snowing up there in Massachusetts. "Then again," Joanna had added, "it's *always* snowing up here in Massachusetts."

The phone was in the dormitory corridor, at the far end of the hall from Joanna's room. Susan waited.

"Logan Hall," a young girl said breathlessly.

"Hello, may I speak to Joanna Hope, please?" Susan said.

"Who's this, please?"

"Her mother."

"Second, I'll see if she's in her room."

Susan waited.

A moment later, another girl's voice came onto the line.

"Hello, is there someone there?" she asked.

"Yes," Susan said, "I'm waiting for Joanna Hope."

"Oh, sorry," the girl mumbled. "I thought somebody'd left the phone off the hook."

"No, there's someone here," Susan said.

"Sorry," the girl said again.

Susan could hear her footsteps hurrying off down the corridor. She kept waiting.

"Hello?"

Joanna's voice.

Thank God.

"Honey," she said.

"What is it?" Joanna asked at once. "What's the matter?"

"Honey . . ."

"Oh, Jesus, no," Joanna said. "What is it? Did he have a heart attack or something?"

She marveled, as always, at her daughter's powers of intuition where it came to anything concerning Matthew, felt again the slight pang of jealousy she always felt whenever she recognized the depth of their love for each other.

"Your father's in the hospital," she said.

Ever since the divorce, Susan had stopped referring to him as "Dad" or "Daddy" when speaking to her daughter. It had formally become "your father." Your father's in the hospital.

"What happened?" Joanna asked. Same imperative, impatient tone in her voice.

"He was shot."

"What?"

"Someone shot him."

"When? What do you mean? Shot? How . . .?"

"Friday night. He was meeting someone in Newtown . . ."

"Newtown?"

"And he was shot. He's in semicoma now."

Better to give her the highly unscientific layman's term than to try defining the various levels of consciousness.

"What does that mean?" Joanna asked at once. "Semicoma?"

"He's neither alert nor comatose. The doctor said . . ."

"Who? Which doctor?"

"Spinaldo."

"Who's he?"

"The man who operated on your father."

"Where was he shot?"

"The shoulder and chest."

"Then how can he be in *coma*?" Joanna asked, her voice rising. "I thought only head wounds . . ."

"He's *not* in coma. They can still wake him. But . . ."

"Is he conscious then?"

"No. But. . ."

"Then he's in coma."

"No, darling. The doctor . . ."

"Mom, is he in *coma* or isn't he?"

"The doctor used the word semicoma. That's the word I used with you. It's not a scientific term, but it best describes your father's condition. That's exactly what the doctor said."

"I'm coming down there, Mom. I'll . . ."

"No, I don't think that's necessary."

"I'll find out when the next plane leaves, and I'll be on it."

"Honey, there's no need for that just yet."

"What do you mean 'just yet'?"

"I mean, there's no danger that your father . . ."

"Yes, what?"

"That he's going to *die* or anything. The doctor didn't . . ."

"I want to be there when he wakes up, Mom."

"All right, darling."

"Can I use my Visa card for the ticket?"

"Yes, fine. Call me when you know what flight you'll be on. I'll pick you up at the airport."

"You don't have to. I'll take a cab straight to the . . ."

"I want to."

"Mom?"

"Yes, honey."

"Mom . . . how bad is he?"

"I don't really know."

"Okay, Mom, let me go make my calls."

"Call me when you have the flight information."

"I will. I hope I can still catch one this afternoon."

"Call me."

"Yes, Mom. Later."

There was a click on the line.

Susan put the receiver back on the cradle.

She wished she knew what she was feeling.

When Warren and Toots got to the circus grounds that Tuesday afternoon, they were told that Steadman was in a business meeting with his various marketing people and would not be able to talk to them till four or five that afternoon. The time by Warren's digital watch was 2:57 P.M.

"What do you think?" he asked Toots. "Should we wait?"

"Let's find the McCulloughs meanwhile," Toots said.

"Why?"

"Ask them about Sam's mother."

"Sam's *what*?"

"His mother. Aggie. The one Peter Torrance ran off with."

"Oh. Yeah. Why?"

"I like skeletons in the closet, don't you?"

"Not particularly."

"I love them," Toots said. "Hey, *you!*" she yelled at a guy running by with a mop and a pail of water. "Where do we find the McCulloughs?"

"Which ones?" the man said. "There're six of 'em with the circus."

"Sam and whatever her name is," Toots said.

"Marnie?"

"Whatever."

"Probably flying around the top of the tent," the man said, and began giggling unexpectedly.

Warren looked at him.

"Where are they when they aren't flying?" he asked.

"Trailer up top," he said. "You'll see their name painted on the side in red. The Flying McCulloughs. That's what they call theirselves."

"Thanks," Warren said.

"You ought to take a look in the tent first, though," the man said. "They practice day and night, practically."

"Thanks," Warren said again.

With the easy familiarity of a man who'd been here countless times before (once, actually) and knew the way, he led Toots to the opening in the big tent, and ushered her inside. The tent was empty except for six people on pedestal boards some forty feet above the ground. They were dressed in skintight pink costumes, a man and a woman on each of the opposite pedestals, two men sitting on trapezes that were hanging motionless between the pedestals. Warren guessed these were the Flying McCulloughs. All six of them. He and Toots took seats on the backless bleacher benches and looked up to where the man on the pedestal to the right was saying something to the woman beside him. Toots had just noticed that all of the McCulloughs were blond. She wondered out loud if they were bleached. Warren guessed they probably were. "Part of the act," he said. He wished he could hear what they were saying up there. He loved all kinds of backstage talk, all kinds of inside jargon. He even loved the argot of the criminal underworld. Regional dialects, slang, cant, all of it tickled him. He told this to Toots now. She looked at him and said, "Yeah?"

"Really," he said.

Their eyes held a moment.

"Me, too," she said, and turned away, looking up to where the man on the closest pedestal board had now swung out a trapeze, setting it in motion.

"Just the double passing leap, one more time," he called to the two men still casually sitting on the center trapezes. Warren guessed they were catchers, though they weren't hanging upside down just yet. What he and Toots were looking at was a pedestal on the right and a pedestal on the left, a goodly distance of naked air between them. The two so-called *catch* trapezes divided this space into thirds. There was the pedestal on the right, and then a catch trap hanging some distance out from it and slightly lower than it, and then another stretch of empty air and the second catch trap, and then the pedestal to the left of it. All of this forty feet above the floor of the tent. Blonds wherever you looked. Pink tights, too. A blond man and a blonde woman on each pedestal, the two blond catchers now setting their own traps in motion.

What they saw up there now were four moving pendulums, swinging back and forth toward each other and away from each other in a rhythm Warren knew had been carefully calculated and timed. He guessed they were counting in their heads up there. He guessed the flyers on the pedestals were premising their moment of flight on the swing of the catch traps between them. He didn't yet know what they were about to do. He'd have covered his eyes if he'd had the slightest inkling.

Not a sound up there now, not a whisper.

Just the traps swinging, and the flyers silently counting, the traps to the left and right rushing back toward the separate pedestals – and suddenly they were off!

A simultaneous leap on the right and the left, each flyer catching the fly bar as it reached the apogee of its swing toward the pedestal, the trap moving out again, this time with a flyer hanging from it, moving in an inevitable arc toward the catch trap moving forward in its own inevitable arc. And then—

Jesus!

In what seemed the mere tick of a hcartbeat, each flyer suddenly let go of the fly bar and somersaulted past . . .

Warren's eyes popped wide open.

Toots grabbed his hand and squeezed it hard.

Passing each other in midair . . .

Warren had never . . .

God, he had *never* . . .

"Are you *seeing* this?" Toots shouted, and squeezed his hand again . . .

. . . each flyer somersaulting past the other in midair, coming out of their singles, arms outstretched toward their respective catchers. Left and right, catcher and flyer met and grasped and held, hands locking on wrists, each catch trap swinging back toward the pedestal left and right, each flyer releasing, back arched, feet touching the pedestal, a long-haired blonde reaching to grab and assist, arms going up in the traditional ta-*ra* salute. Warren and Toots burst into spontaneous applause.

Warren kept remembering the way she'd squeezed his hand.

They were sitting on the performers' side of the cookhouse,

sharing – or at least Warren was – a second afternoon drink with Sam and Marnie McCullough. Toots was abstaining, though she could have *used* a drink after what she'd just seen up in the air out there. McCullough was pouring again into plastic cups from a pint bottle of Johnnie Walker Black. Marnie came walking back from the ice machine on the far side of the tent, long blonde hair swinging, hips and behind swinging in the pink tights, face deadpanned though she had to be noticing the admiring glances of the men sitting at tables hither and yon. She plunked down the small black plastic bucket she'd refilled with ice cubes, swung one long shapely leg over the bench, and sat alongside Toots, who was still raving over what the McCulloughs had done up there at the top of the big tent.

"Far as I know, we're the only aerialists can do that trick," McCullough said. "It's much harder than throwing a quad . . ."

"By a mile," Marnie said. "Little soda in mine, please, Sam."

". . . cause you've got two flyers in motion at the same time, *plus* the catch traps also in motion . . ."

"*Plus* the flyers passing each other in those singles. If they don't pass clean, they can knock themselves *and* their catchers down to the net."

"My uncle invented that trick," McCullough said, and grinned, obviously pleased that it had gone off so well, so early in the rehearsal period. He seemed pleased, too, that Toots had been so effusive with her compliments. Warren noticed that his gaze kept swinging back to her as he poured the Scotch.

"Sure you won't have one, Toots?"

"Positive, thanks. I don't drink."

"Really?"

"Really."

"Is that what I call you? Toots?"

"That's my name."

"Here you go, Mr. Chambers."

"Warren," Warren said.

He was also remembering that Toot's eyes had met his and held when they'd recognized their shared affinity for jargon. Somehow, this seemed important to Warren.

"Cheers again," Marnie said, and raised her cup.

"Cheers," Warren said, and wondered if Toots disapproved of him having a little drink – well, *two* little drinks, counting this one – while they were on the job. But, hell, he wasn't a policeman, he was a private entrepreneur. No such thing as being on duty. Still, he detected some kind of *attitude* there, some kind of tiny little frown between her eyes that seemed to say Watch it, Warr, we need clear heads here. But his head *was* clear. He was listening to every word, wasn't he? And he knew exactly what he wanted to ask McCullough and his shapely wife bursting out of her skintight pinks there, although talking to them had been Toots's idea in the first place. He suddenly wondered what Toots might look like in the same pink costume. Or in *any* skimpy costume, for that matter. Bra and panties, for that matter. Pink or otherwise.

Sitting alongside the other blonde, Toots looked by comparison clean and sweet and somewhat girlish, even though she'd suffered through a long period of substance abuse and withdrawal, an ordeal Warren doubted the high-flying McCullough woman had ever experienced. Threw your timing off, cocaine did. So could Scotch. The second drink was getting to him. He put down the glass at once, and focused on what Toots was saying.

". . . yet they became close friends afterwards."

"Yeah, go figure," McCullough said.

"Did you know Willa at the time?"

"Oh, sure," McCullough said. "I was just ten or eleven at the time, but everybody knew her. She was a *star*, you know."

Warren guessed McCullough was currently thirty-two or thirty-three. He also supposed that Marnie was in her late twenties, though she looked a lot older and a lot harder than that. Maybe circuses did that to people.

"Sam and I didn't know each other back then," Marnie said. "I didn't join the circus till after we were married."

"Which was when?" Warren asked.

"Seven years ago."

"She's only been doing this for seven years," McCullough said. "She's a natural."

"Oh, sure," Marnie said, and waved him away modestly, almost blushingly.

For a moment, there was a flash of the girl she must have been before becoming a circus performer. Warren wondered what sort of girl young Jeannie Lawson had been. Or, for that matter, young Willa Torrance.

"Were you old enough to know what was going on?" Toots asked.

"Oh, sure," McCullough said. "In a circus, eleven years old is *old*, believe me."

Warren guessed so.

"Also, when your mother takes off with a slime ball . . ."

"Was he?"

"Torrance? Oh, sure. Dumped her in Seattle, sent her back east without a cent to her name. I wanted to *kill* the son of a bitch."

"Sam's aunt was taking care of him and his sister," Marnie said. "After Aggie left. His mother. Aggie. His father was dead, you see . . ."

"Died when I was seven," McCullough said.

"A fall from the top of the tent . . ."

"Broke his neck when he hit the net wrong. So Torrance takes advantage of a widow trying to raise two kids . . ."

"Who's at the same time still performing, don't forget."

"Tell me about it," McCullough said. "You don't concentrate up there, you can get in serious trouble. Well, look what happened to my father."

"Thirteen shows a week, she had to do."

"Moving all over the country. My mother had it rough after my father died, believe me. So Torrance steps in and promises her the moon. My sister and me wake up one morning and there's nobody there but us chickens, boss. Mama's off with a slime ball, twenty-four-hour man."

Marketing director, actually, Warren thought.

"But the marriage was supposed to be a good one, wasn't it?" Toots said.

"Whose?" McCullough asked.

"The Torrances. Peter and Willa."

"Yeah, well, circus marriages, you know," McCullough said, and winked at his wife.

"I'll break your head," she said, smiling.

"Little Miss Goody Two-Shoes," Warren said. "We understand that's what they used to call her."

"Willa, yeah. Even the kids knew that name. We also called her the Virgin Runt."

"That bad, huh?"

"That *good*. Well, what do you suppose all that stuff years later was about?"

"What stuff?"

"With Jeannie Lawson. Good versus Evil, is what that was all about. It was almost as if . . . well . . ."

"Yeah, go ahead," Toots said.

"It was as if . . . I'm just speculating, you understand . . ."

"Sure, go ahead," Toots said.

"What I'm saying is she was a good little girl when she came aboard, but after her son of a bitch husband ran off with my mom, she got even worse."

"*Better*, he means," Marnie said.

"I mean she got to be a *crusader*," McCullough said. "That's what all that stuff with Jeannie Lawson was, all those years later. A crusade."

"In other words," Marnie said, "she got too good for her own good."

4

When she was good . . .

EARLY ON Wednesday morning, the twenty-third of March, Matthew telephoned the Byrd residence, and asked to speak to *Mrs.* Byrd, please. When she came onto the line, he told her he was a lawyer who'd met with her husband the day before to discuss some land his client was hoping to purchase . . .

"What land is that?" she asked.

"On Barrington and Welles," Matthew said. "The state fairgrounds. I'm not calling about that, though . . ."

"What *are* you calling about?" she asked. "Who'd you say this was again?"

"Matthew Hope," he said. "Mrs. Byrd, I understand you once knew Willa Torrance . . ."

"Oh God, is it *that* time of year again?"

"I'm sorry?"

"I get a call every year around the anniversary of her death. You'd think she was Marilyn Monroe or somebody."

"Actually, that won't be till May," he said.

"Terrific," she said. "Give me something to look forward to."

He visualized her rolling her eyes.

"I was wondering if I could talk to you about her," he said.

"Why?" she asked.

"Well, as I may have mentioned to your husband . . ."

Actually, he hadn't mentioned this to him at all.

". . . there's been a challenge . . ."

"I don't like to meddle in any of Andy's projects. If this is something you've already discussed with . . ."

"No, it . . ."

". . . him, then . . ."

"It isn't."

"Then what is it?"

"There's been a challenge to the will," he said, figuring if the lie had got by Davey Sheed, it should be good enough to get by Jeannie Lawson Byrd as well. "I was hoping . . ."

"What will?"

"Mrs. Torrance's will."

"How would I know anything about her will? I was seventeen the last time I saw her. That was a good five years ago."

"But you knew her pretty well back then, didn't you?"

"No. She was a grown woman, you should pardon the expression, and I was a teenager."

"The challenge is coming from someone you might have known while you were with the circus," he said.

Oh, what tangled webs we weave . . .

"Who?"

"I'm not at liberty to reveal that, Mrs. Byrd."

. . . when first we practice . . .

"Why not?" she asked.

. . . to deceive.

"Not on the phone," he said.

"Anyway, I hardly knew Willa."

"I was wondering if I could come out there, Mrs. Byrd . . ."

"No, I'm sorry."

"Or perhaps . . ."

"No."

"I know how keen your husband is to have this deal go through . . ."

"My husband's in Mexico just now. You can talk to him when he gets back."

"The point is . . ."

"I told you . . ."

"If I can put this other matter to rest, we might be able to move ahead more swiftly on the land deal. I'm aware that the Lawson-Byrd company . . ."

"All I do for Lawson-Byrd is sign papers and checks. I have nothing else to do with the company."

"I understood otherwise."

"You understood wrong. My husband will be home on Friday morning, you can talk to him then, if you like. As for Willa . . ."

"Mrs. Byrd," Matthew said, "she may have been murdered."

"I'm not surprised," she said, and hung up.

Timucuan Acres was situated on what had once been a cattle ranch, but an enterprising and foresighted developer had purchased the land for a song some twenty years back and just three years ago had turned it into a golf course surrounded by million-dollar homes on two-acre parcels. Man-made lakes now interrupted the monotonous green of the landscape. Fountains abounded. A stone wall ran around the entire property, a pillared entrance gate and security box guarding the homeowners within from intrusion.

On the telephone with Jeannie Lawson Byrd this morning, Warren had learned that Matthew had spoken to her sometime last week. She'd voluntarily given Warren this information the moment he'd told her his friend had been shot and was in critical condition at the hospital. Warren also knew by now that she and the young Willa Torrance had butted heads five years ago, and he was wondering now what *that* had been about.

According to the high-flying Sam McCullough, Jeannie's single season with the circus had been quite a stormy one. As Sam remembered it – and, oh, how he loved remembering it – Jeannie had started with a pair of ignorant gazoonies, and then had moved onward and upward through the circus ranks. In fact, there wasn't a man or boy on the show who hadn't known her intimately – "Including me," he whispered in an aside to Warren while Marnie and Toots were chatting it up.

Apparently, Willa hadn't appreciated all this activity.

Her "prudish attitude," as McCullough called it, may have been the result of her husband having run off with none other than McCullough's own mother sixteen years earlier, who the hell knew? McCullough chose not to speculate on matters psychosexual, especially since his mother and Willa had become good friends again by the time young Jeannie Lawson began rampaging through the circus's male population. But he wondered, nonetheless, about what had triggered Willa's animosity.

So did Warren.

He was here today because he wanted to know what, if anything, Willa's battle with Jeannie had to do with her subsequent suicide-murder-what*ever* two years later – God, how he *hated* cheap mysteries, especially those with solutions buried in the deep, dark past. But if any of this had anything whatever to do with whoever had shot Matthew, he damn well wanted to know about it. In truth, he didn't care why Matthew had been shot, he was interested only in whodunit, yet *another* thing he hated about mysteries. One of these days, he was going to quit the job and join the post office.

Meanwhile, it *also* seemed odd to him that Steadman had known Jeannie Lawson back then when she was sleeping with everything but the bull elephant she rode (and maybe even that), but he'd never met her husband, Andrew Byrd, the man who was now seeking a mortgage judgment on the very land Steadman hoped to buy. Small world indeed, as Steadman had reported mentioning to Matthew last Tuesday.

The security guard was big and sweaty and white. He was wearing a wrinkled gray uniform that made him look like one of the elephants Jeannie Lawson must have ridden back then when she was a teenager. Warren rolled down his window. A blast of hot air suffused the car, overwhelming the air-conditioned interior.

"Mrs. Byrd," he said.

"Who wants her?" the guard asked.

"Warren Chambers," he said, and opened his wallet and flashed his P.I. ticket. The laminated ID card was a smaller replica of the license hanging on his office wall. The guard glanced at it, picked up a phone, hit a button. Warren turned away, totally uninterested. In the near distance, the sprinklers were going. A small rainbow curved over an emerald-green lawn. Through the shimmering mist, he could see beyond to where a lake sparkled blue in the morning sun.

"Go on through," the guard said, hanging up the phone. "Round the oval, first road on your right is Palm Drive . . ."

One of twenty thousand in the state of Florida, Warren guessed.

". . . the address is twelve-twenty Palm."

"Thanks," he said.

The guard nodded and belched.

The striped barrier went up. Warren drove on through, past the sprinklers and the lake, and around the oval, and onto Palm Drive, and into the long driveway on the right of 1220. He got out of the car, stretched, and then went up the front walk to a low, redbrick ranch with a pebbled white roof. He rang the doorbell and waited.

He was ready to show his ticket again if he had to.

A woman opened the door. Well, a girl maybe. Seventeen or eighteen, he guessed that was still a girl. Black girl wearing a black uniform with a little white apron and cap. He figured he'd accidentally stepped into a French movie.

"Mrs. Byrd," he said. "I have an appointment."

The girl looked at him blankly.

"Warren Chambers," he said. "Chambers Investigations."

"Oh, yes, suh, come right in, suh, she's 'spectin you," the girl said, in a southern black accent that immediately dispelled any notions of *La Belle Paree*.

Warren stepped into the foyer. It was cool and dim and it opened onto a huge living room decorated in whites, blues, and greens, hung with abstract paintings.

"Juss have a seat, suh, ah'll go fine her," the girl said, and left him standing near a white grand piano. He looked around the room, and then sat on a white leather sofa that matched the piano. He was staring through the sliding glass doors, at the pool and golf course beyond, when she came in.

She was wearing tight green shorts and a snug dark blue T-shirt that together complemented the throw pillows scattered on the thick white nubby carpet near the glass doors. High-heeled white sandals, long suntanned legs, and long blonde hair – this was a week for blondes, all right. First Toots and Marnie and now Jeannie Lawson Byrd, twenty-two years old if she was a day.

"Mr. Chambers?" she asked.

She did not seem surprised that he was black. Many people were taken aback when they met him after only a phone conversation. But she was married to a black man, and perhaps this rendered her truly color-blind. Her hand was extended, there was a welcoming smile on her face. He felt immediately at home.

"How do you do?" he said, and took her hand. "I'm glad you could find time for me."

"Not at all," she said, and shook hands briefly, and then walked to a tufted ottoman opposite the sofa and sat. "When you told me on the phone that Mr. Hope had been *shot* . . ."

"Yes, I . . ."

"I'll do anything I can to help you. As I told you, he called me last week . . ."

"Yes."

". . . and I'm afraid I was somewhat rude to him."

"Well . . ."

"No, I was, truly. I'm assuming you *knew* he'd called . . ."

"No, I learned that from you this morning."

"Oh. Then . . . I'm not sure I understand. I thought you were investigating his shooting . . ."

"Yes."

". . . and talking to people he'd . . ."

"Yes, but I didn't know he'd called you. I wanted to see you because . . ."

"Yes, why *did* you want to see me, Mr. Chambers?"

A sudden change in her manner? Or was he imagining things? And yet, she'd just told him she'd been rude to

Matthew on the telephone. Was he about to be subjected to the same behavior? He didn't want this to go badly. There were too many things he needed to find out.

"Mrs. Byrd," he said, "lots of people in this day and age in America get shot for no reason at all. They just happen to be in the wrong place at the right time."

"You mean the *wrong* time, don't you?"

"No, I mean the *right* time. If someone's in the wrong place at the *wrong* time, nothing's going to happen to him. Two negatives . . ."

"Yes, I see what you mean," she said.

"Matthew Hope went to Newtown to meet somebody," Warren said. "This wasn't just an accidental drive-by shooting that happened to claim an innocent victim. Someone *knew* he'd be there, someone wanted him *dead*."

Jeannie said nothing.

"He'd been asking around about Willa Torrance's death three years ago," Warren said.

"Yes, I figured as much. On the phone he told me she may have been murdered."

"How'd you react to that, Mrs. Byrd?"

"I told him I wasn't surprised. And I hung up."

"Is that what you meant about being rude?"

"I was rude even before that."

"Why?"

"Because he was asking questions about Willa Torrance. Willa and I did not get along, Mr. Chambers. I do not enjoy talking about her. In fact, if you're here to . . ."

"I'm here for any information that might lead me to whoever shot my friend."

"I have no such information."

"How do you know?"

"I'm sorry, what . . .?"

"Sometimes people don't realize . . ."

"Yes, but I *really* have no idea who shot your friend."

"Can we at least *try*?"

There was a long silence.

Jeannie looked at him.

"Please," he said.

She kept looking at him. Sat primly on the ottoman, sleek suntanned knees together, hands folded on them. Staring at him. At last, she sighed heavily and said, "What do you want to know?"

For the seventeen-year-old who was Jeannie Lawson, the circus was a wonderland of fantasy and fulfillment. Secure in her own good looks, cognizant of the fact that Rudi Kroner, the best elephant trainer in the business, had chosen *her* as a protégé, aware too of the notoriety she'd achieved in Calusa, where everyone on the circus seemed to know about her high school affair with a black man, she became that rarity among traveling shows of any kind, an instant celebrity.

That she chose, at first, to squander her luster on a pair of dim-witted Mississippi gazoonies Steadman had rescued from dishwashing jobs in one of Calusa's sleazier fish joints, was more a matter of willfulness than appetite. The two young black men, respectively seventeen and nineteen, were in fact much handsomer than Andrew Byrd, but this wasn't why she'd bosomed and bedded them.

"It was a matter of pride," she told Warren. "Wasn't anyone in town going to tell *me* what to do."

Reverting to a kind of cracker English she must have spoken as an adolescent, replaced over the past five years by her current carefully honed and honeyed voice.

"I deliberately picked two black kids," she said. "To show 'em."

Warren guessed that was showing 'em, all right.

A circus is not unlike any other road show. The touring company of a hit Broadway play, a band playing town after town, a ballet troupe wending its way across America, each and all become small incestuous universes responsible only unto themselves. But Jeannie knew that the rules and regulations governing black-white behavior in a circus weren't very different from those governing such behavior in the wider universe that was the U.S. of A. After a week and four days of "showing the rednecks," she advised Jordan and Neal, as their names happened to be, to get the hell back to the fish joint in Calusa before somebody on the show hurt them. She was, in fact, fearful for her own safety as well. Some of the less reasoning gazoonies had taken to calling her either "nigger lover" or "The Licorice Stick Kid." It was Rudi Kroner who came to her rescue after the two kids from Mississippi speedily caught a bus back to Calusa.

Reasoning avuncularly, Rudi explained that among the many other reasons for his having thought she would make a good elephant girl were her splendid tits, ass, and legs. When she asked him what the many *other* reasons were, he told her there *were* no other reasons. He explained, too, that in the world of the traveling circus, there were hierarchies and pecking orders, which she might think were one and the same thing, but which in a circus were not.

"I found all of this interesting," Jeannie said now.

The *pecking* order, Rudi explained while patting her knee, was the circus's method of categorizing its lower-class citizens: the billing crew, the barkers, the candy butchers, the hammer gang, and so on. The *hierarchy*, on the other hand . . .

"Und, inzidentally," he said in his guttural Teutonic way, "a memper of zie *hierarchy* neffer calls a *vorkman a gazoonie.*"

The hierarchy, on the other hand, was a ranking of the upper classes, Rudi explained as he slid his hand up under Jeannie's skirt and onto her panties. And, incidentally, there was a very big difference between the words *category* and *rank*.

"I was still finding all of this interesting," Jeannie said, and lowered her eyes like a nun. Warren wondered if she was coming on with him. Somehow, he hoped not.

The point of Rudi's discourse was that no one in the lower classes would *dare* question the actions of anyone in the hierarchy. Never, never, never would any of the redneck *workmen* question the words or deeds of an *animal* trainer, for example. The animal trainers were the very pinnacle of the circus hierarchy, higher even than the equestrians – which was a lie – or the aerialists, and here Rudi began chuckling at his own inadvertent pun, while simultaneously toying with the elastic legholes of Jeannie's panties.

"I'm trying to tell this exactly the way I remember it," Jeannie said.

"I'm grateful," Warren said.

"I'm trying to be as honest as I know how," she said.

A daring young man on a flying trapeze, for example, could not very easily direct an elephant to squash a person flat in his tracks, as Rudi could have done if any of the workmen . . .

"Those *verstinkener* gazoonies . . ."

. . . ever again called her some of the names he'd heard them calling her while she was "foolink aroundt" with those two "*Negeren*."

"You shouldt haff know bezzer zen to be so shtupit," he scolded, and kissed her all over.

Oddly, she used his "Hierarchy Argument" – as she came to call it – to great effect later on when she dumped the wire-walker, Evgeny Zvonkova, for the cat trainer, Davey Sheed.

"I think Rudi was getting tired of me when he let Evgeny move in," she said, and smiled prettily. "Men get tired of women. Even beautiful women," she added modestly, and crossed her long suntanned legs. "I used the same 'Lions are gonna *eat* you!' threat when Willa began crowding me – but I'm getting ahead of myself. Would you like something to drink, by the way?"

"Thank you, no," Warren said.

"What time is it, anyway?"

"Almost noon."

"Shall I ask Reggie to make us some lunch?"

"Well, I don't want to put you . . ."

"Be no trouble at all," she said, and rose smoothly from the ottoman, and walked into the entrance foyer, and looked off to the right someplace, presumably to the kitchen, and called "Reggie!" and waited, and then, again, "Reggie?"

"Yes'm?"

"Could you come in a minute, please?"

"Yes'm."

The maid who'd earlier let Warren into the house rushed into the foyer now, and stood there in what looked like an uncertain curtsy, waiting for instructions. Warren wondered how Andrew Byrd felt about having a black maid in his house.

"Do you know that cantaloupe I brought home yesterday?" Jeannie asked.

"Yes'm?"

"Could you cut that in half and serve it with a nice little mixed salad? The melon first, then the salad. With the dressing my sister sent for Christmas. Would that be all right, Mr. Chambers?"

"That'd be fine, thank you."

"And to drink?"

"Some iced tea?"

"Two iced teas, Reggie."

"Yes'm. Did you want this in the dining room or outside on the terrace?"

"Outside, I think."

"Yes'm."

"Call us when you're ready."

"Yes'm," the girl said, and backed out of the room.

There was an awkward silence for just a moment.

"Andy thinks I should hire a redhead," Jeannie said, and shrugged.

Warren said nothing.

"How would *you* feel about that?" she asked.

"I can't afford a maid," he said.

"If you could."

"I guess a black one might bother me. Because of the stereotype."

"I kicked over all the clichés when I was seventeen," Jeannie said.

"Not everyone has."

"Then *fuck* everyone," she said. "Where were we?"

Just about right there, Warren thought, but didn't say.

"You were telling me how you'd scared Willa with the . . ."

"Yeah, that's right," Jeannie said, and burst out laughing.

"They think if you're sleeping with a guy who can order cats around, he'll send one over to pay a visit some night. I think I was a little scared of that myself, come to think of it. Davey was a very crazy man. Some of the animal trainers begin thinking they're indestructible, you know, it's funny. They start bonding with the animals, it's as if they have a better relationship with *them* than with human *beings*. Davey used to do this trick where he put his head in a lion's mouth, scared me half to death. Didn't bother him at all. Used to tap her under the chin, her name was Sadie, she'd open her mouth, he'd stick his head inside, come out grinning a few minutes later. Never mind her *breath*, that was another thing altogether," Jeannie said, and began laughing again.

Warren was beginning to find her delightful. He was beginning to think she *wanted* him to find her delightful. And desirable. Which he was also beginning to find her. Twenty-two years old, he thought. He suddenly wished he were sharing a cup of coffee with Toots somewhere out on Whisper Key.

". . . how or why Willa became interested in *my* goddamn business," she was saying.

Willa.

She had got around to Willa at last.

"Little Miss Goody Two-Shoes, you had to know her back then," she said, and shook her head in wonder at the memory.

"What was she like?" Warren asked.

The prod.

She didn't need one.

"Actually, she was terrific," Jeannie said, sounding somewhat surprised. "I mean that, I'm not being sarcastic. She was a complete pain in the ass, don't get me wrong, but she was gorgeous, and talented, and sexy besides. *Sexy*, yes. This kind of little-girl manner in a woman's body. She was a grown woman, you understand, with a woman's breasts and legs and hips, it just happened she was *tiny*, that's all. But she was a perfect miniature, really, a terrific shape, men used to go crazy for her. Which was what made them want to carry her into the desert on their camels, if you know what I mean. I think she was kind of a tease, too. I mean, I think she *knew* men were thinking they'd like to pull down her white cotton panties and sample her golden goodies . . . she was a blonde, you know, well, a sort of reddish blonde, not a true blonde like me . . . and she took *advantage* of this girl-woman contradiction. Turned them on, and then slammed them down. '*Hey*, guys, this is just little Shirley Temple here, you can't go having thoughts like that about *me.' That* sort of thing. Do you know the Judy Garland joke?"

"No, I don't," Warren said.

"Well, when she was shooting *The Wizard of Oz*, one of the Munchkins came over to her and said, 'Judy, I'd just *love* to eat your pussy.' And she said, 'Well, if you ever *do*, and if I find *out* about it' . . ."

Warren looked at her deadpanned.

"Maybe you have to be a midget," Jeannie said, and shrugged and shook her head. "It's like the drummer joke."

"Which one is that?" Warren asked.

"This little six-year-old boy is banging on pots and pans in the kitchen, and this five-year-old girl comes in and says, 'What are you doing?' The boy says, 'Shhhhh, I'm playing the drums, I'm a drummer.' Well, the little girl shouts 'A *drummer*?' and she grabs him by the hand, and drags him into the bedroom, and lifts her skirt, and says, 'Kiss me on the wee-wee.' And the boy says, 'Oh, I'm not a *real* drummer'."

"Uh-huh," Warren said.

"Like I said, you've got be a drummer," Jeannie said, and shook her head again. "Anyway, what I was saying was that Willa coming to see me was *ridiculous* when you think about it. I mean, seeking *me* out and trying to show *me* the error of my ways? While she herself was doing her sexy little-girl dance on the midway? Thirty-five years old and showing half her ass in a tiny little skirt, smiling her dimpled come-hither smile? Where'd she come off, man, telling *me* how to behave? I knew she was talking about me, bad-mouthing me all over the place, but then to have the nerve to *come* to me? To *confront* me that way?"

"When was this?" Warren asked.

"Sometime in August. The season was winding down, I forget which town we were playing. It was hotter'n hell, I remember that. I was sitting in Davey's trailer in just a bra and panties when she came around . . ."

The August heat on this night in Alabama . . .

She remembers now that it was someplace in Alabama . . .

. . . is stifling hot. Outside, the insects are raising a racket in the tall canes lining the parking lot. They have set up the big top on land bordering a swamp, delightful during the daytime, sort of, but not too terrific at night when the mosquitoes begin swarming and you're afraid an alligator might lumber up onto the bank and bite you on the ass.

The trailer is air-conditioned, and it has its own toilet, which beats having to share the donniker with the roust-abouts, who leave it smelly and messy. Davey Sheed is sitting at the banquette table, wearing his little Ben Franklin glasses, and reading *Penthouse* – or, rather, just leafing through it for the beaver shots. He's wearing shorts and nothing else. His body is scarred from his many tussles with the big cats he trains, but she finds this emblematic of his manhood and his courage, and therefore alluring.

The tap at the door is almost drowned out by the incessant drone of the insects outside, audible even over the hum of the air conditioner. Davey looks up from his magazine, and then says, "See who that is, willya, hon?"

In black bra and panties – black to hide the dirt, an axiom of road-show travel – Jeannie goes to the door and opens it. The screen protects her from the barrage of insects fluttering around the small outside light. Standing in that light is the Virgin Runt, wearing shorts, halter, and heels that add two inches to her diminutive stature, ducking away from the bugs flapping all around her and threatening to pick her up and fly off with her.

"Okay to come in?" she asks, and yanks open the screen door without waiting for an invitation, barging right in, and walking to the banquette where Davey quickly closes the magazine as if he's been suddenly confronted by the minister's wife.

"Davey," she says, "why don't you run over to the cook-house, have a beer with the guys?"

"What for?" Davey asks. "I'm perfectly comfortable right where I am."

"I'd like to talk to Jeannie," Willa says. "Woman-to-woman."

Jeannie flashes Davey a look that says, "Don't you dare move!" but he either misses it or ignores it. "Shit," he says, causing a tiny frown to crease Little Miss Muffet's brow, and then he gets up from where he's sitting and goes over to one of the trailer cabinets where he keeps his insect repellent. He sprays some all over his naked arms, chest, and legs, sprays some into his hair for good measure, and then slips on a pair of sandals and leaves the trailer.

"What do you want from me?" Jeannie asks.

Willa tells her that she knows this is no Sunday-school show, there are bally girls turning tricks and ticket sellers shortchanging customers, she knows all that. But something has come to her attention recently regarding Jeannie's sex life, and she'd like to discuss it now, if Jeannie doesn't mind. Jeannie *does*, in fact, mind. Jeannie *is*, in fact, incensed by the notion that Little Miss Priss here is poking her nose into her sex life, which is none of her goddamn business. Willa climbs onto *her* high horse, too, which is not easy for someone her size to do, and tells Jeannie that it *is* her business when it reflects on her and her act, and Jeannie tells her she doesn't know what the hell she's talking about, and Willa says I think you know damn *well* what I'm talking about, and the two of them are ready to tear out each other's throats right there in the middle of the Alabama swamp.

"What *was* she talking about?" Warren asked.

"Well," Jeannie said.

"Yeah?"

"Well . . ."

Warren waited.

"There was a little girl," Jeannie said.

"What do you mean?"

"In her act. Two of them, in fact."

"Uh-huh."

"Two *genuine* little girls. Eleven-year-olds."

"Uh-huh?"

"Little *girls*, do you understand what I'm saying? No boobs, no hips, no shapely legs like Willa's, these were just little prepubescent *kids*. Willa was a *woman*. These were little *girls*."

"Uh-huh?"

"Both of them *taller* than Willa."

"Uh-huh?"

"Don't you get it?"

"No."

"They were *taller* than she was."

"Uh-huh?"

"She used them as *bookends*."

"Oh."

"These two skinny, spindly-legged, flat-chested, eleven-year-olds wearing little-girl skirts and blouses identical to hers . . . well, not exactly. *They* wore black skirts and white blouses, and *she* wore a white skirt and a black blouse. For contrast, hmm? Also, *they* wore Mary Janes, and *she* wore high heels – which even so, she was *still* shorter than they were."

Warren was nodding.

"You're beginning to see it," Jeannie said.

"I'm beginning to see it."

"The girls made Willa look even smaller than she actually was! Here's this tiny little thirty-five-year-old *woman* you can fit in your vest pocket, this sexy little thing making you come in your pants, and she's shorter than the two *eleven*-year-olds dancing and singing their hearts out on either side of her."

"Okay," Warren said. "But . . . so what?"

"Well . . ."

"Yes?"

"Willa had the nerve to tell me . . . how can I put this delicately?"

Warren waited. He had not before this moment realized that Jeannie Byrd had any qualms whatever about putting anything *in*delicately. But apparently she was seriously trying to think of a way to phrase something that might offend his maidenly ears, so to speak. He kept waiting.

"She accused me of doing to Maggie . . ."

"Maggie?"

"One of the little girls. They both had black hair, did I mention that? For contrast. Like the skirts and blouses."

"Uh-huh."

"She accused me of doing to Maggie . . . well . . . what the Munchkin wanted to do to Judy Garland."

Warren worked his way back.

"I see."

"What the little girl asked the drummer to do to her."

"I see."

"The nerve," Jeannie said.

Indeed, Warren thought.

"And . . . uh . . . *were* you?" he asked. "Doing these things she . . . uh . . . *said* you were doing?"

"That's none of your business," she said.

"Of course not, forgive me, I shouldn't have . . ."

"It was none of *her* business, either. Even if I was."

"But you weren't."

"Who said I wasn't?"

"I thought . . ."

"I said it was none of your business."

"I guess it wasn't," Warren said.

"It wasn't. Or hers, either. I asked her what made her think I needed advice from a *shrimp* like her who was probably muffing those sweet little girls *herself*, Maggie and Connie, *both* of them, those were their names. I told her if she didn't get out of the trailer right that very minute I'd go get Davey and he'd stuff her head in Sadie's mouth and tell her to bite it off. I told her she might be half owner of S&R, but without Davey and his cats there'd be no goddamn circus at *all*! I think she got the message."

"I take it she left the trailer."

"She left the trailer. And never bothered me again."

"I see. And in November . . ."

"October. Near the end of October . . ."

"You left the circus."

"Left the circus."

"And never saw Willa Torrance again."

"Never."

"Did you know she supposedly killed herself?"

"Of course. I told you. Every *year* they call me to . . ."

"I meant at the *time*. Did you hear about it when it happened?"

"They called me then, too."

"Oh? Why?"

"They were calling anyone who'd known her."

"Who called you?"

"Newspapers. Magazines. Television people."

"The Missouri police?"

"No. The police didn't call me."

"Sam McCullough was wondering why . . ."

"Him," Jeannie said, and rolled her eyes.

"You knew him?"

"I knew him. He used to tease Davey's cats. If one of those cats had ever got hold of him . . . cats never forget, you know."

"Neither do bears," Warren said.

"Bears are the worst," Jeannie agreed.

"He was wondering why she'd got so agitated."

"Agitated?"

"Willa," he said, and watched her eyes.

When he was a cop, he'd been taught to watch the eyes. Watch them whenever you're questioning anyone, watch them whenever anyone was holding a gun. The eyes were always the tip-off. He had taught Matthew to watch the eyes, too. He wondered now if he'd had the opportunity to see the eyes of the man or woman who'd shot him. He kept watching Jeannie's eyes. They flicked toward the terrace. The black girl, Reggie, was sliding open one of the doors.

"Excuse me, ma'am," she said.

"Yes, Reggie?"

"Lunch is ready, ma'am."

"Thank you," Jeannie said, and rose from the ottoman and said, "Shall we?" and led the way out to the terrace.

Warren wouldn't let it go.

As they dipped spoons into their cantaloupes, he asked, "What do you make of that?"

"Make of what, Mr. Chambers?"

"Willa getting so upset by . . . well, whatever it was you were doing."

"What'd *Sam* say I was doing?"

Eyebrows arched, faint smile on her mouth.

"Well, according to him, you were . . . well, you said so yourself."

"Said what myself?"

"That you were, well, promiscuous."

"Sam used to steal my panties from the clothesline," Jeannie said, "do you know that? Threw them in the cage with the big cats." She smiled again, and then added, "Drove them wild."

"How do you account for it?"

"The scent, I guess."

"I meant Willa getting so upset. By your behavior."

"I have no idea. As I told you . . ."

"Yes?"

"The last time I saw her, I wasn't even eighteen yet. Everyone else kissed me goodbye," Jeannie said, and thrust her spoon into the cantaloupe again. Lifting the spoon to her mouth, she added, "Except her."

"I never trust anyone who says, 'I'm trying to be as honest as I know how,'" Toots said.

They were driving north on U.S. 41, looking for a Thai restaurant that had just opened. It was close to six o'clock and Warren was ravenously hungry. Cantaloupe and a salad weren't quite what he considered the makings of a substantial lunch.

"I think she was telling the truth," he said. "Up to a point."

"I once knew a girl who used to say, 'I'll be perfectly honest with you' every time she was about to tell a lie."

"I think Jeannie was . . ."

"Oh? When did it get to be Jeannie? Last I heard, it was Mrs. Byrd."

"During lunch she asked me to call her Jeannie."

"Was that when she was telling you how she used to abuse a couple of eleven-year-old girls?"

"Believe it or not, Toots . . ."

"There's *another* red flag."

"Huh?"

"'Believe it or not.' Anyone says that, you know he's about to tell a lie."

"I'm not about to tell any lie."

"Then why'd you say 'believe it or not'?"

"Because I knew you *wouldn't* believe me when I told you that's when the story began to veer off."

"I don't know what the hell you're talking about."

"The eleven-year-olds."

"Her beautiful tender *romance*, you mean?"

"What the hell's wrong with you, Toots?"

"Nothing. I'm listening to you report on your pleasant lunch with a child molester . . ."

"Jesus, I'm trying to tell you . . ."

". . . who didn't tell us a damn thing we don't *already* know about Willa Torrance . . ."

"Well, that's true."

". . . but who charms you out of your shoes . . ."

"Well, she *is* a charming . . ."

". . . while Matthew's in the hospital in *coma*! Yesterday, you get drunk . . ."

"I was *not* drunk, Toots!"

"No?"

"No!"

"What'd you drink at lunch *today*?"

"Iced tea."

"I'll bet."

"Listen, Toots, *I'm* not the reformed . . ."

"Yeah, *what*? You're not the reformed *junkie*? That's right, I am! And I know when somebody ain't *sober*, damn it! And *you* weren't sober yesterday!"

"No? Then why do you think I went to see the Byrd woman?"

"Oh, now she's the Byrd woman."

"What the hell would you *like* me to call her?"

"Fine, fine, the Byrd woman. That's fine. The Byrd woman."

Warren turned from the wheel to give her a look.

"I said that's *fine*," Toots said. "Watch the goddamn *road*!"

"I went there because McCullough . . ."

"Because McCullough wondered . . ."

"Because he wondered why the hell Willa had taken such a fit about . . ."

"Yes. A good reason to go. Let's drop it, okay? She told you the truth, the whole truth . . ."

"I'm trying to tell you she *didn't*! I got the feeling she was lying about those kids in Willa's act. I got the feeling that *wasn't* what she and Willa argued about."

"Then what did they argue about?"

"I don't know."

"In other words, your visit was a complete waste of time. We *still* don't know a fucking thing. What'd Bloom have to say?"

"About what?"

"The burglary. Is he going to call Missouri?"

Warren looked at her blankly.

"Did you call Bloom?" she said.

"No. Was I supposed to call him?"

"Do you remember our meeting with Steadman yesterday afternoon?"

"Of course I do."

"After you and McCullough knocked off a whole bottle of Scotch?"

"A *pint* bottle. And I only had *two* drinks!"

"Do you remember what Steadman told us?"

"Yes."

"But you didn't call Bloom."

"No."

"You said you were going to call him as soon as you got home."

"All right, I *didn't* call him."

"I thought you weren't drunk."

"Goddamn it, Toots! I had two lousy . . ."

"Do you remember Steadman telling us about a burglary?"

"Yes. No. What burglary?"

"In Willa's trailer."

"Willa's . . .?"

"Two nights before her death."

Warren glanced over his right shoulder, and then pulled the car into the curb. He cut the ignition. He turned to look at her.

"Tell me," he said.

*   *   *

The police officer Bloom spoke to in Rutherford, Missouri, at seven o'clock that Wednesday night was the lieutenant who'd handled the so-called Circus Burglary while S&R was playing the town three years ago. He was not the same man who'd handled the so-called Circus *Suicide* two days later that same year. Captain Leopold Schulz had investigated that one. Lieutenant Heinze told Bloom up front that the Rutherford P.D. did not believe the two incidents were related. They had been investigated separately and there were separate files on each. The burglary file was still open, in that the perp had not yet been apprehended. Perp, Bloom thought. Even in Missouri. The other file had been closed out as a suicide.

"Why?" Heinze asked. "Have you got a lead for us on the burg?"

Even burg, Bloom thought.

"No," he said, "but we're working a shooting down here, and we're running background checks on some of the people in the victim's orbit."

"What kind of shooting?"

Bloom told him.

"And a burglar was in his orbit, is that it?" Heinze asked.

"No, we're just trying to find out what the victim may have known."

"Yeah?" Heinze said.

"Yeah. He didn't happen to call you, did he?"

"What was his name again?"

"Hope. Matthew Hope."

"No, I haven't had any calls from anybody named Hope."

Which means Matthew didn't know about the burglary, Bloom thought.

"Why would he've called me?" Heinze asked.

"I just thought he might've."

"No, he didn't. I have to tell you . . . this seems like a long way around the mulberry bush."

"Maybe it is, but we haven't got much to go on here."

"Calling Missouri about a burg happened three years ago."

"Yeah," Bloom said. "Can you give me the details?"

"What happened was somebody broke into her trailer . . ."

"Mrs. Torrance's trailer?"

"Yeah, the one she shared with her daughter. Though, from what we could gather, she wasn't spending much time there, the daughter."

"What do you mean?"

"She was shacking up with the cat trainer, man named Davey Sheed."

"So she wasn't in the trailer during the burglary?"

"Nobody was. It happened during a performance. He'd've been in even *deeper* shit if there'd been people inside there when he done it. *If* we'da caught him, that is."

"Any suspects at the time?"

"Yeah, we rounded up the usual," Heinze said, and waited for a response.

"Like who?" Bloom said.

"Townies who victimize people passing through. Also persons of less than spotless repute on the circus itself. Plenty of those traveling with circuses, you know."

"What'd you come up with?"

"Nothing. That's why the case is still open."

"What'd the burglar get?"

"I told you. We never did catch him."

"I meant what'd he *steal*?"

"Oh. Just some doodads and gewgaws."

"Like what?"

"Jewelry mostly."

"What else?"

"Oh, some negotiable securities. What it is, you see, he ran off with the whole damn safe."

"There was a *safe* in the trailer?"

"Yeah, one of these little fire safes ain't worth a damn. You know them lightweight things you can pick up and pack in your pocket? That's what this was. He just carried it right off."

"Where was it? Out in plain sight?"

"No, she kept it in the fridge."

"The fridge?"

"Yeah. Thing didn't measure but about fifteen, twenty inches all around. She took out some shelves, stuck it in the fridge. Kept her diamonds nice and cold."

"*Were* there diamonds?"

"Oh, yeah. Diamonds, rubies, emeralds, she had a nice little collection, the lady did."

"You said securities, too. What . . .?"

"Government bonds."

"Anything else?"

"That's all she told us. Well, a wristwatch or two, and a silver rattle from when she was a baby, and some things belonged to the daughter was shacking with the cat man."

"Like what? The daughter's things."

"Oh, pretty much the same. Baubles and such."

"Expensive?"

"Some of them."

"In the diamonds, rubies, emeralds class?"

"Well, there was a string of pearls she listed as costing in the thousands. And a sapphire ring was a sweet-sixteen birthday gift."

"Was there a gun in the trailer?" Bloom asked.

"Wasn't a gun on her list of things, nossir."

"I'm not talking about in the *safe*. Did you people find a gun in the *trailer*?"

"We weren't looking for a gun."

"But was there one?"

"We weren't looking for anything 'cept traces of the perp."

"Was anything missing except the safe?"

"Not according to the lady."

"Then if the lady owned a gun, it would've been left behind. She didn't mention a *gun* being missing, did she?"

"No, sir, she did not."

"I'm thinking specifically of . . ."

"I know what you're thinking specifically of, Detective Bloom. I'm familiar with the suicide, though I didn't investigate that particular case."

"Then you know the weapon used was . . ."

"Yessir, a thirty-two-caliber Colt Detective Special."

"Was such a weapon found in the trailer during your search?"

"We did not make a search of the trailer, per se, sir. The lady provided a *list* of what was missing, and we accepted that as . . ."

"But you did check for latents and such, didn't you?"

"We did, sir, latents *and* fibers, *and* hair samples, *and* footprints inside and outside in the mud, but we weren't looking for any weapons, and we didn't find any."

"Do you know whether Willa Torrance owned a thirty-two-caliber Colt?"

"I do not."

"Did her daughter mention her mother owning a gun?"

"I did not ask her daughter that question."

"What questions *did* you ask her?"

"The usual. Whether she'd seen anyone lurking about the past few days, whether she'd invited anyone into the trailer who might've been nosing around the fridge, whether she'd ever come into the trailer and found anyone there who had no right being there, and so on. She told me she hadn't been home much the past few weeks, referring to the trailer. Referring to it as home. Where she'd been was with the cat man."

"Davey Sheed."

"Yessir. Living in his trailer, for the most part."

"Did anyone . . . during *either* of the two investigations . . . ask Maria Torrance whether her mother had ever owned a Colt thirty-two?"

"I never asked her that, sir. A gun had not figured in any crime at the time. We were investigating a *burglary*. We had no reason to ask about any gun. I don't know what Leo . . . Captain Schulz . . . asked the daughter, or what questions were asked at the coroner's inquest. You'd have to speak to him about the investigation he conducted. So far as the inquest goes, you'd have to . . ."

"Can you transfer me over to him?"

"I'd be happy to, sir, but he's on vacation right now. March ain't the best time of year in Missouri."

"Where is he, would you know?"

"Matter of fact, he's down in Florida," Heinze said.

The drive from Calusa to Bradenton took Bloom less than twenty minutes on I-95. Captain Leopold Schulz was staying with his wife in a motel on the Tamiami Trail and was unhappy about having to conduct police business while he was on vacation. As a matter of fact, as he'd told Bloom on the telephone, him and the wife . . .

"Me and the wife," he said, "have an eight-thirty dinner reservation, which means we have to leave here at a quarter past, which means, you've got half an hour to ask whatever questions you may have in mind. Frankly, Detective, I don't understand why you couldn't have asked your questions on the *phone*. Same way that lawyer did."

"What lawyer?" Bloom asked at once.

"Lawyer from down here, called me last week."

"Matthew Hope?"

"That's the one."

"When last week?"

"Wednesday morning, must've been nine o'clock my time."

Ten o'clock in Florida, Bloom thought. Matthew had called the minute he figured they'd be awake in Missouri.

"Did he happen to ask about a thirty-two-caliber Colt Detective . . ."

"Yes, he did."

". . . Special?"

"Yes, he did."

"What'd you tell him?"

"Same thing I'm telling you now."

Bloom watched him. He had not told Schulz that he wanted to see his face and his eyes when he asked him about a gun that might have been a murder weapon. Which was why he hadn't asked his questions on the phone. He watched Schulz's face now. Across the room, Schulz's wife was watching television, all dolled up and ready to go to dinner. She, too, seemed annoyed by Bloom's presence. Hell with her, he thought. Hell with them both. And kept watching Schulz's face and eyes.

"I told him there was no question in my mind but that Willa Torrance had used that pistol to shoot and kill herself. That's what I told your Mr. Hope."

"Was there any question in your mind about who *owned* that pistol?" Bloom asked.

"You train your people well," Schulz said, and smiled thinly. "He asked that very same thing."

"He's not one of my people," Bloom said.

"I got the impression he was with your State Attorney's Office down here."

Maybe because he *wanted* you to get that impression, Bloom thought.

"What'd you tell him?" he asked.

"I told him we assumed the gun belonged to Mrs. Torrance."

"Who's we?"

"Me and my team of investigating detectives."

"*Assumed* the gun was hers?"

"A reasonable assumption, considering it was in her hand."

"Did you *ask* anyone if the gun was hers?"

"I believe we asked the daughter."

"And what did the daughter say?"

"The daughter said she believed the gun to be her mother's."

"On what evidence?"

"She said she'd heard her mother say something about wanting to buy a gun. After the burglary they'd had."

"The burglary two days earlier?"

"That's the one. You're pretty much up on this case, aren't you?"

"Maybe because Matthew Hope got shot last Friday night," Bloom said dryly.

"I'm terribly sorry to hear that," Schulz said.

Mrs. Schulz looked over from the television set. She, too, seemed terribly sorry to have learned that Matthew had been shot – but she turned back to the set almost at once.

"*He* didn't happen to mention that burglary, did he?" Bloom asked.

"No, he didn't. *I'm* the one mentioned it to him. When I told him the daughter'd said her mother wanted to buy a gun, he asked me why, and I told him there'd been a burglary in her trailer two days before she killed herself. He wanted to know what the perp had stolen, all that. I told him everything I could remember."

"Did you mention that Lieutenant Heinze had investigated the burglary?"

"No, he didn't ask me that."

"Just wanted to know what'd been stolen . . ."

"Yes, all that."

"Did he ask whether the police had found a gun in the trailer? On the night of the burglary, I mean?"

"Yes, I believe he *did* ask that."

Of *course* he would've asked that, Bloom thought. But how come nobody on the Rutherford P.D. had thought to ask it? Half a dozen cops must've crawled all over that trailer, dusting for prints and vacuuming for fibers and hairs and looking for footprints to cast, but two days later nobody thought to ask Hey, was the *suicide* weapon in there while we were investigating that burglary?

"So you figured she'd gone out to buy a gun after the trailer was burglarized, is that it?" Bloom asked.

"*I'm* not the one who figured that. Her *daughter* figured it."

"Her daughter figured Willa Torrance had bought a gun after . . ."

"Something like that."

"Well, I've got a man in the hospital here," Bloom said, "so I really wish you could be a bit more specific about what her daughter figured or didn't figure."

The tone of his voice caused Mrs. Schulz to turn from the television again, a surprised look on her face; apparently not too many people talked to her husband that way. The tone also caused Captain Schulz to put on his best *Hey, You're Fucking with a Police Officer Here* look, which had no effect whatever on Bloom, who happened to be a police officer himself – not to mention in his own jurisdiction.

Both men glared at each other.

Schulz blinked first.

"She told me her mother had *mentioned* wanting to buy a gun. She did not say her mother had actually gone out and *bought* one."

"Then you didn't really know for a fact that the gun you found in Willa Torrance's hand actually *belonged* to her."

"We did not find any evidence that would have led to that conclusion."

"In fact, the gun could have belonged to anyone," Bloom said.

"It was in *her* hand," Schulz said firmly, and looked at his watch.

"You won't be late for dinner, don't worry," Bloom said. "Did you know that at least one physician on the autopsy board . . ."

"Yes, Abel Voorhies."

"Dr. Voorhies, that's right, didn't agree . . ."

"Voorhies *also* does abortions," Schulz said.

At the television set, his wife nodded emphatically.

"Whatever *else* he may do," Bloom said, "he *did* write a minority report on the Torrance case. It was his opinion . . ."

"Yes, I know his opinion."

". . . that homicide was a distinct possibility. In fact, he recommended further police investigation. *Was* there further police investigation, Captain Schulz?"

"The Rutherford Police Department, *and* the Rutherford Medical Examiner's Office, *and* the Rutherford coroner's inquest, *all* concluded that Willa Torrance had died by her own hand. There was no need for any further investigation. I think you should *also* know, Mr. Bloom . . ."

"Leo, we'd better get moving," his wife said, and rose from where she was sitting, and snapped off the television set, and went immediately to the dresser, where her handbag was resting.

"I think you should know," Schulz repeated, "that there hasn't been an unsolved homicide in Rutherford in the past thirty years. We suffered *enough* bad publicity with that damn circus suicide, can you imagine what . . .?"

"Leo!" his wife said sharply.

Bloom nodded.

"Enjoy your meal," he said, and walked out.

All the way to Charlotte, she had deliberately willed her mind blank, using a trick Sarah Harrington, her roommate, had taught her. What you did, you conjured up all things white, like snow and bridal gowns and swans and clouds and frosting on a cake and turtledoves and mashed potatoes and Santa's beard and fluffy bath towels and cotton in bloom, and then you made your entire *mind* go white, a field of endless white into which no bad thoughts could intrude except when your father was lying in coma a thousand miles away.

She'd called her mother moments before she raced downstairs to the cab waiting outside the dorm, and then caught USAir's flight 1577 out of Boston by the skin of her teeth. They'd landed in Charlotte at seven-fifteen, twenty-three minutes late, which meant she'd had to run like hell to catch the seven-forty-five connecting flight to Calusa, even though all the smiling flight attendants assured her it would wait. The plane was due to arrive at the Calbrasa tri-city airport at nine twenty-nine that night. Her mother would be waiting. Now all she had to do was get there.

She tried to think white again, but all she could think was gray. The gray of Sebastian's fur, except for his belly. She thought of the belly all soft and white, but white wasn't working just now, all she could conjure was poor gray Sebastian the cat and the day he'd got hit by the car, oh how she'd loved that big old smiley-faced cat.

"I got home from school about three-thirty," she'd told her father, "and I looked for Sebastian, but he wasn't anywhere around. I was going to the mailbox to see if there was anything for me, and I just happened to look across the street – do you now where that big gold tree is on Dr. Latty's lawn? Right there, near the curb. Sebastian was . . . he was just lying there in the gutter. I thought at first . . . I didn't know what I thought. That he was . . . playing a game with me, I guess. And then I saw the blood . . . oh, God, Dad, I didn't know what to do. I went over to him, I said, 'Sebastian? What . . . what's the matter, baby?' And his eyes . . . he looked the way he sometimes does when he's napping, you know, and he still has that drowsy look on his face . . . only . . . oh Dad, he looked so . . . so twisted and broken. I didn't . . . I just didn't know what to do to help him. So I came back in the house and called your office, but they told me you were out. I didn't know what to do. I didn't know where Mom was, and I couldn't get in touch with you, so I just went in the bedroom and hit the burglar-alarm panic button. I figured that'd bring everybody running. Mr. Soames from next door came over, and then Mrs. Tannenbaum and she drove her station wagon to where Sebastian was lying against the curb and we . . . we picked him up very carefully. We made a stretcher from a board Mrs. Tannenbaum had in her garage. We lifted him only a little, enough to get him on the board. Then we came right here to the vet's, I knew where it was from when Sebastian had his shots last time. Daddy," she said, "Dr. Roessler doesn't think he's going to live."

They buried him in the backyard.

There was a spot under the poinciana tree where Sebastian used to lie flat to watch the pelicans swooping in low over the water, his eyes twitching, his tail snapping back and forth like a whip. They buried him there. It was twenty-five past six, and beginning to get dark. Her mother wasn't home yet. Her father asked Joanna if there was anything she wanted to say. She knelt by the open grave and placed a small orange seashell onto the Styrofoam chest they'd bought on the way home. "I love you, Sebastian," she said, and that was all. Her father shoveled back sand and then topsoil and replaced the rectangle of grass he'd earlier carefully removed. Joanna put her arm around his waist. Silently, they went back into the house together. He poured himself a stiff hooker of Scotch over ice, and he asked Joanna if she wanted a beer. She nodded. He opened the can and handed it to her. She took a sip and said, "I hate the taste of beer," but she kept drinking it, anyway.

Her mother stormed into the house ten minutes later.

She'd come out of her hairdresser's to find the right front tire of her Mercedes flat. She'd called their local gas station for help, but it had taken them an hour to get there, and another twenty minutes to put on the spare. Then, on the way home, the causeway bridge got stuck open for another –

"Is that *beer* you're drinking, Joanna?"

"Yes, Mom."

"Did you give her *beer* to drink?"

"Yes, I gave her beer to drink. Susan . . . the cat's dead. Sebastian's dead."

"What?"

"He got hit by a car, honey."

"Oh," her mother said, and put her hand to her mouth. "Oh," she said, "oh," and began weeping.

Joanna thought now of Sebastian's big masked face and those emerald Irish eyes of his, and the way he stalked lizards as if they were dinosaurs and the way his ears twitched when he lay between the speakers with his head on his paws, listening to modern jazz. She thought of running to her father one time to tell him about the game she and Sebastian had been playing, and saying to him, "We had the *most* fun. I was chasing him around the sofa, and he was laughing and laughing . . ."

She thought of Sebastian the cat now because she did not want to think of her father. Thought of Sebastian laughing. Thought of how her father used to talk to him in a thick Irish brogue, and the way Sebastian laughed whenever he tickled the cat's soft, white furry belly – yes, *he* was sure, too, that Sebastian was laughing.

She squeezed the love rock in her hand now, and thought, Please don't let him die, dear God.

The three of them met in Bloom's office at close to nine that night. They were there to snowball the thing, a procedure familiar to all of them. They were there to recap what they'd separately learned in the expectation that they'd be able to deduce what *Matthew* had learned.

That was the compelling impetus behind each question they asked themselves. What had he discovered? Which single piece of information had led to the attempt on his life? Or which *combination* of facts was responsible for placing him in jeopardy? Where else had he been during the days and hours before the shooting?

His calendar was infuriatingly mute beyond Tuesday, the twenty-second day of March, a week ago yesterday. He'd been very busy that day. A meeting with Andrew Byrd at nine that morning, and another meeting with John Rafferty at noon. He'd gone from there to the circus . . .

This was not in his calendar, but Steadman had reported the meeting to Warren and Toots when they'd spoken to him yesterday . . .

. . . and then on Wednesday morning, apparently prompted by whatever he'd learned from Steadman, he'd spoken first to Jeannie Byrd, and next to Captain Schulz in Rutherford, Missouri. They knew this only because both Jeannie and Schulz had volunteered the information. But had Matthew phoned anyone after his call to Missouri? If so, the telephone company might – and Bloom stressed the word – *might*, without a court order, be willing to supply them with a list of numbers he'd dialed either from his office or his home.

Meanwhile, his activities after that last call to Missouri were a blank. Whom else had he seen or spoken to between ten o'clock on Wednesday morning, the twenty-third of March, and ten-fifteen on Friday night, the twenty-fifth, when someone pumped two bullets into his shoulder and chest?

What else had he *learned*, damn it!

The gallery opening was still going full blast when Matthew got there at a little past nine. The poster in the window read:

MAXINE
JANNINGS
NEW PAINTINGS
MARCH 23 – 8:00 P.M.

The long, narrow room was thronged with the usual Calusa wine-cheese-and-crackers set, a gathering of has-been, would-be, and wanna-be artists who flocked to these things as if Picasso himself were honoring them with a one-man show. The fact was that any artist of true importance, with a few notable exceptions, rarely showed work in Calusa. Maxine Jannings was a somewhat ditsy dame in her early sixties who painted nothing but cats.

The only cat Matthew had ever loved was Sebastian.

There was one specialty bookshop in all Calusa – "specialty" being a euphemism for "mystery, science fiction, and comic books." Matthew had stopped in there shortly before Christmas, hoping to find a good mystery novel for Cynthia Huellen, the firm's receptionist and factotum. To his great dismay, he had found an entire *section* devoted to mystery-solving *felines*. Cute cats who actually *solved* mysteries. He'd be damned if he'd buy an intelligent woman a novel about a sleuthing cat. Instead, he bought a novel about a letter carrier who solved mysteries in his spare time. When he'd mentioned to Bloom that there were actually books about cats trying to put the police out of work, Bloom said he would get his dog to eat them. Matthew didn't know whether Bloom actually owned a dog, but the sentiments were his exactly. Cynthia later told him the letter-carrier detective stunk, too.

Maxine Jannings painted cute cats.

Point of fact, Your Honor, she looked somewhat like a cat herself. Or, rather, like one of the performers in the musical *Cats*, who tried so very hard to look like cats, but succeeded only in looking like dancers in cat ears and cat whiskers. Maxine Jannings didn't have whiskers, and her ears were hidden by a massive hairdo that gave her the appearance of someone who'd just been struck by lightning. But she was long and lithe and her green eyes were heavily outlined to look like cat eyes and she was wearing a long gray shimmery gown that matched the color of her hair and strengthened the image of a tall tabby. She was also wearing fire-engine-red lipstick and dangling red garnet earrings, and she was holding a cigarette in a red cigarette holder in her right hand and puffing out dense billows of smoke in an already smoke-filled room. Matthew felt like calling in a three-alarm fire.

Delilah Phibbs, the "art" critic for the *Calusa Herald-Tribune*, asked Maxine where she'd ever found the inspiration for her playful cat paintings, and Maxine bridled instantly, telling her at once that she did not consider her paintings "playful" in any way, manner, or form, that instead they were quite serious metaphors for human behavior.

"As for example," she said, turning regally, "the painting we're standing in front of this very moment is titled 'Cat-rimony,' which, of course, has much to say about the sexist male judicial control of the purse strings in any divorce settlement. The painting to its right . . ."

Matthew was here to talk to Maria Torrance.

His reasoning was as simple as a cat's: Maria had been the last person to see her mother alive.

He found her wearing her slinky red wig and talking to a group of young men who were trying to look down the front of her white silk blouse. The blouse was unbuttoned down to the third button from the top, the way Burma's used to be in the old *Terry and the Pirates* comic books, valuable copies of which Matthew had seen in the same specialty bookshop selling the cat-detective novels. The Dragon Lady had looked more like a cat than any of those slinking around Maxine Jannings's paintings demanding alimony in some dark alley. Matthew was no stranger to alimony payments. He still made them like clockwork every month – no hard feelings, Suzie baby.

Maria spotted him as he came across the room, broke away with seeming reluctance from the gang of breast fetishists surrounding her, sidled over to him at once, and whispered urgently under her breath, "Let's get *out* of this dreadful place!"

They walked from the gallery on Julian Street, past Pace Avenue, and onto Dorothy's Way, where a truly excellent gourmet restaurant had just opened its doors in tribute to the culinary skill of the lady after whom the street had been named. He'd caught Maria at home just before she was leaving for the opening, and neither of them had eaten dinner yet. But eager as they both were to try La Vecchiaccia, as the new place was called, and even knowing that in Calusa a gourmet restaurant had about as much chance of surviving as a wren in a fox's mouth, they were both dressed far too casually for elegant dining.

Most of the snowbirds had already headed north, the better to catch Easter Sunday in their natural habitat. After the middle of March down here, you could go to any restaurant of your choice without having to worry about a reservation. They chose Marina Lou's, which was on the water, and where they could enjoy a sandwich or a light snack on what had turned into a hot and sticky springtime night. Matthew was wearing a pale blue cotton jacket over darker lightweight slacks and a white shirt open at the throat. Maria was wearing a jungle-green mini, high-heeled leather sandals to match, and the recklessly unbuttoned white silk blouse. Matthew kept remembering that she was bald under all that red hair cascading to her shoulders.

They each ordered a drink, and sat watching the running lights of the boats out on the water, cruising Calusa Bay in the shimmering dark, the scene peaceful and idyllic, a favorite among real estate agents trying to impress prospective house buyers. *Home* buyers, Matthew remembered, excuse me. Down here, the real estate agents sold *homes*, not houses. One of the boats began signaling to another one. You rarely saw that down here, he thought, boatsmen blinking lights to each other. Maybe because none of them knew the Morse code.

Maria ordered the French dip, and Matthew, watching his cholesterol, ordered the grilled grouper, even though he knew it was as difficult to find a good fish in Calusa as it was to find a snake in Ireland. He'd been told this was because the commercial fishermen had to go out too far for a good catch, and by the time they got back to shore, the fish was already a day old. He didn't know whether this was true or not. He knew only that the last truly delicious fish he'd eaten was while he was on vacation in Italy almost a year ago. He told this to Maria now. She seemed inordinately uninterested. He guessed she wasn't a fish lover. Or an Italophile.

"So what is it you were wondering?" she asked. "When you called, you said . . ."

"Yes. Two things, actually."

She sipped at her drink, watching him expectantly. Out on the water, the second boat was signaling back.

"First, the burglary," he said.

"What burglary?"

"Two days before your mother killed herself."

"She was murdered," Maria said.

A blonde sitting at the table closest to theirs turned suddenly to look at them.

"Two days after a burglary occurred," Matthew said, nodding.

The blonde was all ears now.

He lowered his voice.

"Do you know what was stolen?"

"Some things of hers, some things of mine. Nothing terribly valuable."

"How much would you say . . .?"

"I have no idea."

"Ballpark."

"I really don't know. My mother gave a list to the police, and also to the insurance company. My pearls were worth five or six thousand dollars, I guess, and the sapphire ring she'd given me for my birthday cost something like eight thousand. But I don't know what *her* jewelry cost."

"How about the bonds?"

"I don't know."

"Do you think there was any connection?"

"Between the burglary and her murder, do you mean?"

The blonde had tilted in toward them. She'd alerted her boyfriend to the conversation as well, and he was listening, too. Matthew gave them both a look, but it didn't help. They thought they were watching television here. They thought they were watching a mystery show where a goddamn *cat* would eventually unmask the killer.

"Yes, between the burglary and the murder," Matthew said, and shot them another look, more withering this time. The blonde turned away first. The guy with her indulged in a little macho eyeball-wrestling before he, too, went back to his own business, which happened to be eating an overcooked steak. Maybe he figured Matthew was a contract hitter down here to murder eavesdroppers. Matthew gave him another look, reinforcing the image.

"I don't see how," Maria said.

"Tell me again about the day of her murder," he said, and realized all at once that he now completely accepted her conviction that her mother had been killed. "From when you woke up that morning," he said.

Maria sighed deeply, and took a long sip at her drink. At the other table, the blonde and her boyfriend were busily occupying themselves with their food, but Matthew knew they were still listening attentively.

"I got up at four-thirty," Maria said by rote, "I'd set my alarm for four-thirty. Mother was still asleep. I knew she'd set her alarm for five-fifteen, even though she'd told me she wanted to be on the road by six. She always cut things close to the wire. I went over to the cookhouse, met Davey Sheed there for breakfast. We were lovers at the time . . ."

Sheed was out of sorts that morning. His cats didn't like rainy weather, it was his opinion that cats were at their most dangerous whenever it rained. He'd had a difficult time loading them, and . . .

"What time was that? When you went to the cookhouse?"

"Five o'clock."

"And you got back to the trailer when?"

"Five thirty-five. I must've started back around five-thirty."

"And you were with Sheed all that time?"

"Yes."

"From five to five-thirty?"

"Yes. He was angry I hadn't slept with him the night before. He blamed that on Mother, said she was jealous of our relationship."

"Jealous?" Matthew said.

"Yes," Maria said, and hesitated. "From . . . from what I could gather, he and Mother had once been intimate."

"Who told you that?"

"No one, actually. It was hinted at."

"By whom? Your mother?"

"No, no. My mother? *God*, no! It was Davey who did all the hinting."

"What kind of hinting?"

"Dropped little things that made me think he'd known her intimately."

"Like what?"

"Oh . . . like once he mentioned a beauty spot she had. Which he couldn't have known about unless he'd seen it. It was in a very private place, you see, a very personal place. And once he . . . well, this is too crude."

Matthew waited.

"Men can be so goddamn *crude*," she said, and shook her head.

Matthew said nothing.

"Anyway, he led me to believe . . . by things he said while

we were, you know, making love . . ." She shook her head again. "I was only nineteen, you know, some of the things he said were pretty shocking. The things he *did*, too. He trained wild animals, you know, he was sometimes like one of them himself, the things he made me do. Anyway," she said, and sighed heavily, "he led me to *believe* he'd made love to my mother when I was still a little girl."

"Did you think that was true?"

"I guess so."

"Did you ever ask her?"

"No. Never. My mother? Never."

"And you say he was angry that morning?"

"Yes. We had an argument, in fact, because he . . ."

The cause of Sheed's anger was that Maria had chosen to sleep in her *mother's* trailer the night before rather than in *his* trailer. On a night that was *raining*, no less, when she *knew* how the cats reacted to thunder and lightning, he had told her a million *times* how storms affected them. So instead of staying there with *him* when he needed her comfort and solace because he *knew* what lay ahead in the morning when he tried to load cats who'd be skittish and feral . . .

"That was a favorite word of his, feral. It means . . ."

"Yes."

"*Reverting* to the wild, you know. Going *back* to the wild after being domesticated. Davey's theory was . . . well, I guess you know you can never really *tame* a wild animal . . ."

"Yes."

". . . you just *train* them. But his theory was that training *is* a sort of domestication, and every now and then the animals turn *feral* on you. They go wild again, they get savage again, they get unpredictable. Like women, he used to say. Like *me*, he used to say. Like my *mother*, he used to say. And *Jeannie*. And *Marnie*. And every *other* damn woman he fucked on that show!"

The blonde at the table alongside theirs let out a gasp. The man with her turned sharply, as if ready to punch out Maria for uttering words he shouldn't have been listening to in the first place. Matthew braced himself. The blonde calmed her escort down. Loudly, he asked for a check. He gave Matthew a dirty look. And then another one. The waiter brought Maria's French dip and Matthew's grouper just as the couple got up to leave. The waiter knew something had happened but he couldn't figure out what. All he knew was that the couple had stiffed him.

"Why do you think it was Davey who killed her?" Matthew asked.

"Because of something he said."

"What did he say?"

"He said . . . really he could be so crude."

"What was it he said, Maria?"

"He said he felt like going over to the trailer and forcing her to *choke* on it."

"When did he say that?"

"While we were at the table. While he was still fussing about my having spent the night home."

"Home," Matthew repeated.

"With Mom."

"Did you mention this at the inquest?"

"No."

"Why not?"

"Because it wasn't really a threat. He was just being . . . sexy, I guess."

"Mm-huh, sexy," Matthew said.

"Telling me how big he was. You know."

"Mm-huh."

"Making Mom choke on it."

"Mm-huh."

"I'm not saying *I* found it sexy. I'm saying *he* thought he was being sexy."

"I understand."

"Besides, I wasn't positive about the time."

"What do you mean? What time?"

"When he left."

"Left?"

"The table."

"You told me you were with him from five to . . ."

"Yes."

". . . five-thirty, when you went back to . . ."

"Except for the few minutes he was gone."

"Are you saying he *wasn't* with you all that time?"

"That's right, he wasn't."

"Did they ask you this at the inquest?"

"The inquest already had the medical examiner's report. They were looking to show suicide. And I wasn't sure about the time, you see. He might've left *after* . . ."

"How long was he gone?"

"About ten minutes. Said he had to use the donniker."

"The donniker?"

"The portable toilet. That's what we . . ."

"What time do you *think* he left?"

"I'm not sure. That's the thing of it. That's why I didn't mention it at the inquest."

"Try to remember now. Your mother's clock was stopped at . . ."

"I know. Ten after five. But I'm not sure whether he left the table *before* then or *after* then."

"Well, you say he was gone for ten minutes . . ."

"No longer than that."

"Where was the toilet?"

"Just outside the tent. He could've gone back to his trailer, I suppose, but it was raining."

"He was gone for ten minutes . . ."

"Yes."

". . . and then he came back to the table?"

"Yes. And had another cup of coffee."

"Was he still angry?"

"Oh sure. Davey was *always* angry."

"But I mean . . ."

"Yeah, he was still annoyed that I hadn't spent the night with him."

"Did your mother know you were sleeping with him?"

"Yes."

"Say anything about it?"

"Just to be careful."

"Any reason for that advice?"

"I guess she knew him," Maria said, and shrugged.

"Meaning?"

"Well . . . you know."

"No, I don't."

"Davey could be rough when he wanted to."

"Mm-huh."

"You know," she said.

"Mm-huh."

"Men," she said, and shrugged again.

"After he came back to the table . . . how long did you sit there together?"

"Another fifteen minutes, maybe."

"And you say you left at five-thirty?"

"Yes."

"To go back to the trailer."

"Yes."

"Was he still sitting there when you left?"

"Yes."

"He didn't leave before you did?"

"No. Well, just that one time."

"I mean *after* he came back."

"No, he didn't leave again. Not before I did."

"You were there at the table with him for another fifteen minutes before you left the tent . . ."

"That's right."

". . . at five-thirty."

"Yes."

"That means he was *back* at the table by five-fifteen."

Maria looked at him.

"He *could've* been in your mother's trailer at ten past," Matthew said.

Maria kept looking at him. Nodding, seeming to be running the timetable in her mind, she picked up the roast beef on roll, dipped it into the gravy, and brought it dripping to her mouth. It seemed to Matthew that she kept running the timetable as she chewed, going over it again and again in her mind.

"Tell me what happened when you got back to the trailer," Matthew said.

The first thing she sees is the blood. It is the blood that shouts at her the moment she closes the door behind her.

The rain is beating down fiercely, she has turned to close the door behind her, pulling it shut behind her against the wind and the rain, and then she steps fully into the vehicle, shaking rain from her yellow raincoat, turning toward the bed, and seeing the blood shrieking red at her from across the room, the straps of her mother's white gown stained with red, the aluminum trailer wall behind her splashed with red. She begins screaming. Stands rooted just inside the door, screaming.

The first person to burst into the trailer is George Steadman, wet and bluff and yelling What the hell . . .? and then stopping dead in his tracks when he sees the body on the bed, the hole in the forehead, the blood spattered all over the wall, Oh Jesus, he says, Oh Jesus, Willa. And then the trailer is suddenly full of other people, roustabouts running from God knows where, the McCulloughs crowding in with the entire Chen family whose first year with the circus this is. A man named Barney Hale from London pushes his way past the others so he can get to the bed where her mother lies bleeding and dead. He's an aerialist who's been on the show for as long as Maria can remember, back to when she was a little girl, he does this trick where he hangs from a cable by his hair, spinning in the air from this long black lock of hair. Davey Sheed bursts in looking surprised and pushes his way to the bed as well, stopping just alongside Barney, putting his hand on Barney's shoulder where he's kneeling and sobbing beside the bed where her mother lies with her eyes wide open and her mouth wide open and the back of her head wide open. Someone yells that the police are here, and a cop in a soaking-wet black rain slicker and a peaked hat with a hood falling over the shoulders of the coat steps into the trailer bringing wind and water with him, and pushes through the crowd yelling Back away, folks, nothing to see here, let me through, folks, pushing his way to the side of the bed where Davey is standing and looking down at her, and Barney is still sobbing, his long black hair tied back with a black woolen cord and draped over his shoulder. The cop stops cold when he sees the woman on the bed. He goes pale, almost turns away, gets a grip on himself. Maria is still screaming. She cannot stop screaming.

Matthew looked up from the grilled grouper on his plate.
"What'd you say his name was?" he asked.
"Who?" Maria said.
"The one with the long black hair."

5

She was very very good . . .

THE ONE-ARMED bear trainer was out in the backyard doing a handstand when Matthew showed up there on Thursday morning, the twenty-fourth of March. A bear of a man himself, big-boned and thickly muscled, Harry Donovan balanced himself on his only hand, his hairy chest, shoulders, buttocks, and legs revealed in the neon-blue thong swimsuit he was wearing.

Matthew had called ahead and had been warned by his wife not to express any surprise over her husband's handicap. Harry's left arm, she'd explained, had been torn off by a bear some eight years ago, and he was still quite sensitive about it. Matthew immediately thought that asking someone not to notice a person's missing arm was akin to warning him not to mention Cyrano's nose. As if to fortify the warning, the blonde woman in the swimming pool put her fingers to her lips the moment he turned the corner of the house. Matthew assumed this was Aggie McCullough Donovan, trapeze high flyer, mother to Sam, mother-in-law to Marnie, and runaway paramour to Peter Torrance some twenty-one years ago, my, how the time did fly when you were enjoying yourself.

She climbed out of the pool the moment she saw him, shaking her head in warning again while her one-armed husband, his back to her, now hopped across the lawn upside down on that single arm; Matthew wondered if the man was perfecting an act he hoped to audition for George Steadman. Aggie was a woman of about forty, he guessed, the same age Willa would have been if she hadn't been the victim of a suicide or a homicide, whichever the case turned out to be. Like her husband, Aggie was wearing a thong swimsuit, but perhaps because she was expecting company, hers wasn't topless. Instead, it was a very brief yellow maillot that concealed and revealed, here and there and everywhere, the well-muscled, well-toned, and at the moment richly tanned body of an athlete; not for nothing had Aggie vaulted repeatedly from fly bar to catch trap in her days as a performer. Smiling, extending her hand, moving like a ball player or a ballet dancer, she walked in seeming slow motion across the lawn to where Matthew was standing.

"Mr. Hope?" she said.

"Mrs. Donovan?" Matthew said, and just then Harry pushed up on his single arm and leaped to both feet.

"Hey, you're here!" he said.

He was sweating profusely. Matthew didn't feel like taking his hand, but the man was advancing on him now, offering it, a wide grin on his face. The handshake was sticky and wet. Perspiration poured from Donovan's face and neck and hairy body. Matthew felt like taking a shower.

"Time for a beer," Donovan announced, although it was still only ten in the morning. "Can I get you one?"

"Thanks, no," Matthew said.

"I'll have one, hon. Have a seat," Aggie said, and offered Matthew an aluminum folding chair with bright yellow webbing. She herself sat on the lawn, more or less at his feet. The chair's webbing matched her swimsuit. He wondered if she knew he could look down the front of it and see the areola of her left nipple. He resolved not to look. First Cyrano's nose, then Donovan's arm, and now Aggie's left nipple. It was turning into a very trying day, and it was only a little past ten in the morning.

Donovan came out of the house, carrying in his single hand four bottles of beer he was holding by their necks between his spread fingers. A bottle opener was tucked into the waistband of his thong swimsuit. Aggie was careful not to help him as he struggled the beers upright onto a small, round table with a clear plastic top. He plopped down into a twin to the chair Matthew was sitting in, picked up one of the beer bottles, clamped it between his knees, pulled the bottle opener from his waistband, uncapped the bottle, and handed it to his wife. He uncapped a bottle for himself, put down the opener, clicked his bottle against Aggie's, said, "Here's to golden days and purple nights," and brought the bottle to his mouth.

Matthew felt an irresistible urge to ask, "So how'd you lose your arm?"

He squelched it.

"It was nice of you to see me on such short notice," he said.

"Happy to oblige," Aggie said. "Willa was a very good friend of mine." She took a sip from the frosted bottle, and then brought the bottle to her chest, and casually nestled it there between her breasts. "If this has something to do with her death, however . . ."

"Yes, it does."

"Because, you see, I left the circus after Harry . . ."

Matthew tensed.

". . . decided to quit," Aggie said smoothly, not mentioning that the *reason* he'd decided to quit was that some inconsiderate bear had eaten his left arm. "That was eight years ago. Willa, as you know . . ."

"Yes."

". . . died only *three* years ago. Harry and I were already living here in Bradenton. Not in this house. We had a different house. We bought this one a year ago. Because it has the big lawn and the pool. Harry loves to swim."

Matthew tried to visualize him swimming. Although Aggie had warned him repeatedly about the missing arm, everything she said seemed to point directly to it.

"Also, I can do my workouts in the yard back here," Donovan said, and took another long pull at the beer. "My push-ups, my handstands, my chinning . . . I've got a bar set up right there between those two palms . . . my lifting, all my regular routines. When I had the act . . ."

Never once mentioning bears.

". . . it was important to keep in shape. To stay strong. It gets to be a habit. I don't have the act anymore, and I miss it sometimes, but . . ."

"Oh, you do not," Aggie said, and waved the comment aside. "He *loves* doing nothing," she said to Matthew. "There's a lot to say for being retired. Living down here. Lying around in the sun all day. A lot to say for it."

"Like what?" Donovan asked.

"Oh, come on, you love it."

"I miss the circus," Donovan said. "Eight years, I still miss it."

"Well," Aggie said, and lifted the bottle to her mouth and drank, and returned it to its nesting place between her breasts.

"I guess I'll run inside and shower," Donovan said. "I must smell like a . . ."

Matthew guessed he'd been about to say "bear."

Instead, he said, "Nice meeting you, Mr. Hope, I know you and Aggie've got a lot to talk about." He nodded, picked up the opener and tucked it into his waistband again, snatched the two unopened bottles of beer from the table, and went lumbering toward the house. The sliding screen door rasped open and then closed again behind him. Somewhere in the thick foliage separating the Donovan lot from the one next door, a cardinal cried its distinctive *rich-ee, rich-ee, rich-ee* call. The yard went silent again. Sunlight slanted onto the pool, dappling the water. Aggie rolled the bottle of beer between her breasts and drank again.

"Mrs. Donovan," he said, "while . . ."

"Aggie," she said. "Please." And smiled.

"While you were on the show," he said, "Aggie, did you know a performer named Barney Hale?"

She looked up at him.

"How do you happen to know that name?" she asked.

"Someone mentioned it to me."

"Who?"

"Maria Torrance."

"Willa's *daughter*?"

"Yes."

"Maria? Why would Maria . . .?"

"She was remembering the people in the trailer. The night her mother died. The people who came into the trailer afterward."

"And she said Barney was one of them?"

"Yes. Did you know him?"

"I couldn't tell you if he was in that trailer. I wasn't there. I'd already left the show by then. I was already gone five years when Willa killed herself."

"How about *before* you left the show?" he asked. "Did you know him then?"

She said nothing for a moment.

"He was an aerialist from London," Matthew said, goading her. "Barney Hale. He spun around in the air, hanging by his hair."

Aggie looked up into his face.

"Long black hair," Matthew said. "Wore it braided over his shoulder."

She searched his eyes. It seemed to him she was wondering how much he knew, which in fact was very little. He said nothing, simply waited. At last, she nodded in acceptance, apparently deciding he knew it *all* already, so what the hell? He kept waiting.

"I learned all of this later," she said. "Peter told me in Seattle."

Yes, but *what*? Matthew thought.

And still said nothing.

"I was too busy with my own career," she said, "to know . . . or frankly to *care* . . . what Willa was doing or why she was doing it. The McCulloughs hadn't perfected the act yet, you see. After my husband died, we were still working on it day and night. We called ourselves the *Flying* McCulloughs, but I don't think any of us had even thrown a quad yet, this was back . . . well, it was before Peter Torrance, before I got involved with Peter. This had to be twenty, twenty-five years ago. We hadn't even started *thinking* about the double passing leap . . ."

Actually, it was more like twenty-*three* years ago, Aggie

remembered now. Her husband had already been dead for four years by then, she and his two brothers were running the act. They'd brought back her brother-in-law Jimmy, who'd sworn he never wanted anything more to do with circuses, but there he was again in winter quarters. So now there were six Flying McCulloughs all over again, Aggie and her late husband's brothers Jimmy and Jack, and Jack's wife, Tillie, and the two kids, Sammy and Jenn. Her brothers were the catchers, she and Tillie were the two flyers, and the kids decorated the traps, tossed imaginary bouquets to the crowd, grinned a lot, helped the flyers back onto the platform when they sailed back – getting on again wasn't as easy as it looked. They were both adorable little blondes . . . well, everybody in the act was, even Jimmy and Jack, who actually bleached their hair.

"Both my kids are terrific aerialists now," Aggie said, "why'd he take all the goddamn beer with him? So's Marnie, my daughter-in-law. Terrific flyer. You should see her throw a triple."

That first season with S&R was a really exciting time for the McCulloughs. Steadman was breaking in a lot of new acts that season, the McCulloughs, and Barney Hale, and also Harry Donovan . . .

". . . who you just met, the one-armed wonder who can carry off a case of beer without his wife even noticing."

Donovan had an act called Harry and the Dancing Bears, three of them. Gordo was the one who finally chewed off his arm eight years ago. But this was long before that. Aggie had no interest in him at the time. She was still a relatively recent widow, busy perfecting the act, trying to raise her kids to be good and decent, which wasn't easy in a circus environment. Barney Hale was a very handsome guy, on Choosing Day half the girls in the show went after him. He had this Brit way of talking, he sounded a lot like Cary Grant, a bit more Cockney perhaps, but something like Cary Grant. And a smile that knocked people out of the bleachers whenever he flashed it. What he used to do, he'd hang from a cable by his hair, which sounded ridiculous, but it was a very dangerous stunt. There was a woman named Marguerite Michelle who used to work with the Big One, she did a similar act. Had a hook wrapped in her hair, used to hang from a cable, juggling flaming torches while she spun around up there. One day, her hair pulled loose in the middle of a spin and she dropped twenty-five feet to the sawdust and broke her neck. This was around the time the McCulloughs joined S&R; the Ringling accident was in all the newspapers, it made aerialists *everywhere* stop and think.

Barney didn't juggle torches, he worked with parasols instead. What he did up there, he dangled from his hair on the cable while he juggled these open silk parasols. The parasols were weighted so he could juggle them without losing them, he'd start with two of them and gradually work his way up to five. It all looked so simple and soft, all those pretty red and yellow silk parasols floating around up there while the band played this tinkly, airy Japanese music, Barney barechested in silk tights, one leg red, the other yellow, his long thick black hair wound with red and yellow silk ribbons and fastened to the cable hook. It all looked so lovely and languid and so simple a child could safely do it, but nothing in a circus is simple and nothing in the air is safe.

Willa had been married to Peter Torrance for almost three months when Barney joined the circus. From all appearances, she was totally devoted to her husband, a good and perfect wife who pined for him whenever he was gone and adored him whenever he was there. As marketing director, Peter traveled ahead of the circus and was on the road much of the time. Willa sometimes invited the girls in for poker in her trailer . . .

"Everybody plays cards on a circus . . . well, not the gazoonies. They're into crap games, for the most part . . ."

. . . which the girls, even the snobby equestrian *elite*, considered an honor because she was truly a very big midway star. The midway back then was the curtain-raiser to the big show. The entertainers out there put the crowd in a real circus mood, and made lots of money besides. Willa was the undisputed queen of the midway, this darling little eighteen-year-old who was cute as a button and sexy as hell, with a great sense of humor and a real *concern* for people. Whether you were invited into the trailer for an evening of cards, or merely for tea on a cold wet day, you had the feeling Willa cared personally about you. She had this way about her that just inspired confidence. The girls told her about their boyfriends or their marital problems or their career ambitions or even when their periods were late, it was amazing the way this *teenager* really – she was only eighteen, after all – could be so maternal with girls and even women much older than she was. What it got down to, Aggie guessed . . .

"Well, she was simply this very good and decent person, and this goodness communicated itself to anyone who came into her presence. Even Peter . . . even when he left her . . . what I'm saying is that even he found it difficult to say anything bad about Willa. She was just that kind of person."

"Then why'd he leave her?" Matthew asked.

He waited, fearful he'd blown it. He was wondering what Frank would say when he told him he'd been too damned impatient to just shut up and listen. He was also wondering what Frank would say when he told him he'd been following a painted circus wagon for the past six days, instead of working on the real estate transaction that had set the entire quest in motion. Patiently now, belatedly now, he waited for Aggie McCullough Donovan to explain whatever mad passion had caused Peter Torrance to run off to Seattle with her.

"I thought you knew," she said, and hesitated.

"Knew what?"

"Lovelock," she said.

"What?"

"Well . . . the little girl."

"I'm sorry, I . . ."

"There was the little girl, you see."

Maria Lovelock Torrance was born ten months after Willa and Peter were married. Although the newborn infant baby was perfectly beautiful and seemed entirely normal, there was concern at the time that she might one day develop the same pituitary problem that had caused her mother to remain eternally diminutive. By then, however, there was talk in medical circles of shots that could correct hormonal deficiencies, and Willa – in her levelheaded, pragmatic way – figured she would cross that bridge if or when she ever came to it. She had no idea, of course, that her subsequent sobbing confession would cause her husband to run off with a highflying trapeze artist who by then had learned to throw a quite respectable triple, in and out of bed.

"I don't understand," Matthew said. "What confession?"

"If it'd been me, I wouldn't have told him in a million years," Aggie said.

Told him what? Matthew wondered.

"Told him what?" he asked.

"That the baby was Barney's."

Naked in bed, sleepless in Seattle in a room overlooking the houseboats on Puget Sound, Peter told his runaway young lass on the flying trapeze that Barney Hale was the father of his wife's child. Aggie was naturally all amazed until he explained that the middle name, "Lovelock," was Willa's artful little tribute to the baby's true father, he of the long black braid from which he dangled. Willa swore that she'd been to bed with the man once and only once – then why the goddamn homage? Peter wondered – and then on a night when she'd drunk a bit too much champagne in celebration of a telegram she'd personally received from John Ringling North, telling her she was the most extraordinary entertainer he'd ever seen on any midway, and promising her a starring niche with Big Bertha if ever she decided to leave S&R. Barney happened to be playing poker with Willa and some of the girls that night . . . "Maybe they mistook Barney for one of them," Aggie said now, somewhat snidely, "that long sexy hair of his . . ."

. . . and had stayed to help Willa clean up after the game, which was when the telegram arrived. Beside herself with joy, Willa popped the cork on a bottle of Moet & Chandon she had on ice in the fridge, a gift from an unknown admirer who'd caught her act on the midway one night and sent the bubbly around anonymously the next morning. One thing led to another, as they say in confessional boxes and girls' college dorms. Barney Hale was twenty years old and far from family and friends in London, and Willa was eighteen and sympathetic by nature. Barney let his hair down, so to speak, and Willa offered generous aid and comfort.

It was Aggie's opinion, when she gave it deeper thought, that the affair could have been reasonably expected, had anyone been paying closer attention. Peter was, after all, seven years older than Aggie, a mature grown-up who was on the road a great deal of the time. Barney, on the other hand, was constantly hanging around, if only spectacularly from the top of the tent. As Aggie had mentioned, he was a singularly good-looking young man, and Willa could not have failed to notice him dangling from that heavy lock of hair, his lithe young body in silk tights, twirling his parasols and pectorals and whatever else up there, nothing but a healthy scalp standing between him and imminent disaster. As she had further mentioned, Willa was adorably winsome and lusciously seductive besides. If Barney had ever seen her – as most certainly he must have – flashing her little-girl panties and kicking her shapely legs in performance, might he not have entertained fantasies of possibly more extravagant exhibitions in the privacy of her trailer one night, where conceivably he could dangle more than a thick braid of hair before the dimpled darling of the midway?

By her own subsequent admission, Willa and Barney had been together on just that one tipsy occasion – but who could say how many *other* midnight trysts there'd been? If this had been a mere inebriated one-night stand, why the sly inclusion of "lovelock" into the baby's given name, an insertion that seemed to point not only to Barney's trademark mane but also to the very *act* that had created the child: a couple locked in embrace, locked in love, a love lock. And if their ardor had been a mere passing fancy, why the later tearful confession to her husband? It was Aggie's guess that the affair had been a long-running one, even though no one had ever witnessed them holding hands together, or exchanging soulful glances, or dining *tête-á-tête* in the cookhouse tent, or behaving in any way other than circumspect. Then again, no one was particularly looking.

"Did *she* tell you this?" Matthew asked.

"No. I'm guessing."

"Even when you became friends, years later . . ."

"Never. She told me it was just that once. A one-night stand. She said Barney'd meant nothing to her."

"How'd she know the baby was his?"

"She didn't use any birth control that night."

"That doesn't sound conclu – "

"No, she was always very careful about birth control. She was afraid a child would inherit *her* problem, you see. But that night with Barney, she was drinking champagne. I guess we do things when we're drinking champagne."

"Does Maria know any of this?" Matthew asked.

"God forbid," Aggie said.

"So you and Torrance were together for a year or so . . ."

"Eleven months, actually."

". . . and then you came back to Florida."

"Yes. Well, not Peter. I didn't know where *he* went. He lives in Atlanta now."

"But you went back to the circus?"

"Yes. Until eight years ago, when Harry had his accident."

"Have you seen Torrance since?"

"Yes, last week."

"What?"

"He stopped by last week to say hello."

"You mean he's *here*? In Bradenton?"

"Well, in Calusa."

"Doing what?"

"He thinks he owns thirty percent of a circus."

In a fit of extravagance and generosity, the telephone company *messengered* a list to Bloom's office at ten-thirty that morning, the last day of March. Actually, the list was not what Bloom had requested, in that it was merely a record of the calls made from the offices of Sumerville and Hope, and did not supply the calls Matthew had made from his home. Bloom guessed that someone had simply pressed a print button, but a call from a young man at the telephone company made it appear that the entire office staff had been energized in a major effort to supply the document. Going along with the game, Bloom thanked him profusely; he had learned over the years that dealing with the telephone company was akin to waging war with a foreign power.

He called Matthew's office the moment he received the business-bill printout, and spoke to a woman there named Cynthia Huellen, who promptly matched most of the phone numbers with those of familiar clients, banks, law firms, accountants, state attorneys' offices, clerks of the court, and various other regulars Summerville and Hope dealt with on a daily basis. There were two numbers she didn't recognize, however, and judging from the prefixes, they were both on the mainland. She told Bloom she'd check further and get back to him.

At ten forty-two, she called back to say that she'd talked to all the attorneys in the firm, and learned that one of those calls had been made by Mr. Summerville last Tuesday afternoon, to a restaurant where he and his wife would be dining that night. None of the other lawyers could identify the remaining number. The phone company printout indicated that the call had been made at 11:51 A.M. on the twenty-fourth of March. That would have been last Thursday, a week ago today. Cynthia offered the information that Mr. Hope hadn't been in very much last week, but she *did* remember him coming in at a little before noon that day, and going directly into his office. She suspected he might have made the call at that time. In any event, he went out again shortly afterward.

"What time would that have been?" Bloom asked.

"Around one."

"Did you see him go out?"

"Yes, sir, I was just coming back from lunch."

"Did he say where he was going?"

"No, sir, he didn't."

"Thank you very much," Bloom said. "If you ever want a job with the police department, just let me know."

"Thank you, sir, it was my pleasure. Mr. Bloom?"

"Yes?"

"Is . . . is he going to be all right?"

"I hope so," Bloom said.

*   *   *

She had told them if they wouldn't let her stay by his bedside, she would slit her wrists and bleed all over the hospital. They believed her. People tended to believe hysterical fourteen-year-olds. Besides, she *was* his daughter, after all, and by then they were fearful he'd *never* wake up for more than a few seconds at a time. They did not want it on their collective conscience that they had kept the man's daughter from working her primitive magic. Not when the man might remain a vegetable for the rest of his life. Besides, they were all familiar with magic. They were all doctors, and the practice of medicine was not too far removed from the magic Joanna had begun performing late last night when she'd got to the hospital, and was still performing now at ten-thirty in the morning.

She had pressed the love rock into the palm of his hand.

His fingers had not closed on it, there had been no response, so she had kept it pressed there with her own hand, holding his bigger hand under hers, the love rock pressed into his palm. The love rock was a small stone he had given her when he and her mother separated. It had a little white heart painted on it, outlined in red, and lettered inside with the single word LOVE, also in red. When he gave her the rock, he told her he wasn't divorcing her, he was only divorcing her mother. He told her he would always love her. He told her if ever she doubted his love, she should look at the rock, stare at the white heart with its red outline, and then squeeze the rock and the word LOVE would pop right out of that heart, it would jump right out of that heart, and shout LOVE at her, and she would know he was still there, always loving her.

She kept the rock pressed into his hand now, wishing his fingers would close on it, wishing she could feel some movement in his hand, because then she would know that he was going to be all right again. The doctors had told her that they'd been successful in provoking minor responses from him, but that these were not significant and they still could not form any realistic prognosis.

She had begun the litany last night at ten minutes past eleven, when they'd allowed her to go into the room where he was lying alone in the semidark, and she continued the litany now, twelve hours later, sitting beside his bed in the same room, sunlit now, holding his hand with the love rock pressed into his palm. She spoke the litany in a soft, murmuring voice, because prayers didn't count unless you said them aloud, he had taught her that when she was just a little girl.

She wanted the litany to remind him of all the things they'd done together, since as far back as she could remember. The litany promised him all the things they were going to do together once he got better and got out of here. She led him through the litany the way he used to lead her across the playground when she was a little girl, his hand in hers . . .

"Do you remember when we were in Italy that time?" she told him in her soft murmuring voice, "and you and Mom were having a fight, and you shook off my hand? You were holding my hand, and you yelled that my hand was all sticky because I'd been eating *gelato*, do you remember? And I burst into tears because I thought you were mad at *me*, too, and you knelt down and looked into my face, and you wiped my tears with your handkerchief, and then you took my hand again, which was *still* all sticky with *gelato*, and you walked me over to one of those fountains they have all over Italy – I guess this was Rome, you'll remember better than I do, you can tell me when you wake up if it was Rome or not. And you wet your handkerchief in the fountain, and you washed my hands with it, and then you kissed me on the nose and said, 'I love you, Jinkies,' which you used to call me when I was a very little girl, I still don't know why. You'll have to tell me when you wake up, okay? Do you promise?

"And, Dad, do you remember when you taught me the *alternate* lyrics to 'Jingle Bells'? I'll sing them for you now, but when you wake up, we'll have to sing them together, okay? Now don't laugh, I *know* you know them much better than I do. I must've been eight, wasn't I? When you taught them to me? Wasn't I eight at the time? Are you ready? Squeeze my hand if you're ready, okay? Well, ready or not, here I *commmme*! 'Jinkie Burrs, Jinkie Burrs, Jinkies all the way. Oh, what fun it is to hide in the closet every day.' I can't remember the rest, you'll have to sing the rest for me when you wake up. I think you used to call me Jinkies long before then, though. Joanna Jinkies, or Jinkie Joanna, which one was it? You also used to sing 'When Joanna Loved Me,' do you remember that? I love the name Joanna, you know, Mom told me you were the one who chose it, she wanted to call me Deborah. Deborah Hope. Which isn't bad, I suppose, but Joanna is so much nicer. Joanna Hope. I love that name, I may keep it even when I get married, if I ever *do* get married, the way things are going.

"By the way, don't forget to remind me when you wake up. There's this boy I want you to meet, his name is Louis, he's an upperclassman, and real cool. Louis Klein, he's Jewish, he lives in West Newton, he invited me to his parents' house for Passover. Don't you think it's the *dumbest* thing that we had our spring break *before* Passover and Easter, when all the kids really *want* to be home? I would've missed you if you'd gone to Little Dix a week sooner than you had, do you realize that? Well, now I have this excuse to be home *again*, how about that, but it's not gonna be much fun till you wake up, so hurry up, willya, please?

"I like Patricia, by the way, she's a real cool lady. In fact, I'm sorry we didn't get to spend more time together. But you were leaving on vacation at the end of the week, and I had to split *my* vacation time with Mom . . . it's a pain in the ass having divorced parents, you know, I don't think I'll *ever* get used to it, Dad. This isn't a pitch, I really *do* like Patricia. I mean, she's beautiful, and smart, and I think she really does care for you. So please don't take it as a pitch, I'm not expecting you and Mom ever to get together again, I've outgrown that, you don't have to ever worry about that ever again. Although I have to admit, there was a time there, when you and Mom were getting kissy-facey all over again, I sort of got my hopes up. Anyway, forget that, the important thing is that you wake up soon, and you and me and Patricia can go on a boat trip or something together, maybe down the Caloosahatchee, so I can get to know her better.

"Do you remember the time we went fishing for bigmouth bass on Lake Okeechobee? It was raining, do you remember, and you said you wanted to go to a movie, and Mom and I said we hadn't gone all the way down there – on a *boat*, no less – just to go see a movie. This was when we had the *Windbag*, do you remember? Anyway, I think you had some kind of idea from when you were a kid in Chicago that if it rained you were supposed to go to a movie. We finally convinced you to come out on the lake with us, and oh Dad, it was so *gorgeous*, do you remember? The mist rising in the rain, and the boat gliding over the surface, and everything so silvery and still. We caught so many fish!

"I want to go back to Chicago soon, Dad, I mean it. That's a promise you have to make me. It's been too long a time since I've seen Grandma, and also I love that city, I really do. I think if I ever get married, I may move to Chicago. On the other hand, Louis hasn't even *kissed* me yet, so chances are pretty good I'll get to be an old maid. Anyway, when you wake up, let's check our calendars and see when we can get away, okay? Just squeeze my hand if you can hear me, Dad, I just want to know you can hear me. That's the love rock in your hand, the one you gave me, I want you to squeeze it so it'll shout love at me, do you remember telling me it would shout love whenever I squeezed it? Why don't you squeeze it now, Dad? Then you can wake up and we can talk about all these plans we have to make.

"You know, I've been meaning to tell you. This girl in my dorm . . . her father's a judge someplace? He sent her this transcript of the Barton trial . . . it was in some law journal, did you know that? Well, it was. He told her he'd never read a better defense in his life. How about that? She wanted to know if you were actually my father! I'm famous, do you realize it? I was planning to send the article down to you, I'll do that when I get back to Mass. I plan to sit here till you wake up, you know, so don't be too long about it. I don't want to get old and gray while Louis chases every other girl on campus.

"Would you like to know what he looks like? Welllll, he's got sort of muddy-brown hair, which isn't a particularly picturesque way of describing it, I know, but that's what it is, Dad, the color of mud, so what can you do, right? And he's got dark brown eyes, and a fox face . . . oh, by the *way*! I know you'll appreciate the fact that Mr Summerville's method of categorizing faces has caught on up at school. Everybody's either a fox face or a pig face now, ever since I told the kids about his system. Louis is a definite fox face, and he's on the lacrosse team, and he knows all the lyrics to *Evita*, which I think is cool.

"Dad . . . could you just squeeze my hand a little? Just so I'll know you're hearing me, okay, I'm not rushing you or anything, I'll sit here forever if I have to, but if you feel like telling me you know I'm here, that'd be okay, too. You don't have to squeeze the love rock, that might be too difficult for you right now. But I've got my hand resting on your palm, can you feel it? So if you want to give it a little squeeze . . . I mean, we don't have to go for a *shout* here, like with the rock, we can just go for a tiny little *whisper*, okay? Just an itty-bitty squeeze, Dad, how does that sound to you? If you feel like it, of course. There's no hurry, you just take all the time you need.

"Dad . . .

"Daddy . . .

"I love you so much, Daddy.

"Please wake up, won't you? I'll sit here forever, you know, so don't think you're going to get rid of me by pretending you're asleep. I'll just sit here and keep telling you over and over again that I love you, until you'll simply *have* to wake up, how's that? Then we can go to as many movies as you like, never mind fishing, I know you don't like fishing. We'll go to five movies in a single day, if you like, one after the other. Have you ever been to a seder? Maybe you can teach me what a person does at a seder. Meanwhile, how about squeezing my hand, Dad?"

His hand lay just beneath hers, his fingers curled but motionless on the cool white sheet.

She tried very hard not to cry.

The supervisor's name was Miss Finch.

Bloom couldn't believe she worked for the telephone company. Instead of spouting the party line about company policy and reasonable cause and reasonable suspicion and court-ordered Trace-and-Traps and MUDs and LUDs and other arcane terms known only to policemen requesting eavesdropping warrants and judges reluctant to sign them and telephone company personnel eager to protect their own asses, Miss Finch actually told him she understood the difficulties the police faced in reconciling criminal investigation with protection of the individual's privacy.

He almost fainted on the spot.

Instead, he listened carefully and made detailed notes as she gave him the name and address of the subscriber someone had called from the offices of Summerville and Hope at 333 Heron Street in Calusa on March twenty-fourth at 11:51 A.M. And he listened in total amazement as dear Miss Finch in her appropriately squeaky, high-pitched, tiny-bird voice told him she would get to work immediately on compiling the names and addresses of anyone called from the residence of Matthew Hope on Whisper Key between Monday last week, the twenty-first of March, and Friday last week, the twenty-fifth of March, when he'd been shot outside a bar in Newtown.

And then, making the telephone company's unexpected transformation all suddenly clear and understandable, Miss Finch asked, "What is Mr. Hope's condition at the moment?"

Bloom knew many of the attorneys in town, but he wasn't familiar with the one Matthew had visited last Thursday afternoon. The sign outside the whitewashed cinder block building on the South Tamiami Trail read:

ARTHUR D'ALLESSANDRO
ATTORNEY AT LAW

A trim brunette wearing a tan suit and a pale lavender blouse with a stock tie sat behind a desk in a sparsely furnished outer office. Bloom told her who he was, said he had a two o'clock appointment with Mr. D'Allessandro, and then waited while she announced him to the inner office.

D'Allessandro was a sweaty little man in his mid-thirties, Bloom guessed, prematurely bald, wearing a dark brown suit too heavy for the climate; Bloom supposed he'd recently moved south, probably from someplace in the Midwest. He was growing a mustache, an attempt to add maturity to his pudgy little face. His fingers resembled small Vienna sausages. There was a college ring on his right hand. Bloom couldn't read the name of the school, but two framed diplomas were on the wall behind his desk, one from the University of Pennsylvania, the other from Ohio State.

"I must tell you at once exactly what I told Mr. Hope," he said. "That whatever transpired in this office between me and Peter Torrance was privileged communication."

"Oh, sure," Bloom said. "But that was before Mr. Hope got shot, hm?"

"I'm sorry he got shot, but . . ."

"Because now we're looking at attempted murder, hm?" Bloom said.

"If you suspect my client of . . ."

"Who said anything . . ."

". . . a crime, then I suggest . . ."

". . . about suspecting anybody? I'm here . . ."

"You're threatening me with . . ."

"No, I'm not."

". . . attempted . . ."

"I'm trying to find *out*, Counselor," Bloom said sharply, "why Matthew *Hope* was here. Because then maybe I can find out why someone tried to kill him. Now I can understand why you're protecting lawyer-client confidentiality, but surely that doesn't apply to whatever Mr. *Hope* said, does it? Or was *he* your client, too?"

D'Allessandro looked at him sourly. "*Can* you tell me why he was here?" Bloom asked reasonably.

"He was here," D'Allessandro said, "because someone told him Mr. Torrance had sought my advice."

"There," Bloom said, and spread his hands wide as if to say *See? That wasn't too difficult, was it*? "Who was the person who gave Mr. Hope this information?" he asked.

"A woman named Agnes Donovan."

"Told Mr. Hope that Torrance had sought your advice?"

"Yes."

"About what?"

"*That* is privileged."

"However, if Mr. Torrance had . . ."

"Privileged," D'Allessandro repeated.

"Do you think Torrance *may* have mentioned to Miss Donovan . . .?"

"*Mrs.* Donovan."

"Do you think he may have told her why he was coming here?"

"I have no idea what he told her or didn't tell her."

"Well, did Mr. *Hope* seem to know why Torrance had sought your advice?"

D'Allessandro said nothing.

"Did he?" Bloom asked.

D'Allessandro remained silent.

"Counselor," Bloom said, "why are you making me pull teeth here? I've got a friend in the hospital and I'm trying to find out who put him there. Whatever Matthew Hope said to you is *not* privileged communication. He was *not* your goddamn client! Now how about it? You want to play golf here, or you want to fuck around?"

D'Allessandro seemed ready to inform Bloom that in the state of Florida the use of open profanity or indecent or obscene language was a misdemeanor of the second degree, punishable by sixty days in the slammer. Instead, he controlled himself admirably, and said, "Mr. Hope came here with several suppositions. I can tell you what those were, but I can't affirm or deny the truth of them. I told him the same thing. I'm afraid his visit was a waste of time."

"What were the suppositions?"

"Apparently Mrs. Donovan had told him . . ."

"Did he say that?"

"Yes. She'd told him that Peter Torrance had come to see me regarding a will probated three years ago at the time of his wife's death."

"His *former* wife, you mean. Willa Torrance."

"It was Mr. Hope's supposition – and apparently he got this from Mrs. Donovan, and I am neither affirming nor denying the truth of it – it was *his* supposition that Mr. Torrance believed he was still married to Willa Torrance. And was therefore entitled to a fair share of her estate. As her spouse. At the time of her death."

"Can you tell me *exactly* what Mr. Hope said to you?"

"Well . . ."

"Please."

"He called me first, you know . . ."

"Yes."

"And asked if he could come by sometime that afternoon . . ."

"This was last Thursday?"

"A week ago today, yes. We set up an appointment for two that afternoon. He arrived a few minutes earlier. The problem of confidentiality came up almost at once. On the phone he'd told me only that he'd seen a woman named Agnes Donovan that morning, and hoped I could give him some time regarding a matter that had come up during the visit. But the moment he sat down . . ."

"Yes, tell me *exactly* what he said."

Bloom listened now as D'Allessandro described the meeting the week before, Matthew explaining that Agnes Donovan had been an aerial performer with the Steadman & Roeger Circus back when a man named Peter Torrance was marketing director, explaining further that she'd gone by the name of Aggie McCullough back then, a flyer with the trapeze act known as the Flying McCulloughs. It seemed that this morning she had told him that Peter Torrance was now claiming . . .

Well, the moment D'Allessandro heard the name of his client, he told Matthew at once that if this conversation was to be about Peter Torrance . . .

"No, no," Matthew assured him. "Merely about what he told Mrs. *Donovan*."

"I fail to see the distinction," D'Allessandro said dryly.

What Mrs. Donovan had been told – and what D'Allessandro then listened to despite his better judgment because his visitor was not only persuasive but seemingly somewhat *obsessed* – what the garrulous Peter Torrance had told Aggie Donovan was that he'd never been informed of Willa's intention to get a divorce, that she had gone down to the Dominican Republic on her own, without his knowledge, consent, or participation, that he'd received no notice beforehand *or* afterward, was unaware of any publication of notice, and did not in fact learn she was presumably no longer his wife until she killed herself eighteen years later, at which time all the newspapers referred to him as her *former* husband.

"In short," Matthew said, "Torrance is claiming his wife

obtained an *ex parte* divorce that is not a binding one. According to him, they were still married at the time of her death. Under Florida law, and as a surviving spouse, he now intends to elect a statutory share of her estate. At least, that's what Mrs. Donovan told me."

"You understand I can neither affirm nor deny that."

"Of course. You're aware, though, that in Florida, the statutory share is thirty percent of the fair market value of the net estate."

"Yes, I'm aware of that," D'Allessandro said.

"The major part of Willa Torrance's estate was her fifty-percent share of the Steadman & Roeger Circus."

D'Allessandro said nothing.

"Which Willa left entirely to her daughter."

He still said nothing.

"In short," Matthew said, "Peter Torrance is going for thirty percent of that."

"If all of this is what Mrs. Donovan told you . . ."

"It's what she told me. Well, not the part about the will. I knew that part already."

"And if it's true," D'Allessandro said, "which I can neither . . ."

". . . affirm nor deny," Matthew said.

". . . affirm nor deny," D'Allessandro said, nodding, "what would you – as an experienced Florida attorney – advise Mr. Torrance?"

"If I were representing him, do you mean?"

"Yes. You understand, I'm new in Calusa."

"Oh? Where from?"

"Pittsburgh."

"Nice city."

"Cold."

"I'd advise him that he's too late. Section 732.212 gives him four months from the date of first publication to file for elect – "

"There was no publication."

"Or so he claims."

"He knew nothing about any divorce."

"Please understand, Mr. D'Allessandro, I'm not here to discuss whether or not Mr. Torrance has a case. My personal opinion is that he doesn't, but you're his attorney, not me."

"Then why *are* you here, Mr. Hope?"

"Because I think Willa Torrance was murdered."

"And what, if anything, does my client have to do with the murder of his wife?"

"His *former* wife."

"According to *her*. According to *him*, they were never properly divorced, and he's entitled to thirty percent of her estate."

"Don't you think it's ironic," Matthew said, "that I've been telling people all over town – even people *out* of town, for that matter, people in *Missouri*, for that matter – that there's been a challenge to Willa Torrance's will, and here it turns out . . ."

"Peter Torrance isn't *challenging* the will. He knows the will is valid. He's claiming . . ."

D'Allessandro cut himself short, apparently remembering the lawyer-client confidentiality he'd earlier defended to the death.

"He's claiming he was improperly cut out of it," Matthew said. "Sure. Even so, I find it ironic."

"I still don't know why you're here," D'Allessandro said.

"I'm here because shortly after Willa's death, Peter came to see Maria Torrance . . ."

"His daughter," D'Allessandro said.

"Maria Torrance," Matthew repeated, "and asked if he'd been left anything in his former wife's . . ."

"No, *not* former," D'Allessandro said. "They were never divorced. The divorce wasn't binding."

"Be that as it may . . ."

"Be that as it *is*."

"Have it your way," Matthew said. "The fact is he came to see Maria three years ago to ask if he'd been named in the will. And now he's surfaced again, and he's claiming thirty percent of the estate. I'd like to talk to him, Mr. D'Allessandro."

"Why?"

"I'd like to ask him if he was in Missouri on the night Willa Torrance got killed."

"I see. You think he killed her, do you?"

"I don't know who killed her."

"Why do you feel it's your obligation to find out?"

"I don't."

"Because that would seem to be a job for the police, wouldn't you say?"

"Yes, I would."

"Then why . . .?"

"Because I don't believe anyone should get away with murder."

"I don't admire amateur detectives, Mr. Hope."

"I don't admire amateurs of *any* sort."

"Then why are you chasing . . .?"

"I admire murderers even less," Matthew said. "Can you tell me where to find Torrance?"

D'Allessandro's office was silent now.

Bloom watched him across the desk, wondering whether he'd told Matthew what he wanted to know, wondering if he would now compromise confidentiality and tell a police officer where to find Torrance. The silence lengthened.

"As I told your friend, I'm new in town," D'Allessandro said at last. "I had to take the Florida bar exam twice before I finally passed it last year. On the money we got for the house in Pittsburgh, I figure we can hold out down here for another six months at most, till I get started, establish a clientele, make a name for myself. I'm a fair enough lawyer, but I'm no great shakes. I wasn't in the top ten of my class, I wasn't *Law Review*, nothing spectacular like that. But I was earning a decent living in Pittsburgh, and I liked it up there. It was my wife who wanted to move down here, I don't appreciate this kind of heat, I really don't. She's four months pregnant with our first child right now, and I've got, what, half a dozen clients I'm working for on a contingency basis? Peter Torrance is one of them. I don't want him running for the hills. If you ask me does he have a case, I'd have to answer who the hell knows? In Pittsburgh, I'd have told him to take a walk. But this isn't Pittsburgh. If I win this one, there may be a little money in it for me. I'm living on borrowed money here and borrowed time, Detective Bloom. If I don't make it in the next six months, we'll have to pack it in and head back north."

D'Allessandro stopped.

For a moment, Bloom thought that was it.

Instead, he took a deep breath.

"Your friend Hope," he said, "seems to have the time and money to run around playing detective . . ."

"I assure you he doesn't."

"It seemed that way to me."

"It seemed that way to me, too," Bloom said. "Once."

"He comes here wanting to know where my client's staying. He only *suspects* Willa Torrance was murdered, but even if she was . . ."

"But *if* she was, and if her killer is *still* . . ."

"Oh, *please*, Detective, someone gets murdered every hour of the day in this country! There are thousands of killers running around loose all over the place, but *I'm* not out there trying to catch them, am I? Maybe your friend wouldn't have got shot if he'd paid more attention to lawyering instead of . . ."

"Maybe so. But maybe that's why it's important."

D'Allessandro looked puzzled.

"Did you give him Torrance's address?" Bloom asked.

"I did not."

"Will you give it to me now?"

"I will not."

"You're starting on the wrong foot down here," Bloom said, and stood up.

"Who cares?" D'Allessandro said. "I like Pittsburgh better, anyway."

"Good. Because what I'm going to do the minute I leave here is head for the State Attorney's Office, where I'll ask for a grand jury subpoena ordering you to reveal the local address of Peter Torrance."

"Such a subpoena might be seen by some courts as intruding on attorney-client privilege."

"Fine. You move to have it quashed, Counselor. Maybe you'll enjoy litigating this."

"I'm sure I won't. But tell me something, Detective Bloom . . . what makes you think the shooting in Newtown is in any way related to Peter Torrance? Is it your contention that Mr. Hope went to see him?"

"I consider that a definite possibility, yes."

"And you're asking me to breach lawyer-client confidentiality on such a flimsy supposition? Forget it. My regard for the law isn't quite that slight. The fact is, I did not reveal my client's whereabouts to Matthew Hope, and you don't have a scintilla of evidence to show that he ever even *found* Peter Torrance."

"Fine. I'll go get my subpoena. Meanwhile, don't leave for Pittsburgh."

"Oh, I've still got six months," D'Allessandro said airily. "But you're a detective, Mr. Bloom. Wouldn't it be easier and quicker to find Torrance some other way?"

Bloom knew he could get the subpoena he'd threatened, but he also know that if D'Allessandro moved to quash it, the ensuing litigation would consume more time than he chose to spend getting a lousy address. He was delighted, therefore, to find Miss Finch's promised list waiting on his desk when he got back to the office.

Matthew had made a great many calls from his home in the week before he'd been shot. Most of these were to his office; Cynthia Huellen confirmed that he'd called in frequently to check on his telephone messages. Many of them were to the State Attorney's Office and/or to Patricia Demming's home on Fatback Key; Patricia confirmed that he called her often, sometimes three or four times a day. Others were to people they already knew he'd later visited: George Steadman, Maria Torrance, Andrew Byrd, John Rafferty. The calls to Brandenton were the ones that most interested Bloom.

The first of these had been made early Thursday morning. The next one had been made on that same Thursday at 3:10 P.M., an hour and ten minutes after Matthew's meeting with D'Allessandro. Figuring the meeting had lasted some forty-five minutes, Bloom calculated that he'd made the call the moment he got back to his house on Whisper Key. The next call was to the same number, not a minute later. And then another call to that same number a minute after that.

The number in Bradenton was listed to a man named Harry Donovan, whom D'Allessandro had identified as Aggie McCullough's husband. Bloom dialed the number and waited while it rang. Once, twice, three times, four . . .

"Hello?"

A woman's voice.

"Hello, this is Detective Bloom, Calusa Police Department," he said. "Am I speaking to Mrs. Donovan?"

"Yes?"

"Mrs. Donovan, I'm calling about several telephone calls a man named Matthew Hope made to you last . . ."

"How *is* he?" she asked at once.

"He's fine, thank you," Bloom said, not knowing at all whether he really was, but not wanting to waste time talking about Matthew's condition. "Mrs. Donovan, he called you four times last Thursday. One at eight fifty-seven in the morning . . ."

"Yes."

"Three more at ten past three, and eleven past three, and twelve past three. Do you remember him calling you?"

"Yes, I do. I was so *shocked* when I heard what . . ."

"I wonder if you can tell me what these various calls were about?"

"Do you have any idea who did it yet?"

"No, ma'am, not yet. Do you remember your conversations with him?"

"Of course, I do. I'd seen him just that morning. That was what the first call was about. To set up a time for him to come over. We had a long talk here. I was really surprised when he called back."

"Why was he calling, ma'am?"

"He wanted to know if I'd possibly heard from Peter again. He was still trying to find him, you see."

"Had he asked you *earlier* how he could find him?"

"Yes, that morning. While he was here. I told him Peter was staying in Calusa someplace, but I didn't know where. I suggested that he call Peter's lawyer, see if he could help."

"Arthur D'Allessandro?"

"Yes. On the Trail."

"And *had* you heard from Mr. Torrance again?"

"No, I hadn't."

"Then you still didn't know where he was staying."

"No, I didn't."

"Is that all Mr. Hope wanted?"

"Yes, that's all. I'm sorry I couldn't help him. He seemed like a very nice man. I hope . . ."

"Do you know whether Mr. Torrance is still in town?"

"I'm sorry, I don't."

"Would you do me a favor, please?"

"Sure."

"If he does call again, would you ask him where he can be reached? And then call me right away?"

"Is he in some kind of trouble?"

"No, no," Bloom said at once. "I was just hoping I could talk to him."

"What about?" Aggie asked.

The tone of her voice had suddenly changed. He knew at once that if Torrance *did* call, she would tell him the police were looking for him. There was that in her voice. However long ago her relationship with him had been, however trivial it might have been, there was still some attachment, Seattle still held a place somewhere in her heart. He was sorry now that he'd called.

"Let me give you the number here," he said, and reeled it off before she could ask again what he wanted to talk to Torrance about. "Detective Morris Bloom," he said, "just ask for me."

"Do you think Peter shot him?" she asked.

"No, ma'am," he said. "We don't know who shot him."

"But you think Peter did," she said, and hung up.

Bloom looked at the list of calls again.

The next call Matthew had made last Thursday was to Warren Chambers.

Bloom pulled the phone to him at once, and dialed the number. Warren picked up on the second ring.

"Warren," Bloom said, "this is Morrie. I've got Matthew calling you at a quarter past three last Thursday. What was that all about?"

"He wanted to know if I could lend him a tape recorder."

"What do you mean?"

"Something he could use to tape a person without the person's knowledge."

Bloom was silent for what seemed an eternity.

"Morrie?" Warren said.

"Why didn't you tell me this?"

"I just didn't think about it."

"*Did* you lend him one?"

"I dropped a NAGRA reel-to-reel at his house."

"Gave it to him personally?"

"No, he wasn't home. I left it inside the kitchen screen door."

"When was this?"

"Thursday afternoon sometime. Five, six o'clock. In there."

"Did he say who he was planning to tape?"

"No."

"Did you ask?"

"No. Morrie, I didn't know he was gonna get *shot* the next night."

"You know it now. You should have told me about this."

"I'm sorry, I wasn't thinking."

"Man borrows a fucking NAGRA . . ."

"I'm sorry."

"Plans to go in someplace *wired*, how the hell could you possibly . . .?"

"Please," Warren said.

"Okay."

"I'm sorry."

"Okay. We all make mistakes," Bloom said, and then told him about the one he himself had just made.

"I got a call from Bloom two minutes ago," Warren told her. "I fucked up."

"How?"

"Forgot to tell him Matthew borrowed a NAGRA from me."

"When?"

"Last Thursday."

"You fucked up, all right."

"Yeah, rub it in."

"Who was he planning to tape?"

"I don't know."

"Didn't you *ask*?"

"No."

"Great work, Warren."

The phone went silent.

"But not the end of the world," she said.

Warren sighed.

"You hear me?"

"I hear you," he said. "Anyway, Bloom's got his people running checks on all the hotels, motels, and B&Bs in Calusa . . ."

"What for?"

"He's trying to get a lead on Torrance. Meanwhile, he just had a bad experience on the phone with Aggie McCullough . . ."

"What kind of bad experience?"

"He thinks he may have stepped into a tip-off."

"What do you mean?"

"She claims she doesn't know where Torrance is staying, but Bloom's not sure she's telling the truth. He's afraid she'll tell Torrance we're looking for him. He wants us to go see these next two in person."

"What next two? What are you talking about, Warren?"

"Matthew made a lot of calls from his house last week. Some of them were to people we've been tracking."

"Like who?"

"Aggie McCullough, for one."

"Never met the lady."

"Matthew went to see her last week."

"And the other two?"

"Jeannie Byrd and . . ."

"I'll take Jeannie," Toots said.

"How come?"

"So *you* won't take her."

"Don't you even want to know who the other one is?"

"No. Who is she?"

"Maria Torrance."

The offices of Hair and Now were situated in a building that had been designed by one of Calusa's better-known architects.

Meant to look like an old Spanish Colonial monastery, it resembled instead a pink and blue three-story office complex – which was what it actually happened to be.

The original intention had been to rent the street-level spaces as shops, but the architect had cleverly designed the building so that there were no display windows on the street side. Well, after all, did a monastery have any reason to display lingerie, bangles, or beads? Instead, to reach the shops, you first had to go inside the building, where they were arrayed around an interior cloister. From outside on the sidewalk, you never knew there were any shops in there at all. Unless you chanced to read the ladder of signs announcing the building's occupants. Which Warren did before he headed around the cloister to the largest office compound on the ground floor.

The walls of Hair and Now's curving, all-white reception area were hung with huge color photographs of women wearing different hairstyles in different colors. Warren wondered if Hair and Now was a beauty salon. He didn't see any women sitting around in blue smocks, though, their heads under dryers. He went to the reception desk, told the woman there who he was, said Miss Torrance was expecting him, and waited as she picked up the phone and tried to locate her.

A door the color of cotton candy opened at the far end of the room. Warren glanced toward it as a young black girl in a purple mini and a white blouse came breezing through, dropped some papers on the receptionist's desk, smiled at Warren, and breezed out again. He hadn't seen any women in curlers beyond that pink door, either. The receptionist was trying another extension. Warren began wandering the room. To the right of each photograph was a chic little clear plastic label lettered in black, identifying the color and style of the model's hairdo. Sunset Brown Cascade. Autumn Blond French Twist. Red Mahogany Poodle. Winter Wheat Wedge. Oak Brown Shag. Garnet Gold Bouff . . .

"Mr. Chambers?"

Warren turned.

"Miss Torrance is in the shipping department just now. She said if you'd care to join her there . . ."

"Yes, I would."

"It's just through the pink door, to the end of the hall, and then a sharp right. It's a huge room, you can't miss it."

"Thank you," Warren said, and walked to the pink door she'd indicated, and opened it, and walked down a hallway of small offices with wide-open doors. In each of the offices, someone was either on the telephone or sitting before a computer screen. There was an air of hectic activity, men and women placing calls and taking orders, telephones ringing, cursors blinking. From one of the offices, the black girl in the purple mini smiled and waggled her fingers at him. He returned the smile and went on by. At the end of the corridor, he made the sharp right as instructed and found himself in a truly vast room at one end of which was a loading bay, its doors open to the blinding sunlight outside. The room was furnished with long tables upon which sat what appeared to be . . . *wigs*?

Yep, that's what they were, wigs in various colors and various hairstyles, many of which he recognized from the photos lining the reception area. The wigs sat on polymer molds shaped like human heads and marbleized like John Grisham book jackets. There were wigs everywhere he looked, in every hair shade and style he could imagine. At each of the tables, women in blue smocks but no curlers stood packing into wooden boxes the multitude of manes on their eyeless, lipless, marbleized molds. The boxes, taller than they were wide, seemed designed expressly to accommodate them. A helper in a similar blue smock stuffed little Styrofoam pellets into each box, guaranteeing a safe and uneventful journey for each marbleized head and the wig topping it. Over near the loading bay, silhouetted by the sharp sunlight that streamed through the open doors, a man with a clipboard was in earnest conversation with a redheaded woman. The entire scene seemed to Warren like something out of a James Bond movie.

Maria Torrance had been described by Toots as a tall, blue-eyed, zaftig redhead who did cocaine. The woman standing silhouetted in sunlight at the far end of the room was indeed tall – five-nine, if Warren was any judge – with long red hair falling straight to her shoulders. She turned as Warren approached, her blue eyes flashing sunlight, and immediately walked toward him, leaving the man with the clipboard standing abandoned for a moment before he went outside to supervise the loading of some very large wooden crates.

"Mr. Chambers?" she said, and extended her hand to him. She was wearing a clingy blue dress the color of her eyes, confirming at first glance the "zaftig" label Toots had hung on her. The eyes were as clear and as cool as an arctic ice floe. She shook hands cordially, told Warren how sorry she was to learn about Mr. Hope's "accident," and repeated what she'd told him on the phone, that she was willing to help in any way possible.

"Though you caught me at a bad time, actually," she said. "We ship every two weeks, around the fifteenth and the end of the month."

"Those *are* wigs, aren't they?" Warren asked.

"Yes, that's our business, we make wigs. Hairpieces. Toupees. Rugs. Call them what you will. I'm wearing one myself, in fact."

Warren figured she was putting him on. He smiled, but made no comment.

"We ship all over the country," she said. "We've got distributors in every state, including Alaska."

Warren guessed that being bald *could* get cold away up there in Alaska. He was still wondering if she was really wearing a wig. Toots hadn't mentioned anything about a wig. Had Matthew known about it? When he'd gone to see her early last week, had *he* discovered she was wearing a wig? If so, was she *bald* under the wig, or was her natural hair pinned up? He still figured she was putting him on.

"You told me on the phone that you're trying to locate my father," she said.

"Yes."

"Why is that?"

"We think Matthew . . . Mr. Hope . . . may have gone to see him."

"Why?"

"Well, we don't *know* why, actually."

"Who's we?"

"His associates."

"Do the police think so, too?"

"We're more or less working *with* the police."

"And you all believe Mr. Hope went to see my father?"

"That's where it seems to be leading."

"There's where what seems to be leading?"

"The investigation. We're walking in Matthew's footprints, you see. And he seemed to be trying to locate your father."

"I wonder why," she said, and shook her head.

"Miss Torrance?"

Maria turned toward the loading bay. The man with the clipboard was standing there again, without the clipboard this time, his hands on his hips.

"Yes, Jeff?" she said.

"Talk to you a minute, please?"

"Excuse me," she said, and walked over to him. She ducked her head under the overhead door, and stepped out onto the sidewalk. Both of them disappeared around the side of the truck. Warren walked over to one of the tables, stood there watching the women in their blue smocks packing the wigs into their tall boxes, stuffing the boxes with Styrofoam pellets. He picked up one of the molded marbleized heads, kept turning it over and over in his hands. Androgynous, with an aquiline nose, no eyes, and no lips, the polymer piece was smooth to his touch. It had a good heft to it, too. He realized it wasn't merely a shipping device, but something that could later serve as a permanent wig stand for the owner. In some homes, it could even pass for a piece of sculpture. Like his own ratty little aparment, for example. He wondered if he could buy one.

"Sorry," Maria said, coming up behind him and almost startling him into dropping the head. He put it back quickly on the tabletop. "There was a problem with one of the shipping labels," she explained. "Two hundred wigs going to a little town in Iowa by mistake. Instead of to Chicago. Do you think there are two hundred bald people in the entire state of Iowa?"

"Do you think there are two hundred *people* in the entire state of Iowa?" Warren said.

"Anyway, we caught it," Maria said. "Or rather, the trucker

caught it. I noticed you admiring one of our pedestals. They're quite attractive, don't you think?"

"Wouldn't mind owning one," Warren said. "Are they for sale?"

"I'm afraid not."

"Too bad."

"Sorry."

"No, no. Hey."

"Mr. Chambers," she said, abruptly changing the subject, "why do *you* think Mr. Hope was looking for my father?"

"I can only guess at that."

"And what's your guess?"

"He wanted to ask him whether he was in Missouri at the time of your mother's death."

"I see."

Behind her, men were at the long tables now, packing the wig boxes into larger wooden crates already in place on forklifts. The image persisted of a James Bond movie, a tall, voluptuous, blue-eyed redhead in a clinging blue dress standing loose-hipped in the foreground, men and women in lighter blue uniforms working like automatons behind her, boxes being packed into crates, forklifts moving the crates out to the loading bay, crates being hoisted into the trucks waiting in the sunlight beyond.

"Would you happen to know?" Warren asked.

"Know what, Mr. Chambers?"

"Whether your father was in Missouri when your mother died?"

"When she was *killed*, you mean. When Davey Sheed killed her."

Warren said nothing.

"Why was Mr. Hope looking for my father?" Maria said. "I *told* him it was Davey. Why was he wasting time . . .?"

"You still think Davey . . .?"

"Of course."

"Why?"

"Because my mother warned him to stay away from me."

"And you think that was reason enough for . . ."

"Reason enough."

"How so?"

"Because . . . never mind."

"Miss Torrance, if you really believe Davey Sheed . . ."

"I believe he did, yes. I believe he killed her. Because he and my mother were . . . involved, let's say, before he started up with me. And she knew the kind of man he was, and she warned me to stay away from him, and when that didn't work, she went to him."

"What kind of man was he?" Warren asked.

"An animal," Maria said. "King of All the Beasts, in every sense. I only learned that later. After it was too late. After she was dead. So you see, your Mr. Hope was after the wrong person. My father . . ."

"Matthew must have felt . . ."

"No, my father wasn't in Missouri that morning. Nor at any time during our stand in Rutherford. My father didn't come *anywhere* near us from the time he left my mother till the time he came to see me after her death."

"When was that, Miss Torrance?"

"The minute he heard she was dead. He wanted to know if he was in her will. He wanted to know if she'd left him anything."

"Where was this?"

"Right here in Calusa."

"And now he's back in Calusa."

"Not to my knowledge."

"He hasn't dropped in on you again?"

"No."

"Hasn't called you?"

"No."

"Yet he called Aggie McCullough," Warren said.

"He used to *love* Aggie once," Maria said. And then, somewhat wistfully, "He *never* loved me."

Jeannie Lawson Byrd was another young twerp.

Toots hated twenty-two-year-olds who lived in luxurious houses, lying on chaise lounges, reading romance novels, and eating bonbons. Twenty-two, twenty-three, anyway. Give or take a few months, she was the same age as Maria Torrance, who lived in yet *another* expensive house in yet another part of Calusa. One of them a redhead, the other a blonde. Warren had told her that Jeannie Byrd had virtually admitted a relationship with one of the eleven-year-old girls who'd been in Willa Torrance's act. There was a little girl, hmm? Hmmm, indeed. Warren hadn't believed her for a minute.

Willa had the nerve to tell me . . . how can I put this delicately? She accused me of doing to Maggie . . . one of the little girls. They both had black hair, did I mention that? For contrast. Like the skirts and blouses. She accused me of doing to Maggie . . . well . . . what the Munchkin wanted to do to Judy Garland. What the little girl asked the drummer to do to her. I asked her what made her think I needed advice from a shrimp *like her who was probably muffing those sweet little girls* herself, *Maggie and Connie,* both *of them, those were their names. I told her if she didn't get out of the trailer right that very minute I'd go get Davey and he'd stuff her head in Sadie's mouth and tell her to bite it off. I told her she might be half owner of S&R, but without Davey and his cats there'd be no goddamn circus at all! I think she got the message.*

That had been five years ago. Seventeen, eighteen at the time, whatever the hell. But Warren hadn't believed her, and Warren was an experienced investigator. So what *had* Jeannie and Willa battled about back then? It seemed too coincidental to Toots that three of the women Matthew had visited before the shooting had shared an intimate relationship with the King of All the Beasts. She was here to learn whether or not Peter Torrance had tried to contact Jeannie while he was here in Calusa. But if anything else came her way . . .

"Why would he try to contact *me*?" Jeannie asked.

They were in the greenhouse behind the main house. Jeannie wasn't eating bonbons, nor was she reading the latest piece of pulp paperback trash. Instead, she was potting plants, barefoot, wearing shorts and a T-shirt, and a long striped butcher's apron. Her slender fingers worked delicately among the blooms, picking off dead leaves and petals, molding moist earth around the stems of the plants.

"Did you know him back then?" Toots asked.

"Never met him. He was gone long before my season with

S&R. Everyone said he'd left Willa for Aggie McCullough years ago, ran off to Seattle with her."

"This was common knowledge, huh?"

"Oh, sure. Aggie was back with the circus by then, she and Willa were tighter than Dick's hatband."

"Any idea why he left Willa?"

"Rumor had it that she was sleeping with an aerialist who used to hang by his hair."

"Would that have been Barney Hale?"

"I really don't remember his name. You know how circuses are."

"No, I don't. How are they?"

"Trapeze artists aren't the only things that fly. Rumors carry on the wind. You hear this, you hear that. Next day, you hear something else. It's all very incestuous," she said, and looked up over the potted petunias, or whatever the hell they were. "Do you understand what I'm saying? A circus is a very tight, enclosed, claustrophobic community. Everybody knows everybody else's business, everybody's poking his nose into everybody else's affairs."

"Affairs?"

"Well, yes. Literally."

"Uh-huh."

"There," Jeannie said, and stepped back to admire her handiwork.

Toots was wondering if this might not be an opportune time to explore some of these incestuous relationships running rampant with the elephants and horses.

"I understand," she said, and cleared her throat, "that you knew Davey Sheed pretty well."

"I knew *everybody* pretty well," Jeannie said, and cocked an eyebrow, and smiled knowingly, and reached for another leafy, flowering plant in a pot. Toots suddenly wished she knew the names of plants. This suddenly seemed an alarming gap in her education. Then again, she could tell you each and every nickname for cocaine. Snow or Peruvian lady or blow or white gir—

"How well did *Willa* know him?" she asked, biting the bullet.

"I haven't the foggiest."

A lie, Toots thought. In a class with *Believe it or not* and *I'll be perfectly honest with you*.

"Never any rumors circulating about that, huh?"

"None that I heard."

"Nothing flying on the wind, huh?"

"Nothing."

"How about the daughter?"

"The daughter?"

"Maria. Was *she* sleeping with Mr. Tiger Piss?"

Jeannie looked up from the pot, a dead leaf in her hand.

"Not that I know of."

"Just you, then, huh?"

"I don't believe I said I was."

"Oh. I thought you said you knew *everybody* pretty well."

"Yes, that's what I said."

"Forgive me, I thought that was a euphemism."

"I don't know what euphemism means."

"It means saying 'pretty well' when you mean 'fucking,'" Toots said, and looked her dead in the eye. "As I understand this, Mrs. Byrd, the night you and Willa had your big to-do, you were in Davey Sheed's trailer."

"That's right."

"In your bra and panties, is what I was given to understand."

"Mr. Chambers is garrulous, I see."

"I don't know what garrulous means," Toots said.

Jeannie pulled a face.

"So, uh, I don't mean to pry," Toots said, "but we've got someone in the hospital, you see, and a lot of shit seems to be pointing toward the great white hunter. The way we have it, Sheed was training more than cats. You already told Warren . . ."

"I find it easier talking to men than to women," Jeannie said.

"Well, try me," Toots said. "*Was* Willa sleeping with the cat man?"

"I told you. I haven't the . . ."

"Foggiest, right. And that goes for the daughter, too, right?"

"I hardly knew the daughter."

"That wasn't my question."

"I have no idea who the daughter was sleeping with. She was only seventeen at the time."

"So were you," Toots said. "What'd you and Willa fight about that night in Alabama?"

"I already told Mr. Chambers . . ."

"Could you tell me, too, please?"

Jeannie took a deep breath.

"She accused me of unseemly behavior with one of the little girls in her act."

"Maggie, right?"

"Maggie, yes."

"Which is just what you told Warren."

"Yes. And that's the God's honest truth."

Believe it or not, Toots thought.

A ghetto is a ghetto, Bloom figured, regardless of how it looks.

Calusa's black neighborhood was called Newtown, and its wintertime look wasn't at all like that of the South Bronx, or Manhattan's Harlem or Brooklyn's Bed-Stuy. As Bloom drove through searching for the 1100 block on L Street, he saw no crumbling tenements, no graffiti-assaulted walls, no soot-stained, urine-stained banks of snow, no heaps of black-bagged garbage waiting for pickup someday, no old men warming their hands and staring into fires in sawed-off oil drums.

This was Florida.

And here in Newtown, at four on a Thursday afternoon in March, there was pale sunshine and palm trees, and flowering bushes, and houses with lawns, and children riding around on bicycles and skateboards. Most of the houses were small and constructed of wood siding with asphalt shingle roofs. Some of them were badly in need of paint, but none of them were ramshackle. A few of the lawns could have used a trim, but for the most part, the neighborhood looked tidy and neat. Most of the people living in Newtown were black. There were some

Hispanics and Asians as well, yes, but no white people lived here. The thing that made this a ghetto, Bloom figured, was that the people who lived here *had* to live here.

Oh, sure, in a democracy you could live anywhere you liked, certainly. There was no reason why any of the blacks living here in Newtown couldn't buy a house on Flamingo Key tomorrow, for example – provided they had the five hundred thousand dollars or more such a house would cost. But, you see, the blacks living here in Newtown couldn't in their wildest dreams ever *hope* to live on any of Calusa's eminently desirable keys, ever *hope* to buy into any of the mainland's luxurious condos. Yes, there were black lawyers and even a black judge in Calusa, and there were black doctors and black bank tellers and black dental hygienists, and other black professionals with high-salaried jobs – but none of them lived in Newtown. And now and again, yes, true, you found a black car salesman or department-store clerk living in Newtown, but for the most part, the small, affordable houses here were owned or rented by blacks who worked in any of the so-called *service* occupations, the gardeners, dishwashers, cleaning women, garbagemen, busboys, all the others who performed menial labor that required long hours and paid short wages.

There was a lot of crime in Newtown.

When dreams are denied a huge portion of the populace, those dreams will be sought elsewhere. There's instant gratification in a crack pipe, you see, true democracy to be found in the smoking of cocaine. Anyone – black, brown, white, yellow, red, purple, blue – can journey to the moon for the price of a hit. But selling crack and doing crack are crimes – yeah, sorry about that, Bloom thought. And they foster yet other crimes, because the lotus-eaters need money to support their habits, and no gardener in the state of Florida earns enough to keep a full-time crack habit going. Therefore the gun.

Bloom wished he had a nickel for every gun on the streets of Newtown. One of those guns had seriously wounded Matthew Hope last Friday night, right here in this black part of town. And now a white man named Peter Torrance had been located in a rooming house on L Street. Bloom hadn't called ahead.

Bad enough the desk clerk had already been alerted by the canvassing phone call from the police.

He parked the unmarked sedan in front of what had been a small hotel when Calusa was a smaller, friendlier place, long before this part of the city was renamed Newtown. Back then when the Shelby Arms was built, this section of town was simply called Temple's Fields after a landowner named Jason Temple, who'd owned all of the acreage running from Berringer Road to the bayfront. It wasn't until 1937 that the Hannah Lewis School of Art was built on the site of what had been Jason Temple's main house on what was by then called merely *Temple* Field, the possessive having been dropped years ago. This name, too, was promptly changed to Newtown, by unanimous vote of the city council.

Newtown.

New town indeed.

A brand-new town with a new grid pattern for streets on what had once been soybean fields bordered by scrub oak and cabbage palm, A to R running west to east, the names of presidents for the wider north-to-south roads. A new art school with four hundred and twenty students, for whom five wooden dormitories were built just this side of the Tamiami Trail. New shops and markets, and a new hotel as a convenience to the students' parents, who enjoyed coming down to see the kids, especially during those brutal winter months up north.

Well, the area turned almost exclusively black after a fire demolished the art school and three of the dormitories. The school never reopened. It was rumored that it had been in financial trouble before the fire, and that the fire had been deliberately set. The remaining two dormitories were purchased by a man who converted them into storage sheds for his lumberyard. The Shelby Arms survived, though now there were no parents of art students to inhabit it. Instead, it became first an inexpensive hotel for the rare black couple who wandered down to Florida on vacation, and next a haven for color-blind hippies who liked the easy proximity to Newtown marijuana, and finally – after the hippies disappeared and after it was possible for blacks to check into any Holiday Inn anywhere in America – the place became a rooming house still called the Shelby Arms, but operating now almost exclusively for the convenience of hookers and their johns. Why Peter Torrance had chosen the place was a question Bloom intended to ask – if in fact the man was still here.

The desk clerk said Mr. Torrance was out just now.

Bloom asked if he had *checked* out.

The desk clerk, a rake-thin man of uncertain heritage, with pale blue eyes and skin the color of tea, told Bloom that if he'd meant to say *checked* out he'da *said* checked out. What he'd said was that Mr. Torrance was out just *now*. Bloom hadn't yet flashed the tin. He still didn't. He told the clerk he would wait. From the newspaper articles he'd read about Willa's death, he had some idea what Peter Torrance would look like. Besides, he suspected not too many white men would be coming through the doors of the Shelby Arms. Prepared to wait however long it might take, he sat in a red velveteen easy chair opposite the desk. The chair had seen better days.

At twenty minutes past six, just as dusk was beginning to settle upon the street outside, a tall, angular man wearing a white suit out of a Tennessee Williams play came up the front steps to the hotel, walked into the lobby and over to the desk, and asked for his key. Bloom knew at once that this was Peter Torrance. He rose from the threadbare easy chair, approached the man as he was turning, key in hand, and said, "Mr. Torrance?"

The man's pale blue eyes opened wide in a gaunt but still handsome face. Remembering the newspaper articles, Bloom figured Torrance for a man in his fifties, but he looked a good decade or more older. Perhaps it was the very pale face, unusual for this part of the country, or perhaps it was the faintest sign of graying beard on that face, the sort of whiskery trace you saw on men too old or too tired to shave every morning, an echo of the spiky white thinning hair on his head. Or perhaps it was the anachronistic white suit, rumpled and graying, or the matching scuffed white sneakers. Or perhaps it was the fact that he was wearing a white shirt without a tie, the top button unbuttoned. The total effect was one of a beachcomber. Perhaps an alcoholic beachcomber. Bloom no longer had to ask what Torrance was doing in a fleabag like the Shelby Arms.

"Mr. Torrance?" he asked again.

"Who are you?" the man said.

"Detective Morris Bloom, Calusa Police," he said, and showed his shield. "Are you Mr. Torrance?"

"What is this?"

"Some questions I'd like to ask you," Bloom said.

The man turned to the desk clerk.

"What is this?" he asked him.

The desk clerk shrugged.

The man turned back to Bloom.

"I'm Peter Torrance," he said. "What do you want?"

"Few questions I'd like to ask you."

"What kind of questions?"

"How long have you been here, Mr. Torrance?"

"Why do you want to know that?"

"Routine investigation," Bloom said.

"Why am I in a routine investigation?"

"Do you know a man named Matthew Hope?"

Torrance blinked.

"We think a man named Matthew Hope was trying to make contact with you. Can you tell me whether he did or not?" Bloom asked, and noticed that the desk clerk was listening intently. "Let's go outside, okay?" he told Torrance. "Find a place we can talk."

"Well, all right," Torrance said reluctantly. "But I must tell you . . ."

"Be easier outside, okay?" Bloom said, and took Torrance's arm and gently guided him toward a pair of French doors that opened onto an unkempt garden at the rear of the hotel. They sat on a curving stone bench in the waning sunlight. The bench was considerably more comfortable than the easy chair inside. Flowering shrubs grew rampant everywhere. The last of the sun's rays slanted in through trees hanging moss.

"*Did* Matthew Hope ever reach you?" Bloom asked.

"I don't know anyone by that name."

"Sure?"

"Positive."

"How long have you been here, Mr. Torrance?"

"Since the twentieth. Why?"

"Are you here on business or pleasure?"

"I came here to see an old friend."

"On business or pleasure?"

"I was passing through, I thought I'd drop in to say hello."

"Passing through from where?"

"I came over from Miami."

"What were you doing in Miami?"

"Taking the sun."

Bloom looked at his face.

"How long were you there?"

"Three or four days."

"And you came here on the twentieth," Bloom said.

"Yes. On the twentieth."

Five days before Matthew got shot, Bloom thought.

"Excuse me, Detective – Bloom, is it?"

"Bloom, yes."

"Excuse me, but I really *would* like to know what this is all about."

"Who was the friend you dropped in on?"

"A woman named Aggie Donovan. Now, listen, *really*. I refuse to answer any more questions till you tell me . . ."

"Mr. Torrance, an attorney named Matthew Hope was seriously wounded last Friday night outside a bar not seven blocks from here. The day before, he had gone to see an attorney named Arthur D'Allessandro, hoping to get your address from him. We're wondering now . . ."

"I know nothing at all about any of this."

"Mr. D'Allessandro didn't call to tell you . . .?"

"He did not."

"How about Mrs. Donovan?"

"I don't understand the question."

"Have you spoken to her recently?"

"Not since I visited her last week."

"When last week was that?"

"Last . . . Monday, I believe it was."

"And you haven't spoken to her since?"

"No."

"Did you mention to her that you were seeing a lawyer here?"

"Yes, I did."

"Did you tell her why?"

"No."

"You didn't mention that you intended to elect a statutory share of your former wife's . . ."

"We were never properly divorced," Torrance said.

". . . a statutory share of her estate? You didn't mention this to Mrs. Donovan?"

"No, I don't think so."

"Didn't tell her that you were looking for thirty percent of the estate?"

"I really don't remember."

"This was only last *Monday*, and you don't remember?"

"We're old friends, we talked about a lot of things."

"Mrs. Donovan seems to think you told her all that. At least, that's what she reported to Matthew Hope."

Torrance sat in silence for a moment, a pale wraith in the lengthening shadows, his hands clasped, his head bent, looking down at the cracked and crumbling flagstones that formed a path to the bench.

"I may have told her that," he said at last.

"Whether you told her or not," Bloom said, "it *is* true, isn't it? That's why you went to see Mr. D'Allessandro, isn't it?"

"Actually . . . well, yes."

"Did Matthew Hope eventually find you, sir?"

"No, I don't know anyone by that name, I'm sorry."

"Mr. Torrance . . . were you in a town named Rutherford, Missouri, on or about the eleventh of May, three years ago?"

"If you're asking whether I was there when Willa killed herself, I was not."

"You know when she killed herself, do you?"

"Yes, of course, I do. Mr. Bloom, I want you to know that I'm answering your questions only because you seem to believe I had something to do with the shooting of this Hope person you keep mentioning. I want to repeat that I do not *know* the man, I've never *met* the man, and I had *nothing* whatever to do with his shooting, *whenever* that may have been."

"Last Friday night," Bloom said. "The twenty-fifth."

"Whenever."

"Were you anywhere near the Centaur Bar & Grill that night? That's on Roosevelt and G."

"I don't know of any such place."

"Were you anywhere near the circus grounds in Rutherford, Missouri, on the night Willa shot herself?"

"What's one thing got to do with the other?"

"That's what I'm trying to find out."

"Well, I'm afraid I can't help you there. As you just said, Willa shot *herself*. From what I can gather, Mr. Hope was shot by someone *else*. If you're seeking a link somehow . . ."

"I'm trying to learn *why* he was shot, Mr. Torrance. On the day before the shooting, he went to your lawyer's office to ask questions about *you*. Presumably because you're seeking thirty percent of Willa Torrance's estate. What I want to know . . ."

"We were never divorced. I'm *entitled* to a proper share of the estate."

"But there wouldn't *be* an estate if she was still alive, would there?"

"If she chose to kill herself, that's none of my affair. I was not there at the time."

"When *were* you there?"

"Not when she killed herself. Mr. Bloom . . . let me get something straight, may I?"

"Sure."

"Are you attempting to reopen Willa's case?"

"Not unless it's tied to Matthew Hope's shooting."

"I do not *know* this fucking person! You're really upsetting me, Mr. Bloom," he said, and abruptly stood up. "If you have any *real* police business here, perhaps you'd better arrest me. Otherwise . . ."

"Otherwise I can go to the State Attorney for a grand jury subpoena," Bloom said.

Torrance blinked again.

The ploy hadn't worked with D'Allessandro, but D'Allessandro was a lawyer, and Torrance wasn't.

"A subpoena?" he said. "What the hell for?"

"To order your testimony before a grand jury."

"*What* testimony?"

"Regarding the shooting of Matthew Hope."

"I've told you a hundred fucking *times* . . ."

"Shall I go make application, Mr. Torrance? Or can we talk quietly and peacefully here in this lovely little garden?"

Torrance let out his breath in hissing exasperation. Seething, he sat on the stone bench again, and clasped his hands again, tightly now, as if constraining them.

"What do you want to know?" he said.

"Were you anywhere near the circus grounds on that date?"

"No, I wasn't. Willa's case was a suicide, Mr. Bloom. If you're trying to . . ."

"Matthew Hope didn't think so."

"Fuck Matthew Hope. He doesn't work for the Rutherford Police, does he? Or the Rutherford Coroner's Office? *They* determined . . ."

"Did the Rutherford police discuss Willa's case with you?"

"No. Why would they? I was nowhere *near* Rutherford when Willa took her own life."

"Where were you?"

"Gone by then."

"So you *were* in Rutherford *before* then."

"All right, let's get this over with," Torrance said, shaking his head in utter disbelief, making no effort to conceal his extreme impatience and annoyance. Clenching and unclenching his fists as if struggling not to strike this impossible *boor* who had no right to be questioning him this way about an event that had taken place in ancient times – all of three years ago – he said, "I was there, yes. But I was gone before . . ."

"When would that have been, Mr. Torrance?"

"I got there several days before she killed herself," he said, the words forcing themselves from a tight-lipped mouth, the voice constricted and angry.

Bloom was unaffected.

"What were you doing there, Mr. Torrance?"

"I have friends there. I have friends all over. When I was with the circus, I knew anyone of importance in any town we showed. I was there to see some old friends."

"And coincidentally, the circus was there at the same time, is that it?"

Torrance said nothing. Just kept clenching and unclenching his hands, not deigning to look at Bloom.

"Do you remember the *dates* you were there?"

"I told you. I arrived three or four days before her death."

"That would've made it the seventh, the eighth, around then."

"If you say so."

"And you left when?"

"The day before she shot herself."

"Did the Rutherford police know this?"

"I have no idea."

"No one ever questioned you about your presence there?"

"Not until this *moment*," Torrance said.

"Mr. Torrance," Bloom said, "did you happen to see Willa while you were there in Rutherford?"

"Yes, I did. So what?"

"When did you see her?"

"I don't recall the date."

"What was the purpose of your visit?"

"I'd heard certain things while moving around . . ."

"What do you mean, moving around?"

"Visiting old friends here and there. In circus towns I used to visit."

"What things did you hear?"

"Things I thought Willa should know."

"Like what?"

"If I tell you, Mr. Bloom, will this be the end? Can we then *end* this stupid . . .?"

"What things did you hear, Mr. Torrance?"

"I heard . . ."

"Yes?"

"Well, I heard . . ."

Bloom waited.

"I heard there was a little *girl*, you see."

What it got *down* to . . .

There was a little *girl*, you see, who was doing a little *girl*.

In other words . . .

Wee Willa Winkie was doing cocaine.

When Bloom was working with the Nassau County police, cocaine was often called *the white lady* or simply *white lady*, possibly because it was an expensive drug preferred by effete white folk and largely ignored by blacks, whose drug of choice back then was horse. Nobody called heroin *horse* anymore – nowadays, it was *scag* or *smack* or simply *H* – the same way nobody called cocaine *white lady* anymore, either. But the word *girl* had come to mean cocaine through a sort of perverse evolution.

Bloom thought it supremely ironic that all the feminists out there had fought so hard to get themselves called *women* rather than *ladies*, while at the same time cocaine was undergoing an indifferent sexist-pig change from white *lady* to white *girl* and then simply to *girl*. Sad, when he thought about it, which he rarely did. Nonetheless, "The brighter the blue, the better the girl" was an expression common to cops and thieves alike, and it referred not to the color of a lady's eyes or dress, but merely to a chemical test for the purity of cocaine. What you did, whether you were an undercover narc or a mere dealer, you dribbled a drop of cobalt thiocyanate onto the suspect white powder, and if the stuff turned blue, it was cocaine. The fewer times the coke had been stepped on, the brighter was the blue reaction you got. The brighter the blue, the better the girl, *verdad, amigo*? When she ees good, she ees very, *very* good, eh, *señor*?

Bloom listened with increasing interest as Torrance told him he'd heard about Willa in more than one town, most recently in Rutherford, from contacts who still had a great deal of regard for him – *and* for her, of course – and who didn't want to see her get in trouble with the law. Why Torrance should have cared whether Willa was doing girl or pot or smack or adam or whatever the hell her drug of choice happened to be, was something Bloom couldn't quite comprehend. The woman had been unfaithful to him; in fact, she'd had a baby by another man. Yet Torrance had felt *obliged*, as he put it now, to inform Willa that his old circus cronies all over were saying she'd turned into a Grade A *nose*.

"So you went to see her, huh?" he said. "To tell her what you'd heard."

"Yes."

"But you don't remember when this was."

"It was probably . . ."

"Yes?"

"The day I left Rutherford."

"And when was that?"

"The tenth."

"You remember now, do you?"

"Yes. It was the tenth. I saw her that morning, and left town later that day."

"How'd she greet you, after all those years?"

"Well, she was surprised to see me, of course . . ."

"I'll bet. How long had it been?"

"Eighteen years. But she was extremely cordial. I guess she realized I was doing her a favor."

"By telling her what you'd heard."

"Yes, what people were saying about her."

"Did she say it was true?"

"She said it was an absolute falsehood. But she was nonetheless grateful I'd told her. She said it made her realize she had enemies out there."

"She said that, huh? That she had enemies out there?"

"Yes."

"She didn't happen to *name* any of these enemies, did she?"

"No."

"How long were you with her?"

"An hour or so."

"And she was cordial all that time, huh?"

"Oh yes."

"No hard feelings between the two of you?"

"No, no. Why should there have been?"

"Well . . . her and Barney Hale."

"That was years ago."

"You and the McCullough woman."

"Willa and Aggie were good friends by then."

"So how'd it end? Your conversation with her?"

"She said she'd try to track down the rumors . . ."

"Did you believe her, by the way? That none of this was true?"

"No."

"You thought she was, in fact, doing coke."

"Yes."

"Did you tell her that?"

"No. We shook hands, and said goodbye, and I told her I'd see her again sometime."

"Did you? See her again?"

"How could I? I left town that afternoon, and she killed herself the very next morning."

6

But when she was bad . . .

AT SEVEN o'clock on Friday morning, the first day of April, a
chambermaid making her rounds at the Shelby Arms happened
to notice that the door to room thirty-seven was slightly ajar.
Curious, she knocked on the door, and then pushed it open a
bit further and peeked inside. A man in white undershorts was
lying face-downward on the bed. The back of the man's head,
the back of his neck, were covered with blood. The chambermaid merely nodded, left the door open, went downstairs to
the lobby, and mentioned to the night clerk that somebody
was dead upstairs in room thirty-seven.

Then she took her coffee break.

The night clerk told Bloom he'd come on at midnight and
wasn't due to be spelled till eight in the morning. Although
Bloom needed no identification, the clerk told him the dead
man in the white undershorts was Mr. Peter Torrance. He told
Bloom that Mr. Torrance had checked in on the twentieth. That
would've been two Sundays ago. Gratuitously, he mentioned
that Mr. Torrance was the only white man in the house at the
present time. Or *had* been the only white man, since now that
the gentleman was deceased the night clerk figured he could no

longer rightly be considered a guest, wasn't that so? In fact, he wanted to know who'd be paying Mr. Torrance's bill now that he'd gone to his final reward. Bloom said he didn't know.

The room was surprisingly large, with a double bed against one wall, the corpse still bleeding on it, a dresser against the other, an easy chair near the windows, a standing floor lamp behind it. The bilious green paint on the walls was peeling and the ceiling plaster was falling, but the windows opened onto a good view of the small garden three stories below. Outside, the mobile lab techs were chatting with the assistant M.E., who'd just arrived. Nobody was in a hurry to come upstairs where a corpse awaited them. Voices climbed the early morning air, drifting.

The night clerk said he had to go downstairs now, get things in order for the day man's arrival any minute. Bloom assured him he'd be okay up here alone, and realized all at once that the man was fearful of leaving him unattended in the room. Maybe he was afraid Bloom might run off with the gorgeous lamp there, or one of the tattered window shades. Bloom told him to send up one of the uniformed cops, they'd keep an eye on him, keep him honest. The night clerk didn't know whether he was kidding or not. Still suspicious, he left the room, looking back over his shoulder, hoping to catch Bloom in the act.

On the floor beside the bed, close to Torrance's dangling hand, Bloom found what looked like an Iver Johnson .22-caliber Trailsman Snub revolver. He figured this might be the gun that had shot Matthew. He did not touch it. Left it right where it was. Looked down at the corpse. Nodded. Went to the one closet in the room.

A beige sports jacket and vanilla-colored slacks hung side by side in the closet. A matching tie was draped over the hanger holding the jacket. A pair of tan leather shoes rested on the closet floor, alongside a zippered, black cloth valise with a tiny combination lock hanging from it. Bloom hoisted the valise off the floor, carried it to the bed, and sat on the bed beside it.

A name tag hanging from the handle gave Torrance's address as 2314 Littlejohn Way in Atlanta, Georgia. The space for a telephone number had been left blank. The combination lock was open. Apparently, there was nothing of value in the valise. Bloom unzipped it.

There was a coach airline ticket to Atlanta in the valise.

There was a copy of Willa Torrance's will in the valise.

There was a small black notebook in the valise.

There was also a box of .22 long rifle cartridges in the valise.

She had put an exhausted Joanna into a cab at a little past eight A.M., instructing and paying the driver to take her back to her mother's condo. Now Patricia sat beside Matthew's bed, holding his hand, talking to him much as his daughter had, reciting a different sort of litany, but a litany nonetheless.

She was reminding him of their history together.

Reminding him that they already shared a considerable *back* story, you know, which, if they played their cards right, might just possibly turn into a bright and promising scenario for the future.

"If only you'd wake up, Matthew," she said.

She had already reminded him about the first time they'd met, when she'd crashed into his car in the rain, and now she began telling him about their *next* little accident. A collision between humans this time, rather than automobiles.

"Do you remember that day in the police gym?" she asked. "Neither of us knew the other was there running on the indoor track – and *whammo*, we suddenly crashed into each other, and got all entangled, and fell to the floor . . . which, by the way, is probably when I fell in love with you. Though actually I think it was the very *first* time I saw you, when I skidded into your car. The thing is, I probably *kept* falling in love with you over and over again, every time I saw your sweet little face. That time with the car, *and* that time in the gym, *and* the time you turned down my breakfast invitation . . ."

Want to have breakfast with me? I'll open some champagne. Celebrate your victory.

Thanks, but I'm exhausted. Some other time, okay?

Sure. See ya.

". . . turned me down cold, I couldn't believe it. I figured you probably had another date, probably with that Vietnamese girl, the translator, whatever her name was. Me walking off trying to look indifferent, swinging my hips, tossing my hair, 'Hell with you, bub,' was what the body language said. But I was *furiously* jealous, don't ask me why, I hardly knew you. Do you remember how *outrageously* I flirted that night we met on the Barton case, when you thought I was going to offer a deal? Both of us drinking martinis . . ."

To justice.

Fair enough.

Mmmm.

Indeed.

Hard day.

You don't look it.

I went home.

So did I. Otherwise we'd have frightened the horses.

"Did that *really* come from my mouth? An allusion to making *love*? The very first time we're in a social setting together, people everywhere around us? It's a wonder I didn't frighten *you*, never mind the horses. A wonder you didn't run for the hills . . ."

I have a bottle of twenty-year-old cognac at the house. A gift from one of my clients. When I was still practicing on the Coast. Never found the right occasion to open it.

"The way you looked at me, I thought 'There he goes, I've lost him.' But, what the hell, in for a penny . . ."

Want to sample it?

". . . staring into your eyes, dropping my gaze to your mouth, thinking 'He's going to run for sure,' leaning over the table and trying to melt you with my eyes, hoping I didn't look like six kinds of brazen hussy, waiting for your answer, praying . . ."

Sure, why not?

"It was perfect from the very first minute, wasn't it, Matthew? Neither of us had to learn anything, we knew it all from the very start. The more I think about it, the more I'm *sure* I was planning it from the moment I ran into your car. In fact, I think it may have been *fated*, my running into your car . . ."

Do you believe in destiny?

No.

You don't think it was fated?

Yes, I do.
Then you do believe in destiny?
No.
I'm a very jealous person, you know, I'd rip out your eyes. This is crazy. I think I love you, Matthew.
I think I love you, too.
Yes, say it.
I love you, Patricia.
Ahh, say it, say it.
I love you.
I love you.
I love you, I love you, I love you, I love you.

"Oh, God, we were crazy," she said, and squeezed his hand. "Do you remember the . . .?"

"Nuts," he said.

". . . night you . . ."

—and realized all at once that he'd spoken.

She stood up instantly and leaned over the bed and looked into his face. His eyes were still closed.

"Matthew?" she said.

Nothing.

"Matthew?"

Still nothing.

"Matthew," she said, "we *were* nuts, you're right, we were crazy. Totally. Totally nuts. Crazy, insane, nuts. Say it again, Matthew, tell me how nuts we were, *please*. Say it again. Please."

She stood looking down into his face, his hand caught between both her hands, willing his eyes to open, willing his lips to part, squeezing his lifeless hand hard, willing him to speak, begging him to speak again, "Please, darling, please, please, *please*," but he said nothing more, and at last she wondered if she hadn't imagined him muttering that single word.

She sat beside the bed again, his hand still between hers.

"Do you remember," she started again, "the night you . . .?"

Still sitting on Bloom's desk when he got back to the office at nine that morning was Miss Finch's list of the calls Matthew had made from his home last week. Bloom placed it alongside Torrance's little black book and Matthew's calendar entries for March 19 through March 23. His handwritten breakdown looked like this:

	TORRANCE	*MATTHEW*
SAT 3/19	Still in Atlanta	9:00 AM meeting with Steadman @ circus
SUN 3/20	Arrives Calusa	Maria Torrance @ 4:00 PM Patricia afterward
MON 3/21	D'Allessandro 10:00 AM	Phone Felicity Codlow FSU Steadman-Sheed @ circus 2:00 PM Lonnie McGovern – Sun & Shore 4:00 PM
TUE 3/22	Aggie Donovan 9:30	Andrew Byrd – 9:00 AM John Rafferty – 12 Noon Phone MEMO Steadman @ 2:30 PM
WED 3/23	Maria Torrance 1:00 PM	*CALENDAR ENTRIES END*

Torrance had told Bloom that he hadn't gone to see his daughter since his arrival here in Calusa. Maria had told Toots the same thing. But Torrance had also claimed that he didn't know anyone named Matthew Hope. Bloom's focus zeroed in on Torrance's actual calendar entry for:

FRIDAY, MARCH 25
MATTHEW HOPE
10:00 AM

Bloom pulled the phone to him, and quickly punched out Aggie Donovan's number again. She picked up on the third ring.

"Hello?" she said.

"Mrs. Donovan?"

"Yes?"

"This is Detective Bloom, I'm sorry to bother you again, but . . ."

"Yes, what is it?"

"I'm wondering if you've given any further thought to those calls Matthew Hope made to you in Bradenton last Thursday afternoon. Specifically . . ."

"Mr. Bloom, I have nothing else to say to you."

"Mrs. Donovan, he was shot the very next . . ."

"I don't know anything about who shot him."

"Did you tell him anything that might have . . .?"

"I don't remember what I told him."

"Did you tell him where Peter Torrance was staying?"

"No," she said, and hung up.

Lightning kept flashing in the darkness, lightning crackled incessantly inside his head. He could remember telephone wires crackling . . .

"This is a terrible connection," she'd said.

"Shall I call you back?"

"No, don't bother, Mr. Hope."

Click and another flash of lightning, the sound reverberating inside his head, ricocheting off the walls of his head like tracer bullets, everything echoing and resonating. He punched out the number again.

"Hello?"

"Mrs. Donovan . . ."

"Look, I told you . . ."

"Aggie, don't hang up again. If you do . . ."

Another *click*, louder this time, remembering it now, the shattering sound of the **CLICK**. Adamantly, he punched out the number again.

"If you hang up, I'll come there."

"Mr. Hope, please . . ."

"Where's Peter Torrance staying?"

"I don't know."

"You do know. I have to see him."

"Why?"

"I want to know what he can tell me about Willa Torrance's murder."

A long silence on the line.

"She wasn't murdered, she . . ."

"She was murdered, Aggie."

Another long silence.

"I thought she was your friend," he said.

"She was, yes."

"Then tell me."

"Peter had nothing to do with it."

"Then he has nothing to hide."

"They'll say he did it."

"Not if he didn't."

"He was in Missouri, they'll say he did it."

"What?"

"Mr. Hope, please, I don't . . ."

"Are you saying he was in *Missouri* at the time of her . . .?"

"I don't want to get anyone in trouble."

"Just tell me where he's staying. I just want to *talk* to him."

He waited.

Patience, he thought. I'm learning, Frank. Patience, patience, come *on*, Aggie, let *go* of it.

"Aggie?" he said.

"The Shelby Arms," she said.

The day clerk Bloom spoke to was the one with the jade eyes and a complexion the color of strong tea. His name was Muhammad Azir. He looked at the newspaper photo of Matthew Hope and said he'd never seen the man before in his life.

"He might've been here last Friday morning, around ten A.M.," Bloom said.

"Don't recognize him."

"He would've been visiting the dead man," Bloom said.

"Still don't know him."

"Let's talk about the clientele here, okay?"

"Nothing wrong with the clientele here," Azir said.

"Except they're mostly hookers and johns."

"Not to my knowledge."

"Get many white johns in here?"

"White, black, we get all kinds of guests here."

"Equal opportunity employers, huh? The hookers?"

"I don't know of any hookers here at the Shelby Arms."

"You'd've noticed a white man if he walked in here, though, wouldn't you? White man at ten in the morning?"

"We get white men walking in here all the time. White, black . . ."

"All kinds, sure. White man visiting the only white guest in the hotel? Now you'd've noticed *that*, wouldn't you?"

"I notice *everything* that goes on here."

"But you didn't notice . . ."

"Except when I have the day off," Azir said.

The man who'd had the day shift behind the desk at the Shelby Arms on Friday, March 25, was a thirty-eight-year-old black man named Abdul Shakhout. Bloom found him in a room he was renting in a house not far from the hotel. The house was a single-family structure with part of it remodeled to accommodate a tenant. There was a separate path along the side of the house, a separate entrance door at the rear of the house. The room was a fifteen-by-twenty-foot rectangle that contained a bed, a dresser, an easy chair, a small enamel-topped table under the backyard window, two chairs at the table, a stove, a fridge, several lamps, a kerosene heater for frosty nights, and a television set. An open door led to a tiny bathroom. When Bloom arrived, a white girl wearing nothing but a slip was sitting on the bed reading a magazine. He figured her for sixteen, seventeen, in there. Shakhout introduced her as his wife. Bloom made no comment.

"Were you working the desk at the Shelby Arms last Friday at ten in the morning?" he asked.

"Yes, I was there last Friday morning," Shakhout said. "It's my second job. I'm also a bellhop at the Hyatt."

"You got a warrant?" the girl asked, looking up sharply from her magazine.

"Did a white man come in asking for Mr. Torrance?" Bloom said, ignoring her.

"You got a warrant?" she asked again.

"Miss," Bloom said, "I don't have any business with you. So butt out."

"Oh, you don't, huh?" the girl said, and pulled a snotty face and went back to her magazine.

"Recognize this man?" Bloom asked, and showed Shakhout the newspaper photo.

"Yeah, I seen him," Shakhout said.

"When?"

"When you said. Around ten last Friday."

"Asked for Peter Torrance?"

"Told him room thirty-seven."

"What then?"

"Went upstairs. Elevator was out again, he had to climb up."

"When did he come down again?"

"Around quarter to eleven."

"So he was up there almost an hour."

"Well, forty-five minutes or so."

"Say anything to you when he left?"

"Nope."

"Okay, thanks," Bloom said.

"Sure hope you got what you needed," the girl said snottily from where she was sitting on the bed.

They were taking a short lunch break away from the hospital. Frank was eating a hamburger and alternately drinking a Coke. Patricia was dipping a spoon into a bowl of yogurt and sliced banana. She was telling him that Matthew had spoken to her. She'd reported this to Dr. Spinaldo as well, and he'd thought it was a good sign. Frank sounded skeptical.

"Just that single word, though, huh?"

"Yes, but it was relevant to what I was saying."

"So you think he understood you, is that . . .?"

"Yes, and was commenting. The way people . . ."

"Yeah."

"Will keep up a running commen—"

"Yeah."

"The way you're doing now," she said.

"Yeah. Well, I hope so."

Patricia sipped at her iced tea. Frank took another bite of the hamburger. High on the wall above their table, an air-conditioning unit hummed noisily. It was a familiar sound in Florida, a sort of background leitmotif. In Florida, you stepped from one air-conditioned space to another, and you got used to the incessant drone of air-conditioning wherever you went.

"Have you spoken to Bloom?" Frank asked.

"Not this morning. He was out on the Torrance murder."

"Related, do you think?"

"I don't know."

"Because Matthew was tracking him, wasn't he?"

"From what Bloom told me, yes."

"He's been terrific, you know."

"Yes."

"Keeping us informed."

"Yes."

Frank nodded.

They were both silent for a moment.

Patricia sipped at her tea again.

"I wonder what Matthew had," Frank said.

"If we knew that . . ."

"Oh sure. I went through his desk yesterday, his filing cabinets, everything in his office. To see if there was anything there. We've been partners a long time now, I know how he works. He's a very meticulous man, I don't know if you know that about him, keeps detailed notes on whatever he's working on, a closing, a brief, a deposition, whatever. So where are the notes here?"

"Well, there's his appointment calendar . . ."

"Yeah, but that's not . . ."

"You mean . . . stuff he would've dictated?"

"Yes, or written by hand. I just can't believe there's *nothing*."

"Did you check with Cynthia?"

"Yeah. Nothing there. He was really on the go last week, popped in and out, hello, goodbye, no dictation, no typing, nothing."

"He was probably still working it all out. Piecing it together."

"Yeah, I guess."

Frank sighed heavily, picked up his Coke, idly swished the lemon wedge around with his straw.

"Still," he said, "it's funny there aren't any."

"Notes," she said, and nodded.

"Yeah."

She was lifting another spoonful of yogurt and bananas to her mouth when suddenly the spoon stopped midair and her eyes opened wide. For an instant, Frank thought she'd spotted something horrible in the spoon. A bug or a hair or . . .

"Not nuts," she said. "*Notes!*"

She was as familiar with the house on Whisper Key as she was with her own. Matthew had given her a key almost as soon as they'd begun seeing each other, and she used it now to open the front door, remembering him charging out of that door the day she'd slammed into his brand-new car, the house silent and washed with morning sunlight now as she waited for Frank to follow her in, and then closed the door behind them.

"Where do you suppose?" he said.

"The study," she said, and led him knowledgeably through the living room, and then back toward the rear of the house to where Matthew's office occupied an alcove just off the bedroom. Through the open bedroom door, she could see that he'd left the bed unmade. This was unlike him. He had probably gone out of here in one hell of a hurry last Friday. Frank noticed this, too. He said nothing, but she remembered him describing his partner as a meticulous man. Together they went into the study.

The room was a smallish one, with a teak desk and teak bookshelves bearing the Florida Statutes, and Weinstein on Evidence, and LeFave on Search and Seizure, and McCormick on Criminal Law, and a novel called *Closing Arguments* by someone named Frederick Busch. There was a combination telephone answering machine on the desk, and a fax machine on the waist-high counter that ran under the bookshelves. Resting on that same counter was a framed picture of Joanna lying in a lounge chair by the pool and grinning at the camera.

On one wall, there was a framed cartoon someone on the *Calusa Herald-Tribune* had drawn while Matthew was trying the Mary Barton case. It showed him questioning his client, who was caricatured as an absolute harridan. The caption under the photo said, "Tell us, Miss Barton, can you *also* fly through the air on a broomstick?" On that same wall, there was a framed front page headlining the acquittal Matthew had won in the so-called Three Blind Mice case, the one he'd been trying when first she'd met him. Seeing the headline almost brought tears to her eyes.

The house seemed so empty, so still without him.

Frank appeared reluctant to touch anything in the room. Patricia sighed deeply, and opened the top drawer of the desk. Together, they began.

His notes were disjointed and scattered, written in a hurried hand that sometimes defied scrutiny, personal memos to himself in a scrawl decipherable only *by* himself. Here and there, Patricia and Frank caught glimmers of the track he was on . . .

He'd been trying to trace parallel time frames.

Pinpointing the year Willa DeMott had joined the circus, the year she'd married Torrance, the year her daughter was born, the year Torrance ran off with the high-flying Aggie, the year Jeannie Lawson joined S&R, the year Willa's trailer was burglarized, the year she was murdered.

Like a spaceship zooming into an uncharted sky, his notes rocketed off in six directions at once, tracking the relationships between Willa and Barney Hale, Torrance and Aggie, Willa and Davey Sheed, Willa and Jeannie, Jeannie and the two little girls in Willa's act, and lastly Willa's daughter and Sheed.

In one section of his notes, he had jotted a timetable for the morning of May eleventh, three years ago:

4:30 AM: Maria's alarm goes off. She awakens, dresses.
5:00 AM: Maria goes to cookhouse to meet Sheed.
5:05 AM: Sheed leaves cookhouse.
5:10 AM: Bullet stops Willa's alarm clock.
5:15 AM: Time Willa's alarm is set for. Sheed returns to cookhouse.
5:30 AM: Maria starts back to trailer.
5:35 AM: Maria reaches trailer, finds mother dead.

At another point in his notes, Matthew had outlined the Byrd/Rafferty/Lawson triangle:

1) Byrd knows Rafferty in high school.
2) Rafferty hires Jeannie for summer job. She is 16 at the time. Rafferty is 31. Byrd, also working for Rafferty, is 27. Jeannie begins affair with Byrd.
3) Jeannie and Byrd leave town. He goes to South America. She joins S&R.
4) She quits circus after single season, marries Rafferty.
5) Byrd returns a rich man one year later. She divorces Rafferty, marries him.

At yet another point, Matthew seemed trying to understand what had happened on the tour during Jeannie's single season with S&R.

1) Jeannie joins circus at age 17. Willa's daughter is same age.
2) Jeannie sexually promiscuous.
   a) Takes up with two young black men.
   b) Takes up with elephant trainer.
   c) Takes up with Sheed.
3) Willa warns Jeannie to stay away from two girls in her act. Jeannie threatens her. Willa backs off.
4) Jeannie quits circus at end of season.

On the page following this outline, Matthew lettered in a large, lucid hand:

JEANNIE IS LYING!

NONE OF his notes were dated, so they assumed the ones at the bottom of the sheaf were the most recent ones. These were headed PETER TORRANCE, the name underlined. In an abbreviated style similar to many of his other entries – as if he were jotting down only the bare bones of ideas, hurriedly getting them on paper before they eluded him – Matthew had scrawled:

Torrance says went Missouri . . .

"Means he *did* talk to Torrance," Frank said. "Yes."

. . . see old circus friends. Stopped by say hello Willa.

Arrived before burglary, gone before murder.

And then:

TORRANCE IS LYING!

And then:

See Maria's statement re no visit Calusa.

And then:

MARIA IS LYING, TOO!

And then:

Play Torrance tape again.

"*What* Torrance tape?" Frank asked.

The notes ended there.

They searched the desk from top to bottom, every drawer, every hidden corner, and found no tape. They went through every shelf in the study, and found nothing. They went into the bedroom and searched through the bedside night tables, finding the condoms Patricia had brought over one night before she and Matthew had both taken tests for AIDS, and finding a plastic nose-spray container, and five pairs of cuff links, and four Japanese watches, and a dozen or more mail-order catalogs from L.L. Bean and J. Crew and Lands' End . . . but no tape.

"The night he was shot," Frank said, "did he have a tape recorder with him? You had dinner with him . . ."

"Yes, but . . ."

"Did you see a tape recorder?"

"No."

"If he was going around *taping* conversations . . ."

". . . he'd've had it with him, yes."

"But where? Was he carrying a briefcase that night?"

"No. We had dinner out, this was after office hours, Frank, no briefcase, no dispatch case. We'd planned on going back to my house later, but he told me something had come up. He said he didn't know how long the meeting would take, he'd try to stop by later."

"No phone calls while you were in the restaurant, isn't that what you told me?"

"That's right."

"Which means that even *before* dinner, he knew he'd be going to Newtown."

"Yes."

"So . . . if he was running around *taping* people . . . and he needed to have a recorder with him . . . where would he have kept it?"

"Of course," Patricia said at once. "His *car*."

No one had thought to ask how Matthew had *got* to Newtown. In a town where most people drove wherever they went, and where public transportation was inadequate at best, it must have been assumed that Matthew had *driven* himself there, but the detectives initially investigating the shooting had made no attempt to locate his automobile. This was Newtown, after all, where drive-by shootings were common. Detectives Kenyon and Di Luca weren't anticipating any big murder mystery plot here; this was just an unfortunate white man who'd got himself shot because he was someplace he shouldn't have been. They never even *thought* of looking for his car, which was parked on M Street, a block from the bar.

Similarly, the uniformed cop who'd tagged the car with a parking ticket and had it towed off to the pound on the day after the shooting never once connected the name he saw in the newspaper headlines with the name provided by Motor Vehicles, whose computer had located the registered owner of the vehicle. Bloom kicked himself in the ass for having been so stupid. Then he rushed over to Good Samaritan, retrieved Matthew's car keys from the personal belongings they'd confiscated when he'd been admitted, and drove over to the car pound.

In the trunk of Matthew's Acura, Bloom found a tan leather attaché case with the initials W.C. monogrammed in gold on the front panel. Inside the case, fastened to the frame, was a battery-powered, reel-to-reel tape recorder. Bloom had recovered the NAGRA Warren Chambers had loaned to Matthew on Thursday of last week.

The instrument's microphone was constructed to look like part of the hinge holding the top half of the case to its bottom half. The button in the clasp at the front of the case activated the recorder. Once the tape was rolling, the batteries were capable of recording four hours of conversation before they gave out. A tape was already in position on the pickup reel, and from the look of it, half of it had already been used.

—Mr. Torrance?

Matthew's voice.

—Yes?

Bloom recognized Torrance's voice, but it sounded as if it were coming from the bottom of a well. He realized all at once that Matthew had been calling from his car phone, and that Torrance was on the speaker. The *car* phone. *Another* thing Bloom had missed. How many calls had Matthew made from that same car phone last week? Again, he kicked himself in the ass for not having asked the productive Miss Finch if any other phones were listed under Matthew's name.

—hoping I could talk to you sometime this . . .

Bloom hit the stop button, rewound the tape, hit the play button again.

—Yes?

—My name is Matthew Hope, sir, I understand you're in town seeking redress on exclusion from your former wife's will. I was hoping I could talk to you sometime this evening . . .

—How do *you* know why I'm in town?

—I'm an attorney, sir. I may be able to help you in this matter. It happens . . .

—Did you talk to *my* attorney? Did he ask you to . . .?

—Yes, I did. But no, I'm calling on my own.

Playing it straight, Bloom thought. Just in case D'Allessandro had told him about Matthew's visit.

—Did *he* tell you where to find me?

—No.

—Then who did?

—A woman named Agnes Donovan.

Who wouldn't give *me* the right time, Bloom thought.

—Mr. Torrance, I'm assuming you obtained a copy of your former wife's will from Probate . . .

—*Deceased* wife, not *former* wife. And a will is a matter of public record, there's nothing wrong . . .

—Nothing wrong with that at all, sir. I'm calling because I think I may be able to help expedite matters for you. If, indeed, you're interested in getting this settled as soon as possible.

Bloom was wondering what he had up his sleeve.

—As I said, I can stop by sometime this evening, if you like. I'm on my way to the mainland right this minute, I can be at the Shelby Arms in, oh, half an . . .

—Are you representing my daughter?

—Maria? No, sir.

—Oh, you know her, do you?

—I've had several conversations with her, yes.

—What about?

—She thinks Davey Sheed killed her mother.

—Ridiculous.

—In any case, if I can come by . . .

—I'm busy right now.

—How about later tonight?

—Busy then, too.

—Tomorrow morning?

—What time?

—Nine o'clock?

Eager to get to him, Bloom thought.

—Too early.

—How does ten sound?

—I'll look for you.

There was a click.
Bloom kept listening.

—Friday, March twenty-fifth, nine fifty-five A.M. Entering Shelby Arms Hotel on L Street . . .
  Sound of footsteps, background noises, indistinct voices.
—Mr. Torrance, please.
—Who shall I say is here?
—Matthew Hope. He's expecting me.
—Second.
More background buzz.
—Mr. Torrance. Man here by the name of Hope, says he . . . yep, right away. You can go on up, it's room thirty-seven. Elevator's broke, you'll have to walk it.
—Thanks.
Ambient noise, sound of somewhat heavy breathing. Little out of shape, Matthew? The sound of knocking. A muffled voice. Then:
—Matthew Hope.
The muffled voice again. A clicking sound.
—Mr. Torrance?
—Come in.
The sound of a door closing. Another clicking sound. The lock turning?
—Have a seat.
—Thank you.
—So what's this all about?
—Let me cut to the chase, Mr. Torrance. From what I understand, you're electing a statutory share of your former wife's . . .
—Where'd you get all this stuff?
—I have friends at the courthouse.
—I didn't discuss this with anyone at the courthouse.
—I have friends who have friends.
—Someone who knows D'Allessandro?
—Does it really matter? If my information is correct, and if I can help you get thirty percent of Willa's estate without any fuss or bother . . .

—How can you do that?

—The problem is not *how* I can do it, it's whether or not I can do it without opening a bigger can of worms.

—What are you talking about?

—I'm talking about Willa's murder, Mr. Torrance.

—She wasn't murdered, she killed herself. And I had nothing to do with her death, either way.

—Well . . . there seems to be a bit of a cloud in Missouri.

—Fuck the cloud in Missouri. I'm not a weatherman.

—I'm suggesting that if the other side brings this up in litigation . . .

—What other side?

—Your daughter, of course. I'm sure she's not eager to give up thirty percent of what she inherited.

—Are you sure you're not representing her?

—Positive.

—Who *are* you representing?

—I'm *hoping* to represent you.

—What are you, some kind of ambulance chaser?

—Let's say I'm an opportunist who'd like to own ten percent of a thirty percent share of half a circus.

—Huh?

—Maria inherited half of S&R, didn't she?

—You know that, huh?

—I know it, yes, sir.

—And you're looking for ten percent of whatever I get.

—Only if I win. If I lose, you go home to Atlanta without paying me a dime.

—You know that, too, huh?

That you live in Atlanta? Yes, I do.

—You've been busy.

—Mm. What do you say?

—What makes you think there'll be litigation? Did my daughter tell you that?

—No, she didn't. By the way, have you seen her since you got here?

—No.

—A lie, Bloom thought. His appointment calendar for Wednesday of last week had read:

<u>*WEDNESDAY, MARCH 23*</u>
MARIA
1:00 PM

—makes you think she'll bring up Willa's suicide.

—Because you're claiming a share of her estate, Mr. Torrance. And you happened to be in Missouri at the time of her death.

—What?

—You sound surprised.

—Who told you that?

—Aggie Donovan.

Playing it straight all the way down the line, Bloom thought. Best way to do it. No lies to remember later on.

—I was nowhere *near* Missouri when . . .

—Please.

—I'm telling you . . .

—Do you want my help, or don't you?

—If you're going to keep saying I was in *Missouri*. . .

—Well, fine. If you weren't, you've got nothing to worry about. The other side can't possibly claim you had anything to do with Willa's death.

—But I *didn't*!

—But you *were* in Missouri, weren't you?

Silence.

—Well, listen, lots of luck, Mr. Torrance. Maybe they won't bring it up, after all.

—Sit down.

—Sure.

Another long silence. The sound of a bird twittering somewhere in the distance. Then:

—I was gone before anything happened.

—But you *were* there?

—I was there.

—*In* Rutherford, Missouri, *on* or about the eleventh of May, three years ago.

—Yes. But . . .

—When did you get there, Mr. Torrance?

—On the eighth.

And now the conversation followed pretty much the path that Bloom's *later* conversation with Torrance had taken, with much of the information jibing almost exactly. He had told Bloom, for example:

I arrived three or four days before her death.
That would've made it the seventh, the eighth, around then.
If you say so.
And you left when?
The day before she shot herself.

And now Bloom heard on the tape:

—When did you get there, Mr. Torrance?
—Several days before she killed herself.
—Can you pinpoint that for me?
—The seventh, I believe it was.
—When did you leave?
—On the tenth.
—Did you see Willa while you were there?
—I did.

Mr. Torrance, did you happen to see Willa while you were there in Rutherford?
Yes, I did. So what?
When did you see her?
I don't recall the date.

—Do you remember when that was?
—Yes, I went to see her shortly after I arrived.
—The eighth? The ninth?
—I saw her on the eighth. And again on the tenth.
—Twice, then?
—Yes. Twice.

And now the two accounts began to vary even more widely:

What was the purpose of your visit?
I'd heard certain things while moving around . . .
What things did you hear?
Things I thought Willa should know.
Like what?
I heard there was a little girl, you see.

—Why'd you go see her, Mr. Torrance?
—The first time simply to . . . to say hello, to tell her there

were no hard feelings.
—About what?
—Well . . . the separation.
—But *you* were the one who'd left *her*.
—Yes. I wanted to tell her I was sorry. That was all.
—I see. But the separation had been a long time ago . . .
—Eighteen years. Almost nineteen years.
—Hadn't told her you were sorry in all that time, hm?
—Well.
And yet, while you were in Missouri, you saw her *twice*, is
that it?
—Yes. I'd heard there'd been a burglary in her trailer. I
wanted to tell her how sorry I was.
—About the burglary this time.
—Yes.
Bloom thought it amazing that Torrance had expressed all
this remorse to a man he later claimed he'd never met:
*Mr. Bloom, I want you to know that I'm answering your questions
only because you seem to believe I had something to do with the
shooting of this Hope person you keep mentioning. I want to repeat
that I do not* know *the man, I've never* met *the man, and I had
nothing whatever to do with his shooting, whenever that may
have been.*
He figured Torrance had merely been trying to distance
himself from an attempted murder. In much the same way,
while speaking to Matthew, he seemed trying to convince him
he'd had nothing to do with either of those long-ago felonies
in Missouri.
—What did she say when you appeared on her doorstep?
I'm talking about the *first* time. After twenty years.
—She was surprised, of course. But . . .
—You said this was *before* the burglary?
—Yes. The day before the burglary.
—The eighth of May.
—Yes.
Was she cordial? After her initial surprise, I mean.
—Oh, yes. Offered me a drink. Sat and chatted for . . .
—Champagne?
—What? No, not champagne. Champagne? No.

—I understand she used to keep champagne in the refrigerator.

—I really couldn't say.

—She didn't offer you any that day?

—No. I drank Scotch and soda.

—With ice?

—Yes.

—Did she take ice cubes from the refrigerator?

—Yes. I'm sorry, what . . .?

—Club soda, too?

—Yes, she did. From the fridge, do you mean?

—Yes.

—Well, yes, she did.

—You didn't happen to see a *safe* in there, did you?

—A what?

—When she opened the refrigerator. A small safe. Apparently that's where she kept the safe.

—I didn't notice any safe in there.

—This was on the eighth, is that right?

—Yes.

—And you went back to see her again after the burglary.

—Yes.

—That would've been the tenth.

—Yes.

—But you left *town* on the tenth, didn't you?

—Later that day, yes.

—So this would've been when? The morning? The afternoon?

—When I went by her trailer, do you mean?

—Yes.

—The morning.

—You'd heard about the burglary by then?

—Oh, yes. Word travels fast in a circus.

—Where'd you hear about it?

—What?

—You said word travels fast . . .

—Oh. Well . . . I . . . I was there on the grounds that morning. Not to see Willa. Merely to talk to some old friends. When I heard about the burg –

—Which old friends did you talk to?

—George Steadman, actually.

—What'd you talk about?

—The burglary mostly. Everyone was talking about the burglary. Excuse me, Mr. Hope, but you said you thought you could help me. So far, all you've done . . .

—Did you talk to your daughter?

—No.

—Why not?

—Maria and I never got along. I don't think she's ever forgiven me for having left her mother.

—How about Willa? Had *she* forgiven you?

—Well, we're both adults, you know.

—How'd she treat you when you stopped by again? *After the burglary*, I mean.

—She was still very cordial.

—You didn't discuss what'd happened all those years ago, did you?

—No, we didn't. We talked mostly about the burglary.

—No mention of Aggie McCullough? Or Barney Hale?

—No.

No hard feelings between the two of you?

No, no. Why should there have been?

Well . . . her and Barney Hale.

That was years ago.

You and the McCullough woman.

Willa and Aggie were good friends by then.

—Was that a usual habit of hers, by the way? When you were still married, I mean.

—We *are* still married, Mr. Hope. That's the basis of my *claim*. We were never properly . . .

—Of course. But did she usually keep a safe in the refrigerator?

—I don't remember her keeping a safe in the refrigerator. I don't even remember her *having* a safe.

—Odd place to keep a safe, wouldn't you think?

—Yeah.

—I wonder how the burglar knew to look there.

—Burglars know to look everywhere.

—Did you know Maria had a combination to that safe?

—Yes. Willa mentioned that she did.

—Oh? Why was that?

—It just came up.

—How?

—Well . . .

—How did Willa happen to mention that her daughter had a combination to the safe?

—Because of what was stolen.

I'm not sure I'm following you, Mr. Torrance.

—Well . . . there was a little *girl*, you see.

"What?" Bloom said aloud, and missed the next few words on the tape. He rewound at once, hit the play button again:

—a little *girl*, you see.

—A little *what?*

—Cocaine.

—I'm sorry, what . . .?

—Girl. Cocaine. Maria was keeping cocaine in the safe.

Willa told you this?

Yes.

Wait a minute, Bloom thought, hold it one goddamn minute. Didn't you tell me . . .

I'd heard about Willa in more than one town, most recently in Rutherford, from contacts who still had a great deal of regard for me – and for her, *of course – and who didn't want to see her get in trouble with the law.*

"Damn it," he said, and rewound the tape again, and played it back from where he'd started losing it.

—Maria was keeping cocaine in the safe.

—Willa told you this?

—Yes.

—She felt comfortable enough to confide this to you?

—Oh, yes. Well, she'd only discovered it the day before the burglary, you see. She told me . . .

No, Bloom thought. *You* told me . . .

I felt obliged to inform Willa that my old circus cronies all over were saying she'd turned into a Grade A nose!

But no. Now it was turning into something else again. Now it was turning into there was a little girl who had a little *girl* who was doing a little girl. Now it was turning into Willa's daughter *Maria* who was . . .

—doing cocaine, you see. Maybe even . . .

The tape was running ahead of him again. He rewound it, played it back:

—discovered it the day before the burglary, you see. She told me . . .

—When you say she'd just *discovered* it . . .

—Yes.

—Do you mean she just opened the safe and *found* it there?

—Yes. And immediately figured it was Maria's.

—Why Maria?

—Because she was the only other person who knew the combination to the safe. Which meant she was doing cocaine, you see. Maybe even dealing it. Because this wasn't just a couple of *ounces* in there, this was a real *stash* she'd found in that safe.

—Did she tell you how much?

—She guessed about two kilos. She . . .

"Jesus," Bloom said.

—told me she thought Maria *had* to be dealing the stuff. She was afraid that whoever had stolen the safe might come back to blackmail her.

—Did she think he'd known beforehand?

—I'm not following you.

—The thief. That there was cocaine in the safe?

—No, no. She just thought he'd lucked out. And would try to take advantage of the situation.

—Well . . . what'd *Maria* have to say about all this?

—She denied the stuff was hers.

—Then how'd it get in the safe?

—Oh, she'd *put* it there, all right, but she said it didn't belong to her.

—Then whose was it?

—Davey Sheed's.

The cat man again, Bloom thought.

Maybe the son of a bitch *did* kill her.

—The point is, whoever it belonged to, and whoever put it

in the safe, somebody *else* had it now. And Willa was afraid he'd come back to blackmail her.

Or *kill* her, Bloom thought. Whenever dope is on the scene . . .

—Did she confront Sheed?

—I don't know.

—I'm assuming she didn't go to the police. If she was afraid of blackmail . . .

—No, I don't imagine she went to the police.

Me neither, Bloom thought.

—So what do you think?

—About what, Mr. Torrance?

—My chances of getting a proper share of the estate. I mean, with all this funny stuff going on back then . . .

—Which funny stuff do you mean?

—All of it.

—Like what?

—Well, Maria living with Sheed, for one. I happen to think that's pretty damn funny. A nineteen-year-old girl sleeping with a man old enough to be her father? Man who used to be her mother's lover? Man who incidentally gives her two keys of *dope* to hide in her mother's safe? I find that pretty *peculiar*, don't you? What I'm trying to say . . . well, if Maria's *dumb* enough to bring up my accidental presence in Missouri, we can counter with all this other stuff, can't we? The dope, her sleeping with Sheed, intent to sell, all of it. Can't we nail her that way?

—Do you want to know what I think, Mr. Torrance?

—Of course. Why do you suppose I . . .?

—I think you know damn *well* that you and Willa were properly divorced . . .

—What?

—and that you're not entitled to a nickel of her estate. I *also* . . .

—Hey, listen, you . . .

—think you're lying about what happened back there in Rutherford, Missouri.

—What?

—I think you spotted that safe when Willa opened the fridge . . .

—Goodbye, pal.

—and came back to steal it. You're the one who found all that coke, Mr. Torrance. You're the one who tried to blackmail . . .

—Get the hell out of here!

—Sure. Nice talking to you.

"You've come at a bad time, Detective Bloom."

Bloom wondered if there ever was a good time.

It was now four P.M. on the afternoon of April first. At exactly ten-fifteen P.M. on Friday a week ago, Matthew Hope had been shot outside a bar in Newtown. Now, as the circus band began playing the music for the show's finale, the entire S&R troupe lined up for the dress-rehearsal blow-off, waiting to be led into the tent by Steadman in jodhpurs, boots, red ringmaster's jacket, and black top hat.

"Wait here," he said sourly, and signaled to the workmen standing by to throw open the tent flaps. Under the big top itself, the trumpet blasted an entrance cue fit for a Roman emperor. The workmen pulled the flaps back wide and Steadman stepped through, a smile magically lighting his face as he went out to greet an imaginary audience, his right hand moving to the top hat as he removed it in a salute.

And now, as Bloom watched in wide-eyed wonder, the performers moved past him all twinkling and bright, a sequined Fellini movie parading before him close enough to touch. Here were horses led by sylvan sylphs in flowing white, and behind them were leapers and vaulters and tumblers and clowns, and now the Zvonkovas dressed in forest – green tights and looking somehow smaller on the ground than they did while balancing high in the air. The Chen family came somersaulting through the flap in ascending order, and there were yet more horses, and acrobats and balancers, and here came the aerialists in their skintight pinks, Marnie and Sam and the flying McCulloughs, and there were girls and more girls stepping out in sequined high heels now rather than the practical ballet slippers they wore in performance, and now came Davey Sheed in star-spangled tights and a glittering silver vest open over his bare chest, a matching silver band crossing his forehead, snapping a whip as he entered the tent and stepped out grandly. And there were yet more girls, girls, girls, and dogs pulling carts, and jugglers, and ponies, and a ventriloquist with his dummy, and clowns on bicycles, and finally the elephants draped in silk thundered past Bloom, one of the elephant girls grinning down at him and winking, and the last of the parade disappeared into the tent to the blaring of the band and the flashing of the lights and there was a climactic flourish and the lights dimmed, and the tent went black for just an instant before the lights came on again.

It was show time.

Steadman was breathing hard and sweating profusely after his stint around the tent. He had taken off the top hat the moment they'd entered the office trailer, and now he tossed it impatiently onto one of the cabinets. His white shirt clinging to him under the red jacket, his hair matted and damp, he looked flushed and cross, his manner clearly indicating that the only thing on his mind right now was getting his goddamn show on the road tomorrow morning. He seemed annoyed, too, that Bloom was here when there were important matters to discuss with S&R's major attraction, the King of All the Beasts. Sheed looked no less annoyed. His sun-bronzed body glistening with sweat, and rippling with muscles, and bristling with the scars he wore like bravery medals, he paced the trailer in his glittery silver vest and blue tights sprinkled with oversized stars, violently waving away the clouds of smoke Steadman created while lighting his cigar.

"What'd you think of it?" Steadman asked him.

"Everything ran too long," Sheed said.

"I know it."

"Including my act."

"Well, a little."

"Sakti's beginning to think *she's* the star, instead of me."

"Cute, though."

"Also, the band missed almost all its cues."

"I know. What else?"

"The Chens were too cute by half. They want their own circus, tell 'em to go buy one."

"Uh-huh."

"Marnie missed the triple. Again. In fact, she almost missed the fuckin *double*."

"Tell me about it," Steadman said sourly.

"One of the elephant girls was flashing. Olga? Whoever. The redhead."

"I didn't notice."

"Ask her to put a tuck in that costume."

"What else?"

"Actually, I thought it went – oh, by the way, what spooked that horse?"

"I don't know."

"Something the band did?"

"Maybe."

"That band needs talking to, George."

"I know it."

"Did you think the charivari worked?"

"Not enough yelling."

"Not only the yelling. Too mild altogether."

"I'll talk to them."

"Otherwise it went okay, I think."

"Yeah, not too bad."

"For beginners," Sheed said, and smiled.

"Beginners, yeah," Steadman said, and returned the smile, and then turned to Bloom. "How'd *you* like it?" he asked.

"All I saw was the climax," Bloom said.

"Best part," Sheed said, and winked.

"Well, how'd *that* look?" Steadman asked, puffing furiously on the cigar.

"Terrific," Bloom said.

"I'll leave you two alone," Sheed said, and started for the door.

"I'll go with you," Bloom said.

Sheed looked at him.

"Few questions I want to ask you."

"Sure," Sheed said, and opened the door. "See you, George."

"Early!" Steadman warned, and waved to them both as they went out.

The grounds were littered with performers discussing their first full dress rehearsal. All of them looked somehow exhilarated and exhausted at one and the same time.

"Want a beer?" Sheed asked.

"No, thanks."

"I do," he said, and walked Bloom to the cookhouse, where he bought a bottle of Heineken, had it popped by the guy behind the counter, and began drinking it as they walked outside again. Dusk was gathering quickly; it happened that way in Florida.

"So what's on your mind?" Sheed asked.

"My friend made some notes . . ."

"Which friend would that be?"

"Matthew Hope."

"Right, the lawyer. Notes about what?"

"Notes about Peter Torrance."

"Come on, willya? First Hope, and now *him*? You guys must think I'm running around shooting everybody in town."

"You know about Torrance, huh?"

"I watch television," Sheed said. "Same as anyone else."

"When's the last time you saw him?"

"Years ago. After I joined S&R, he used to pop in every now and then. Talk to his old buddies, shoot the shit, share a few brews. But I thought he was dead by now. In fact, he is, come to think of it."

"You didn't happen to see him in Missouri, did you?"

"Once or twice, I guess. Why?"

"I mean recently."

"How recently?"

"Three years ago come May eleventh."

"Oh, *that* again, huh?"

"Meaning?"

"Meaning Willa's suicide."

"*Did* you see Peter Torrance in Missouri, three years ago?"

"No. I heard he was there, but I didn't see him. He was

broke. Tried to borrow money from Willa. She turned him down cold."

"My friend thinks Torrance broke into Willa's trailer, carried away her safe . . ."

"Your friend is right."

Bloom looked at him.

"Torrance stole the safe, found cocaine when he opened it . . ."

"Two keys," Bloom said.

"Two keys. And then tried to shake Willa down."

"Where'd you get this?"

"Maria told me," Sheed said, and shrugged.

"When?"

"The night before Willa shot herself."

And now, as Bloom listened, he had the distinct feeling that he was watching a Japanese movie titled *Rashomon* . . . well, not quite, but certainly close enough. As he recalled the film, none of the characters was actually *lying*, but everyone's perception of the *truth* was a different one. In effect, everyone was seeing the same event through different eyes, making it impossible to know which retelling of the story was the real one. Torrance had already related two different versions of his visit to Missouri three years ago, one to Matthew and another to Bloom. In each of his tellings, he'd been the friendly former husband offering solace in a time of crisis, but this time around – if Sheed was to be believed – Torrance was the villain of the piece.

"Nobody likes to believe a thief's working a circus," Sheed was saying, "but half the gazoonies come aboard with jail-house time behind them, and you never know who you can trust. This was the night after the burglary, you understand, and that's all anybody could talk about, anyway. The rain was . . ."

. . . coming down in sheets, turning the circus grounds into an ocean of churning mud, dripping into the cookhouse tent, seeping into the bones, slanting into the cages where the big cats are restlessly pacing. Maria doesn't want to sleep with Sheed that night. After the burglary, her mother's afraid to be alone, and Maria thinks she should stay with her. Sheed tells her he wants her there with *him*, where she belongs, in *his* trailer, what's this on-again, off-again shit? Is she his woman, or some fuckin teenybopper firefly?

She spills it all then, tells him Torrance went to her mother to tell her there was cocaine in that safe, enough to presume trafficking, and whereas he doesn't plan to blow the whistle, what he *would* enjoy is a little piece of the action for old time's sake. After all, if sweet Wee Willa Winkie had once upon a time fucked another man who hung from his hair at the top of a tent while Torrance was out slaving on the road, wasn't it now fair – if indeed this miniature treacherous *cunt* was now dealing dope – that she should share the proceeds with her wronged husband? Or so Torrance had argued reasonably.

Willa knew the dope wasn't hers. She also knew her daughter had a combination to the safe. In tears, the wind and the rain raging outside Sheed's trailer, Maria told him about the confrontation that afternoon between her and her mother, Maria swearing she'd merely been holding the dope for someone else . . .

"*Me*, Davey Sheed . . ."

. . . and would never again do such a stupid thing in her life, oh, how *could* she have been so stupid?

Truth of the matter was that Maria had been doing this stupid thing for more than a year now, selling coke to half the gazoonies and performers on the show, distributing it like candy to the eager street dealers all along the circus route. Torrance had already left town, but he'd told her mother he'd catch up with her again in Tennessee, at which time he wanted her decision on what his cut would be. Otherwise, contrary to his benevolent nature and fond feelings for her, he might be compelled to inform the authorities.

What to do, oh, what to do?

"What Maria did was call her partner for advice," Sheed said.

"What partner?" Bloom asked.

"Her little girlfriend from when she was seventeen."

"Who do you mean?"

"Who do you think I mean? Jeannie Byrd."

Di Luca and Kenyon – the two detectives who'd originally caught the Matthew Hope shooting – questioned Maria Torrance in an interrogation room on the third floor of the Public Safety Building. In a room next door, Bloom questioned Jeannie Byrd. Neither of the women knew that the other had been brought in. It was explained to each of them that they were in police custody and entitled to an attorney if they wished one. It was also explained that they did not have to answer any questions if they chose not to. Maria Torrance asked for an attorney. Jeannie Byrd opted to answer questions without any legal representation. They figured Jeannie would be the weak link, simply because she was so goddamn supremely sure of herself.

"Miss Torrance," Di Luca said, "there's something we'd like you to hear, if you . . ."

"Oh? What's *this*?" her attorney asked at once.

His name was Howard Mandel, and he was one of the best criminal lawyers in Calusa, something Matthew would have been the first to admit. In fact, when Patricia learned that Maria had called him, she rolled her eyes in despair. Now, standing some six feet tall in a brown, tropical-weight suit, maize-colored shirt, and hunter-green tie, Mandel waited with his hands defiantly on his hips, back ramrod straight, chin thrust out, trying to terrify Kenyon and Di Luca, who'd both been cops for almost twenty years, and who had seen it all and heard it all, and who were not about to back away because of any body language. Eyes bright, pert attentive look on her face, wearing her red wig and a green suit with matching high-heeled pumps, Maria Torrance sat looking serenely secure in the knowledge that her appointed champion would protect her from any harm or discourtesy.

"Counselor," Kenyon said, "this is a tape Matthew Hope made of a conversation between him and Peter Torrance."

"Have you seen him lately, by the way?" Di Luca asked.

"Mr. Hope is in the hospital," Maria said.

"Just a minute here . . ." Mandel said.

"I meant your father," Di Luca said.

"No, I haven't."

"Have you *talked* to him lately?"

"Nope."

"Don't know he's in town, right?"

"News to me," she said, and smiled.

"Because his appointment calendar had you written in for a one o'clock last Wednesday," Di Luca said, and then, "Sorry, Counselor, didn't mean to interrupt."

"Are you finished now?" Mandel asked.

"Yes, sir, sorry about that."

"How do I know this tape is what it purports to be?" Mandel asked.

"Well, I guess you'll have to take my word for it. I'm sure you'll advise your client accordingly if you think the tape's a fake."

"I'm assuming you have some specific charges in mind here. Otherwise . . ."

"What we're thinking is homicide, sir," Kenyon said. "Plus attempted murder and conspiracy. And illegal possession of a firearm."

"For starters," Di Luca said.

"So if you'll accept that this is Mr. Hope and Mr. Torrance talking on this tape and not some actors we got from Burt Reynolds's dinner theater over on the east coast . . ."

"What's your purpose in playing this tape?"

"We just want Miss Torrance to listen to it and answer some questions about it."

"She may listen to it, but as for answering any questions, I'll hold judgment on that in abeyance."

"Well, sure, Counselor. As you know, though, she can call this off anytime she likes. That's what Miranda's all about, right?"

Mandel shot him a dirty look.

"Okay to play it, then?" Kenyon asked.

"Go ahead and play it. You don't have to answer any questions about it if you don't want to," he advised Maria.

"I have nothing to hide," Maria said.

Famous last words, Di Luca thought.

*   *   *

"According to a record of calls I obtained from the telephone company," Bloom said, "Matthew Hope made a call to your home on Flamingo Key last Friday morning at . . ."

"Yes, I remember," Jeannie said at once.

"Can you tell me what that call was about, Mrs. Byrd?"

"He was trying to reach my husband. I told him Andrew was still in Mexico."

"Reach him about what?"

"I have no idea. I don't pry into my husband's affairs."

"I thought you were partners," Bloom said.

"We are."

"But you don't pry into his affairs."

"I don't know why Matthew Hope called him."

"This would've been after a conversation he'd had with a man named Peter Torrance. Do you know him?"

"No."

"Never met him while you were with the circus?"

"I was only with them for one season."

"Didn't run into him at that time?"

"No. I just told you, I don't *know* the man."

"Do you know Davey Sheed?"

"Yes, I do."

"I wonder if you'd care to comment on some things Davey Sheed told me earlier today."

"Depends on what things he told you."

"Well, let's start with this," Bloom said, and flipped open his notebook. "Davey Sheed says Maria sought your advice the day after her mother's safe was stolen. Care to comment?"

"I won't bore you with the whole tape," Kenyon said, and opened the lid of a dispatch case monogrammed with the letters W.C. "I've got it set where I . . . let me see . . . yeah, here it is . . . I can start it whenever you're ready."

"I'm ready now, Detective," Maria said, and smiled.

Kenyon hit the play button.

—discovered it the day before the burglary, you see.

—When you say she'd just *discovered* it . . .

—Yes.

—Do you mean she just opened the safe and *found* it there?

—Yes. And immediately figured it was Maria's.

—Why Maria?

—Because she was the only other person who knew the combination to the safe. Which meant she was doing cocaine, you see. Maybe even dealing it. Because this wasn't just a couple of *ounces* in there, this was a real *stash* she'd found in that safe.

—Did she tell you how much?

—She guessed about two kilos. She told me she thought Maria *had* to be dealing the stuff. She was afraid that whoever had stolen the safe might come back to blackmail her.

—Did she think he'd known beforehand?

—I'm not following you.

—The thief. That there was cocaine in the safe?

—No, no. She just thought he'd lucked out. And would try to take advantage of the situation.

—Well . . . what'd *Maria* have to say about all this?

—She denied the stuff was hers.

—Then how'd it get in the safe?

—Oh, she'd *put* it there, all right, but she said it didn't belong to her.

—Then whose was it?

—Davey Sheed's.

Kenyon snapped off the recorder.

"Boy," Maria said.

"Excuse me," Mandel said, "but are you . . ."

"Some fairy tale," Maria said.

". . . investigating a *narcotics* case here?"

"No, sir, this was a long time ago, the event they're talking about on the tape. I think Miss Torrance knows about the event, if she'd care to discuss it with us."

"What dope is he talking about?" Maria asked, eyes wide. "That man on the tape."

"That's Peter Torrance," Di Luca said. "Your father."

"The dope that was in your mother's safe," Kenyon said.

"Where is this dope?" Maria asked. "Do you have this dope?"

"No, miss, we surely don't," Kenyon said.

"Neither do I," Maria said, and smiled again.

"If you have questions regarding homicide and attempted murder," Mandel said, "or conspiracy, or whatever else was on your laundry list, I wish you'd . . ."

"He must've made all that up," Maria said, and paused for the merest tick of an instant. "And he's dead now, isn't he?" she said.

"Davey Sheed confirms his story," Di Luca said.

"Davey killed my mother. He'd confirm anything."

"Just a minute here," Mandel said. "You understand you don't have to answer any of these questions, don't you, Maria? Questions relating to crimes other than . . ."

"Yes, I understand that."

"What'd Jeannie advise when you called her?" Di Luca asked.

"Jeannie who?"

"Byrd."

"When was this?"

"The day after the burglary."

"What burglary?"

"Come on, a hundred people have already told us . . ."

"Oh, *that* burglary."

"Miss Torrance," Mandel said, "I feel I should advise you. These felonies they keep . . ."

"Not to worry," Maria said calmly.

They were beginning to think *she* was the one who'd outsmart herself.

"Mrs. Byrd?" Bloom said. "Any comment?"

"Davey Sheed is a foul-mouthed, ill-mannered, totally amoral *animal* who would say anything or do anything to extricate himself from a threatening situation. I imagine you were asking him about Willa Torrance's murder . . ."

"No, as a matter . . ."

"Which everyone is *still* convinced he committed, by the way. That he would lie to protect himself comes as no . . ."

"Who's everyone?" Bloom asked.

"Anyone familiar with the circumstances of her death."

"Are *you* familiar with the circumstances of her death?"

"I'm called every year at about this time by journalists who want to know all about Willa. Yes, I'm familiar with the case."

"Who told you Davey Sheed killed her?"

"No one had to. I know Davey."

"What'd you and Willa argue about?"

"When?"

"You know when. You were only with the circus for a single season, when do you *think* I mean?"

"I thought Warren Chambers was working with you."

"He is."

"Then go ask *him*. I told him all about it."

"I'm asking *you*," Bloom said.

Jeannie heaved an enormous sigh.

Bloom waited.

"She thought I was *bothering* the two little girls in her act."

"That's not why Sheed says you argued."

"I told you. Davey is . . ."

"He thinks Willa came to see you about her daughter."

"I hardly knew Maria."

"About you and her daughter."

"Why would . . .?"

"About you and her daughter being lovers."

"How well do you know Jeannie Byrd?" Di Luca asked.

"We're casual acquaintances," Maria said.

"Still know her, though, do you?"

"As I said . . ."

"Casually, right," Kenyon said. "How well did you know her while she was with the circus? When she was still Jeannie Lawson."

"Casually."

"Casually then, casually now."

"Correct."

"Did you call her the day after your mother's safe was stolen?"

"No. Why would I have done that? Who even knew where she *was*?"

"You didn't know where she was, huh?"

"No. Well, Calusa, I guess. I heard she'd gone back to Calusa, married someone . . ."

"Didn't you know who she married?"

"Not then."

"But you know now?"

"Yes, I do."

"What'd Jeannie say when you called her?"

"I didn't call her."

"She's already *told* you she didn't call her," Mandel said.

"I heard her. Davey Sheed thinks you called her."

"Anything to say about that, Mrs. Byrd?"

"Davey has a lively imagination. It comes from sleeping with cats."

"So there's no truth to his claim that you and Maria . . ."

"None whatever."

"You were *not* lovers."

"We were not."

"Not then, not now . . ."

"Not ever."

"Yet she called you for advice on what to . . ."

"She never called me for advice."

"Called you in tears, Sheed said, wanting to know what to do about that dope."

"What dope?"

"The dope Torrance found in her mother's safe."

"I don't know what dope you're talking about."

"You know there was a burglary two days before Willa's murder, don't you?"

"Yes, I know that."

"You know that a safe was taken from her trailer . . ."

"Yes."

"But you don't know what was in that safe?"

"No."

"You don't know that two kilos of cocaine were in that safe?"

"How would I know that?"

"Because Maria called you about it."

"Maria did not call me about *anything!*"

"Maria called you to say Torrance knew about the dope
. . ."

"No, she did *not!*"

". . . her *mother* knew about the dope . . ."

"Listen, Detective . . ."

"Maria called wanting to know what the hell to *do!* Isn't that
so? Isn't that what happened?"

"Maria did not call me," Jeannie said flatly. "Are we finished here?"

"Not quite."

"Well, I *am,*" she said.

Which left them with just Maria Torrance, after all.

"Let's talk again about the night your mother's safe was stolen
from that fridge, okay?" Kenyon said.

"Sure," Maria said.

"Toward what end?" her lawyer asked.

"Try to clarify a few things," Bloom said.

He had joined them not a few moments earlier. Now there
were three cops in the room. Three cops were always more
impressive than two, especially when an attorney was present.
Maria sat at her end of the table with her legs crossed, one foot
jiggling. Bloom read this as a sign of nervousness. Either that,
or she had to pee.

"Where was your mother that night, would you know?"
he asked.

"Doing the show. She was an entertainer, you know."

"Came back to the trailer and found the safe gone, huh?"
Kenyon said.

"Apparently. I didn't learn about it till the next day."

"When your mother told you about the cocaine, right?" Di
Luca said.

"I don't know anything about any cocaine."

"As she's already told you ad infinitum," Mandel said. "If
you gentlemen have any *new* questions to ask . . ."

"We'll get to them, Counselor," Kenyon said.

"When? My client's already been here . . ."

"No one's breaching her rights, Counselor," Di Luca said.

"I'm suggesting that either you charge her or let her go," Mandel said.

"In a hurry to have her charged, huh?" Di Luca asked.

"No, but I know a fishing expedition when I see one," Mandel said. "You're dredging up ancient history here because you haven't got a damn thing . . ."

"Language, language," Bloom scolded.

". . . that links her either to the Hope shooting *or* the Torrance murder. Nothing at all. So you've invented a cockamamie story about a stolen safe . . ."

"The burglary's a matter of record," Bloom said. "Check with Missouri, if you like."

"How about the cocaine? Is *that* a matter of record, too?"

"No, but . . ."

"I didn't think so."

"Peter Torrance told me there was cocaine in that safe," Bloom said.

"My father is dead," Maria said dryly.

"I'm not. And that's what he told me."

"My father is a liar," Maria said. "Was."

"What'd you and he talk about when you saw him?"

"I haven't seen him in years."

"What'd he call you about yesterday?"

"He didn't call me."

"Mind if I show her something, Counselor?"

"What now?" Mandel said.

Bloom took a folded computer printout from his jacket pocket, spread it on the table so that both Maria and her lawyer could look at it.

"Recognize any of those numbers?" he asked.

"What is this document, anyway?" Mandel asked.

"A log of the phone calls charged to room thirty-seven at the Shelby Arms. We figure that Matthew Hope left Torrance at about eleven on the morning of the twenty-fifth. Here's a call Torrance made at a few minutes past eleven. Recognize the number, Miss Torrance?"

"Yes, it's . . ."

"Maria . . ."

". . . my home phone number."

"Maria, I think it may be time to . . ."

"Relax, Howard," she said coolly.

That was when Bloom knew he had her. The way she said the word "relax."

"Didn't you tell Detective Di Luca that you didn't know Torrance was in town?"

"That's right."

"Hadn't seen him . . ."

"Right."

". . . or talked to him . . ."

"Right."

"Yet here's a phone call to your house on Fatback Key at eleven-oh-seven on March twenty-fifth . . .

"I wasn't even home at that time yesterday."

"Then he must have talked to someone else there."

"I have no idea," she said.

"You have a maid, don't you?"

"Yes?"

Somewhat cautious note in her voice now.

"So maybe he talked to her, is that possible?"

"That's entirely possible. I know he didn't talk to me."

"So he must have talked to her, right?" Bloom said, and hit her with the hammer. "For forty-five minutes, right?"

Maria looked at him.

"That's what the hotel's computer says. Forty-five minutes. A Mr. Muhammad Azir there provided the information, if you'd like to check on its authenticity, Counselor. It says that the call Torrance made from *his* room to Miss Torrance's number was forty-five minutes long."

"Who is this Muhammad Whatever?"

"Day clerk at the Shelby Arms. What'd you talk about all that time, Miss Torrance?"

Maria took a deep breath.

"Want to tell us?" Bloom asked.

"Sure," she said, "why not? He was trying to blackmail me. He told me he'd just had a meeting with a lawyer named Matthew Hope, and it occurred to him during the meeting that if I opposed his claim, he'd reveal everything he knew about . . . well, the burglary."

"What about the burglary?"

"That there was cocaine in the safe. Or so he said. It was nonsense, of course. There was only jewelry and . . ."

"Then you *knew* about that, huh?" Kenyon said. "The cocaine."

"Only after we talked about it on the phone."

"But when I played that tape for you . . ."

"What tape?" she asked, eyes wide, tone mocking.

Oh, yes, we have you now, Bloom was thinking.

"The tape Hope made of him and your father . . ."

"Oh, *that* tape."

Sure, Bloom was thinking, play it big, honey, we are about to *nail* you.

Kenyon flipped open his notebook.

"After I played the tape, you said, 'Boy, *some* fairy tale, what dope is he *talking* about, where *is* this dope, do *you* have this dope, he must've made all that up.' Isn't that what you said?"

"Possibly."

"Well, more than just possibly, because it's what I wrote down here. When all the while you knew about the cocaine because that's what you and your father talked about on the phone, isn't that right?"

"So what?" Maria said.

"Miss Torrance," Bloom said, "did you have occasion to call Jeannie Byrd after your phone conversation with your father?"

"No, I didn't."

"I think you did. And I can always get a court order asking the telephone company to release information regarding . . ."

"Okay, I called her."

"The way you did in Missouri?" Bloom asked.

"I didn't call her in . . ."

"To tell her your father knew about the dope?"

"I didn't . . ."

"The same way you did on the twenty-fifth?"

"That's enough, Maria. Don't answer . . ."

"In panic about the dope again?"

"No!"

"Maria!"

"This is all *bullshit*, Howard!"

"You didn't know anything about that coke in Missouri, right?" Bloom said.

"How many times do I . . .?"

"How about the coke *here*? In Florida?"

"What?"

"What I'm going to do, Miss Torrance, is make application for a warrant to search your house for cocaine."

"On what grounds?" Mandel said at once.

"On information and belief that . . ."

"What information?"

"Information from a licensed private investigator named Toots Kiley that on the patio of Miss Torrance's home on Fatback Key, at or around four P.M. last Sunday . . . that would've been the twenty-seventh . . . Miss Torrance asked her if she'd care for a drink, and when Miss Kiley declined, then asked, 'How about a toot instead?' Miss Kiley declined this as well, at which point Miss Torrance said, 'I think I'll have one,' and walked back into the house. Isn't that true, Miss Torrance?"

Maria said nothing.

"May I have a word with my client?" Mandel said softly.

7

She was horrid

PATRICIA was wearing her other hat.

Assistant State Attorney, Twelfth Judicial District, in and for Calusa County, Florida. This time, Jeannie Byrd had elected to have an attorney present. Perhaps that was because she was being charged with a string of felonies, including but not limited to the murder of Peter Torrance and the attempted murder of Matthew Hope.

Her attorney's name was Benny Weiss.

He was a smallish person – five feet eight at the outside – slight of build, with a narrow face, the soulful brown eyes of a cocker spaniel, and unruly brown hair that he raked with his fingers every three or four minutes. Conventional courthouse wisdom maintained that he was an even better lawyer now that'd he stopped smoking. Patricia had never come up against him before. But here he was now. Benny Weiss. Unquestionably the very best criminal lawyer in the state of Florida. Never mind Howard Mandel, never mind Matthew Hope, *this* was Benny Weiss. But this was Patricia Demming, too, and she wasn't here to play golf.

"I've advised my client not to answer any questions," Benny said at once.

"Fine with me," she said. "But meanwhile . . ."

"No meanwhiles, Pat," Benny said.

First mistake.

At Brown University, Patricia Demming had broken the nose of a quarterback who'd insisted on calling her Pat instead of her full and honorable name.

"It's Patricia," she told Benny now, her eyes as cool and as baleful as a shark's. Not for nothing had she been called the Wicked Bitch of the West when she was practicing private law in Los Angeles. Benny should have known this, but he hadn't bothered to do a quick background check. Instead, obliviously unaware, he stood by his seated client, confident he'd be out of here in five minutes, further confident that Jeannie Byrd would be released the moment he asked a judge to set bail.

"I understand Mrs. Byrd doesn't wish to answer any questions," Patricia said, "but I was hoping she wouldn't mind *listening* to a few things I have to say."

"Like what?" Benny asked.

"Like why I think I can fry her," Patricia said sweetly.

Benny smiled.

"Why should we be interested in that?" he asked.

"Well, at the very least," Patricia said, and shrugged, "it might help you prepare your case."

"Thanks for the offer, Pat, but I respectfully . . ."

"That's twice," she said levelly.

"What?"

"It's Patricia."

"Patricia, Pat, whatever you say."

"I say Patricia. Never Pat. Always Patricia."

"Fine. Patricia. Fine. Meanwhile . . ."

"No meanwhiles, Counselor. *Always.*"

"Always, fine."

"Care to listen?"

"I don't see what purpose it'll serve. If you're intending to frighten my client . . ."

"Perish the thought."

"Then what possible purpose . . .?"

"I'd like to hear it," Jeannie said.

"Thank you," Patricia said. "Mrs. Byrd . . ."

"You can listen," Benny advised, "but don't say a word."

Jeannie nodded.

"Maria Torrance made a statement not half an hour ago that implicates you in . . ."

"Wait a minute, wait a minute, hold it," Benny said, "where's this statement, what statement, what is this?"

"I have it right here," Patricia said. "I was going to summarize it for you, save a little time . . ."

"I can read, thanks. And I have all the time in the world. Let me see it, please."

"Sure," Patricia said, and handed him a Xerox copy of Maria Torrance's signed statement.

"How'd you get this?" he asked.

"Detective Bloom gave it to me," Patricia said.

"How'd *he* get it?"

"He mentioned obtaining a warrant to search her home, and – depending on what he found there – a *second* warrant to search her place of business. One thing led to another . . ."

"Such as?"

"I thought you could read, Counselor."

Benny shot her an angry glare.

"Such as she *knew* there was a sizable amount of cocaine in her house . . . try six ounces . . . and she *further* knew the dope was in a manila envelope with her business address on it. A little sidebar with her lawyer advised her that this constituted reasonable cause to believe the dope had been *transported* from her place of business to her home. Her lawyer explained that this gave Bloom all he needed for a warrant to search Hair and Now as well. That's the name of her business. Hair and Now. It ships wigs – *and* dope – all over the country. Apparently a whole *lot* of dope passes through that little old wig emporium, Counselor. *Much* more than the hundred and fifty keys specified in 893.135. They ship it inside these hollow polymer heads they put the wigs on. Bloom's got his dogs over there right this minute, sniffing around."

"My client has nothing whatever to do with Maria's business."

"Well, maybe not. In any event, a kilo of cocaine, as you know, is two-point-two . . ."

"I know what a kilo is, thank you."

". . . pounds," Patricia went on. "A hundred and fifty keys

come to three hundred and thirty pounds of the stuff. The section states that any person who knowingly sells, purchases, manufactures, delivers, brings into the state . . ."

"I'm familiar with the section, thank you."

". . . Or is knowingly in possession of a hundred and fifty keys or more," Patricia continued, unperturbed, "commits the first-degree felony of trafficking in cocaine. Which is punishable . . ."

"I'm well aware," Benny said.

"Perhaps Mrs. Byrd isn't," Patricia said pleasantly, and went on, unruffled. "Punishable by a term of lifetime imprisonment without the possibility of parole. Maria has admitted that she and her partners were dealing cocaine in the amounts specified in the statutes." Patricia paused and then said, "By the way, Mrs. Byrd, she named you and your husband as her partners."

Benny had been scanning Maria's statement. He now looked up sharply.

"What I was able to offer her," Patricia said, "in return for testimony stating that you and your husband have been in business with her for the past four years, from when she was still traveling with the circus, actually, distributing coke at every whistle-stop in . . ."

"That's her word against . . ."

"Well, not entirely, Counselor. Maria has records of so-called *wig* orders, and bills of lading, and cash bank deposits, and phone calls to people with full heads of hair. Speaking of phone calls, by the way, she *also* says she called you from Missouri the day before her mother was murdered, which I find a rather odd coincidence . . ."

"Willa committed suicide," Jeannie said.

"Yes, so I hear. But I think I can try that case . . ."

"In Missouri?" Benny said. "Don't be ridic—"

"No, in Florida, under Florida law. No statute of limitation on murder, right, Counselor? And that phone call gives me jurisdiction, doesn't it? The call to Mrs Byrd here in Florida, followed almost immediately by Willa's suspicious death in Missouri? That would constitute conspiracy, wouldn't you say? If I can show motive related to the threat of exposure? That's my reasoning, anyway. But as I was saying . . ."

Benny was studying her closely now.

". . . Maria called you in panic again last Thursday, after her father threatened to do an encore of his whistle-blowing routine . . ."

"Is that in this statement?"

"Yes. And we've also made application for a corroborating telephone company log. Once again, Mrs Byrd, you came to the rescue. First you tried to take out Matthew Hope who was getting too close for comfort, and next . . ."

"I'm sure *that* isn't in here," Benny said, and rattled the statement.

"That's right, Counselor, it isn't. It's all in my head."

"That's what I thought," Benny said, and handed the statement back to her. "I see nothing here to worry about," he told Jeannie. "So, if it's all right with you, Counselor . . ."

"I told Maria Torrance that if she pleaded to possession of four hundred grams, we'd go for the mandatory minimum and we wouldn't oppose parole after she'd done the fifteen. A matter of her getting out of jail when she's thirty-eight instead of spending the rest of her life there. As a condition of the plea, we agreed to drop all conspiracy charges on the murders and the attempted murder. Her attorney recognized the sense in . . ."

"Who's her attorney?" Benny asked.

"Howie Mandel."

"Shmuck would cop a plea on his own mother."

"How about you?" Patricia asked.

"You're blowing air, Patricia."

"Maybe you weren't listening. Her partner's already flipped, she's already been burned on a drug charge with a lifetime penalty."

"Until I put Maria on the stand and start questioning her about the little deal you cut."

"Sure, you do that. Be the first time in history anyone copped a plea, right? But you know, Counselor, I feel I should point out to Mrs Byrd that if a person trafficking in a hundred and fifty kilos or more of . . ."

"Please, spare me."

". . . cocaine *also* happens to cause the intentional *killing* of an individual . . ."

"Mrs Byrd hasn't killed . . ."

". . . then it becomes a *capital* felony. We're talking the chair, Counselor."

"You're still blowing air."

"I've got two panic calls from Maria, followed by two murders."

"Talk about flimsy."

"You may call it flimsy. I call it motive."

"Weak, Patricia, very weak. If that's all you've got, I would welcome a trial."

"I also have a witness who can identify the car the shooter was driving the night Matthew Hope got shot. We know you drive a red Mercedes, Mrs. Byrd, but Bloom's people are out checking rental car companies right this minute. Maybe they'll learn you rented a black two-door Mazda on the day of the shooting, him?"

"No answers, Jeannie," Benny warned.

"Because, you see, we're getting all *kinds* of cooperation from the phone company, even *before* we applied for our court orders. For example, we have a log that has you making a call from your home on Palm Drive to Matthew Hope's home . . ."

"No answers," Benny warned again.

". . . at five o'clock last Friday. Why'd you call him, Mrs. Byrd? To set up a meeting at the Centaur Bar & Grill? So you could shoot him?"

"No, I called to . . ."

"Jeannie!"

". . . to tell him when Andrew would be coming home."

"Oh? And why'd you do that?"

"Because when we'd talked earlier in the week, he wanted to know when my husband would be home."

"I see. So you called to tell him . . ."

"That Andrew would be home tonight."

"I see. You felt it necessary to call Mr. Hope a week in advance to give him this information, is that right?"

"He seemed interested," Jeannie said, and shrugged.

"Well, I'm sure Detective Bloom will be interested, too. He may want to meet your husband at the airport, in fact, welcome him back to Calusa."

"Are we chatting here, or what?" Benny asked.

"You asked me what I have," Patricia said. "I'm telling you what I have."

"Which isn't very much."

"Unless we include the gun," Patricia said, and smiled nicely. "We have the gun, too."

"What gun?" Benny asked. "The statement didn't say anything about . . ."

"The Iver Johnson .22-caliber Trailsman Snub revolver your client dropped alongside the bed in Peter Torrance's room," Patricia said, and smiled again. Somehow the smile enhanced her momentary sharklike appearance.

Benny looked at Jeannie.

"Nice try, Mrs. Byrd," Patricia said.

"I think we've heard enough here," Benny said.

"Wipe the weapon clean, drop it on the floor, then plant a box of cartridges in Torrance's valise, hoping we'll figure the gun . . ."

"I gather *this* is in your head as well," Benny said.

"I'm afraid it is."

"In which case, I'll see you in . . ."

"But the bill of sale isn't," Patricia said.

"What bill of . . .?"

"On the gun."

Benny looked at his client again.

"The gun was purchased at F&G Arms on the South Tamiami Trail on October fifteenth last year," Patricia said. "Birth date of great men," she added, but did not amplify. "We located the merchant through the serial number. The gun was sold to a man named Andrew Byrd, who gave his address as 1220 Palm Drive, in Timucuan Acres. I believe that's where you live, isn't it, Mrs. Byrd? Andrew's your husband, isn't he?"

"Andrew was in Mexico when . . ."

"Yes, but you weren't. I think you'll agree, Ben, that her . . ."

"It's Benny."

"Sorry. I think you'll agree that her husband's ownership of the murder weapon establishes her link to it, *especially* since he was out of town at the time of both shootings – probably buying dope, if I might hazard another guess."

"Never mind the guesses," Benny said. "Stick to what you've *got*, okay?" He was scowling now. Patricia figured that was good.

"I've got a link to the gun," she said, "and I've got motive . . ."

"Motive, motive, what motive?"

"The threat of exposure. Under 893.135 . . ."

"Stop reading me the statutes."

"You asked," Patricia said. "I've also got a common, virtually *identical* scheme on the two murders, the one here and the one in Missouri. I think you know that evidence of similar crimes is very powerful stuff, Counselor. Admittedly prejudicial, but nonetheless powerful. The beauty part is I can use evidence of one murder as evidence in the other. Even if I'm willing to forget the *attempted* murder . . ."

"Wait a minute, wait a minute," Benny said, holding up his hand like a traffic cop. "Who says we're dealing here?"

"Excuse me, I thought we were dealing here," Patricia said.

"Even if her husband *does* own the gun you described, that doesn't mean . . ."

"Well, I think it does."

"It could have been lost . . ."

"Oh sure."

"Or stolen."

"Sure. But I think it was used by your client to shoot two people, incidentally killing one of them."

"You don't have any evidence to support that," Benny said. "But let me hear your deal, anyway. Just for the fun of it."

"I don't want any *deals*!" Jeannie said, and whirled on Patricia. "You have nothing but Maria's word on any of this. Why'd she *tell* you any of this? Is she crazy?"

"No, just angry."

"About *what*, for Christ's sake?"

"Well, gee, maybe she didn't expect you to kill her mother."

"I was in *Florida* when Willa . . ."

"Or *have* her killed. Either way, it was murder."

"I had nothing to do with Willa's death."

"Then you have nothing to worry about, right?"

"Can she really drag Missouri into this?"

"Yes, she can," Benny said.

"Then fuck her. Let her."

"Oh, I will," Patricia said.

"Go ahead, do it. You've got nothing. And you know it."

"Well, I'll admit I'm not too bowled over by the evidence, either. Then again, I'm not the one who'd be gambling my life on it. If you'd like to hear the plea, I'd be happy to . . ."

"No, I told you, I don't want to hear any goddamn plea."

"Okay, fine. Roll the dice."

"Maybe you ought to hear it," Benny said.

Jeannie looked at him.

"I'd hear it, if I were you," Benny said.

Patricia waited.

"Let me hear it," Jeannie said.

"The way I see it," Patricia said, "if I forget the Missouri murder and the attempt on Matthew Hope's life . . ."

"Forget the Torrance murder, too," Benny said.

"No way."

"Give her the same deal you gave Maria."

"No. I'm offering life for the Torrance murder."

"Just give us the basic black and pearls," Benny said. "We'll admit to four hundred grams if you forget the thirty-year max. We'll take the mandatory fifteen, no opposition to parole . . ."

"No. She's looking at the chair, Benny. That can be in twelve years or it can be in three years, depending on how your appeals go. But what's certain is she's going to die young. I'm offering life in prison, take it or leave it."

"Make it twenty without parole."

"Thanks, I'll go for the death penalty."

"Okay, we'll do the Torrance murder if you'll agree not to oppose parole after twenty-five years."

"*Life*, Benny."

"Patricia, twenty-five is the *minimum* on a capital felony!"

"Why does she deserve the minimum?"

"Make it forty, then. We'll take the Torrance plea if you don't oppose parole after forty years."

"No, Benny."

"She'd be sixty, sixty-five years *old* by then!"

"I'd rather be dead," Jeannie said.

"She's going to tough it out," Patricia told Bloom.

They were in his unmarked police sedan, on their way to the hospital. This was now nine thirty-seven that night, almost a week to the minute since Matthew had been shot.

"I was hoping she'd deal," Patricia told him. "What we've got isn't very strong."

"Unless we can zero in on the car."

"How does it look?"

"Still working it."

"I'll settle for parole in forty, if I have to," Patricia said. "But not if we have her renting that Mazda."

"We'll see."

"What'd the dogs find?"

"Oh, they were busy, busy, busy. A shipment went out yesterday, while Warren was there visiting. But new stuff has already come in. She was wise to cut a deal, young Maria."

"Who's waiting for Byrd at the airport?"

"Kenyon and Di Luca."

"Won't *he* be surprised."

"Maybe not. There are phones in Mexico, you know. His wife may have got to him before he boarded his plane."

"I hope not. He might just be the one to nail her coffin shut."

"*Aluvai.* One thing I've learned in this business, you offer anybody a good deal, he'll burn his partner in a minute. And there's nobody in the world who'll choose ten seconds in the electric chair over life in a prison cell."

"Tell that to Jeannie."

*   *   *

Dr. Spinaldo was tired and hungry and he wanted to go home, but the five of them had him surrounded in the corridor outside the intensive care unit. The daughter was the most aggressive of the lot, wanting to know *when* her father would wake up, what they were doing to *help* him wake up. The woman from the State Attorney's Office came next in the pecking order, firing questions as if he were being examined on a witness stand. What is the prognosis, Doctor? What is the significance of his occasional speech? Is this a sign that his condition is improving?

Well, yes, certainly, if the man wasn't previously saying anything at *all*, and he is now muttering an infrequent word or two, then one could say with guarded certainty that his condition does seem to be improving moderately, yes, one might conceivably say that.

They want me to be God, Spinaldo thought.

They want me to say he will live or die, he will recover completely or he will remain as he is until . . .

"Can't we do something to *help* him?" the daughter asked.

Pray for him, Spinaldo thought.

There were tears in the girl's eyes, she was looking up plaintively into his face. The five of them waiting, all of them waiting. The big police detective, and the blonde state attorney, and the other two, the black man and the other blonde, all of them waiting for the word of God, all of them wanting him to promise that Matthew Hope would definitely come back.

"We're watching him closely," he said, "monitoring his progress, doing everything we can to keep his condition from deteriorating. But you see . . ."

What can I tell them? he wondered. What can I possibly say?

"I just don't know," he said.